A Daughter's Gift

Maggie Hope

EBURY

This edition published by Ebury Press in 2018
First published as 'A Blackbird Singing' in 2000 by Piatkus Books

15

Ebury Press, an imprint of Ebury Publishing
20 Vauxhall Bridge Road,
London SW1V 2SA

Ebury Press is part of the Penguin Random House group of companies
whose addresses can be found at global.penguinrandomhouse.com

Penguin
Random House
UK

www.penguin.co.uk

A CIP catalogue record for this book is available from the British Library

ISBN 9780091949174

ays Ltd, Elcograf S.p.A.

sustainable future for our
book is made from Forest
fied paper.

This book is dedicated to my sisters.

Chapter One

On the day that Elizabeth, Jimmy and their two younger sisters were to go to the workhouse, Elizabeth rose early, washed and dressed in her best dress, the one she had kept for school in the old days, the days before Mam had died. She was dry-eyed; after all it was too late. Both she and Jimmy had prayed and prayed for days now that their father would come back and say to Auntie Betty and Uncle Ben, 'Of course the bairns aren't going to the workhouse! What on earth were you thinking about? I've come back to look after them.' And then he would open his arms and grin his bright, devil-may-care grin and hug all the children to him. Sometimes he would have a travelling bag with him and would open it and bring out presents for them all, just like Father Christmas did at the Sunday School Christmas party. But she didn't really care whether he had presents or not, so long as he came himself.

Maybe it wasn't too late, she thought as she combed her hair and tied it back from her face. Maybe he would still come before the man from the Welfare. She glanced at Jimmy, his teeth clenched together and his brow wrinkled with a frown even in sleep. Downstairs she heard the back door open and someone come in. Elizabeth hurried down. She hadn't even lit the fire yet, her aunt might be angry. Auntie Betty was there, holding Kit against her shoulder for all the world as though he were *her* baby. And he wasn't, was he?

'Give him to me, I'll give him his bread and milk,' Elizabeth said, holding out her arms.

'He's had his breakfast,' said Auntie Betty, and held the baby closer. She didn't like giving him up at all. But this time, when Elizabeth gave her a hard stare, she did. Elizabeth sat down on her mother's chair and rocked the baby gently. Kit put up a hand and patted her cheek and smiled, showing milky gums, and Elizabeth's heart overflowed with love and grief, but she bit her lip hard and by sheer force of will didn't cry.

Betty looked down at her niece and nephew. 'I can't help it, you know, Lizzie,' she said. 'I'll take Kit but I can't take the rest of you. Ben has put his foot down. When you're older you'll understand.'

Elizabeth looked hard at her. 'Don't call me Lizzie. Only my mam called me Lizzie. My name is Elizabeth – I was called after you, remember? And anyroad, I know you always wanted a baby. Now you've got our

2

Christopher.' She turned her attention back to the baby, cooing to him, and he gurgled back.

'Don't cheek me,' said Auntie Betty, 'I'm your mam's sister, remember? Our Jane would have wanted me to look after Kit.'

Elizabeth turned her face away and Betty sighed and turned her attention to the fire, raking out the still-warm ashes, laying paper and sticks from a pit-prop offcut, placing cinders carefully on top. Elizabeth watched her silently. She touched the top of the baby's head with her lips. The hair felt soft and downy.

I'm nearly ten, she thought. If I'd been older they would have let me keep the bairns here. But I'm not and Auntie Betty has given us away to the Welfare and we're going to the workhouse. It is a fact, and Miss High says facts can't be changed. Miss High was her headmistress at school and so knew everything.

Betty sat back on her heels, watching the flames lick round the cinders and coal, listening to the sticks crackling. A faint warmth crept into the kitchen.

'You're letting us go to the workhouse,' said Elizabeth, her tone accusing. She had screwed herself up to say it and Kit, who had been leaning against her thin chest, felt the rapid increase in her heartbeat and looked up into her face uncertainly. She took his little hand in hers. 'Mam always said she would do anything but let us go to the workhouse. That's what she said.'

And that was why she had been working in the turnip

field when she died and Elizabeth had been working with her. She shut her mind to the memory though, it hurt too much.

'Elizabeth, it's not the workhouse where you're going. How many times do I have to tell you?' Betty rose to her feet and picked up the iron kettle, taking it to the tap in the wall by the door, bringing it back full and settling it on the fire. 'It's the Children's Home, the one along Escomb Road. It's a nice new building, and you'll like it there.'

She sighed again. What was the good? She could say it as often as she wanted but Elizabeth and Jimmy had it set in their minds that they were going to the dreaded workhouse, the place most feared by the pit folk. And yet surely Elizabeth, never mind Jimmy, wasn't old enough to know what the workhouse was? She blamed it on their mother.

Betty had had one last try with Ben the evening before. 'We'll get help from the Welfare,' she'd said. 'Howay, Ben, think of the little 'uns.'

'One's enough to have in the house.' He had gazed steadily at her. 'If you hadn't been barren, me girl, we'd have had one of our own by now and then they'd all have gone. Think yourself lucky you've got to keep one. I'm not one for bringing up other men's bairns.'

Now, as she watched Elizabeth holding Kit so possessively, thinking what a proper little mother she was and no mistake, Betty hardened her heart. It was no good, the others had to go, Ben wouldn't let her keep them. But she could keep Kit. That was the most important thing, not to have to give *him* back to anyone now that Jane was gone. Kit was hers and these last few days had been so sweet with a baby of her own to fill her empty arms, stilling the hunger. Before, Jane had always taken them back.

After all, the other children were only going a couple of miles away into the town; they could still see their brother occasionally. People said the new Children's Home was a great improvement on the old system, they would probably like it there. Times had changed. It was 1910, the old Victorian poor laws were going. The old folk had pensions now. The Poor Law Guardians were enlightened folk, more humane. Yes, the children would be well looked after and Elizabeth would get to go to school instead of slaving in the fields with her mother. She was doing them all a favour, Betty reckoned. The bairns would thank her for it when they were old enough to understand properly.

So Betty excused herself but in her heart she knew she would send the others to the opposite ends of the earth, anywhere, just so she could keep her baby. That's what he was now, hers. And Elizabeth had held him long enough.

'Now then, Lizzie, give me the baby and you go and get the others out of bed. It's nearly time for us to go.' Betty's voice was confident, happy, she had convinced herself she was taking the right course and going about it the best way. That was one thing she'd promised them: the workhouse cart wouldn't be calling for them, showing them up in front of the neighbours. No, she was going to take them into Bishop Auckland herself, say goodbye properly.

Elizabeth nodded and did as she was told, though as she handed the baby over she said, 'Don't call me Lizzie, my name's Elizabeth,' yet again to her aunt.

'Oh, Lizzie . . . Elizabeth . . . what does it matter?' said Betty impatiently.

Elizabeth went upstairs and woke little Jenny, who was only three and didn't know what was happening, and Alice who was four and cried for her mam every day and all day. Jimmy was awake, lying at the foot of the bed which had his sisters at the top, curled up so that his legs didn't disturb them.

'Is it time to go?' he asked Elizabeth. His dark blue eyes, fringed with long black lashes that Mam had said were a waste on a boy they were so beautiful, were open wide with fright, his face white.

'It's time,' said Elizabeth. 'Howay, pet, you get dressed while I see to the bairns.' Jimmy was six and quite capable of dressing himself, though the laces of his boots were often trailing on the ground; he couldn't get the knack of tying the knot. So his sister, who was nine and almost grown-up – for hadn't their mam left school and gone to work when she was nine? – dressed Jenny and the grizzling Alice and tied Jimmy's laces.

'Lizzie! Howay now, we have to go,' Auntie Betty shouted, and they went down the stairs to where she was waiting to take them away from Morton Main.

'Don't call me Lizzie,' Elizabeth said again to her aunt, but Betty didn't look at her. They drank hot tea with condensed milk and ate a slice of bread with the last of Mam's plum jam, then Elizabeth took a hand of each of the girls and led them out of the house, Jimmy trailing behind.

'Ta-ra, pets,' said their neighbour Mrs Wearmouth who had come out to the back gate to see them off. 'You look after yoursels, mind.'

'Ta-ra,' chorused the children politely.

Elizabeth pulled on the thick, black, hated cotton stocking and fixed the garter above her knee. Then the black boy's boots with the toe caps and steel segs in the heels and toes to prolong wear. The boots she hated even more than the stockings. It was almost a year since she had come to the Home and had to wear the stockings and boots but still she hated putting them on in the mornings. Not but what she'd worn black boy's boots at home in Morton Main, she conceded as she pulled on the other, but these were worse somehow, heavier.

'Pit boots,' Julia Perkins called them, smirking sideways at the group of girls who always followed her around. Like a queen's court, Elizabeth thought, having just done the Tudor queens in history class. Julia was the daughter of a builder in the town and lived in Cockton Hill, the posh end. She was the scourge of the girls from the Home, her contemptuous tongue as sharp as a knife.

Elizabeth took no notice of her, not outwardly at any rate. As she always told Jimmy whenever she got chance to have a talk with him, which wasn't very often, the boys being in a separate building: 'Never let them see they had got to you.' She would have told Alice and Jenny an' all, but they had left the Home, been fostered. Elizabeth had found out where they were, though. Oh, yes, she'd been determined on that. When Matron had refused to tell her she had managed to get into the office early one morning, slipping in when the cleaner went to the cloakroom for a pail of hot water, and she'd found the records. It hadn't been *so* hard. Elizabeth had worked out what she would do for days beforehand, getting up early and watching and listening.

Anyway Alice was fostered with a shopkeeper and his wife out Coundon way, and Jenny (at the thought Elizabeth's heart raced with worry) miles away up the dale, on a sheep farm. Jenny was so little and she had a bad cough. What would she do on a cold, bleak moor up in Weardale? And how could she, Elizabeth, keep an eye out for her there? Jimmy had been fostered there too for a while but he had run away and gone back to Morton Main. Uncle Ben had dragged him back to the Home, though, after first giving him a clout around the ear which made it ring and still gave him trouble.

'You should have stayed!' Elizabeth had shouted at him. 'You should have looked after Jenny.'

'Eeh, it was bloody awful, man,' said her brother. 'I had to sleep in the barn wi' the cow, I never got a hot dinner neither. And I had to work all the time. The farmer wouldn't let me go to school and when the kiddy-catcher came, he said I'd been playing the nick!' He gazed at Elizabeth with eyes now definitely too big for his face and she saw how thin he was.

'You're just after a bit of sympathy, you,' she said. 'The guardians wouldn't let it happen.'

'Aye, well, they did. They don't believe me, do they?' he answered. 'Our Jenny'll be all right, man, o' course she will. She sleeps in the house. She doesn't have to go out on the moor after sheep, does she?'

'She's only little.'

'Aye. Well, I tell you, she's all right. The missus there, she'll look after our Jenny.' And with that, Elizabeth had to be content.

Sighing, she pulled on the blue and white checked dress which all the girls in the Home wore. It was cut straight, with just some bunching at the back of the waist, and reached to the top of her boots, showing every ugly little bit of them. She pulled on her apron and combed her unruly hair, tying it back as best she could with cotton tape. Ah, well, she thought as she joined the other girls in her room, standing in a long line at the foot of the beds, waiting for Matron to do her rounds, there was nothing she could do about her dress or her boots or stockings so there was no use fretting about them.

The door opened and Matron swept in, tall and stern, her eyes raking the room so that every girl there felt guilty and cast an involuntary glance back to make sure her bed was made properly, every personal possession packed away neatly in a locker.

'Good morning, girls,' Matron boomed and without pausing walked round the room.

'Morning, Matron,' chorused the orphans as they did every morning but Sunday. That was Matron's day off and the highlight of the week because her deputy ruled that day. Miss Rowland was everything Matron was not: warm and loving with the young ones, always ready to talk and smile and even laugh with the older ones. And, best of all, she was always ready to listen to them, interested in all their doings. Elizabeth had asked her why Jenny was to stay on the farm up Weardale when Jimmy had said how awful it was but Miss Rowland just said she thought the guardians would have checked the farm out and Jenny would be fine.

Today, though, was Saturday and Auntie Betty was coming to take Elizabeth and Jimmy out. It was the first time for three months and Elizabeth could hardly contain herself, waiting to see little Kit. Betty was coming at two o'clock sharp and right on the dot Elizabeth and Jimmy were waiting in the entrance of the Home. Half an hour later their aunt was there, walking along Escomb Road as if she had all the time in the world. But what could they say? Kit was walking by her side, his hand in hers. After all, he was only eighteen months old. Elizabeth's heart swelled with love as she saw him.

'Hello there, you two, I see you're ready and waiting,' Auntie Betty said cheerfully. Jimmy's eyes were a bit too bright. He found it so hard to wait about, and he'd been waiting since early morning for the clock to get round to two and every minute after that was as long as an hour to him. He'd thought Auntie Betty wasn't coming, like the time she hadn't turned up at Easter, just sent a couple of dyed eggs for them. She looked away now and pretended she hadn't noticed his tears so close.

'By, it takes a long time with our Kit,' she remarked to Elizabeth, 'his little legs don't go very fast.'

Kit was hanging back, hiding his face in Betty's skirts. She pulled him round and swung him up into her arms. 'Look now, Kit, see who we've come to see. It's your sister Lizzie and that's your brother Jimmy. Don't you remember them?'

Elizabeth held out her arms to him. 'Hello, Kit,' she said. 'Mind, what a big boy you've grown, haven't you?' But he buried his head in his aunt's neck and refused to look and Elizabeth was cut to the quick even though he was changing from a baby into a little boy already and she wouldn't have recognised him herself if it hadn't been for his eyes, the same dark blue as his mam's had

11

been. And, of course, his Auntie Betty's and Jimmy's and her own too.

'Are we going for a picnic in the park, Auntie Betty?' asked Jimmy, looking doubtfully at the empty basket she was carrying.

'Well, I haven't got much time . . .' she began, but stopped as she saw the disappointment in his and his sister's expression though Elizabeth's was quickly masked. Kit began to struggle in her arms and she covered the moment by bending down to stand him on his feet.

'You hold his other hand, Lizzie,' she invited. 'In fact, you can hold one of his hands each.'

'I don't want to,' said Jimmy, looking mutinous.

'Ah, well, maybe you think you're too old for your little brother,' Auntie Betty snapped. She took one of Kit's hands and Elizabeth took the other and they walked slowly to the corner and on down South Road, Jimmy trailing behind even more slowly. But when they came to a butcher's shop, Auntie Betty must have been feeling guilty for she bought penny dips and had the butcher wrap the bread buns dipped in gravy juices carefully. Further down, in Newgate Street, she bought three bottles of liquorice water and they went off down the park. By this time Betty was carrying a sleeping Kit and Elizabeth the basket. So they had their picnic after all.

Elizabeth and Jimmy paddled in the stream and looked for tiddlers and afterwards they ate the picnic sitting on the grass. They'd had mince and taties for their dinner at the Home but they still ate the penny dips and drank the liquorice water, and Jimmy pronounced it to be grand, better than the lemonade Miss Rowland sometimes made them on Sundays (using ingredients she had bought in herself, of course).

Elizabeth made a daisy chain and hung it round Kit's neck but she had to take it off again because he tried eating the daisies. But it was lovely, a lovely day, only spoilt a bit when she brought up the subject of Jenny.

'Have you been to see Jenny too, Auntie Betty?' she asked. Her aunt frowned and got to her feet and dusted the bits of grass from her skirt.

'Best not to worry about Jenny,' she said. 'I haven't been to see her, no, I'd only upset her. But I'm sure she's having a grand life, up on a farm with fresh milk and butter and everything. Come on, we'll walk along the path and then I'll have to take you back. Uncle Ben will be wanting his tea.'

'But – will I never see her again?' asked Elizabeth.

'Never's a long time, lass,' her aunt replied.

'The only time I got milk up there was when I sucked the old cow in the barn,' Jimmy muttered.

'What? Are you making up stories again, our Jimmy?' Auntie Betty snapped at him, and he hung back and began kicking at the grass on the side of the path.

They walked along the path which came from Coundon. Where Alice was, thought Elizabeth, but she was nervous of mentioning it to Auntie Betty who seemed to get into a mood so easily. But one day, she thought, maybe next year, I'll go there myself, I'll find her.

At the railway station Auntie Betty stopped. 'You can find your own way back to Escomb Road, can't you?' she asked them. 'I have to get back.'

So Elizabeth and Jimmy walked back along the road, quiet now their lovely outing was over.

'Do you think she'll come back soon, Elizabeth?' Jimmy asked, but there was no hope in his voice.

'I wouldn't bet on it,' said his sister.

A few months later, on a Friday afternoon, school was over for the week and Elizabeth was walking behind the rest of the class as they came out of the school gates.

'Will you look at Lizzie Nelson?'

Julia Perkins and her cronies were just in front and suddenly Julia turned round and smirked at Elizabeth. 'We're going to the seaside tomorrow on the train, my dad's taking us,' she said. You can't come, though. I *bet you've* never seen the sea.'

'I have! Yes, I have,' said Elizabeth. Well, she'd seen it in pictures, hadn't she? And there was a poster of Redcar-on-Sea at the entrance of the railway station, wasn't there?

'Gerraway! You've never been anywhere. You haven't got anybody to take you, you're the queen of the bastids. You've only got your Jimmy and he's a bastid an' all.' The other girls looked at each other and at Julia Perkins who was fairly dancing with enjoyment as she jeered at the orphan from the Children's Home. They tittered uncertainly.

Elizabeth was determined not to be drawn though her heart was beating wildly. She was looking forward to the weekend for Auntie Betty had sent word she was coming to take her and Jimmy out, the first time for months and months. And she wasn't going to let Julia Perkins spoil that for her. No, she wasn't.

'My name is Elizabeth,' she couldn't stop herself from saying, though.

'And you're a bastid!' sang Julia, and laughed, a cackling unbearable sound. 'I bet you don't know what that means, do you? My mam and dad say that's what you are 'cos you never had a dad.'

Elizabeth was stung. 'I did! Of course I did. He went to America, went to make his fortune, and he's coming back for us, he is!'

'You're telling lies. You're always telling lies. You have no mam and no dad and you're a bastid. My mam says folk like you should be put down, 'cos it's folk like us has to pay for your keep.'

Elizabeth crossed her fingers behind her back. It was just a little lie she'd told. 'I'm not lying and I'm not a bastid neither. My mam died and my dad's coming back for us – he is! And I'm going out tomorrow, my auntie's coming for us. We're going to . . . to . . .' Elizabeth paused, trying to think of somewhere better than the seaside. 'We're going to London!' she shouted, inspiration coming.

Julia and all her friends laughed this time. They laughed loudly, bending over and holding their sides, their mouths open, their faces red with laughing. Elizabeth turned and ran from the hateful sound, running along the pavement in her clumsy black boots with the steel segs which struck sparks off the stones. But even when she turned the corner she could still hear them. She leaned against the wall, tears springing to her eyes, panting with rage.

'Howay, man, what's the matter with you? Come on, we won't get any tea if you don't hurry up.' It was Jimmy, coming from the boys' school. He stopped beside her on the pavement.

'It was Julia Perkins. She said . . .'

'Why, man, take no notice what she said. Anyway, you know Auntie Betty's coming tomorrow. She might buy us sweets, bulls' eyes maybe. She'll take us out anyroad. Come on, I'll race you back. I'll give you a start, if you like.'

And they were off, running like the wind. To hell with Julia Perkins, Elizabeth told herself. Tomorrow they were going out with Auntie Betty and Kit would be there. She was dying to see how he had grown.

They waited all day by the front gate of the Home. It

was sunny in the morning and they didn't go in for their dinner, just in case they missed her. But it rained in the afternoon and Miss Rowland came out to them and persuaded them to go in for their tea. On Monday morning a comic postcard came from Auntie Betty showing a picture of Cockerton Green, wherever that was. *'Sorry I couldn't come,'* she had written. *'Don't worry, I'll come to see you soon.'* But she never did.

That night Elizabeth dreamed about the day her mother died. She did that sometimes.

Chapter Two

Elizabeth was back in her dream, reliving that terrible day.

'Lizzie! Ah, Lizzie . . .'

The voice was faint, had she really heard it? She turned over in her bed and suddenly the dream was reality: she was snagging turnips. She paused in her work and looked about her. Was that a voice? She pushed her thick dark hair back from her face, leaving a smear of mud on her forehead. Had someone spoken or was it just a voice from the story she was telling herself in her thoughts, one of the stories she told herself all the time when she was out in the frozen fields, chopping away at the turnips – or snagging them as the farmer called it – so they provided extra fodder for the sheep and cattle.

All was quiet, the field deserted, nothing moving except for the curl of smoke from the farm in the distance, a dark stormy grey yet barely perceptible against the leaden colour of the sky. Where was Mam? Elizabeth got to her feet, stiff as an old woman after a couple of hours crouched on the frozen earth. Mam could snag turnips standing up but Elizabeth had to get closer to them. After all, she was only nine, going on ten, and her wrists were thin as matchsticks, much like the rest of her.

'What d'you bring the lass for then?' the farmer had asked Mam on Monday morning when Elizabeth had turned up with her. 'She doesn't look strong enough to snag a turnip.'

'But she is,' Mam had said. 'She's good at it an' all, will she show you?'

And Elizabeth had stood as tall as she could in her old black boots with the cardboard soles Mam had cut for her only the night before. 'We'll get them soled properly on Friday, pet,' Mam had said then, 'both of us together. We'll make a deal of money in a week, me and you, see if we don't. And we'll have butcher's meat on Sunday.'

Elizabeth hadn't been so sure about the money. In her experience they never did make as much as Mam thought they would. And anyroad, the kiddy-catcher might find out she was working in the fields on a school day and Mam would be fined and then where would they be? Elizabeth sighed now as she bent back to her work. Mam must have gone off into the coppice at the side of the field; that was where she had told Elizabeth to go when she had to answer a call of nature. Anyroad, she thought as she resumed chopping the top from a mud-caked turnip, the farmer hadn't really cared whether Elizabeth was helping her mam or not. All he was interested in was that the work was done, and done cheaply. And as Mam said, there was always work for such as her for no labour is cheaper than that of a woman on her own with a family to support.

'Lizzie? Where are you, Lizzie? Eeh, for God's sake, pet . . .'

Lizzie sprang to her feet this time. Oh, yes, that had been her mam calling all right and there was something desperately the matter. Her voice had sounded so funny. She gazed round frantically and then, dropping her snagger, began to run towards the coppice.

'Mam? Mam?'

The cry burst from her as she ducked under a straggling branch of hawthorn. Thorns clutched at her, scratching her face, tearing her dress and the skin of her forearms. And she knew what she was going to see: her mother lying on the ground, hands clutching her belly, face whiter than the frosted leaves on the bushes around her. And even as she watched her mother's hands loosed their grasp on her stomach and fell to the ground on either side, palms uppermost, open, fingers bent and the broken nails pointing to the sky. Her eyes were closed, her lips almost as white as her face. The only colour was in the red pool soaking the earth about her, staining her patched old working skirt. The stain widened even as

20

Elizabeth watched for a frozen second before snatching
up her mam's old shawl which had caught on a bush and
been pulled from her shoulders.

Elizabeth knelt by her mother, covering her with the
shawl, taking the one from her own shoulders, pushing
it under her mother's inert body, frantically trying to
warm her hands, patting her cheeks, crying, 'Mam! Oh,
Mam!' A wailing, desolate cry. And her mother opened
her eyes and looked up at her. Elizabeth couldn't bear
that look. It was faraway though a faint smile came into
the eyes, came and went so swiftly that a second after
seeing it Elizabeth wasn't sure it had even been there.
And then they were blank and staring and Mam's mouth
fell open and her head fell back and Elizabeth knew she
was dead for she had that look, that empty look.

Elizabeth wept. She wept and cried for her mother,
and the bushes crowded in on her, and suddenly all she
could see was the bare brown of the hawthorn and the
red, the deep, deep red of the blood, spreading on the
ground and covering everything . . .

Elizabeth screamed and sat up in bed, her nightdress
wet with sweat, hair sticking to her head and neck. Her
heart beat furiously, her mouth was dry as tinder.

'Elizabeth, stop it! You've just had a nightmare, that's
all. Wake up properly now, you don't want to have
Matron in here, do you?'

She turned her head and stared at the girl who was
speaking, barely above a whisper. It was her friend Joan,

standing by the side of the bed, shivering in her cotton nightgown for the night was chilly. Elizabeth drew in a long shuddering breath and lay down again. The immediacy of the nightmare faded. It had happened so long ago, why did it always come back to her when she was upset?

'Oh, Mam, Mam,' she whispered, 'don't haunt me, Mam.'

'What? What did you say?' Joan leaned closer to catch her words.

'Nothing, it was just a dream,' Elizabeth whispered back.

'I'll get you a cup of water,' Joan offered, and went to the washstand by the door where the jug of water stood and there was an old cup for the girls to rinse their teeth. She filled it and brought it to Elizabeth and her friend drank it thirstily and lay down again, shivering.

Joan got into the narrow bed with her: she always did when one of them had a nightmare. The girls lay with arms intertwined until warmth crept back into their bones and they fell into a natural sleep. As dawn was breaking, Joan crept back into her own bed. It wouldn't do for anyone to find them in bed together, especially not Matron.

It was Monday morning and the orphans from the Home were on their way to school. Elizabeth walked beside Joan. There was a poetry test this morning and they were reciting Robert Browning's 'Home Thoughts from Abroad'. Elizabeth spoke confidently, Joan watching her friend's mouth for clues as she stumbled through the difficult bit about 'the brushwood sheaf round the elm tree bole are in tiny leaf', the part she always got muddled about, when Julia Perkins came round the bend, as usual surrounded by her cronies.

'Well, here's Lizzie Nelson. Did you have a good time in *London* then?' She was grinning her disbelief before Elizabeth even spoke, looking sideways at her friends. By, it's a great joke, her grin seemed to be saying, a girl from the Home going on a trip to London, I must say!

Elizabeth turned and ran, Joan shouting after her: 'Hey, what's the matter?' But Elizabeth simply shouted over her shoulder, 'I'll see you tonight.'

'Are you badly then?' Joan took a few steps after her then hesitated.

'No . . . Yes, tell them I've got the runs . . .' And then she was off, hurrying along the alleyway which led to the path along the top of the wood to Old Morton village, and after the village Morton Main.

She slowed down to a walk as she came to the wood and ducked under the fence until she was under the trees, listening to the birds, smelling the wild garlic almost overpowering the damp musty scent of the ground. She was alone in the wood, the trees joining overhead to make a canopy, mysterious and exciting.

She crossed the rickety wooden bridge over the

stream, and walked up the rise to the old railway line and the tunnel beneath, emerging on the other side only a mile or two from home. For Morton Main was home to her still, even though she hadn't seen it during the years she had been in *the* Home. Oh, why hadn't she been brave enough to come before? Everything she saw now was familiar, even after all this time, familiar and dear.

She passed her old school; heard the chanting from the classrooms. The seven times table as she passed class four; 'I before E except after C' from class five. And then she was approaching West Row and her old home. 'I'm a fool,' she said aloud. There was another family living there now, she had to go instead to Double Row, to Auntie Betty's house. She found it and walked up the back yard to knock boldly on the door. Auntie Betty would not turn her away, she thought, even though she couldn't be bothered to come to see her and Jimmy in Auckland.

It was Uncle Ben who opened the door, his collarless shirt open at the neck, braces hanging down over his trousers, a cigarette hanging from his wet lips.

'Aye, what do you want?' he asked, lifting a hand to scratch at the stubble on his chin. Then he took in her blue and white checked dress, black cotton stockings wrinkled around the legs, the hair tied back severely with black tape, and frowned.

'It's not Lizzie, is it? What the hell are you doing here?'

'Elizabeth.' She stared at him, lifting her chin, willing him to let her in, remembering how Auntie Betty had said it was Uncle Ben who wouldn't take them in when Mam died. 'I want to talk to Auntie Betty.'

He stood back from the door, allowing her room to get past, and she walked into the kitchen. There were dirty pots on the table. He'd evidently just eaten a fried breakfast; congealed fat and a crust of fried bread lay on a plate and there was a smell of bacon. The fire was blazing, making the room suffocatingly hot, and the zinc bath stood on the hearth rug, half full of grey scummy water.

Uncle Ben followed her in, grinning. 'Well,' he remarked as though it was the greatest joke in the world, 'you'll have a job to see your Auntie Betty because she's not here.'

Elizabeth's face fell. She hadn't thought her aunt might not be in, it was Monday, wasn't it? Monday was washing day in Morton Main. No woman was out of her house then, she was too busy with the possing stick at the wash tub. Maybe she'd gone to the Co-op?

'But she'll be back, it's washing day. I can wait, can't I?'

'Please yourself.'

Ben Hoddle closed the door and took a seat beside the fire. He nipped the glowing end of his cigarette into the flames and put the stump behind his ear. 'Aye, well, she might be a while.'

'I don't mind, I can wait, I've plenty of time,' said Elizabeth. She glanced around her. 'I'll side the table, if you like?' she offered. She was uncomfortable just sitting there with him staring at her.

He sniffed. 'If you like,' he said, and, taking the stump from behind his ear, lit it again from a piece of paper he tore from a newspaper lying on the steel fender. He sat back and watched her as she tidied away the remains of his meal and washed the dirty pots in a chipped enamel bowl with a ladle of water from the boiler on one side of the fire.

At first she was so full of disappointment at not seeing Kit she was hardly aware of Ben. She worked away, washing and drying pots and putting them in the mahogany press which took up almost the whole of one side of the room. Then she took a bucket and scooped water out of the bath tub, taking it outside to the drain in the brick-paved yard. It was when she bent down to lift the now almost empty bath that she became aware of his eyes on her. Looking up, she saw he was staring intently down the ill-fitting neck of her dress, where it fell open as she stood bent almost double.

Blushing deeply, she seized the handles of the tub and lifted it off the ground, then stood looking at him.

'Open the door for me,' she said, not looking directly at him. Even her ears were blushing, she knew it.

'Yes, right, I will, pet,' he replied and jumped up to do it. She felt her back brush against him as he stood

26

holding on to the door handle and took a deep breath of fresh air as she got outside. She emptied the bath tub and hung it on the nail between the window and the door, and still he stood there. Elizabeth walked to the gate and looked up and down the street but there was no sign of Auntie Betty or Kit. There were a couple of women stringing out drying lines across the street, that was all, but they were strangers to her.

He was still standing in the doorway as Elizabeth reluctantly walked back up the yard. She didn't know what had changed about him since he'd first opened the door to her, she only knew he made her feel squirmy inside. He was looking at her through short, sandy lashes and there was a peculiar grin on his face.

'I don't want to keep you out of bed, Uncle Ben,' she said as she stepped into the house, 'not when you've just come off shift.' If he had just had his bath he must have been on fore shift, she reckoned. Surely he would be wanting his bed? 'I can wait here myself, I'm all right. I might go round and see Mrs Wearmouth anyroad.'

He put out a hand and slid his forefinger under her chin. 'You know, pet, you're growing up, aren't you? How old are you now?'

'Twelve.'

Elizabeth retreated until the backs of her knees were hard up against the wooden frame of the settee. But he stepped forward too and ran his hand round the back of her neck then under her dress.

'Mind, you're growing up into a bonny lass an' all,' he said softly. 'I bet you've got nice little titties under there.' His face was close to hers, she could see the small blue marks where coal had got into his cuts. There were hairs emerging from his nostrils, a different colour from his beard, she noticed. It felt unreal, this couldn't be happening. Auntie Betty would be coming in with Kit any minute, she told herself. Ducking under his arm, she went to the other side of the kitchen, putting the table between them. For a second an expression of irritation crossed his face. He opened his mouth to snap at her, then changed his mind.

'Do you know? I reckon we wouldn't mind having you come to stay with us now. You could help your auntie, couldn't you? I bet you'd like to get out of that place, wouldn't you?'

'Where is she?' Elizabeth burst out, ignoring his question. Oh, if only Auntie Betty would come!

'Never you mind, she'll be along,' said Ben. 'Howay now, I'm not going to hurt you, you look like a frightened rabbit.' He walked round the table and Elizabeth froze. Her brain wouldn't work. He put an arm round her waist and pulled her to him, rubbing himself against her thin little body.

'By, that's nice,' he murmured and his eyes closed. He sagged a little. It was enough for her to slip out of his grasp. She came alive and ducked for the door, wrenching it open and fleeing down the yard.

'Come back here, you little bugger!' he roared after her. In the road women turned in surprise to see her running by. They heard Ben shout but he didn't come out.

'Are you all right, hinny?' one of the women asked, but Elizabeth hadn't time to reply. She fled for West Row.

Mrs Wearmouth was hanging out her washing. 'Why, hello, Elizabeth,' she cried, 'I never thought to see you! And mind, how you've grown. You're shooting up like a bean stalk and about as fat. How are you, love?'

'I'm fine, Mrs Wearmouth,' Elizabeth replied, panting after the run, her face all red, her hair dishevelled. 'Mrs Wearmouth, do you know where Auntie Betty is?'

'Why, aye, I do as it happens. Aw, have you come to see her and her away at Cockerton for a few days? Did you not know? She had to go to see her man's mother. The old woman's had a stroke, they've took her into the workhouse at Darlington. You won't see her today, you'll have to come back. There's nowt else for it.'

'I'm very disappointed in you, Elizabeth,' said Matron. 'What have you to say for yourself?'

'I'm sorry, Matron.'

She gazed at the child. She wasn't a bad girl, not like some of those that came into the Home. Elizabeth was growing up now but she was showing none of the bad habits some of the other girls did and often had to have beaten out of them. She didn't stare after the boys, didn't giggle in corners and scrimp on her chores.

'Where did you go?' Matron asked, more softly.

'Just down to woods, Matron. I . . . I plodged in the beck. It was lovely.' Elizabeth couldn't possibly tell the truth, couldn't mention Uncle Ben. Her mind as well as her tongue was frozen at the thought of him. Anyroad, if she said anything they would think it was her fault, and maybe it was. Maybe she had done something to make him think . . . No, she hadn't.

'You will apologise to the teacher and take whatever punishment she thinks necessary. And you will report to me when you come back from school. Every evening, do you hear?'

'Yes, Matron.'

'Now go to bed, you'll get no supper.' Elizabeth was glad to find herself outside the door. She knew the interview would have gone on and on but it was Matron's early evening off and she wanted to get away. That was lucky anyroad.

She sat on her bed in the empty room, staring out of the window. Fragments of memory had returned to her during the day. She remembered especially the day Mam died. Mrs Wearmouth and Auntie Betty were in the kitchen, the neighbour helping to get the dinner ready.

'Who the hell put another babby in her belly?'

It was Mrs Wearmouth speaking. The children were sitting in a row on the settee watching as she cut potatoes in half and dropped them in the great iron pan with a plop. Even the baby was watching, his fist stuffed in his mouth.

'Shh, the bairns are listening,' Betty had hissed, and the two women turned away.

Elizabeth pondered over this conversation now. Funny how she had forgotten so many things from when she was younger but that day stuck in her memory. It meant something, she knew, and one day she would find out what.

Chapter Three

1916

Elizabeth turned over the card of the everlasting calender which Auntie Betty had sent her for Christmas the first year she went to the Children's Home. There it was, the day she had been waiting for, the day she was free, for today was 23rd June, 1916 and she was sixteen years old. As her mam used to say, she was almost as old as the century.

More important, Jimmy was thirteen next month and he too would be free of the Home and the guardians, for wasn't there a war on? Because of the war her brother could leave school a whole year early and go to work. He'd sat the exam which proved he was proficient in reading and writing and could do sums and recite the kings and queens of England, and in three weeks' time he too would be free.

'Elizabeth! Get yourself down here, you're late, it's almost a quarter to six.'

'Coming, Joan, I'm coming,' Elizabeth called back down the attic stairs, but this morning she wasn't inclined to hurry and turned back to the old looking glass above the deal chest of drawers which she shared with Joan, her friend from the Home and now the maid of all work in the big old house which was doing duty as a hospital for wounded soldiers. And there were plenty of them in this second year of the war.

Elizabeth poured cold water from the jug into the basin which stood on the washstand by the door. She splashed her face and arms and dried them quickly on the thin towel before cleaning her teeth with Odontoline, rinsing and spitting in the water before she emptied it into the slop pail and rubbed the basin around with an old flannel. Within a couple of minutes she was dressed and covered with the green wraparound overall and cap which was as much a uniform as she had had to wear in her orphanage days. But this was different, this was a working uniform, and besides she didn't have to wear black shapeless stockings with it but had some decent beige ones like everyone else.

Downstairs in the kitchen Joan had already eaten her porridge and gone. Bless her, thought Elizabeth gratefully, her friend had cooked enough porridge for both of them and there was a cup of tea in the pot too. After all, there was a whole three hours yet to proper breakfast which was shared by all the staff, including the nurses, and a lot of hard work to be got through before then.

She washed and dried the pots and put them carefully away before going out into the cool morning air. The laundry was just across the yard, a converted coachhouse it was, right next to the stables. As Elizabeth hurried past she heard Jimmy's voice. He was talking to the horses as he worked and she smiled to hear it. Jimmy loved horses, especially the big, patient farm horses which shared the stables with the carriage horses and the pony which pulled the trap to the station for supplies three times a week.

There was no one in the laundry room, the laundress didn't usually come until eight o'clock, but Elizabeth was the laundry maid and it was her job to fill the boilers and light the fires underneath them. Then she had to sort the laundry. Most of it was white, sheets and pillow-cases, but there were nightshirts and hospital blues too. Even the whites which had come in since yesterday evening were to be sorted into grades of soiling and the worst put into cold salted water to soak.

Elizabeth set to with a will. For one thing, work kept her warm and it was cool in this great cavernous place, even in June. Though it would be hot later on in the day when the boilers were at their hottest and the sun was directly overhead.

It was almost eight o'clock. The fires were burning brightly and the huge coppers beginning to sing. Elizabeth picked up the two buckets of ash which she had raked from under the grates and started to carry them, panting slightly, out to the corner of the yard where the ash pit was. She was a little clumsy with the weight of the buckets and only just managed to stop herself from colliding with a wheelchair containing a man in hospital blues being pushed by an orderly.

'Oh!' she gasped and put down the pails with a bump, spilling a ring of grey ash as she did so. A lock of hair had fallen over her forehead and she pushed it back under her cap, unaware that she left a smear of grey on the white skin.

'Watch where you're going, will yer!' the orderly shouted. He had stopped the chair and turned towards her, holding the handle of the chair in one hand and lifting the other in a threatening gesture as though he might swipe her across the face with it. He was a middle-aged man and wore the uniform of a soldier but with a Red Cross armband on his left sleeve.

Elizabeth shrank back involuntarily. Private Wilson was known as a man who bullied anyone he considered to be below him, though he acted very differently towards the officers and nursing staff.

'Stop wasting time, Wilson,' said the man in the wheelchair. 'I told you I fancied a look around the grounds, not the stable yard.'

'Yes, Captain Benson. Sorry, sir.'

The man cast a last baleful glance at Elizabeth and resumed pushing the chair over the cobbles of the yard.

The man in the chair had been looking back at her but now he jerked and gripped the arms with whitened knuckles. A line between his eyebrows deepened into a furrow but he said nothing more.

Elizabeth watched until they were out of sight round the corner of the block. Poor man, she thought, still seeing in her mind's eye the plaid which had covered the bottom half of the captain's body, the flat place at the bottom where his feet were missing. He looked vaguely familiar though his accent was what she would call 'posh', like most of the officers at the Hall, so she couldn't have known him before. None of her acquaintances talked posh. She hadn't seen him at the Hall before either, he must be new.

Benson . . . Now where had she heard that name? He had fair hair that needed cutting. The sun had glinted on it as the chair moved into the light after the shadow of the stable block, the last thing she'd noticed before he disappeared from view. He could have been good-looking but for the scar which ran down from the corner of his left eye and disappeared under the collar of his shirt. Benson . . . Absent-mindedly, Elizabeth went in for the broom and shovel, and began sweeping up the ashes she had spilt.

Of course! Benson was the name of the man who'd owned the mine where her dad had worked before he took off. He'd owned a number of mines. She remembered the name clearly now, had even seen the man when she was little. His son looked something like him, that was why he'd seemed familiar. Mr Benson had often been around Morton when her mam was alive. Probably still was.

'Elizabeth Nelson, will you stop dreaming and get on with your work? Do you mean to say you haven't even got rid of the ashes yet? How are we supposed to get the washing done . . .?'

Elizabeth hurriedly stood the broom and shovel against the wall of the laundry and picked up the buckets of ash.

'Sorry, Mrs Poskett, I'll just take them now,' she said, and hurried away to tip out the ash. Mary Poskett was in charge of the laundry and Elizabeth was her only laundry maid, though there was enough work for another. But she was a nice enough woman, and not afraid to work as hard as Elizabeth if necessary.

She had worn a strange expression when Elizabeth had first turned up for work, as though she was going to mention the old days at Morton Main, but she never did. She had no family, though there was talk in the hospital of a daughter who had disappeared. Probably run off to London, thought Elizabeth when she heard that, and felt sympathy for the older woman and a pang for her own father.

They worked until time for staff breakfast, a substantial one taken in the big kitchen of the old house along with everyone else who worked there, except for

Matron and the doctors, of course. And afterwards they went back to work, putting the linen through the great wooden rollers of the mangle. Elizabeth turned the handle while Mrs Poskett fed in the washing, and then at last, her arms aching from the prolonged effort, it was ready to hang out on the drying green beside the vegetable garden.

Mary Poskett stood back, puffing a bit, her face beetroot red from the effort. 'Eeh, lass,' she said. 'It's getting over much for me. Fair pulls me arms out, it does.' She looked down at the remaining clothes in the basket and sighed.

'You go in, it's nearly tea-time anyway,' said Elizabeth. 'Go on, I'll finish up here.'

'You're not a bad lass,' commented Mary, and trailed up the path to the gate which led to the stable yard and the laundry.

Elizabeth sang to herself as she worked, hardly knowing what it was she was singing, happy to see the white linen blowing on the lines in the afternoon sun. There was ironing to do after tea, but she didn't mind that. Plain ironing it was mostly, bed linen. And there was the never-ending round of washing. Already the dirty skip would be waiting, full to the brim with more sheets to sort and soak.

Jack Benson sat in his wheelchair in the bay of a first-floor window, staring out over the back of the house, not seeing anything much of the rolling fields he had loved to roam as a boy, nor the tall chimney of a colliery in the distance, belching black smoke.

His attention was caught, however, by the movement of white objects closer to the house. He leaned forward and gazed down. It was a drying ground. The white objects were sheets and pillowcases, he could see that now, blowing in the wind. The girl was there, pegging out smaller items, her dark hair blowing too as it escaped from her cap. Her hands were red, he could see the colour even from this distance; she was thin yet she handled the linen well, deftly pegging it out on the lines which were moving as the wind caught the sheets and lifted them to flap and crack in the air. Not pretty, but there was something about her . . .

He sighed and sat back, away from the window. He was bored, that was it, taking such an interest in a washer girl. Now, if he was home it would be different. In Newcomb Hall he was so close. He could walk from here, taking the footpath over the fields, it wasn't more than a mile or two. Or if he still had his feet he could walk. But he hadn't. He needed looking after and at home there was only his mother, frail and living in a twilight world since the death of his father. And old Nancy couldn't look after both of them, of course she couldn't. She was only a cook after all.

His attention was caught by a movement down in the garden near the drying ground, a glimpse of khaki from behind a bush, a hand on top of the garden wall. One of the orderlies having an illicit cigarette, he supposed. Yes, there was a small puff of smoke rising into the air.

Jack leaned forward as far as he could, more out of boredom than anything else. The orderly stepped out into the open as the garden gate opened and the girl came in, carrying her laundry basket. He threw the cigarette end away and it swung in an arc and landed in an onion patch. He was stepping up to the girl, putting out his hand. Jack felt a tiny pang of disappointment. It was an assignation, obviously there was something going on between them.

He would have pushed his chair away from the window but the orderly who left him there had put the brake on hard and he couldn't move it. He tried to look elsewhere: out to the distant stand of trees, at the clothes blowing in the wind, anywhere. It was extraordinarily difficult somehow. And suddenly he heard a cry, quickly choked off, and looked back at the couple.

The orderly, Jack recognised him now, was Private Wilson. He seized the girl. Her basket fell to the ground as she struggled. Private Wilson's hand was clasped over her face . . . Good God! The man was molesting the girl, she wasn't a willing partner at all! He was dragging her behind the bush. The girl was fighting, flailing her arms, grabbing hold of the wall. The man was grinning!

Jack looked about for the bell the nurse had left with him. He rang it, loud and clear. Wilson looked up at the windows for a moment and carried on trying to get the girl behind the bush. Frustrated, Jack pushed himself forward in his seat, cursing his missing feet, trying to reach the window which was open only a couple of inches at the bottom.

He fell to the carpet, catching his forehead a glancing blow which he hardly felt, he was so intent on reaching the window. Why the hell didn't someone come? What was the use of a bell if no one answered it? Dragging himself on to his knees, making his missing feet throb with pain, he managed to reach the window sill. Pushing upwards with his arms, getting his shoulder beneath the sash in the end, hanging on to the wooden frame of the window, he at last got it open another six inches.

'Private Wilson!' he yelled.

The sound reverberated round the garden, bounced against the wall of the house. It was the loudest he had yelled since leading his men against the Turks at Gallipoli, up the hill, in a hopeless charge which had ended abruptly for him when he stepped with both feet on a hidden mine. It was the only time he had yelled since. 'I *am* still alive then,' Jack muttered as his missing feet and the half-healed scar on his face throbbed in unison, and he slid down from the window to the polished wooden boards beneath and on into a pain-filled blackness.

'Captain Benson, what on earth are you doing?' Nurse Turner exclaimed as she burst into the room in answer to the bell which had interrupted her tea. 'Orderly, where are you?' she called, and knelt on the floor to rest the captain's head on her lap. His eyelids flickered and opened. She sighed with relief. Well, thank the Lord, for a minute there she had thought he had done for himself. They were always hearing of maimed young officers finishing themselves off one way or another, though so far none had at this place. She glanced suspiciously at the window. He hadn't been trying to throw himself out, had he?

'What were you doing?' she demanded again.

'Sorry, Nurse, I leaned too far forward, that was all. Trying to see more,' said Jack meekly. The floor orderly came in and between them they heaved the captain back into his chair.

'I see you've banged one of your stumps; now I'll have to dress it again.' Nurse Turner frowned. As though she had nothing else to do but re-dress wounds all day, was the unspoken reproof. Jack looked down at the stump he still couldn't believe was on the end of his leg. There was blood on the bandage, not a lot but enough to cause concern.

'Sorry, Nurse,' he muttered.

'Yes, well, I'm sure you are,' she replied. She brought an enamel dressing tray and undid the bandage and removed the dressing. There was a red patch, angry-looking, on one end of the stump, but the seepage of blood was already drying up. 'Doesn't look too bad,' she said grudgingly as she washed her hands in the basin in the corner. But her fingers, as she dressed and bandaged the wound again, were deft and soothing, she was a good nurse.

'Send Private Wilson to me when you go down, orderly,' said Jack as they were leaving the room. The man looked surprised. Nevertheless he agreed. Jack settled back in his chair and closed his eyes, feeling suddenly exhausted. But before he could doze he wanted a word or two with Private Wilson.

'Where the heck have you been, lady?' Mrs Poskett demanded as Elizabeth ran into the laundry room with the empty basket. Sweat was running down Mrs Poskett's face as she stood at the table and ironed pillow-cases, one after the other, and folded them lengthwise to air on the great clothes-horse.

'I . . . I . . .' Elizabeth felt like bursting into tears, sobbing the whole story out to the older woman, but she bit the words back. They would do no good, there was nothing Mrs Poskett could do for her. It was a hazard the young girls faced daily from a certain section of the soldiers and other men working in the place.

It was the general view in the kitchen that if a girl made it plain she wanted nothing to do with a fellow then he would leave her alone. Eventually. The thing was, Cook said, never let yourself get in a position where a man could take advantage. Never 'ask for it', as they said. Which was all very well for Cook, a comfortable fifty if she was a day, in age as well as round the hips.

'Well, come on now, you'll have to do without your tea. I'm fair clemmed for a cup,' snapped Mrs Poskett. 'Help me fold these sheets, will you?'

'Yes, Mrs Poskett.'

The two women folded and smoothed the clean dry sheets and put them through the mangle to smooth them. Afterwards Elizabeth ironed the hems. It was well after eight when she finally finished and she went straight to her room as the thought of food made her feel nauseous. She was thankful that Joan was still working and she had the room to herself.

Lying on the bed, she thought about Private Wilson. By, he was a rotten, randy old sod, she reckoned. He had been after her for ages even though he bullied her whenever he got the chance. She always tried to make sure she was with Mrs Poskett or Joan when he was about the place. It was just bad luck he had been in the garden when the laundress went back inside.

Elizabeth shuddered, remembering the feel of his hands on her, the animal stink of him. He had hurt her too. There was a bruise on her thigh where he had tried to thrust himself into her most private place; one on her neck where he had held her. For a minute there she had thought it was all up for her, that he had won. A bell had rung somewhere but that meant nothing, all the patients had bells.

Elizabeth had stared at the blank windows of the house with the sun full on them. Why was there nobody looking out when she needed someone? She'd tried to bite Wilson's hand but he was too wily for that, then she had seen a movement at a first-floor window, someone watching there. She'd struggled all the harder but Wilson was succeeding in pulling her behind the bush. Another minute and they would be out of sight.

Then she had heard it. The officer, Captain Benson, had got his head out of the window and yelled at Private Wilson. Suddenly she was dropped, painfully scratching her back on a broken twig; she could feel the place now. And Private Wilson was ducking away behind the raspberries, making for the gate.

Elizabeth had stood up. She'd gazed at the window where Captain Benson had been but it was as blank as the others. Shakily she'd picked up the laundry basket and hurried round to the laundry room. She'd felt bruised and dirty, just as she had done that time Uncle Ben . . . Uncle Ben . . . no, she wouldn't think of that.

Chapter Four

'Will you go with me, Jimmy?'

'Go with you where?' he replied, absently scuffing at the gravel on the path by the side of Newcomb Hall. It was Sunday morning and the staff of the Hall, those who could be spared, had just returned from church.

Elizabeth sighed. All the way back from the village she had been telling her brother how there was a train to Weardale at two o'clock and she was determined to travel on it up beyond Frosterley, as close to the address she had in her tin box of meagre private possessions as she could get. The address where Jenny was living. Elizabeth had hardly slept all night for excitement. The time had come when she was going to see her little sister again. Or not so little now, she reminded herself, Jenny must be ten. It had been a long six years. Now Elizabeth couldn't understand why Jimmy wasn't as excited as she was herself.

'Jimmy, are you coming with me?' she asked again, struggling to keep the impatience out of her voice.

'I suppose,' he said at last. 'Though I was going down the bunny banks with the lads.'

Elizabeth bit back a retort. After all, he was only thirteen and he worked all week. 'Come on then, we'll go straight after dinner, we don't want to miss the train,' was all she said.

She had saved the fare and a bit to spare for extras over the last six months, never spending a penny without looking at it twice, putting cardboard in her boots to cover the holes as Mam used to do, patching her bloomers and petticoat. She smiled, thinking of it. She had even darned over the darns in the heels of her stockings, though it made for hard lumps which rubbed at her skin and caused calluses.

Jimmy was unnaturally quiet as she bought the tickets at Bishop Auckland station, only showing interest when the train came chugging in from the direction of Darlington, enveloped in steam and smoke. He followed her docilely into a third-class compartment and sat staring out of the window, leaving her to her own thoughts.

At the last minute a soldier backed into the compartment, carrying a large suitcase. He had a Red Cross armband on and for a minute Elizabeth's heart fell to her boots, but no, it wasn't Private Wilson, this soldier didn't even work at the Hall.

She bit her lip. She'd had to face Wilson a couple of times since the incident in the garden and both times he had leered at her, a knowing leer which made her flesh crawl. She stared out of the window at the green sides of the cut they were going through, seeing her own pale face reflected there. Why were men so horrible? she wondered miserably. She had a rotten feeling it must be something to do with her. She remembered Cook's words about some girls giving men the 'come on'. But she didn't do that, she didn't.

Shrugging, she determined to think no more of Private Wilson. And all men weren't the same anyroad, she told herself. The captain now, Captain Benson, he wasn't like that, he was a proper gentleman. It gave her a warm feeling to think how he had tried to help, shouting at Private Wilson from his window.

The train had pulled into Witton Park station. The soldier lugged his suitcase off there and she and Jimmy had the carriage to themselves again. Jimmy was blowing on the window until it misted over then drawing marks in it. He stopped as the train pulled away and there was a pit head close by and the straggle of colliery houses.

'After this the ride gets prettier,' Elizabeth offered. 'You'll like it up the dale, the hills and the fields and the river.' She hadn't been herself but she'd heard about it from Mrs Poskett whose grandmother lived in Wolsingham.

'The river's here,' said Jimmy, and it was true, the Wear wound beneath them, they were going over a viaduct. But the banks weren't pretty. There was the black of shale and coal, bricks and stones from old buildings. 'There was an ironworks here,' he said unexpectedly.

'How do you know?'

He shrugged. 'I know. And it's a lot more interesting than old fields and trees and such.' He sat back in the seat and stared at Elizabeth, an odd, defiant stare.

'What's the matter?' she was stung into asking.

'Nothing. Nothing's the matter. I'm going to get a job down the pit. Me an' me mates . . . we're all going to get jobs down the pit.'

'Jimmy, you can't! You're too young. And anyroad, you have a good job now.'

'Call that a good job? I don't know why they bother to pay us at the end of the week, I get nowt. Down the pit I could earn a fortune if I worked hard enough. I'm not too young neither. They're taking lads on my age at Morton Main, an' glad to get them an' all. What wi' the war.'

Elizabeth stared at him. 'The guardians won't let you,' she said weakly.

He nodded his head vigorously. 'Aye, they will. Tommy Gibson's starting next week.'

There was nothing she could say, Elizabeth knew that. Jimmy had been working up to telling her something all day and it was this. And if the guardians said it was all right, no one was going to take any notice of her. She was only sixteen herself. Witton-le-Wear went past, they were coming into Wolsingham. Soon they would be in Frosterley.

'We'll talk about it tomorrow,' she said.

'Please yourself but I'm doing it anyroad,' he said, in the firm tones of a man. Well, lads were about grown-up when they started work, she told herself. And Jimmy had had to be more grown-up than most.

Brother and sister came out of the station at Frosterley and began to climb the hill behind the old lead-mining village. Elizabeth had the piece of paper in her hand with the address on it and the name of the farmer. Mr Peart it was. She had shown it to an old man in the street outside the station. 'Peart? Up along o' there,' he had said, after holding it at arm's length and peering at it. He had indicated with the back of his thumb in the direction they were to go.

'How far do you think it is?' Jimmy asked as they crested yet another hill only to find the path wound down and up again; more up than down, Elizabeth reckoned. They were both tired by now, they had been walking for at least an hour and her heart sank as she gazed around at the bleak moorland which, according to her piece of paper, was Bollihope Common. Though it was not in the least like any common land she had seen before. Not even sheep seemed to be about, though a curlew rose and shrieked mournfully. The wind had risen and moaned in ever-changing directions. Clouds were rushing across the sky before it.

'We'll have a rest,' she decreed, spotting a hollow to one side of the track. It seemed fairly sheltered. She took a couple of apples from the deep pocket of her serge dress and handed one to Jimmy. Sinking down on the turf, which was surprisingly springy, she bit into her own. The climb had made her hungry.

The two of them munched their apples, saying nothing. Afterwards, Elizabeth got to her feet and walked up the slight rise to the path and gazed back down the valley. There was nothing to be seen of Frosterley though away to the west there were old quarries which she surmised had been where the black marble, which the area had been famous for in centuries gone by, had been won. She remembered that from a history lesson of long ago, how Weardale had been under water once and the marble had fossils of sea creatures in it. Or maybe it was a geography lesson? Anyroad, one day she would go to Durham Cathedral and see the marble pillars for herself. But today she had to find Jenny.

They set off again, walking in single file. The track here had degenerated into a stony path with clumps of heather jutting out on to it. It went on and on, winding about the desolate moor.

'Are you sure you know where to go, our Elizabeth?'

asked Jimmy, looking sceptical. 'Or are we going to be wandering up here all night an' all?'

'It's not far now,' she replied, though to be honest she had no idea, really. She'd been a fool to come when she didn't know exactly where the farm where Jenny lived was. The very next farm they came to she would go and ask, she determined. Then, sticking out of a patch of dead, rank grass, there it was, a post with a name nailed to it: Peart. She stopped and turned to Jimmy, beaming with relief.

'There, I told you, didn't I?'

He was trailing behind. He walked up to her and gazed at the sign. 'Doesn't look much, does it?' he asked. 'I'd forgotten it.'

There was a branch off the main path, an even narrower path it was, leading away down a hillside, curving into the heather. On this path they actually had to push the wiry branches out of the way; once or twice their booted feet sank into a patch of swampy ground. Elizabeth's heart sank too with every step.

'Let's go back, sis, eh? Our Jenny cannot be living down here, nobody is,' said Jimmy. 'That sign's an old one, man. They must have flitted.'

It must be getting on for five o'clock, Elizabeth thought. The last train went at nine and they had to get back for it, that would take about two hours. But they had time to press on further. 'Just a little,' she urged.

They trudged on. Once, her foot sank into a boggy bit

of ground almost to the boot tops; she had to wipe it as best she could on a heather bush. Jimmy went ahead as she balanced on one foot and scraped away at her boot.

'Hey, look here,' he suddenly exclaimed. He had rounded a slight bend and she ran to where he stood, her boot squelching, splashes of mud uncomfortable on her stockings and petticoat.

There was a house of sorts, tucked into a fold of the moor; even an old rowan tree by the grey, lichen-covered gate. Her heart jumped. They were there, this was where Jenny was. But Jimmy shook his head. 'No, they can't be here, look, the place is derelict.'

Indeed, it looked as though no one could be living there. There was no sign of any activity, no hens clucking in the yard, the stable door hung open. The gate was intact but the fence in which it was set was broken down, overgrown with bracken. Elizabeth gazed at the blank window by the door. The top half of the house was windowless with rough old stone, crumbling mortar in between. No one could be living there, she thought, then she saw a wisp of black smoke coming from the chimney.

'It's not derelict,' she said. 'Come on, Jimmy.' Without looking to see if he was following she led the way around the gate and over the filthy cobbles to the bare, unpainted back door. She stood for a moment or two, startled. There was a sound coming from inside, a girl humming a tune Elizabeth had never heard before. Lifting her hand, she knocked hard. The humming stopped immediately. It was very quiet. A bird flew up from the rowan tree with an alarmed, clicking whistle; another followed.

Jimmy had caught up. He stepped forward and banged on the door with the flat of his hand.

'A rum do, this,' he said in an undertone, frowning at Elizabeth.

'Hey, what the hell are you doing here? Get out of it, the pair of you!'

Elizabeth whirled round. There was a man tramping over the grass towards them, a gun, broken open, over his arm. At his feet was a cur, baring its fangs and growling low in its throat. Suddenly it darted ahead of its master, rushing at Elizabeth and barking loudly. Jimmy stepped in front of her and yelled at it.

'Gerraway, you stupid mongrel, or I'll boot you in t'ribs!'

The dog stayed and sank to its belly, still growling. Jimmy grinned, pleased with his success.

'I said, what are you doing here?'

Elizabeth gazed at the man. He was wearing an old pair of corduroy trousers tied round the knees with twine. His shirt had once been striped blue and white but was faded and stained to a murky brown. Over it he wore a leather jerkin. The cap on his head sported a couple of holes and his grey-speckled beard bristled as he glared back at her.

'Mr Peart?' she asked. 'I'm Elizabeth Nelson and this

is my brother, Jimmy, remember him? We've come to see our sister. I'm afraid she won't open the door.'

'I'm Peart. Your sister, is it? Nobody told me Jenny had any family but for the lad. It was us that brought the lass up. And fine thanks we got for it an' all. She's a lazy little bitch.'

'She's only a bairn, don't you be saying that about her,' said Jimmy, his fists doubling up, and the dog jumped to his feet and barked again until he was cuffed across the ear by Peart and subsided with a yelp. The cur was ignored by Jimmy. 'Why hasn't she opened the door anyroad?' he demanded.

''Cos she cannot, she hasn't got a key, that's why,' said Peart. 'And I haven't heard enough reason why I should let you in neither, you're still as cheeky as you were as a bairn.'

'Because if you don't I'll go straight to the guardians at Auckland, I will, and I'll tell them you keep Jenny locked up. Where's your wife anyroad? They don't let bairns go to lone men, not nowadays,' Elizabeth protested.

Peart stared at her then he hawked in his throat and spat into the rank grass by the door. 'The wife's ran off,' he said flatly. 'I'm not having Jenny doing the same. There's nowt the matter wi' the lass, though. I'll open the door. I was going to anyway. But you needn't think I'm frightened of the guardians, I'm frightened o' nobody . . . so think on.'

He took an ancient iron key from under a pantile over the doorway and inserted it into the lock. The door swung open and brother and sister looked in, Elizabeth in some trepidation at what she might see.

'Go on then, you might as well get on in,' Peart said, in grudging invitation.

'Thank you,' she answered and stepped over the threshold straight into a large room. Her mind registered the fact that the flagged floor was newly swept, the table scrubbed and set for a meal. A fire burned in the ancient grate and a black kettle stood by the fire. The room was lit by a window set in the opposite wall. A clean window; without curtains or any other adornment, the paintwork cracked and in places the wood bare, but clean nevertheless. On the floor before the fire there was even an old rag rug.

For all this her attention was focused on the slight figure standing in front of the window, not five feet tall, a girl with black hair swept back from her face, a face Elizabeth couldn't see properly because of the way she stood against the light.

'Jenny?' she said. 'Jenny, is that you?'

The girl didn't move but cast a look of apprehension over Elizabeth's shoulder at the man. Peart strode in followed by his dog which slunk into a corner and lay down, facing the room.

'What's the matter wi' you, lass?' snarled Peart. 'Do you not know your own sister? Here's your brother an' all, come to see you. Have you not got a welcome for them?' His voice was loud, unnecessarily hearty, and the girl jumped and came forward.

'By, our Elizabeth,' said Jimmy. 'She's a scrawny wee thing, isn't she?'

'She gets her share to eat,' Peart said sharply. 'I don't starve the lass, if that's what you think.'

'No, well, I'm sure the guardians keep an eye on you,' Jimmy was stung into replying.

Elizabeth didn't hear. She went towards her youngest sister, put her hands on her shoulders and gazed down at her. Jenny looked back timidly and Elizabeth leaned forward and kissed her on the cheek. Jenny still hadn't moved.

'Don't you know me?' Elizabeth asked. But of course Jenny didn't, she wouldn't. Hadn't she been no more than four when she was taken away from the Children's Home? No more than three when their mother died?

'She doesn't look like us,' said Jimmy. No more she did; though her hair was as dark as the others', her eyes were brown, her skin olive.

'Jenny's like our dad,' Elizabeth said softly.

'Howay, lass, bestir yoursel',' said Mr Peart. 'Where's me tea?'

Jenny moved then, hurrying about pushing the kettle on to the embers of the fire, spooning tea into an old pewter pot. She brought half a loaf from a cupboard in the corner and a hunk of hard cheese. A jar of pickle

completed the meal. Then Jenny glanced hesitantly at
Elizabeth and Jimmy and back to her foster father. 'Will
I pour tea for them an' all?' she asked.

'Aye, go on,' he replied, grudgingly.

'Don't bother, we can't stay long,' Elizabeth said. 'We
just wanted to see . . .'

'Aye, well, you've seen her,' he snapped. 'You can
see she's all right. Now you can be ganning away back
home.'

But Elizabeth wasn't about to turn tail and go on his
say so. 'I'd like a word with her first,' she said. So far
Jenny had said nothing at all to her or Jimmy.

'I'm not stopping you,' Peart retorted. He put his
elbows on the table and sat forward over his meal,
cutting chunks from the cheese and putting them in his
mouth. He grinned, showing a mouthful of half-chewed
food.

But nothing Elizabeth or Jimmy said brought a
response from Jenny, though she did give a sort of half-
smile once. And the day was getting on and brother and
sister had to be back in Frosterley for the last train to
Bishop Auckland. At last Elizabeth nodded to Jimmy.

'We'll have to go,' she said. 'Is it all right if we come
back next week?'

'Please yoursels,' said Peart. Jenny started forward as
though she was going to object but she checked herself
and said nothing, simply glanced again at her foster
father.

They went out quietly, going to the door on their own. Peart didn't even get up from the table. Outside the afternoon was turning into evening. They hurried up the yard and out by the rowan tree, on up where the path branched. They didn't speak until they finally got on to the metalled road which led to the station.

'A queer set up that, isn't it?' Jimmy commented, glancing sideways at his sister.

'She was all right though,' said Elizabeth. 'Did you notice? She was clean, her dress was clean too, and it wasn't worn. It was him that was filthy.' She shuddered and wrinkled her nose at the memory of him.

'Never mind, pet,' said Jimmy, in the tones of a father comforting his child, 'we'll go back. She'll be better next time.'

Chapter Five

'Can I have a word, Miss Rowland?'

Elizabeth stepped inside the office and closed the door quietly behind her. Miss Rowland, her dark hair all but covered by the enormous 'Sister Dora' cap she had taken to wearing since coming to Newcomb Hall the month before, looked up from the papers she was studying and smiled at the girl. Encouraged, Elizabeth stepped up to the desk and gazed earnestly at the woman who had been the only one she could talk to in the Children's Home, and who was now Matron of the convalescent hospital. By, she thought, she blessed the day Miss Rowland got the transfer, she would never have dared ask the old Matron.

'Yes, Elizabeth?' Miss Rowland prompted.

'I would like to be a nurse's aide,' said Elizabeth, rather baldly.

'Don't you like it in the laundry then?'

'Oh, yes, it's all right, and Mrs Poskett is nice, but I

want to be a proper nurse when I'm old enough. I know I can't until I'm eighteen, though. I think I would be a good help to the nurses now. I'm strong and fit . . .' Her voice tailed off in a fit of anxiety that Miss Rowland might not agree.

'Oh, I'm sure you would do well, Elizabeth. But if you're needed in the laundry, you may have to stay there, at least for a while.'

Elizabeth's face fell. She had keyed herself up to ask and now it looked as though Miss Rowland would refuse her request. The disappointment was so crushing she hardly heard the Matron start to speak again.

'You may have to stay in the laundry until I get another girl.'

'Oh, yes, I can do that,' Elizabeth cried when it sank in that she was going to be allowed to transfer after all. She jumped to her feet. 'I'll work hard, you see if I don't, Miss Rowland.'

'Indeed, I know you will.'

Elizabeth was elated when she left the office. She took the washing out to the lines, quite forgetting to keep a weather eye open for Private Wilson, and hummed 'Dolly Grey' under her breath as she pegged out the sheets, taking pleasure as she usually did in the sight of them blowing in the wind.

Jack Benson did not forget how the soldier had behaved; he sat in his window and watched, on guard for Private Wilson almost, as he had been wont to do since the last incident with him. He hardly knew why he did except that it was something to do to fill the empty hours. After all, girls from the mining villages were usually well able to look after themselves, but still . . .

As he watched, he pondered what he was going to do when he went back to his own home. The Manor was only a mile away from the pit head and mining village but it was a world away in reality, hidden away in its own grounds, at the end of a long drive.

'I really don't know how we will manage, Jack,' his mother had said on her last visit. She had walked beside his wheelchair, which was being pushed by a VAD, to a bench on the lawns of Newcomb Manor. 'It's so difficult to get servants these days. Things have changed a lot since you went away, you've no idea.'

'Yes, Mother, I'm sure you're right,' Jack had answered mildly.

Now he watched the girl outside as she picked up the washing basket and came back to the garden path. Even in her ugly overalls she was attractive and moved with a natural grace. Tendrils of hair had escaped from her cap. She pushed them back with a reddened hand, which was slim and shapely for all its apparent roughness.

She had approached him after the incident with the orderly, when he was out in the grounds sitting on his own.

'I wanted to thank you, sir,' she had begun hesitantly. 'For stopping him . . . I mean, Private—'

'I don't know what you're talking about,' Jack had said coldly, and the girl had blushed and stepped back. He had returned to his book, staring at the printed page though not taking in a word. Why had he acted like that? Only a prig could be offended at a laundry maid daring to speak to a gentleman. Oh, blow the girl! He would forget about her. The trouble was he hadn't enough to occupy his thoughts.

She had disappeared now, back to the laundry room no doubt. Jack sat back in his chair and contemplated starting another book. But the nurse would be in in a moment, he was going to have his stumps measured for artificial feet. He touched one with the other, experimentally. It was only a little sore. He sighed. No doubt it would be painful getting used to wooden feet. But marvellous if he could walk.

Elizabeth was happy as she worked. She had been unaware of Captain Benson's scrutiny. She scrubbed at stained collars and cuffs with a will and threw the garments into hot soapy water. '"Goodbye, Dolly, I must leave you",' she sang, '"though it breaks my heart to go".'

'Mind, you're in a good mood,' said Mrs Poskett.

Elizabeth looked up from a yellow-stained night-shirt. 'I am,' she said. 'I'm going to be a nurse, Mrs Poskett. As soon as Miss Rowland can get a new laundry maid.'

Mrs Poskett sighed. 'I'll never get anyone else as good

as you,' she replied. 'All the best lasses are working at the munitions. The pay's better there.'

'Somebody'll come, Mrs Poskett,' said Elizabeth. 'I know it. Maybe someone from the Home.'

Her own pay would go up, she thought, even nurses' aides got more money than laundry maids. A whole two shillings more. That was enough for the fare to Weardale, to see her sister.

She stopped singing as she thought of the broken-down, impoverished farm on Bollihope Common. And Jenny, little Jenny. She went over and over in her mind everything she had seen there, particularly the way her sister jumped to do that man's bidding. Like a beaten puppy. And how thin she was. The worried expression she seemed to wear all the time had haunted Elizabeth's dreams. Oh, she wished she could go up there this Sunday, see her sister again. Alice was all right, she was happy at Coundon. Kit would be all right, she knew, with Auntie Betty. (Her mind shied away from the memory of Uncle Ben.)

She had decided she would go to Morton Main this coming Sunday as she couldn't go to Weardale; she could walk there over the fields. She would go to Mrs Wearmouth's first, make sure Auntie Betty was at home. She had let too much time go by without seeing Kit, she knew that.

'I'll come with you,' offered Jimmy. 'Me and Tommy Gibson'll both go.'

'That's grand, Jimmy,' said Elizabeth, delighted that he should be so thoughtful. It was not until they were sitting on Mrs Wearmouth's settee in her kitchen in West Row that she realised why the boys had really come.

They had drunk tea and eaten a slice each of Mrs Wearmouth's excellent cake which the boys had praised lavishly until their hostess had simpered with pleasure and pressed another slice on them.

'Mrs Wearmouth,' said Jimmy, 'we've got jobs at the pit.'

Elizabeth stared at them. She had been about to question Mrs Wearmouth about Kit and Auntie Betty and, if she could say it nonchalantly enough, where she thought Uncle Ben was likely to be this fine afternoon. Elizabeth fervently hoped he would be out behind the pit heaps playing pitch and toss ha'penny, along with the crowd of men they had seen on their way to West Row. Now all that was driven out of her head.

'You haven't!' she exclaimed. The boys ignored her.

'Have you, lads? Well, your dad was a pitman before he went off, Jimmy,' Mrs Wearmouth said. 'And both your grandads an' all.'

'Aye, I know,' he replied. 'But what I wanted to ask you is, do you know where we could get lodgings, like? I mean, we'd love to stay here, wouldn't we, Tommy? We'd be no trouble, Mrs Wearmouth, an' we'd pay the going rate an' all.'

'Eeh, I don't know,' she answered. But Elizabeth could see she was thinking seriously about it.

'I mean, I know widows don't get a big pension. It would help you an' all,' said Jimmy, gazing earnestly at Mrs Wearmouth.

Half an hour later they were on their way to Auntie Betty's house and the boys had completed their negotiations for lodgings successfully. 'Mind, you're only bairns. I know a lot of lads start in the pit when they're thirteen, and my man, he started when he was nine. But that doesn't make you men, you know. I want you in at decent times an' I want you to mind what I say.'

Jimmy and Tommy had glanced at each other but agreed with little hesitation. It was no more than they had expected.

'And,' said Elizabeth, 'I didn't want you going down the pit – remember that when it's hard. And you'll have to square it with the guardians.'

'We've already asked them,' said Jimmy. 'For goodness' sake, our Elizabeth, don't be such a worrit. Anyroad, we won't be going down the pit at first, we'll be working on the bank.'

Mrs Wearmouth had assured them that Auntie Betty would be at home and that Uncle Ben always spent all afternoon on Sunday behind the pit heap with the pitch and toss players. So Elizabeth tried to forget about Jimmy and the pit, she was going to see her other brother after all this time. It was Kit who answered the knock on the door, it could only be him. There he stood, a seven-year-old boy, holding on to the door handle and looking out at them, so exactly like Jimmy had been at his age that Elizabeth felt her heart do a sudden flip.

'Who is it, Christopher?' a female voice called from within the house.

'I don't know, Mam,' he answered.

Mam . . . he called her Mam, Elizabeth had time to think with a stab of pain. But of course he would, wasn't Betty the only mother he knew? It was his so-called mam's fault he didn't know his own brother and sister.

'I'm your sister Elizabeth,' she said firmly to the child. 'And this is your brother Jimmy.' Kit stared at her, uncomprehending. 'It's Elizabeth,' she called more loudly for Auntie Betty's benefit, and stepped past Kit and into the kitchen in time to see the look of surprise and anger on her aunt's face, swiftly masked.

'You'd best come in then. Christopher, open the door properly, pet,' Auntie Betty said.

The two older boys came in after Elizabeth, looking decidedly uncomfortable. They were not asked to sit down. Elizabeth stood by the hearth. Auntie Betty had an oven cloth in her hand. She had been lifting a tray of fairy cakes from the oven. Her face was flushed, whether from the heat or the surprise, Elizabeth didn't know.

'By, what a surprise,' Betty said at last.

'Yes, it's a long while since we saw you,' said Elizabeth.

'Now then, our Lizzie, it's not been easy for me, you know. An' I knew you were being well looked after at the Home.' Auntie Betty sounded aggrieved at the implied criticism. Kit went and stood beside her. He stared at the two boys solemnly. 'Time goes by anyroad, almost before you notice. I was always going to come and see you,' Betty went on.

'Aye, well,' said Elizabeth. 'But don't call me Lizzie.' She smiled at Kit. Oh, he was a bonny lad, well set up and tall for his age. Betty was doing a good job of bringing him up and he seemed fond enough of her. She could forgive her aunt a lot for that.

'I'm your sister – Elizabeth, Kit,' she said again.

'I haven't got a sister, nor a brother neither,' he replied, and she was shocked.

'Auntie Betty! You didn't tell him that, did you?'

'No, I didn't. I suppose he just thought it.' Betty was on the defensive now. She put an arm around the boy's shoulders.

'You didn't tell him about us neither,' Elizabeth said bitterly.

'You leave my mam alone,' said Kit. 'An' my name's Christopher.' His little face was flushed and he stood in front of Betty, fists doubled up. Jimmy and Tommy stood by the window, looking embarrassed, as though they would like to be anywhere but there. Elizabeth glanced at Jimmy, seeing how he felt. She would get no backup there, she realised.

'You two go on out, if you like,' she said. 'I can get back to Newcomb Hall on my own.' They turned as one for the door. Elizabeth wasn't ready to give up yet, though.

'Kit – Christopher, I am your sister, pet,' she repeated. 'I just came to see if you were happy.'

'Why shouldn't he be?' demanded Betty. 'We do our very best for him, me and Ben.'

This had the unfortunate effect of reminding Elizabeth of the last time she had seen Uncle Ben, three years ago now but still fresh in her mind.

'Do you like Uncle Ben, Christopher?' she asked the boy.

'Dad. He calls him Daddy,' Betty put in. 'You love your dad, don't you, Christopher?'

He nodded his head vigorously, face breaking into a smile. 'He's going to make me a rabbit hutch when he gets in from the club,' he confided. 'Mr Allen has some baby rabbits and he says I can have one if I have a hutch.'

'That'll be grand,' said Elizabeth. Suddenly the appalling sense of loss she had experienced when her mother died and the family was broken up came back to pierce her, as painfully as when it had first happened. All these years she had lived with a dream. A dream that eventually she would be able to make a home for her brothers and sisters and they would all live happily together once again. It was what had sustained her

69

through all the bad times, the lonely nights in the Home.

It was no good, she realised that now. Was she the only one who wanted it? Alice wasn't interested, Jimmy was on the verge of striking out on his own, and Kit, her baby Kit, if she was even able to take him away to live with her, would only hate her for it. She would be breaking up his home as surely as her own had been broken. Oh, God, she thought bleakly, what a cruel world it is.

'I suppose you'd like a cup of tea?' said Auntie Betty. Elizabeth studied her. She still wore that defiant expression like a child caught out in wrongdoing. But she had lifted Kit up on to her lap and he was leaning against her breast in an attitude of utter trust. No, Elizabeth told herself, she couldn't break that up. Not that she would have stood much chance. She rose to her feet.

'No, thank you, we had some at Mrs Wearmouth's. Jimmy and his friend are going to lodge with her, did I tell you? No? Well, no doubt I'll be seeing you soon, now he'll be in the rows. He's going to work at the pit.'

Elizabeth bent to her brother and kissed him on the cheek though he made a movement away from her. Then, on impulse, she kissed Auntie Betty too.

'Ta-ra then,' said her aunt, relieved. 'Christopher, say ta-ra to Elizabeth.'

She left the house without looking back and set off for

the path which led via the woods by Bishop Auckland. There was still Jenny. Her sister needed her, Elizabeth told herself.

Chapter Six

'Miss Rowland wants to see you,' said Joan. She was lying on her bed in the room they shared when Elizabeth got back from Morton Main. 'Said you were to go to the office as soon as you came in.'

'I wonder what she wants?' asked Elizabeth wearily. She searched her memory; she didn't think she had done anything wrong. And just at the moment all she wanted to do was curl up on her own bed and sleep. Maybe she could sleep away the melancholy which had enveloped her since she left Jimmy and Kit.

'You'll not know unless you go to see,' Joan pointed out. She sat on the edge of her bed and reached down for her boots. 'How did your visit go?'

'Awful, Joan. The bairn didn't know me.'

'Well, he wouldn't would he? He hasn't seen you for years. Did you expect him to recognise you just because you're his sister?' Joan knew all about Kit and Alice, less about Jenny because Elizabeth found it painful to talk about her. 'When I think of that auntie of yours, I'm glad I haven't got any family.'

Elizabeth watched as her friend splashed water on her face perfunctorily then rubbed it vigorously with a towel. She dragged her light brown hair back and pinned it with a hairpin then pulled her cap over it.

'You'd best get along there now,' she advised Elizabeth when her toilet was finished. 'I think Miss Rowland goes off at six.' She sighed. 'Well, I'd better get down meself or Cook will be laying into me for being late when all the spuds are to do for supper.'

Elizabeth went to the tiny attic window when her friend had gone, gazing out over the darkening fields. How was Jenny getting on? she wondered. If only she could get up to see her next week but she hadn't the fare. She'd had to buy new stockings as the last ones were finally beyond repair.

Miss Rowland had already tidied her desk and taken off her cap but she sat down again when Elizabeth went in.

'Elizabeth, I was expecting you earlier,' she said. 'Never mind, you're here now. I want you to start upstairs tomorrow, we're a girl short on the first floor.'

'But . . . I thought you said . . .'

Miss Rowland didn't wait for her to finish. 'I did, I know. But I have a girl coming from the Home tomorrow. Daisy Jones, do you remember her? She is to start in the laundry room. Mrs Poskett will keep her right. You can pick up your nurse's apron and cap from the sewing room at seven, leave your others there. Now, is that clear?'

'Oh! Thank you, Miss Rowland, I never expected . . .'

'No. Well, that's all right. You can go to supper now.'

Miss Rowland was brisk, she opened a drawer and bent to look inside. When she straightened up Elizabeth was still hovering before her desk. 'Well? Is there something else?'

'If you have a minute, Miss,' said Elizabeth. She had been thinking of it all week, wanting to ask but never summoning the courage. It was now or never, she thought.

'It's about our Jenny, Miss, me sister. She was fostered up the dale – oh, years ago.'

A slight look of impatience crossed the older woman's face. 'Oh, Elizabeth, you know I can't discuss placings with you. At least, I couldn't when I was employed at the Home and now I've forgotten most of them.'

'She's my sister, Miss, and me and our Jimmy went to see her last week.'

Miss Rowland closed the drawer and sat back in her chair. She remembered now, how Elizabeth had found out where her sisters were.

'I suppose now you're older, you're your own boss, so to speak, no one can stop you from visiting her. But you know the guardians liked our placings to have a fresh start with their foster families. They don't like their former families upsetting the children.'

'She *is* my sister, Miss Rowland, and if you saw the place where she is you would understand why I'm worried. She's not with a family, the woman is gone, there's just her and a horrible dirty old farmer . . .'

'That's enough, Elizabeth! It must be all right. The inspectors would have visited the place. And if she was unhappy she would have had plenty of chances to tell them.' Miss Rowland stood up again and moved to the door. 'Now, I must go. I'm sorry, Elizabeth, but I'm sure you're exaggerating. If I were you I'd leave well alone. You have enough to think about, you have to get on with your own life.'

She went to the door and stood holding it open, plainly considering the subject closed. Elizabeth had no choice but to leave.

'I'll go back to Weardale, though,' she said aloud to the empty bedroom when she reached it. 'I'll go back as soon as I can raise the fare. I'll go back to Bollihope Common as often as I can.'

Next morning she presented herself at half-past seven to the desk on the first-floor landing where Nurse Turner, the nurse in charge of the first-floor rooms, together with the VAD, Nurse Middleham, were taking the report from the night nurse. Elizabeth was thrust into the middle of it immediately.

'Oh, you're here,' said Nurse Turner. 'Good. Well,

you can assist Nurse Middleham in making the beds and turning out the rooms. 'Go on, now, no time to spare.'

The young VAD hurried Elizabeth away. There were eight bedrooms on the floor, four with two occupants each and four singles.

'There's never any time to spare.' Nurse Middleham smiled at Elizabeth as she opened the door of the first room. 'Don't worry, though, I'll show you what to do.'

She found herself dusting and sweeping, washing out bowls and urine bottles, helping patients out of bed, making the beds (thank goodness she already knew how to make hospital corners, from her time in the Home), fetching and carrying for the men and giving them breakfast, all in a race to have it finished by nine o'clock and her own breakfast time.

'Doctor's rounds today,' said Nurse Middleham. They had just finished the seventh room and at the door she turned and cast an experienced eye back over their handiwork. 'Just turn that bed wheel in, would you?'

Elizabeth went back and turned in the offending wheel, smiling to herself. It was, after all, only eight weeks since Nurse Middleham had come to the hospital after only the briefest of training. But she had Nurse Turner's voice and manner off to a 'T'.

'Good morning, Captain Benson,' the nurse said brightly as she opened the door to the last room and Elizabeth felt a slight sense of shock. Of course, this would be Captain Benson's, she told herself. The room was on the end, at the back of the house, overlooking the vegetable garden and the drying ground where she caught a glimpse of Mrs Poskett and Daisy already pegging the linen on the lines.

'What are you doing here?' Jack Benson asked baldly. 'Where's Katie?'

'This is Nurse Nelson, Captain Benson,' Nurse Middleham said formally. 'Katie had to leave yesterday.'

Elizabeth glanced at her curiously. Katie had only been here a month or so, she hadn't known who it was she was replacing.

'Hmm.'

Jack said no more, though he frowned heavily. He had an idea why Katie had had to leave; she had been thick with Private Wilson but these last few days she had appeared with red-rimmed eyes and blotchy cheeks and Private Wilson had made some excuse and run every time she came near him.

Elizabeth immediately thought the captain was frowning because of her. She reddened, then lifted her head high and glared at him.

'Fetch the orderly, please, Elizabeth,' said Nurse Middleham. 'We'll need him to get the captain into his wheelchair.'

Elizabeth's heart sank but she went out into the hall where Private Wilson was polishing the brass door handles.

'You're wanted in Captain Benson's room,' she said stiffly, from a distance of about eight feet.

'What? Did you say something?' he asked, cupping his ear and leaning towards her in a parody of a deaf man so that she had to go nearer. She repeated her request, more loudly, and he grinned, dropping the pretence and stepping so close to her she could smell the faint but rather unpleasant body odour which came from him.

'Well, I'd better come then, hadn't I, sweetheart?' he said, and grinned even wider when he saw her expression. 'You'll have to get used to me now, lass, we'll be working together.'

'Leave me alone!' she hissed at him, recovering a little of her equilibrium. She wondered why she hadn't thought of this drawback when she had decided to take up nursing.

'It took you long enough, Private,' said Jack as they went into his room. He frowned as he glanced from Elizabeth to Wilson but said no more about it. 'Come on, you can push me out in the grounds, Wilson.' The nurses were left to finish the cleaning in peace and shortly afterwards the breakfast bell rang and they went downstairs for their break.

Elizabeth was used to hard work in the laundry but now she felt as though she had done a shift down the mine and it was still only nine o'clock.

*

'You can push me down to the lake and back, Wilson,' Jack decreed. He wanted to get away from the other patients who were scattered about the grounds, some in wheelchairs as he was and some on crutches, while one or two of the blind were being led about. He had something to say to Private Wilson and to be fair to the man, it was best said where no one else could hear.

'I have the brasses to finish, sir,' he objected.

'Yes, well, you can do them later. If anyone objects, refer them to me.'

The day was fine and sunny, the dew on the grass just beginning to disappear. A family of ducks was on the water, the youngsters no longer babies but almost fully grown. Behind him, Jack could hear the 'brrr' of a mower as one of the gardeners began to cut the grass.

'It's my half day, sir, I have to get the work done if I want to get away,' ventured Private Wilson.

'Never mind that,' said Jack. They were by the lake by this time, Wilson had turned on to the path which ran alongside it. 'If ever I hear that you are molesting that girl, if I see anything or find her distressed because of you, you'll find yourself in front of Major Davies so fast your feet won't touch the ground. Do you understand me, Private?' Jack challenged him.

Wilson had stopped pushing the chair. Jack could hear him breathing heavily but he didn't answer.

'Do you hear me, Private Wilson?' he roared, losing his temper.

'Yes, sir. I hear you.'

'Well, then, believe me. I mean it. Now take me back to the house, I have an appointment at ten.'

In fact the appointment was with the surgical appliance fitter from Durham who was bringing Jack his new feet for a first fitting. In spite of his doubts, he was looking forward to the chance of looking at the world from an upright viewpoint once again. He'd done his bit for the girl, he reckoned. Major Davies of the RAMC, the doctor in charge of the military staff of the hospital, was a man who believed in discipline. The orderlies, men who were on the whole not A1 physically or else slightly older, were aware that he could send them to the front. Consequently, they had a healthy respect for him.

But as Private Wilson returned to his brass polishing in the upstairs hall, he nursed a bitter resentment against both that workhouse brat of a girl, as he thought of Elizabeth, and the high and mighty Jack bloody Benson. It was his guess the captain wanted the lass for himself, that was the trouble. And he should stick to his own kind, that was a fact.

Jack, for his part, wondered vaguely why he was going to such trouble for Elizabeth Nelson, a pitman's girl, he would put money on it. But there was something about the girl . . . and it wasn't just her lustrous dark hair and eyes so deep blue they were almost the colour of wood violets. Or her white skin, the grace with which she moved . . . His thoughts were interrupted by a knock on the door. His visitor had come.

Elizabeth went up to Weardale again on the last Saturday in September when the hedges flashing past the train window were heavy with brambles and rose hips, bright splashes of colour in among the dusty green. She was on her own this time. She hadn't seen Jimmy all week now he was working at the colliery in Morton Main and living with Mrs Wearmouth. But she had no worries about him somehow; he would be fine there with their old neighbour. Pit work would hold no fears for him either, since mining was in his blood. He would soon make friends, enjoy the camaraderie of his 'marras'.

Elizabeth tramped purposefully up the track from Frosterley, getting higher and higher until she paused for breath and gazed back over the little town and around at the great sweep of the hills, up to the tops of the moors and down into the shadow of the valleys. The wind was quite sharp, an autumn chill had already arrived in this upland place. It brought a deep colour to Elizabeth's cheeks and a sparkle to her eyes. She pulled her old coat closer around her. She had bought it from a second-hand stall in the market and it was a size or two too big. But it was a good wool and a pretty reddish-brown and would last her all through this winter. She even might grow into it before next. She hoped so, she was barely five foot two inches and had an ambition to be tall and statuesque, as she was sure she remembered her mother being.

Coming to the sign with 'Peart' written on it in faded letters, she made her way through the heather and bracken and on to where the path got slightly better, then at last to the gate in the broken-down fence. She noticed a sign nailed to the rowan tree. It had lost one nail and now hung on its side. There were red rusty streaks from where the nail had been. It looked as though the tree was bleeding, she thought.

Funny, she hadn't noticed the sign last time she was here. She turned her head sideways to read it. 'Stand Alone Farm' it said. Stand Alone. Well, it certainly did that. Looking at the desolate yard, the tumbledown house and the moor around, with dead bracken more in evidence than heather or grass and not another habitation in view, she felt the name fitted it exactly.

She gazed at the back of the house, wrinkling her nose at the smell of the ancient midden in the yard. Was Mr Peart in? Would Jenny answer the door? She took a deep breath and went up to it, knocking on the grey wood that was bare of paint.

There was silence. Jenny wasn't singing today. In fact, Elizabeth began to believe she'd had a wasted journey. Her sister must be out, it was so quiet. She stepped back from the door and looked up at the chimney. There was no smoke that she could discern. She put a hand up to the guttering and felt along it for the key as Peart had done when she and Jimmy had come. It was there. She fitted it into the ancient lock and turned it and the door swung open.

'Jenny?'

Hesitantly, Elizabeth stepped inside, straight into the main room of the house. Her sister was huddled up in the corner of an old wooden settle. She lifted her head as Elizabeth spoke then jumped off the settle and stood there, shaking.

'Jenny? What's the matter? It's only me, your sister Elizabeth. Don't be frightened of me, please!'

She took a shuddering gasp of breath. 'You shouldn't have come in. You know he'll think I opened the door and I didn't!'

'No, he won't, the key was outside anyway. And I'll tell him I opened it myself. Jenny, Jenny, come on . . . don't be scared. No one's going to hurt you, I won't let them, I promise.'

Elizabeth stepped over to her little sister and impulsively flung her arms around her, feeling the thinness of the little girl's body, the trembling in her limbs. A fury was growing in her. She longed to burst out in anger, rail against this man who kept Jenny like a terrified rabbit. But she had to hold it in. Instinctively she knew that anger would only make Jenny more frightened.

Jenny stood passively in Elizabeth's arms. She didn't lift her own arms to hold her sister, she didn't move. It was as if she had no idea how to respond. But her trembling lessened, her breathing became easier. And Elizabeth stepped back to look at her.

'Mind, our Jenny,' she cried, 'you look like our dad, did you know that?'

The girl shook her head.

'Well, you do. Just the same bonny hazel eyes, you have, just the same nut brown hair. You were the one who took after him. You'll be too young to remember him, though.'

'Is he dead?' A gleam of interest shone in Jenny's eyes. For the first time her face looked like a child's rather than a little old woman's.

'Come and sit down,' said Elizabeth, 'we'll sit on the settle, will we? And I'll tell you all about him and Mam.'

Jenny glanced once at the door, uncertain, but the pull of talking to Elizabeth, her own sister, after all the hours of being on her own was too much of a temptation. They sat down together on the settle and Elizabeth told her what she could remember of their dad, and of Mam and the rest of the family. And Jenny sat, as quiet as a little lost sparrow.

Chapter Seven

'Dad might still come back for us,' said Jenny, her little face alight with hope. 'I mean, if he's making his fortune in America, he might just have been a long time getting rich and might still come back.' She got down from the settle and took the kettle to the pail of water in the corner, filling it with a ladling can obviously kept for the purpose. She carried the kettle back to the fire in two hands, leaning forward from the weight of it. Elizabeth wanted to help but Jenny shook her head.

The fire, which had been almost out when Elizabeth came in, was freshly made up with small pieces of coal and blocks of peat and was throwing a fair amount of heat out into the room. Elizabeth, who had no experience of peat, watched with interest. It had taken longer to catch hold than coal but the heat from it was impressive.

She had told Jenny that Mam had died and they had had to be split up because they were too young; she had told her about Kit and how he was called Christopher now that Auntie Betty was his mother. And how Alice had a nice new mother in Coundon and Jimmy was working in the pit.

Jenny had listened carefully, her little face rapt. She seemed to have forgotten all about her foster father, even her fear that he would come in and be angry because she had let Elizabeth in. Elizabeth was apprehensive, though. The nights were cutting in now it was the back end of September and surely Peart would be coming home soon? She could have gone, made the excuse she had to get back to Frosterley before dark, but she felt she had to stay in case Jenny needed protecting from the man.

'Does he hit you?' she asked. 'Does he treat you badly?'

'No,' Jenny replied. But she rubbed at her arm as she spoke and the sleeve rode up and there was a purplish bruise encircling the whole of her upper arm. She saw Elizabeth staring at it.

'He didn't hit me,' Jenny said quickly. 'It's just when I'm lazy and don't get something he asks for quick enough, like. He was a bit rough when he caught hold of my arm. It was my fault, I'm too slow.' She stared at the fire. 'He would never let me call him Dad. I went to school for a while and all the other girls had dads. And *she* told me I was a charity case. They took me in out of the goodness of their own hearts. I wasn't their daughter, really.'

Took you in for a slave was what they did, thought Elizabeth. She remembered the way Jenny had jumped and run to Peart's every bidding the first time she was there and felt hot words rising to her lips. But she held them back. She had to be careful, she counselled herself, Jenny had to stay with the man.

'What was it like when Mrs Peart was here? Was she nice?'

Conflicting emotions chased across Jenny's face. She looked down at the faded skirt of her over-large dress. 'It was all right,' she whispered at last.

Elizabeth frowned. 'Was she not nice to you then?'

'Aye . . . Yes, she was,' the child answered, but her voice was hesitant. Elizabeth was about to press her further but just then the door was flung open and the dog rushed into the room, barking furiously. He raced up to Elizabeth and, sticking out his head, snarled and growled and barked. His master was directly behind him, though and Peart flung his stick at the dog, catching it a glancing blow on the shoulder. The cur broke off, growling abruptly, and sneaked into the corner and lay down, whimpering softly.

'What the hell are you doing here?' Peart demanded of Elizabeth. 'Did I not make it clear you weren't welcome the last time you came poking your bloody nose in?'

'I have a right to visit my sister,' she replied, lifting her chin and staring at him defiantly. 'You didn't adopt her, she's still under the guardians, really. And I was told

I could visit her.' It was stretching the truth somewhat but Elizabeth didn't care.

She wrinkled her nose as he came near her. The rank smell from him hadn't improved since she last saw him; she reckoned he hadn't had a wash, never mind a bath, since then. And yet Jenny was clean even if she was dressed in threadbare clothes.

'Aye, well, I should have left her in t'Home. She's nowt but a trouble to me. Wanders off up the moor when she gets the chance, she should have been a bloody sheep! Might as well have been an' all. Once I found her wi' the sheep – sleeping in among them she was – an' nobbut a slip of a bairn an' all. That's why I cannot let her out.' He looked again at Elizabeth, eyes sliding from her face to her feet, lingering on her figure.

'I suppose you could take a cup o'tea? The lass'll be making one for me, if she ever gets hersel stirred. Jump to it, lass!' The last was a barked order and Jenny did indeed jump to it as though she'd been shot. But she glanced at her sister, eyes wide, and Elizabeth guessed she was as much startled by his offer of hospitality as she was by his order. But it was getting late, Elizabeth had to go if she wanted to get back to Newcomb Hall. Besides, she couldn't understand why Peart had changed his mind about letting her come. It was suspicious.

'Thank you but I haven't time,' she said, 'I have to catch the last train from Frosterley.' She turned to her sister. 'Will you walk me a way up the path, Jenny?'

'No, she won't,' Peart said shortly. 'You found your way here, I reckon you can find it back. The lass has my meal to get ready.'

Elizabeth glared at him then turned back to Jenny. 'I'll see you in a fortnight,' she promised. 'You'll be here?'

'Where else would she be?' Peart answered for her. 'An' I'll be here an' all. I'm not having you two talking about me behind me back.'

It was only when Elizabeth was hurrying along the path to Frosterley station in the near dark and going over in her mind the events of the afternoon that she realised something. Jenny had talked to her when they were alone; she had almost seemed like a normal little girl then, asking questions, listening to the stories Elizabeth told her about her parents. But she had never once called Mr and Mrs Peart anything except 'he' and 'she'. And when Peart had come in she had said not one word. Well, Elizabeth promised herself, she would get to the bottom of it. Oh, yes, she would.

Jack Benson sat out on a garden bench until quite late that Sunday afternoon. In the morning he had worn his new feet; wooden they were, with metal joints which he had been warned he would have to keep oiled. He had actually got up on his feet himself, with a great effort of will and some encouragement from Nurse Turner and Elizabeth, or Lizzie as he privately thought of her. He had been reading Jane Austen simply because it was there in the library at the Hall and he was a voracious reader, always running out of books. And Nurse Nelson, the little nurse's aide, for all her lowly status, reminded him of Elizabeth Bennet in *Pride and Prejudice*. She was so sensible for a young girl, instinctively knowing when his legs hurt. She had such a delicate yet firm touch when she helped Nurse Turner gently massage with spirit the new pink skin which covered his wounds, to harden it, or the way she could make a pad of Gangee tissue without a single crease in it to protect the ends when he wore his new feet. She was better at it even than Nurse Turner and definitely streets ahead of Nurse Middleham.

She wasn't there when he triumphantly stood up again that afternoon, even took the step which got him on to the garden bench and off that damned chair. He had glanced around, expecting to see her, strangely disappointed that she was missing.

'Where is Nurse Nelson?' he had asked.

'The nurse's aide? It's her half day. I don't know where she's gone,' Nurse Middleham had replied. 'Now, are you all right there? Only I have such a lot to do this afternoon, it really is a nuisance when she has time off.'

And Nurse Middleham had hurried away over the grass to the Hall, the wings of her VAD's cap floating behind her in the breeze.

Bitch'd never make a nurse in a million years, Jack told himself savagely. He sat back on the bench and carefully crossed his legs. He could feel the weight of the wooden foot which dangled in the air from the straps which wound around his calf. After a while it became uncomfortable and he put it back on the ground, jarring it a little as he misjudged the distance. The feeling of optimism which had been with him since the morning began to evaporate a little. At the back of his mind he could sense the black shadows forming; the demon which had sat on his shoulder since he'd stood on the mine was waiting to pounce again. He deliberately looked up at the sunlit sky.

'I don't know, Jack, do you think you should be out here on your own and out of your wheelchair? No attendant either, it's very worrying.'

The sun disappeared from his view as his mother put herself between him and the sky. The demon crept closer.

'Hello, Mother.'

He hitched himself up on the bench and forced a smile.

'I'm fine on my own, really I am. I like a bit of peace sometimes anyway. How are you, Mother?' He lifted his face as she bent to kiss him on the cheek, the familiar smell of violet-scented face powder and lavender water drifted over him.

'Sit here, Mother, why don't you?' He patted the seat beside him and she took out a handkerchief and dusted the slats of the bench with it before sitting down.

'Oh, don't ask, don't ask, dear boy,' said Olivia

Benson, putting her head to one side so that the stuffed bird on her Queen Mary-style hat tilted perilously. 'How can I complain when such a terrible thing has happened to you? No, I'm fine, I'm fine, though I can't remember the day – or I should say night – when I've had more than two hours' sleep put together. And I can't eat, really I can't. "Rations!" I say. "They make no difference to me, I don't eat anything anyway".' A dot of saliva appeared on her lips from the emphasis with which she spoke and she dabbed at it with a wisp of lace. 'Of course, Nancy eats my share anyway, great lump that she is. It's perhaps just as well I can't get another maid. I certainly couldn't *feed* one.'

She stopped talking and looked at him properly; it was almost like an inspection. Then she pursed her lips and sighed.

'I don't know, Jack, really I don't. What would your dear father have said if he could have seen you now? Really it's just as well he's dead and gone, bless him.' Her look was reproachful as though she blamed Jack for getting injured; obviously she thought he should have watched where he was going and then he wouldn't have stepped on a land mine, would he? Jack smiled as he remembered his schooldays. She had had the same attitude when he fell off his horse, or when a cricket ball thumped him between the eyes and landed him in the sick bay at school. He was just plain clumsy and didn't look where he was going, in her considered opinion.

'Well, Mother, at least I won't be going back to the front, will I? And I suppose I'll get a war pension.'

'Hmm!'

It was a snort, showing what she thought of that. Jack wished fervently that she would go. He knew perfectly well what her next words would be and he was right.

'You know I can't have you home, don't you, Jack? There's no possibility of my looking after you, I'm just not up to it, and neither is Nancy, she's too old.'

'It's my home too, Mother. And besides, I will have to leave here soon. Did you not notice I've got my new feet? I stood up today, I'll be walking quite well soon.'

Olivia Benson sniffed. Her glance at the feet was anything but encouraging. 'I was in at the watchmaker's in Newgate Street on Friday, picking up my pendant watch. Nancy was clumsy enough to knock it from the dressing table last week, but I told her the cost of mending it will be taken from her wages.' Mrs Benson pursed her lips and half shook her head, endangering the stuffed bird once again.

'Well, what I was going to say was that Mrs Buxton was there, the watchmaker's wife. You remember Mrs Buxton, don't you? I was telling her that you were to be fitted with artificial feet and she was telling me that her cousin had an artificial foot but he wasn't able to wear it much, it made his leg far too sore. So how you can possibly expect to walk with two of them is beyond me . . .'

'For pity's sake, Mother, will you shut up?'

Most of the other people in the garden stopped talking and listened as Jack roared at his mother, the demon finally taking over.

'Well, I mean, I was only telling the truth. You have to be prepared for these things—' Mrs Benson stopped abruptly as she saw his expression. She lowered her voice. 'Don't shout, Jack, everyone is looking,' she whispered.

'I don't care who the hell is looking, Mother, do you hear me? Now find me an orderly or a nurse or someone. I want to go back to my room!'

Mrs Benson stood up and hovered and suddenly she looked like a frail old lady and the people about were all looking at Jack as though he were a murderer. She took out her wisp of lace again and dabbed at her eyes.

'Please, Jack,' she whimpered.

He sighed. 'All right. Sit down, Mother, please. I'm sorry I shouted, I won't do it again.'

'No, I think I'd better go, you're obviously over-wrought. Look, there's an orderly over there, I'll ask him to be good enough to take you in.' She walked a few steps away and then came back. 'I'll say goodbye now, Jack, I'll see you next week if I am well enough. But you know the precarious state of my health . . .'

'Yes, Mother. Very well, I'll see you soon.' He watched as she went up to Private Wilson who was standing on the steps of the Hall. He saw her push something into the man's hand and Wilson nodded and touched his forelock and started over the grass towards him. His mother went off along the drive to where her groom was waiting with a governess cart.

Jack's stumps felt sore. The black shadows were clouding in from the back of his mind and taking over altogether.

Chapter Eight

'Did you have a nice time on your afternoon off?'

Elizabeth, who had been gently washing the ends of Jack's legs with a solution of boracic acid, looked up in surprise at his question. Captain Benson had rarely spoken more than two words to her except to say what he wanted her to do for him. But now he was smiling at her. His normally austere expression had vanished and he looked genuinely interested. He lifted an eyebrow and she found her tongue.

'Yes, thank you, sir.'

She bent her head to what she was doing, gently squeezing the liquid over the reddened patches made by his feet the day before. She was suddenly intensely conscious of him. They were on their own, Nurse Turner having gone off to see Miss Rowland and Nurse Middleham on her day off. Elizabeth was gradually being allowed to do proper nursing jobs on her own; in fact, some of the men especially asked for her; she was beginning to get a name for her 'healing' hands. It was not usual for a nurse's aide to do dressings but the hospital was chronically short-staffed. Most trained nurses preferred to be in the larger hospitals or even in the military ones in France.

Elizabeth turned her mind to the afternoon before. How sweet it had been to talk to Jenny after all the years of longing for her, worrying about her. The journey back to Newcomb Hall had passed swiftly as she had gone over every word in her mind. She wished she knew why the girl was so timid, so frightened of her foster father.

Elizabeth finished the bathing and dried the stumps carefully with cotton wool before applying zinc and castor oil ointment. He hardly winced at all, and she felt a measure of satisfaction at that.

'Did you go somewhere special?' Jack asked, surprising her again, and Elizabeth flashed a glance at him from under her lashes, her cheeks tinged with pink. He was such a lovely man, and it was a terrible thing that had happened to him. His poor poor feet. And you could see from his face it had taken a lot out of him. Well, it was bound to.

Jack was sitting up against his pillows. There were shadows under his eyes and the scar on the left side of his face stood out red against his pallor. His legs had ached all night, he had got very little sleep. But now, lying here, feeling her soothing touch, he felt content, almost happy, though it didn't occur to him to realise why.

'On your afternoon off?' he prompted her.

'I went up to Bollihope Common to see my little sister,' she said at last.

'Your little sister? Bollihope Common in Weardale? She's living there?' Jack was surprised. He had thought, taken it for granted, really, that Elizabeth was from one of the mining villages. 'You're from the Dales?'

'No. I'm from the Children's Home, the one attached to the workhouse,' said Elizabeth. 'We were sent there when my mother died.' The statement was made matter-of-factly without a trace of self-pity but Jack was stricken, though it was a common enough story.

'Oh, I'm sorry.'

She was carefully padding his legs with Gangee tissue, ready for him to attach his feet. The doctor had been in earlier and decreed that, despite the soreness, Jack should try to accustom himself to wearing them.

'You'll be surprised how soon the skin will harden, Captain Benson,' he had boomed. Dr Hardy was not an army man but a local general practitioner who put in a number of hours at the Hall. Elizabeth knew him for a good doctor, a gruff red-faced man with a Scottish accent who lived for his day off which he spent at the golf club in the town. He sported tweed plus fours and Argyll woollen socks and brogues, and his hair was parted down the middle and slicked back and to the sides.

It was raining today so Jack was only going to walk across the bedroom and back to his chair in the window. But he was in no hurry to end this pleasant interlude with the little nurse's aide; in no hurry to call in that oaf of an orderly to help him out of bed. He looked down at the knot of glossy black hair which emerged from the back of Lizzie's cap, contrasting so well with the white skin of her nape. He felt something . . . Perhaps he just felt protective, she was so capable and yet vulnerable.

'Tell me about it,' he said to her, then, seeing her expression, 'If you don't mind, of course? I don't want to pry.'

'I don't mind,' she replied. She began to tidy away the enamel basin with the antiseptic solution, the rubber sheet which had protected the bed and the dressing towel which had covered it. As she worked, she told him about how her mother had died and she and her brother had gone into the Home; how her younger sisters had been fostered out and she hadn't been able to get in touch with them for years. She spoke calmly as though it was all something which had happened to someone else. It was the only way she could keep control of herself; even after all this time the wounds were as fresh as ever.

'That's monstrous! They shouldn't be allowed to separate families like that.'

Elizabeth paused, holding the basin ready to tip the contents into the bucket on the bottom of the dressing trolley.

'The Home wasn't so bad. Miss Rowland was there. And they said the bairns should start a new life with new parents. But I missed the little 'uns. Well, after all, in the old days we would just have gone into the workhouse proper, wouldn't we?'

Elizabeth had had enough. She felt wrung out by telling him her story. It was ages since she had tried to explain to anyone, she didn't know why she had now. She must get on with her work, she told herself.

'Are you ready for Private Wilson, sir?' she enquired, and Jack nodded. He swung around so that he was sitting on the edge of the bed and waited for the orderly.

That night Elizabeth had the dream again, for the first time in a long while. The one where her mother was dying in the field and the red, red blood was spreading all around. And her mother's eyes as she gazed at Elizabeth were trying to tell her something, something important, but she couldn't. And then the dreaded moment when all feeling and knowledge began fading away from the eyes until they were blank and staring and it was too late to find out what it was she'd been trying to say.

Elizabeth woke, sweating and panting, and her heart beat so fast she felt it coming up into her throat, the fear was so bad. For Mam had been trying to warn her of something and she couldn't hear, couldn't understand what it was. And now it was too late.

*

'Proper little pet of Captain bloody Benson, aren't you, you little workhouse whore?'

Elizabeth jumped. She was in the linen cupboard, tidying the clean linen in neat piles, sheets on one shelf, pillowcases and nightshirts on another, all ready for the pile which would come up from the laundry room to go on top. The linen room was oblong, barely wide enough for two people to pass, but quite long.

Private Wilson was standing in the doorway, watching her, that sneering look on his face. She walked towards him, keen to get out into the hall where at least there might be other people. The only way was to get past him.

'Let me past, please,' she said, and kept her eyes from his face, cringing from the expression she knew she would see in his eyes. Instead she stared stoically at a brass button on his tunic.

'Let me past, please!' he mimicked. 'Butter wouldn't melt in your mouth, would it? Oh, aye, I'll let you past, once you answer my question. Aren't you Captain Benson's little pet whore?'

'No, I'm not. I'm nobody's.'

'Too namby-pamby to say it, aren't you? Go on, say it. Say you're Captain Benson's whore and I'll let you through.'

Elizabeth's mouth set. She continued staring at the button. Private Wilson laughed and leaned forward. Unexpectedly, he took hold of her breast, his fingers twisting cruelly so that she jumped back in pain and shock. But she had had enough, fury took hold of her. Suddenly she remembered something she had heard a girl boast of in the kitchen, how the girl had stopped a man from attacking her in the woods on her way to work. Elizabeth lifted her knee and rammed it into Private Wilson's privates. He dropped like a stone.

She jumped over his body as he lay squirming on the floor and collided with the laundry basket which he had evidently brought up the stairs. Recovering herself, she ran for the back stairs and her haven, her own attic bedroom. She sank onto the bed, panting and dishevelled. Oh Lord, she had done it now, she had an' all. He would never let her get away with that, no, he wouldn't. She could tell she had hurt him, hurt him a lot.

'And I'm not sorry!' she said aloud as soon as she had got her breath back. She wasn't. Maybe he would want his revenge . . . but maybe he would leave her alone after this. She began to laugh, softly rather than hysterically. By, it had felt good! He had got such a shock, fallen like a felled ox. Private Wilson's privates, what a joke! She felt a sense of liberation, realising she could fight back.

Getting to her feet, Elizabeth went over to the looking glass on the wall by the washstand. Her collar was askew. She straightened it, took off her cap and brushed her hair smoothly. She replaced the cap, anchoring it firmly with kirby grips. Then she grinned at her own flushed face and sparkling eyes in the glass.

'You stick up for yourself from now on, lass,' she

instructed her image. Then she marched to the door. Her hand on the doorhandle, she paused. Sticking up for herself was one thing, foolhardiness another. First she had to make sure that Private Wilson wasn't waiting for her on the first-floor landing. She crept down the uncarpeted attic stairs and peeped round the corner, ready to fly if need be. But there was no sign of anyone. Everyone was outside, the only sounds the distant clatter of pots and pans from the kitchen where, no doubt, Joan and her fellow kitchen maids were washing up after the midday meal.

Elizabeth ran then, past the linen cupboard which had its door closed now and the laundry basket still standing beside it. Down the stairs and into the front hall.

'Nurse!'

Miss Rowland's call brought her up short. The door to Matron's office stood open and she was sitting behind her desk with a full view of the hall and staircase.

'Come in here, Elizabeth, please. And close the door behind you.'

She took a deep breath and went into the office, standing meekly before the desk.

'Is there a fire, Nurse? Someone haemorrhaging? No? Then please explain to me what emergency made you run like that.'

'There was nothing, Matron. I'm sorry.'

Miss Rowland shook her head. 'How you expect ever to make a proper nurse, Elizabeth, I'll never know,' she said sorrowfully. 'I get good reports from your superiors. I was thinking that as soon as you reached seventeen and a half I would write to Durham County or the Royal Victoria Infirmary at Newcastle and recommend you for training. Of course, that can't happen when you suddenly revert to the ways of a harum-scarum little girl, showing no sense of responsibility. You realise you could have knocked down a patient on crutches or even one just unsteady on his feet?'

'I'm sorry, Matron.' Elizabeth was almost ready to burst into tears.

Miss Rowland's voice changed, became concerned. 'You weren't running away from anything, were you? Or someone?'

What could she say? She couldn't tell Miss Rowland the truth; the very thought of explaining made her squirm.

'No, Matron.'

Miss Rowland sighed. 'Well, then, more decorum after this, please, Nurse.'

Outside the sun was shining, though there was a distinct nip in the air. Brambling weather, thought Elizabeth, and felt a sharp longing to be out in the hedgerows filling a basket with ripe fruit. There was a place at the top of the hill by Morton Main, just a hole in the ground really, with fallen masonry all overgrown with brambles and a few wild raspberries. The memory of it came to her over the years – how she would take

Jimmy with her and clamber about the sides, pulling the laden top branches down with a walking stick which had belonged to her granda.

Once it had been the engine house of the aerial flight which carried tubs of coal up the hill from the pit to the waiting coal carts. Now it was just a wilderness of brambles. Elizabeth stood on the steps of the Hall and looked over towards the distant smoke, curling away lazily in the sky above the pit chimneys. It was too far to see where the old engine house had stood.

Elizabeth shook herself mentally. What was she doing, daydreaming about the old days? There was work to be done now; she was supposed to be asking the patients if they needed anything, did they want to come in now it was getting nippy, and anyway it would soon be their teatime. Besides, it was October, she told herself; the brambles wouldn't be fit to eat if a heavy frost had got to them.

She walked down the path to where Captain Benson was sitting on the bench alongside Captain Bell who had the neighbouring room to his. Captain Bell had been blinded in the first chlorine gas attack at Ypres in 1915 and was awaiting a place in St Dunstan's. He sat at the shady end, where the sun, weak though it was, would not irritate the shiny red tissue which had replaced the burnt skin on his face.

'Here's our Nurse Nelson,' said Jack as she approached them. 'Come to take us into tea, I suppose.'

Captain Bell smiled. He was a large, gentle man, with eyebrows which tufted oddly where they had been burned. 'No Private Wilson today, old chap,' he said. 'I'll push you in if you'll be my eyes.'

Elizabeth could have done it but she was well aware that Captain Bell liked to prove he could still do some things. They stood to either side of Jack as he heaved himself to his feet, teetering for a moment so that she put out a hand and he grasped her arm.

'The chair's on your left, Captain Bell, sir,' said Elizabeth, and he felt for it and manoeuvred himself so that he could hold it steady while Jack sat down. 'We can manage now, Nurse,' said Captain Bell. 'Jack will be my eyes.' They set off up the path to the temporary ramp which went up by the side of the steps of the Hall. Elizabeth watched them for a moment, the large man, head thrust forward as he pushed the wheelchair over the stony path, and the only slightly shorter one bumping along in the chair. Her arm tingled where Jack had held it. She went to bring in the other patients.

A cold wind had sprung up from somewhere. In the valley a white mist was rising. Elizabeth shivered. Soon it would be winter. She thought of Jenny in the lonely farmhouse. Oh, she hoped she would be able to go to see her often this winter, would not be cut off by snow. But she knew that was a forlorn hope. Bollihope Common was high and desolate and the wind must sweep across it without hindrance, especially in the wintertime, for there were few windbreaks. But she would go as often as she could, she vowed to herself as she walked beside the last patient, watching him carefully as he hopped up the steps on his crutches and into the hall. Joan was just setting a paraffin lamp in the bracket by the door.

"'The north wind doth blow, and we will have snow",' she said as her friend closed the door against the few dead leaves now swirling in the wind.

'Don't say that, man!' protested Elizabeth, knowing she was right.

Chapter Nine

The day Jimmy was to make his first descent into the pit was supposed to be in January of 1917 but in the event, he went down in early December.

'You're a big strong lad,' said Mr Dunne, the manager. He had come up to the coal-screening shed, which was on the first floor. The coal corves came up one end and the coal was tipped onto the slowly moving screen so that the dust fell through the holes. It went on to the other end to fall into the coal wagons, waiting to be filled and sent along the wagon way to the main railway line. To each side of the screens stood a line of boys and a few women, picking out the stone and cleaning the coal.

It was hard work, bending over the screen, and Jimmy's fingers were sore for the first few weeks. They'd hardened after that and it was better.

'You there – Jimmy Nelson, is it? An' you an' all,

Tommy Gibson. Come here, I want a word with you,' the manager shouted over the clanking of the machinery and crashing of the coal as it hit the wagon below.

Jimmy felt guilty immediately. He had been late for yesterday's shift and it wasn't the first time either. Though Mrs Wearmouth tried her best to get him off to work promptly, asleep, he was dead to the world. It was like struggling through a dense thicket of cotton wool for Jimmy to wake up. So he looked at Mr Dunne warily, expecting the manager to play war with him, maybe even dock his wages. But Mr Dunne had other things on his mind.

'You're a well-grown pair of lads for your age,' he said to them. It was true. Neither of them had to look up to the manager, who was only about five foot eight himself. Most of the boys were smaller and thinner, having come up through the strikes and lockouts which preceded the war. At least the Home had fed the two of them as they grew up. Tommy slid a sideways glance at Jimmy. What was the gaffer on about?

'Come over to the office, lads, will you? I won't keep you a minute.' This last for the benefit of the others working on the screen, all of whom had to work faster while the boys were gone.

Jimmy followed Mr Dunne across the pit yard, Tommy behind. Were they going to get their cards after all? he wondered.

'How would you like to start underground? Straight away, I mean, back shift the morn?'

'Down the pit?' asked Tommy.

'Aye, putting. The pay'll be better, of course. You'll get more than you do working on t'bank.'

Jimmy only just stopped himself from reminding the gaffer that they were not yet sixteen, the age when they could legitimately work on the tubs; not yet fifteen, in fact. He swelled with pride. He was going to do a man's work. He couldn't speak.

'You'll be putting the tubs from the face to where the road way'll take ponies. Mind, you'll have to keep up – the hewers won't stand for it if they can't keep up the output. The seam's only two foot six there. You can do it, lads, can't you? Only with the men deserting the pit in droves to go off to the flaming war, we're short, see?'

For the gaffer actually to feel he should explain his reasons, he must be desperate, thought Jimmy. 'What sort of pay, Gaffer?' he asked.

But the manager had had enough. 'What you damn' well earn!' he snapped, then modified the angry note in his voice. 'No, it's up to you, lad, not me. You know the hewers get paid once a fortnight and they'll give you what they think you've been worth to them. They do a share out. So it's up to you, isn't it, son?'

'Why, aye, Jimmy,' said Tommy. 'Did you not know that?' Jimmy had forgotten. 'Anyroad, I'm game if you are. What do you say?'

110

'I'm on,' he said.

'Right, away back to your work then. You have today's shift to finish,' said Mr Dunne. 'An' don't forget, Jimmy Nelson, if you're late again and miss the cage that will mean a fine. So mend your ways, lad.'

Six o'clock next morning, Jimmy stepped nonchalantly into the cage with the rest of the men working his cavil, the working place allotted to them, his black tin helmet resting on his ears, the pit boots with their steel toecaps which had belonged to Mr Wearmouth, God rest him, padded out with two pairs of thick wool stockings and his Davy lamp in his hand. The boys had been solemnly searched for contraband, matches or cigarettes, and now stood in the midst of the men. The wheel high over the engine house started to turn and the cage plummeted into the depths of the earth, leaving his stomach somewhere at the top and his heart crying out for his big sister, Elizabeth.

Elizabeth addressed the letter she had got up early to write to Jenny, the one which had to take the place of a visit because once again she couldn't get up Weardale the weekend coming. 'Miss Jenny Nelson,' she wrote, 'Stand Alone Farm, Bollihope Common, Frosterley'. She tucked the envelope into the bib of her apron and prepared to go downstairs to begin the day's work.

'Do you think Jenny can read?' Joan had asked when she had seen what her friend was doing. She'd looked doubtful and Elizabeth had stared at her in horror.

'Read? Of course she can read,' she had said. Surely Jenny went to school, didn't she? No, she had gone to school was what she had said. She was absent a lot with Peart wanting her slaving after him all the time. 'By heck, Joan, if she can't, if she's not going to school at all, I'll have the kiddy-catchers on that foster father of hers, I will. I'll raise such a stink—'

'Aye, well,' said Joan as she opened the door to go down to the kitchen to start the patients' breakfasts, 'I wouldn't be surprised.' Elizabeth had told her all about the conditions at Stand Alone Farm, agonising over her little sister's unhappiness.

If Jenny was kept away from school, was that enough of a black mark against Peart to get her away from him? Elizabeth wondered as she sped downstairs to the linen cupboard to fill the trolley with clean sheets ready to change the beds. She brought hot water up from the kitchen, carrying it in huge enamel jugs, panting at the strain on her shoulders and arms. But the geyser in the bathroom was not lit until eight and was only sufficient then for the men's baths, those who were ambulant. They all had to have a dish of hot water to wash and shave before breakfast. Of course, the orderly was supposed to be helping her in this task but Private Wilson was nowhere to be seen; no doubt he would turn up later with a plausible excuse, she thought. She never thought about him now, just got on with the job. At least she was no longer frightened of him, feeling she could look after herself after the episode in the linen cupboard. She smiled at the memory.

At last, all eight patients were washed and sitting up in bed, ready for breakfast. Nurse Turner was shaving Captain Bell and the VAD; Nurse Middleham was on her day off.

'Private Wilson can help you bring up the breakfast trays,' Nurse Turner called over her shoulder.

'Yes, Nurse,' said Elizabeth, thinking that if she waited for him the patients would be eating breakfast at lunchtime. She was on her fourth journey when he appeared, sketchily shaved, the top button of his uniform undone and with a glowering expression as he passed Elizabeth. She pulled away to one side, balancing the tray precariously as she did so, the distaste she felt showing in her expression.

'Don't bloody worry, you damn' tart,' he hissed at her. 'I wouldn't touch you with a flaming barge pole. Captain Benson is welcome.'

'Oh, good,' said Elizabeth sweetly, recovering her equilibrium, and went on up the stairs. She put the tray down on the table outside Jack Benson's room while she knocked.

'Enter.'

Picking up the tray and going in, she was surprised to find him out of bed and already dressed in his hospital blues. He was actually standing at the table, looking down at a paper. She couldn't help but glance at his feet, amazed that they should look so normal. He was even standing naturally. Of course, they were covered with socks and shoes, nothing to see of the wood and metal. He looked up and smiled at her, a frank, open smile which lifted her heart and made her want to sing. By, he was a lovely man, she thought, not for the first time. And not for the first time she half-wished Private Wilson was right about them.

'Oh, it's you, Lizzie,' he said, and his voice was warm and welcoming. 'Just put it down here, will you?'

'Yes, sir.'

She poured his tea and took the cover from the kedgeree which was the standard fare for Tuesday morning breakfast. He watched her, concentrating as she did on what she was doing. Her bent head showed the white nape of her neck below her cap. How neatly she moved. Then she looked up and caught his eyes on her and for a moment, violet-blue eyes looked into hazel and he caught his breath at the glory of them. He couldn't help himself, he reached out and covered her hand with his, feeling the roughened skin from the hard work it did, feeling a great urge to take her away from all this.

'Good morning, Captain Benson, sir.'

Private Wilson was standing in the doorway, the suspicion of a smirk on his lips.

'What the devil do you want, Wilson?'

Jack pulled his hand away quickly and glared at the orderly.

'I wondered if you'll be wanting me to help you down to the garden, sir? After breakfast, of course.'

'Oh, get out, Wilson. If I want you, I'll ring for you,' said Jack and frowned. The mood of optimism which had been on him since he awoke dimmed. He had just about forgotten his disability until the orderly reminded him. He had just been a man with a pretty girl, one he was thinking about asking . . . No, he wasn't, it was all pie in the sky. How could he ask any girl, the state he was in? As if to underline it he moved to sit down at the table and stumbled, reaching out to Elizabeth and knocking over the milk jug. Swiftly she put one arm around his waist and stood, rock-solid, so that he regained his balance.

'It's all right, Nurse, I can manage,' he snapped, though for a minute or two he patently couldn't. But he couldn't bear to feel the outline of her body against his, even covered as it was by a starched dress and apron. Oh, God, what a fool he was.

'I'm here to help,' Elizabeth said reasonably.

'Well, you have. Now go and help some other poor fool!'

Elizabeth withdrew her arm and stood back, watching as he lowered himself to the chair. Then she mopped up the milk with a napkin and picked up the jug.

'I'll go for more milk, sir,' she said.

'Send Wilson back with it, Nurse.'

Elizabeth went down to the kitchen and got the milk. Private Wilson was there, drinking an illicit cup of tea, so she gave him the jug. 'Captain Wilson wants to see you,' she said. There were people about, so he took the milk and went out. It was not his way to say or do anything untoward before others. After that, Elizabeth was unsettled all day – not because of the change in Captain Benson; she felt she could understand that and her heart ached for him. She hugged to herself those few moments when she had gone into his room that morning, seen his welcoming smile, not even noticing his scar, heard him call her Lizzie.

Ever since that awful day when her mother had died beside her in the turnip field, she had hated anyone to call her Lizzie. Lizzie was her mother's name for her, no one else had the right to use it. And yet . . . on *his* lips how sweet it had sounded.

'I think I'll go to Morton Main on Sunday, Joan,' she said to her friend as they walked round the Hall after the midday meal.

'I thought you couldn't afford to go anywhere?' Joan commented.

'I can walk to Morton Main. I've been thinking of Jimmy most of the day.' It was true, his image had popped into her mind at odd intervals all through the dusting and sweeping and bed baths and dressing of sores which had filled the morning.

Joan glanced at her friend. She knew what that meant: Elizabeth thought something was wrong with her brother. And usually when she thought that she was right. What was it about her that she always knew if there was something wrong with any of her brothers or sisters? It was a mystery. Perhaps it was just as well that Joan herself was an only child, or at least, thought she was. She had been a foundling, left in the porch of the Home one night long ago.

'The gaffer's just taking advantage because the lads are orphans,' declared Mrs Wearmouth. She stood, arms akimbo, before the black-leaded range in her kitchen, her face red with anger.

'No, he's not, we wanted to go down the pit,' Jimmy protested, and Tommy nodded his head in agreement. 'Anyroad, lads always used to go down when they were younger than us, didn't they?'

'Aye, they did, an' look at the old ones that did now,' said Mrs Wearmouth. 'It stunts their growth, doesn't it? These low seams are no good for lads.'

'Mind, Jimmy, I wish you hadn't agreed to go down,' said Elizabeth, speaking for the first time. She gazed at her brother, his eyes rimmed with coal dust, tiny pockets of it in the folds of his ears. Sure marks of the new young miner who hadn't learned how to wash it off properly and the cause of much hilarity among his older marras, or workmates. Tommy was just the same.

He, however, didn't have the hangdog miserable expression of her brother. He was actually grinning at Elizabeth.

'It's all right, you know. An' anyroad we're making money, it's grand. An' it's not too hard. The ponies take the corves the main of the way to the bottom of the shaft. I like it,' he asserted. 'I don't know why you don't, Jimmy.'

'I do, really I do,' said Jimmy, managing to sound wholly unconvincing.

'Who're you working with, lad? Who's the main hewer?' It was Mrs Wearmouth asking. A shrewd question, Elizabeth realised.

'Ben Hoddle.' Jimmy hung his head.

'Ben Hoddle? Uncle Ben, you mean?' He nodded.

'Does he treat you right?' demanded Mrs Wearmouth.

'All right,' Jimmy mumbled. He didn't know how the putters were usually treated. He only knew that this last week he'd crawled along tunnels no more than two foot six high and dragged loaded corves after him and been snarled at and cursed at and yesterday . . . he put a hand upon his right shoulder where Uncle Ben had kicked out at him in a fit of temper when he hadn't got back with an empty corf quick enough. The steel toecap of Uncle Ben's boot had connected with the bony part of the joint.

'Hey, Ben, don't you kick the lad, he's doing his best,' one of the other men had said. 'Gan canny, will you?'

'You mind your own business, Jonty,' Ben had

118

snapped venomously. 'He's a lazy little sod, but he'll learn to quicken up if I have the learning of him.' He had laughed in Jimmy's pain-twisted face. 'Or I'll know the reason why not,' he'd snarled. The other men had looked at each other in the murky light of their lamps and muttered but in the end they had turned away and got on with the job of winning the coal. Time was money after all and this war had given them the chance to earn a bit more than they were used to. Though not much. Even Jonty had turned away, telling himself that they had all had to come through it when they started.

Trouble was, this lad was scared of the coal, Jonty could tell that. He was frightened of the noises it made, scared of the roof falling in. Well, he'd have to get over that if he was to make a pitman, Jonty reckoned.

But coming out of the pit he had walked beside the lad. After all, he had no dad to watch out for him. 'You tell me if things aren't right, lad,' he'd said as they hung up their tokens and handed their Davy lamps in to the lamp cabin. He'd pushed the helmet back from his forehead, showing a rim of startling white where it had rested. 'You know what I mean.'

Jimmy remembered that now and felt better. He smiled at his sister. 'I'm all right, Elizabeth,' he said. 'Leave us alone, will you? We're men now, doing men's jobs, aren't we, Tommy?'

'Aye.'

'Well, I would have a word with your blooming Uncle

Ben, Elizabeth,' Mrs Wearmouth declared. 'He's a bully that one, I can see it in his face.'

'No! you're not going to do that, are you?' shouted Jimmy. 'Leave us alone. I said we're all right!'

Elizabeth sighed. 'I won't, I won't,' she said. But there was more to it than Jimmy was letting on, she told herself as she walked back to the Hall in the near dark. And if Ben Hoddle was bullying her brother she knew how to spike his guns all right. A wave of disgust swept over her as she remembered that day, long ago, when he had tried to 'get funny' with her and she only being twelve at the time. Aye, she'd kept quiet all this while but if he didn't behave himself she'd have a word in Auntie Betty's ear, she would an' all.

Chapter Ten

Christmas 1916, and here he was, Jack thought, still in Newcomb Hall Convalescent Hospital. He'd have to go soon, though, whether his mother liked it or not. Now that more and more blind and injured men were filtering through from the front-line hospitals to those in Britain and on to convalescent hospitals such as the Hall, he couldn't continue to take up a room when so many others were waiting.

Morosely, he stared at his legs, moved them against each other, felt the broken skin stinging against the padding.

'You've been on them too much, Captain,' Dr Hardy had announced that morning. 'Best stay in your chair today at least.'

Nurse Middleham had dressed his feet and put on the pads yesterday, that was the trouble. If Lizzie had done them he would have been all right. *Nurse* Middleham? Ha, that was a laugh.

Using his hands to turn the wheels of his chair, he pushed himself out of his bedroom to the top of the stairs and looked down into the entrance hall of the old house. Lizzie and half a dozen others were decorating the Christmas tree with a box of glittering baubles they had found in the attic and which must have been decorating Christmas trees here since Prince Albert first made them popular.

'No candles,' Miss Rowland was saying. 'We don't want to chance setting the place alight.'

'No, Matron,' Lizzie replied. She was on the ladder, stretching to reach the top of the tree to put the shining star in place, her lissom body outlined against the tree.

'Take care!' Jack cried, but no one heard him from his place in the shadows at the top of the stairs. His hands clenched around the arms of the chair, but Lizzie pinned the star successfully and climbed down to look at it admiringly.

'It's grand, isn't it?' she asked as the gold star caught the light from the recently electrified chandelier and glistened. Jack watched her face, the rapt expression as she gazed up at the tree, and his pulse quickened.

He had plans for this Christmas when he went home for three days over the holidays. ('I've got a girl in from the village, Jack,' his mother had told him. 'It's scandalous what she's charging . . . Why, I remember, not so long ago, when they were begging for jobs at the back door. Now, of course, they think the war will last forever, *and* the extra jobs it brings. Well, they're in for a shock in a short time when it's all over. They'll wish they kept in with us then, you mark my words.')

This Christmas he would speak seriously with his mother, tell her he was going to ask Lizzie to marry him, orphan girl though she might be and a miner's child at that. If only he was back on his feet again . . . Could he tie a beautiful girl like Lizzie down to a helpless cripple? Self-doubt returned like a dark cloud. What a mess and a mix-up everything was. One minute his mother's voice sounding in his head, telling him Lizzie was a homeless waif with no family, coming from God knows where; the next thinking Lizzie herself wouldn't have him anyway, not a cripple like him. Sadly he pulled at the wheels of his chair, managed to turn it round and went back into his room where, not without difficulty, he banged the door shut behind him.

On Christmas Eve, Lizzie was allowed time to slip down to Morton Main with the presents she had bought for her family. A lot of the rooms in the Hall were empty as most of the patients who came from round about had gone home for the holiday. As she walked down the path, she was thinking of how her happiness had dimmed when she realised Jack Benson was going to be among those absent. It had been a shock to realise how much she was going to miss him. What a fool I am! she told herself crossly. He was a lovely man, it was true, but far above her. He would never consider marrying such as her, of course he wouldn't. But she could dream, couldn't she?

She was coming to the rows which made up Morton Main now and glanced in her basket with a smile, anticipating the look on Jimmy's face when she gave him his gifts. She'd made him up a parcel. There were two pairs of pit stockings which she had laboriously knitted, going into Bishop Auckland especially for the wool. And a new tie, a blue one, to wear with the nearly-new suit he'd bought from the stall on the market. He had joined the choir at the Primitive Methodists. Jonty was the choir master there and it was he who'd discovered Jimmy had a voice. Not yet broken, it was true, but at the moment a pure alto. The suit had a Norfolk jacket and trousers which buttoned at the knee and it fitted Jimmy very well. It wasn't worn out at all. He'd put it on and come up to the Hall especially to show her, proud as punch of it he was. Elizabeth had had to laugh thinking of him in the choir, scamp that he was.

'Are you getting along better at work, Jimmy?' she had asked when she'd recovered from the laughing fit. His smile had faded and he'd turned away quickly.

'Aye.'

She had let it go at that though her heart ached for him.

There was a parcel for Kit containing a paint box and colouring book she'd bought on that same expedition to the town, and an embroidered card for Auntie Betty and

Ben Hoddle. Elizabeth no longer thought of him as Uncle Ben. She made her first visit to them.

'Oh, you needn't have come, Elizabeth,' was Auntie Betty's greeting. 'We're all coming up to the Hall anyway. The Sunday School and choir are going to call in and sing carols. Christopher is singing, aren't you, pet?' She beamed at the boy who was looking into his sister's basket.

'Is there a parcel for me?' he asked.

'There might be. But it's not to be opened until tomorrow,' she answered.

'Santa Claus is bringing me a lot because I've been a good lad, Mam says so,' he asserted, looking at her as though he thought she might challenge it.

'That's nice,' said Elizabeth. She still couldn't stomach the way he called Auntie Betty 'Mam'– had to bite her tongue to stop herself from correcting him. He soon lost interest in her and went off to play in the corner with a battered toy train. Auntie Betty carried on with the baking she had been doing when Elizabeth went in and she knew her aunt was waiting for her to go. She was dying to say something about Ben Hoddle's behaviour to Jimmy, demand that Betty speak to him about it, the words trembling on her lips. But she had promised Jimmy she wouldn't. Maybe she would just mention . . .

'Jimmy is putting for Uncle Ben and his marras,' she said at last.

'Aye, I know,' her aunt replied and frowned heavily. 'Ben says . . .' She noticed Elizabeth's expression and changed what she had been going to say. 'He says it's a bad cavil, a thin seam.' She rubbed her fingers clean of the dry pastry and picked up the water jug.

Elizabeth was silent for a moment or two, remembering she had promised Jimmy not to say anything. She watched as Auntie Betty rolled out the pastry and lined a pie tin.

'Jimmy's too young for it,' she said at last.

Auntie Betty didn't look up. 'Aye, well, there's a war on,' she replied. After a few minutes, Elizabeth rose and picked up her basket.

'I'll have to be going.'

'Aye. Merry Christmas,' said her aunt. Christopher didn't look up from his game.

Jimmy and Tommy were in from work when Elizabeth got to Mrs Wearmouth's in West Row. Perhaps it was the prospect of the Christmas holiday but Jimmy looked better, more cheerful. He had even managed to remove the coal dust from around his eyes, leaving only tiny specks in the corners.

She handed over the parcels, even a small tin of toffee for Tommy and another embroidered card for Mrs Wearmouth. Jimmy had a parcel for her too, tied elegantly with a piece of bright red ribbon.

'Don't open it until the morrow, our Elizabeth.'

'Nor you neither.'

'I'm going up to the Hall wi' the choir.'

He was wearing his suit and his hair, still wet from his bath, was slicked back from his forehead. Elizabeth smiled. The sadness over her reception from Auntie Betty and Kit eased a little as she saw his happier mood.

'Eeh, lass, when I see you both now, you looking so much like your poor mother . . .' Mrs Wearmouth sank down on the rocking chair which stood by the fire. 'You know, I miss having her next door, I do. That lot who live there now, well, the woman's not the sort to make a friend of. Not like your mam. She'd do anything for you, would Jane Nelson.'

These unexpected words brought a sharp sense of renewed loss to Elizabeth. And she didn't want that now. She felt like walking straight back out of the door.

'Well, she's gone,' she managed to say.

'Aye, an' no need for it, that's what I think,' said Mrs Wearmouth. 'That da of yours going off like that, then her trouble . . . who did that, I'd like to know? Who put—'

'Mrs Wearmouth, please don't talk about it now,' Elizabeth said desperately. 'It's Christmas Eve, a time to be happy, isn't it?' She cast a meaningful glance at her brother, who luckily was saying something to Tommy so that he hadn't caught the drift of Mrs Wearmouth's reminiscences.

The older woman caught the glance. 'Oh, aye, you're

right. Sorry, hinny, I am that.' She stared into the fire for a few moments then changed the subject.

'How're you getting on at the Hall, then, pet? I hear the place is full to the gunnels most of the time. Those poor lads . . . Eeh, it's terrible, isn't it? But I suppose you'll be learning to be a nurse and you wouldn't have got the chance before the war. It's a good trade an' all. I'm pleased for you, I am that, Elizabeth. I—'

'Me an' Tommy have to go now, we've a long round to do tonight before we go to the Hall. See you later, eh, sis?' Jimmy butted in.

'I'll be going too, Mrs Wearmouth, if you don't mind? There's things to do . . .'

'Aye, of course. Well, Merry Christmas, lass.'

'Merry Christmas, Mrs Wearmouth.'

It was dark outside but Elizabeth knew the path like the back of her hand by now. She hurried up the incline, swinging her basket. At least she hadn't to worry about meeting Private Wilson on the way. He was one of the orderlies given forty-eight hours' leave for Christmas since so many of the patients were going home too. As she crested the hill and saw the bulk of the Hall against the night sky, she felt a quickening of her pulse, an urge to hurry. The windows were shrouded so as not to attract any Zeppelin which might stray in from the coast. The great German airships had been preying on the shipyards and ports nearby. It was reported in the *Northern Echo* that one had bombed Hartlepool. Yet the dark Hall did not seem eerie or unwelcoming to her. Not, that is, until she remembered that Captain Benson had gone home that afternoon. He would not be back until the day after Boxing Day. A whole three days. Christmas would be dull without him, she thought. Then, shaking herself mentally, she thought of how the other nurses would laugh if they knew her fancies.

The choir and Sunday School sang in the hall around the tree which Elizabeth had helped to decorate, and Kit's eyes shone with wonder along with those of the other younger children. Christmas trees were rare in Morton Main, not being a necessity of life. The only other one the children had seen was the one in the Sunday School, a small one decorated with homemade paper chains and precious little glister.

Elizabeth's heart swelled with pride when Jimmy sang 'Still the Night' accompanied by the leading cornet of the colliery band, who happened to be Jonty Mason, the choir master. 'That's my brother, singing,' she told Captain Bell, and wished with all her heart that Jack had been there to tell also.

'A beautiful voice,' said the captain sincerely. 'I predict it will be a full-bodied baritone when he's older.' Elizabeth handed everyone mince pies and put twopence in the collecting box when Tommy came round.

Next day, after the festive dinner had been cleared away and the patients were in their rooms having a rest,

Elizabeth found herself with little to do and feeling restless. She wondered about Jenny, what sort of Christmas she'd had, and wished she had been able to go to Stand Alone Farm to see her. But she couldn't, not until her day off, and there were two more days to go. In the end, she decided to go for a walk, even though the sky was glowering with threatened rain. She pulled on her nurse's cape, an old one given to her by Miss Rowland, and slipped along the path by the back of the Hall, not thinking where she was going.

The rain came, of course, as she had known it would but somehow it suited her mood. The path beneath her boots soon became a quagmire so Elizabeth walked on the grass by the side whenever there was space. The ground began to slope away to her left, the rain came in sheets and the grass was slippery with tiny rivulets and patches of mud. Still she did not turn back, the restlessness within her driving her on. Her cape became sodden. She could feel the wet penetrating as far as her shoulders and beginning to trickle down her back. A copse of ash trees was just off to her left but leafless as they were in December they offered little shelter. Further on there was a stone wall, a holly bush beside it. She turned off the path to take what shelter it afforded, at least until the rain eased. She was almost there when her foot slipped on the rank, wet grass and she fell heavily, rolling over and over, unable to protect herself with her arms, as the cape wrapped itself round and round her.

There were a hundred little knocks and scratches, a bang on her head, and then nothing.

It was almost dark when Elizabeth woke. She felt wet wool on her face, heard a quiet baa-ing around her, and sat up in swift alarm. She tried to stand but the sharp pain in her ankle made her cry out. The sheep around her moved sharply then settled down again; the warm, musky smell so peculiar to them would have told her what they were even without the sound. She raised herself to sit on the low wall and felt her ankle. It was puffy but she didn't think she'd actually broken it. Miss Rowland would be angry with her, she was supposed to be back at the hospital by four. Well, there was nothing she could do about that now.

The rain had stopped. A crescent moon came out from behind a cloud and she looked about her, searching for a pit head or farm that would tell her where she was. And then saw the dark shape of a house she recognised. Of course, she knew where she was now. It was the Manor which stood a couple of miles from Morton Main. Without admitting it to herself, she must have been making for it in her long, rain-soaked walk. Drawn to the house where Jack Benson was.

Chapter Eleven

'All right, Nancy, you can go to bed now,' said Jack. 'I can manage myself.'

'If you're sure, Master Jack?' The old woman's voice trembled. She was obviously tired out, not only from preparing and serving dinner but from the excess of emotion she had gone through since he'd come home the day before. Nancy was a woman who lived every emotion to the full, suffering vicariously everyone else's traumas. The tears had welled in her eyes the whole day and Jack reckoned he couldn't stand another minute of it.

'I'm sure. After all, I haven't far to go to bed, have I?' The new girl, Elsie, had helped Nancy make up the bed in the corner. She was a timid little thing, couldn't bear to look at his feet, actually seemed to be frightened of them. She was only fourteen, though, having just left school the week before.

Jack forgot about Elsie, sitting before the fire in what

had been his father's study, a whisky and soda in his hand, the decanter conveniently on the small table at his elbow, his sticks propped up by the table. He took a long swallow and stared into the fire morosely. Hell's bells, he thought, what was he going to do, stuck in this tomb of a house, when he had to leave the Hall? His mother had gone to bed already. There was no one to talk to. Living here, in the back of beyond, he would go steadily crackers. Or descend into alcoholism. Jack took another swallow of whisky and soda and refilled his glass.

A sudden bump against the window made him sit forward, startled, almost spilling his drink. What the hell was that? The window was draped in dark blue velvet, few noises penetrated inside. There it was again, a muffled thump, then a tapping, a scratching. A dog perhaps? A cat? Was that someone calling?

If he hadn't been teetering on the brink between being tipsy and plain drunk, perhaps he wouldn't have tried to do it. He would have rung the bell for Elsie even though she would be tucked up in bed by now. As it was, he reached for his sticks, stood up, and stiffly and clumsily made his way over to the window. Dimly he realised his stumps barely hurt at all. Bloody good pain-killer that whisky. He grinned to himself. It was a distance of perhaps thirty feet, and he was walking better with each yard.

Standing tall, he dropped the sticks and reached up to pull the curtains open. At first he could see nothing. The tall old-fashioned sash window was wet with rain. A bush to one side flapped against the glass, the noise must have been that. Oh, well, back to the fire and the whisky. He reached up again and his hand stayed still: there was a bundle of rags on the ground where the Christmas roses had been blooming only that afternoon. Jack stared at it, swaying slightly when it moved and there was Lizzie, struggling to rise.

'Good Lord in Heaven!' he exclaimed. In a moment his brain cleared. He was not imagining it, she was there, white-faced and soaking wet. Something must have happened to her. He pushed up the bottom half of the window as far as it would go and leaned out, catching her as she swayed towards him. Pulling her in, he closed the window with one hand and made to carry her to the warmth of the fire. But this time he wasn't quite up to it and they ended up collapsing together on the carpet.

'Oh, I'm sorry, I'm sorry!' cried Elizabeth. 'But it was the only place there was a chink of light, you see, and there was nowhere else for me to go.' She was panting with the exertion of hopping and limping over the garden to the window, knocking on the glass, calling to whoever was inside, slipping and falling again in the wet, filthy flower bed. Her ankle throbbed inside her boot which felt incredibly, painfully tight; her face was smeared with blood and stinging from the thorns of the holly bush. She must look a proper sight and of all the people in the house to let her in it had to be Captain Benson. By, she was mortified! She tried to rub the blood from her face with the back of her hand and succeeded only in smearing it with mud which, thankfully, she couldn't see. She couldn't bear to look at him and when she did her mortification was doubled. He was laughing at her! He was sitting on the carpet, head thrown back, convulsed with mirth.

Elizabeth sniffed, dangerously close to howling out her misery. She looked away at the bookshelves on the wall, the fire, the desk in the corner, the bed . . . anywhere but at Jack.

Oh, what a fool she was, coming here at all. He must think she was running after him, her, an orphan from the workhouse Children's Home, a nothing, a nobody. She blinked rapidly, desperately struggling for control.

'Oh, Lizzie, my love, what a pair we are!' cried Jack, but the laughter disappeared when he saw her expression. 'Oh, dear, don't be upset. Look, come to the fire, I don't know what I'm thinking of.' He clutched the back of an overstuffed armchair and pulled himself upright. Though he was stiff and clumsy he did it without thinking. He even bent and held out one hand to her, helping her up too, she wincing as her injured ankle took some of the weight. Together they lurched towards the warmth of the hearth until she could sit in his chair.

'Drink this,' he said, handing her a glass. Elizabeth did as she was told and choked and spluttered as the burning liquid went down. 'All of it,' commanded Jack, and she emptied the glass. A warm, soft glow flooded through her. By, it was lovely! The cold, wet, painful endurance test of the last hour or so faded into the background. He had stirred the fire until the cinders burst into flames and she stretched out her frozen toes to the blaze.

'Let's get that wet cloak off,' he said, and undid the red ties, dropping the offending garment on the floor. He sat on the padded end of the fender and lifted her foot into his lap. 'Let me have a look at this,' he said, and eased off her boot. The feel of her cool skin beneath his fingers, the fine bones of the foot with only a slight puffiness about the ankle, made him tremble. He bent his head to hide the desire which scorched through him.

'It's not too bad,' he said huskily. 'A sprain, I think.' He took a handkerchief from his pocket and bound it tightly round the ankle.

She watched him as in a dream. The warmth and the whisky were having their effect. This really was a dream. She would wake up shortly and be back in her attic bedroom at the Hall. Meanwhile, she was in Heaven and didn't want to do or say anything which would spoil it.

'Oh, Jack,' she murmured. 'Jack, you're a lovely man.'

Exultation surged in him. He leaned forward and kissed her and her lips clung to his, body straining against him. He lowered his lips to her breast, pulling at the material of her dress, fumbling at the buttons. She laughed softly at his ineptitude and brushed his fingers aside so that she could undo them. And then his hand was there, and his lips as he took the rosy tip in his mouth, and Elizabeth moaned and sagged against him, and they were down on the hearth rug. Above her there was Jack's face, his beloved face, eyes intent and absorbed as they looked into hers and his hands found her drawers and the secret place within and Elizabeth thought she would surely die, she was so bombarded with the sensations he roused in her.

There was pain, a sharp pain which made her cry out, and he paused in his movements over her. 'Hush, now, it's all right,' he whispered in her ear. And, 'Whisht, pet,' in the ancient language of the north. And in a moment it was all right and then there was such an explosion inside her that she thought she would indeed die.

Elizabeth remembered little after that. She was vaguely aware that he was lifting her and wanted to tell him not to, she could manage herself, what about his poor feet? But she couldn't somehow, and anyway he did it, and then she was lost in happy, drifting oblivion.

Jack woke with a sense of well-being he hadn't experienced since before the start of the war. He lay for a moment in the dark, gathering his thoughts, before it came back to him why he felt so good. Then he couldn't believe he had forgotten, even for an instant. Especially as she was lying beside him, the whole length of her against him, of necessity of course because the bed was narrow. He lay there, one arm across her, listening to the soft sound of her breathing, the scent of her in his nostrils.

It was a sound outside in the hall which made him sit up and reach for his feet in the half-light which had started to enter at the base of the curtains. Quickly he strapped them on, found the crutches which leaned against the foot of the bed and went to the door to turn the key. There was no way he could let Nancy, or maybe Elsie, discover them.

'Lizzie,' he said gently, sitting back down on the edge of the bed with a sigh of relief, 'Lizzie, wake up.' He thought rapidly of how he could get her out without anyone finding her. He was going to marry her, that was certain, but he had to protect her now. He leaned over and kissed her lips, then her cheeks, rosy with sleep. She smiled and snuggled towards him. 'Lizzie,' he said again, and she opened her eyes and smiled dreamily at him. It was all he could do to stop himself from going further and making love to her again. 'Lizzie, you have to go. Come on, love.'

Elizabeth opened her eyes fully with a dawning realisation of what he was saying. He wanted her to go. Oh, God! She sat up abruptly, causing her head to thump sickeningly, the room to whirl around her. She was ill, she was dreadfully ill . . . no, as memory of the previous evening returned in vivid images which made her blush for shame, she knew she must have been drunk. She had not drunk a drop of alcohol before in her life but she knew the symptoms well, had seen them in others, and the after-effects too.

'You must get dressed, sweetheart, you must,' said Jack. 'One of the maids will be wanting to come in here shortly and you don't want them to see you, do you?'

Elizabeth wasn't looking at him, she couldn't. He wanted to get rid of her – she was mortified with shame. She scrambled out of bed, gathered her clothes together and limped painfully behind a chair. Pulling her clothes on any old how, still she didn't look at him.

There was a knock at the door, the handle was turned but of course the door was locked. 'Captain Benson? Can I come in? I have to light the fire.' It was Elsie, her voice expressing surprise at the locked door. Elizabeth froze, her dress half buttoned, and stared at him in horrified appeal, expecting him to do something, say something.

'Come back in half an hour,' called Jack. 'I don't wish to get up yet.'

'Very well, sir. Sorry,' Elsie replied and there were sounds of her going away. Elizabeth let out her breath and finished dressing. She looked around for her boots.

'Don't look so frightened, please,' said Jack, almost in her ear. She turned quickly and he was there, his arms coming out to draw her to him and hold her. And she let him, an incredible weakness sweeping over her. Oh, she had no shame, no shame at all, she chided herself.

'For your own sake, you have to go, Lizzie,' he whispered. He picked up her cloak from the floor and wrapped it round her. She pulled on her boots, having to leave the right one completely unlaced, and was ready.

'Take one of my walking sticks,' he said. 'Come on, I'll help you out of the window. Go along to the end of the lower path and turn to the kitchen door. Just say you were out walking and hurt your foot. It will only be old Nancy. She'll get the handyman to take you back in the trap. You can't possibly walk on that foot.'

Within ten minutes of waking Elizabeth was bundled out into the cold morning air. He leaned after her to kiss her, began to say he would see her soon and they would decide what to do then. But she didn't hear, she didn't look back. Last night was no longer the wondrous, beautiful night of love it had seemed. Oh, it was still one she would remember for the whole of her life but it was spoiled. She felt dirty and squirmed at the thought of it. She had thrown herself at him, she knew it, offered herself to him and of course he had taken her. Oh, he had been kind but what must he think of her now? She had some ideas. She thought of the sneering, knowing face of Private Wilson. How he would laugh if he knew he had been proved right. She *was* Jack Benson's whore. Her mind flinched from the thought.

Elizabeth had little memory of the journey back to the Hall. How Nancy had looked at her, staring in disbelief.

'But where were you going?' she asked.

'A walk, that's all,' Elizabeth mumbled. By the time old Joe, the handyman from the Manor, had driven her back to the Hall, her foot was throbbing painfully and she felt tired to death. She dragged herself upstairs to the attic, almost fell into the room. Joan was still in bed. Elizabeth could hardly believe it was still not yet seven o'clock. She dropped her clothes on the wooden chair by her bed, shivering uncontrollably in the unheated attic, and crept into bed. Thank goodness it was Boxing Day. She had a whole half-hour to warm up under the clothes before she had to get up and attend to the few patients who had spent the holiday there. And thank goodness Joan was still asleep, no explanations needed there.

'Where were you?'

The question dropped into the silence, just as Elizabeth stretched out her legs and, sighing, turned on her side.

'Oh Joan!'

Tears sprang to Elizabeth's eyes. She closed them tightly and turned her head into the pillow, sobbing.

'What? Someone didn't go for you, did they? It wasn't that bloody Private Wilson, was it?'

Joan was out of her own narrow bed and perched on the end of Elizabeth's in a second, quivering with indignation and anxiety. She leaned over her friend.

'I'll massacre the sod. I will, I will!' cried Joan.

Elizabeth could only shake her head. It was minutes before she could stutter out, 'No . . . not him . . . not Private Wilson. It was nobody.'

Chapter Twelve

Elizabeth couldn't travel up to Weardale until New Year's day, when the swelling in her foot finally went down.

'You really should be more careful, Nurse,' Miss Rowland had said. 'I can barely do without you at the moment, even though some of the patients are away. You'll have to make yourself useful with jobs you can sit down to do.'

So Elizabeth had spent the week rolling newly washed bandages, mixing ointments, and most important of all to her, keeping out of the way of Captain Benson who had returned to the Hall on the evening after Boxing Day. She had been sitting in the linen cupboard, darning sheets and pillowcases, when he appeared at the door.

'Lizzie,' he said. That was all.

'Good evening, Captain Benson,' she replied. She had been rehearsing how she was going to handle this meeting all day but she had not thought it would come so soon. She kept her eyes on her work, threading the needle up and down. Her heart beat uncomfortably. She knew he was going to tell her that it had just been a thing of the moment, something that had happened and now was over. And she was determined not to let him see she cared, couldn't bear to think he should feel sorry for her.

'How is your ankle?'

'A lot better, thank you, sir.'

'Lizzie . . .' He watched her. Did her hand tremble or was that just the light flickering? He couldn't see her face. A lock of hair had escaped from her cap and hung over her forehead as she bent over the darning. The nape of her neck looked bare and vulnerable. Jack sighed.

'Did you get into any trouble after staying out last night?' he asked at last. He couldn't understand why she was being like this. Surely she wasn't shy with him?

Elizabeth was a while answering. Why was he bothering? she asked herself, and told herself the answer. Because he was a kind man, a lovely man. Though he would never marry a girl like her, he didn't want to hurt her, that was it.

'Thank you for asking, sir,' she said formally. 'No one found out.' She looked up at him now squarely, her violet eyes wide and solemn. 'Please go, sir. Miss Rowland will be angry if she catches me talking to a patient instead of working.'

'Why do you call me sir? After all—'

'Please, Captain Benson.'

Jack bit his lip and turned away. 'Of course, Nurse.'

Elizabeth went over the episode in her mind as she travelled up to Frosterley on the train. She had gone over it endlessly in the last few days. Oh, she loved that man, she did, she thought, but it was no use, she knew it wasn't. Yet she couldn't regret the night they were together, she would always treasure the memory of it. As the train drew into Frosterley station Elizabeth picked up her basket with the belated Christmas presents for Jenny and the packet of tobacco she had bought for Mr Peart, not before some soul-searching but after all it *was* Christmas, and got out.

The wind was against her as she climbed the hill. She had to bend into it, holding the collar of her coat together to stop the piercing blast which blew down from the tops from getting inside her clothes. The temperature was noticeably colder than it had been in Bishop Auckland but she had anticipated that and wrapped a scarf around her hat and she wore the woolly gloves which Joan had knitted her for Christmas. Nevertheless she was thankful to find the overgrown pathway which led down to Stand Alone Farm, even more pleased to see the rowan tree by the gate and the homestead.

The farm looked more desolate than ever. The wind eddied around the yard, lifting ancient dried dung and depositing it against the house wall. An old tin can

145

clattered about then lay still until the next gust lifted it
again.

The rowan tree was bare but for a few dried up berries
in the upper branches, disdained even by the birds. But
a desultory line of smoke was coming from the chimney
of the house and inside the dog barked. Elizabeth
knocked on the back door. There was no response at
first. After a minute or two she knocked again and the
door opened. Jenny stood there, looking as small and
thin and pale as ever, and Elizabeth's heart went out to
her. She took one impulsive step forward and flung her
arms around her sister, kissing her on the cheek. Jenny
stood stiff and awkward, obviously not accustomed to
any show of affection. At last she trembled and a faint
pink tinge appeared on her white cheeks. She did not lift
her own arms, they simply hung by her sides, and
eventually Elizabeth let her go.

'Hello, Jenny,' she said. 'Did you have a nice
Christmas? Did you get my card? I'm sorry I couldn't
come before now but I—'

'Will you get in here and close that bloody door? I'm
damn' well nithered!' The voice from inside made Jenny
jump visibly. She stood aside to allow her sister to enter.
Peart was sitting at the table. He rose to his feet as
Elizabeth walked forward, astonishing her as it was the
first sign of courtesy she had seen from him. What was
more, he was reasonably clean. He was wearing a clean
shirt, though minus the collar, and his boots were

polished, his trousers no longer encrusted with filth. Why, she could even tell the colour, they were a faded brown corduroy.

Was this elegance all due to the fact that she had written to say she was coming? Elizabeth couldn't believe it. She smiled tentatively at him.

'Hello, Mr Peart,' she said. 'A happy New Year to you.'

He seemed to have got over his little outburst of temper. 'An' a happy New Year to you an' all,' he replied, with a creasing of his face she took to be a smile. It faded as his glance fell on Jenny.

'Move yourself, lass,' he roared. 'Get your sister a chair.'

'Yes, Peart.' Jenny jumped to pull one forward, the habitual anxious expression she wore deepening. She stood back, her hands clasped together, fingers moving nervously, and Elizabeth was reminded of the picture of a little black slave she had seen on the magic lantern which had come to the Sunday School one social evening.

'Aren't you sitting down, Jenny? Look, I've brought you your Christmas box. Did you have a nice Christmas?'

Elizabeth looked around the bare, comfortless room, the walls devoid of any streamers or decorations, the only card on the mantelpiece the one she herself had sent.

Jenny looked at her doubtfully, gave a darting glance towards Peart. Before she could answer he spoke for her.

'Why, man, we don't bother with such silly goings on here. Christmas? It's just another day. Now New Year, today like, that's summat else. Today's the real holiday for us up the Dales.'

Had Jenny had no Christmas at all? Elizabeth was horrified. She blamed herself. Oh, she should have made more of an effort. She should have got up here before. She wept inside for her little sister who was still standing in the same way, looking anxious.

'Sit down, for God's sake, Jen, will ye?' Peart roared suddenly and she slid onto the edge of a chair. Elizabeth lifted her basket onto the table and began to unpack it. Peart leaned forward to look.

'What you got there then?'

She took out the wrapped parcel for Jenny, the smaller one for Peart. He pulled the paper off immediately and grunted with satisfaction when he saw the tobacco. But Elizabeth wasn't really interested in him; she was watching Jenny. The little girl was looking at the parcel tied with red ribbon on the table before her and her face was a study in bewilderment.

'Aren't you going to take the paper off, pet?' Elizabeth asked gently. Heavens, had she not received a Christmas box before?

'Can I?'

'Yes, you can.' Elizabeth stared coldly at Peart, the

148

supposed foster father. 'Has Santa Claus never been to Jenny?' she asked.

He looked up briefly. 'Santa Claus? Don't be daft, woman. What has a charity lass to do with such fairy tales?'

There was no sign of Christmas here because there hadn't been one, Elizabeth realised. Poor little Jenny. Oh, when she got back to Bishop Auckland she would write a letter to the guardians, she would! One to scorch their ears off.

'I'll help you, will I?' she said to Jenny. She showed her sister a little nurse's apron and cap with red crosses sewn on. Elizabeth had made them herself from sheet remnants she had begged from the sewing room. There was a bag of mint humbugs and one of hazelnuts she had gathered from the woods in the autumn. And a bright red knitted jumper and floppy hat with a band of artificial silk around the edge. And a doll, a second-hand doll with a tiny worn patch on the nose of the waxen head which Elizabeth had disguised as best she could with a little white paint.

'You'll spoil the lass, I won't be able to do a thing with her,' Peart said. 'Anyroad, what does she want a doll for, a great lass like her? She hasn't got time to play wi' dolls, she has work to do.'

Jenny started up from the table at his words. She picked up the doll and took it into the corner where she knelt with her back to the room, cuddling it fiercely.

'Leave her alone,' said Elizabeth. 'She's only a bairn. Every little girl likes a doll.' She glared at Peart, the realisation that Jenny had probably never had a doll before increasing her dislike of him. She went over to her sister and sank down beside her. 'Howay, petal,' she said gently. 'He's not going to take it away, I promise you. What're you going to call her?'

Jenny looked from her to the doll and back again, doubtfully. 'I don't know.'

'Well, look, why don't we take her for a walk? You can wear your new jumper and hat and we can think of a name for her on the way.'

'The lass has the tea to get,' said Peart. But he had a strange look on his face, his tone unexpectedly mild.

'She's a little lass, not a slave,' Elizabeth replied sharply. 'It looks like she's had no Christmas, she's due a holiday.'

'Aw, go on then,' he said, turning away and taking a pipe out of his pocket and filling it with the tobacco Elizabeth had brought. He pointed the stem at Jenny. 'Mind, while you're out you can check on the ewes.'

Jenny opened her eyes wide in obvious amazement but she said nothing, only scampered across to the table and put on the jumper and hat. Still clutching the doll, she turned shining eyes to her sister.

Outside, the wind had died down. The winter's afternoon was grey and bleak but it was still light enough for them to walk a short way up the fell side to where the sheep were clustered by a broken-down fold. There were a few strands of hay about, showing that Peart had subsidised their grazing on the barren moor, but still, to Elizabeth's eyes, they were a sorry lot. She leaned on a stone wall and watched as Jenny went in among them, talking gently to them, and they baaed quietly, moving over for her, reminding Elizabeth of the sheep near the Manor on Christmas Day. Was it only a week ago? She thought of Jack, the feel of his arms around her, and her heart melted within her in sad, aching yearning.

Jenny came back and stood before her, hugging her doll and gazing earnestly at her.

'Elizabeth,' she said. It was the first time Elizabeth had heard her speak before being spoken to. Jenny spoke more easily to the sheep than she did to people, she thought sadly.

'Yes, petal?'

'Somebody else used to call me petal, I think,' said Jenny, her brow wrinkling as she tried to remember.

'Oh, Jenny!' Elizabeth pulled the thin little body to hers, holding her sister close, though the doll was between them.

'Can I call my doll Petal?'

'Why not? Of course you can, Jenny.' They began walking up the fell, Elizabeth holding Jenny's small, work-roughened hand in hers. But they hadn't gone far when Jenny began to look nervous. She kept looking behind to where the homestead lay hidden in a fold of land.

'He'll be wanting his tea,' she said at last.

'We'll go back, then.' Elizabeth was dying to ask all sorts of questions about Jenny's life but decided not to rush at it all at once. But she did ask, 'Did you like going to school, Jenny? You went when Mrs Peart was here, didn't you?'

Jenny considered the question gravely. 'I liked school. Except when the others made fun of me, said I was dirty.' She looked down at the skirt of her dress showing beneath the bright jumper. 'They said I was always raggy. I'm not now, though, am I?'

'Did you like *her* though?'

Jenny put her head on one side. 'When she went, *he* said I had to do everything or he would put me out on the top of the moor. But I'm good, aren't I, Elizabeth? I work hard, don't I?'

They were back in the farmyard by now. Inside, the dog gave a couple of desultory barks.

'You do, pet,' her sister assured her. She stopped walking and, putting a hand on Jenny's shoulder, turned her to face her. 'Jenny, I'm your friend as well as your sister, you know that, don't you?'

Jenny nodded. But now she was back home she was looking careworn and worried again. She pulled away and ran towards the door. 'He'll be wanting his tea,' she said again.

Going back home on the train Elizabeth reflected on the afternoon. By, how she wished she could stay longer, maybe take a room in Frosterley, see more of Jenny. Could her sister even read? She'd sent her a Christmas card, had she read that? I'll have a word with Miss Rowland again, she decided.

Then there had been the peculiar behaviour of Peart. What a strange man he was. It was funny the way Jenny just called him Peart, and Elizabeth had fallen into the same way of thinking of him. Most normal foster fathers liked to be called Dad or even Daddy. But Jenny hadn't been taken in as a daughter, that was plain. She'd been taken in to train up to work, a skivvy, a slave, which was what she was. How could the authorities in Auckland have let it happen?

Another thing, though, Elizabeth brooded over: Peart was looking at her in a way she had learned to recognise. She would have to be careful with him, that was for sure. She was troubled with so many worries and apprehensions, she couldn't think straight.

Joan was in the attic bedroom when Elizabeth got back, sitting up in bed, looking at the pictures in an old *Tatler* she had found somewhere in the house.

'You're back then,' she greeted Elizabeth. 'Was the bairn all right when you got there?'

'All right? I think so.'

Elizabeth hung her coat behind the door and stripped off her clothes. She poured cold water from the jug into the chipped pottery basin and washed, shivering as she reached for her nightdress and jumped under the bedclothes.

'Look at this lot – all la-di-da and dressed up to the nines in their fancy clothes. It makes you think, doesn't it? Aye, well, our turn will come – Elizabeth, what's the matter with you?' Joan flung down the old magazine and jumped out of bed to stand beside her friend's. 'I thought you said Jenny was all right?'

Elizabeth was weeping silently. Now she searched for the piece of rag under her pillow which did duty for a handkerchief and blew her nose and wiped her eyes.

'I don't know, Joan,' she said and pulled back the blankets so that her friend could get into bed with her. Joan doused the lamp first and the two girls lay side by side as they had done so often when they were orphans in the Home and comforted each other.

'What?' Joan asked. 'You might as well tell me it all.'

So Elizabeth related everything about her afternoon at Stand Alone Farm: how timid Jenny was, how quiet, how she ran to do Peart's bidding, how he treated her worse than he did his dog.

'She doesn't go to school, I'm sure she doesn't. I don't think she can read and write properly. And I'm sure that was her first doll and she'd had no Christmas at all, she hadn't. I wish I could get her away from Bollihope Common, I do.'

'If you were married, had a place of your own, mebbe

you could,' said Joan. 'Any chance of that?' Joan was thinking of Christmas Day or, more likely Christmas night, and what had happened then, Elizabeth knew. She felt a great burst of longing. By, it would be perfectly grand, it would, if she were living at the Manor with Jack. A warm glow began in the pit of her stomach at the thought, grew until she could actually feel the warmth of a blush in her cheeks. She could have Jenny to live with her, maybe even Jimmy would come, go back to school, get out of the pits. And there would be Jack, her lovely man.

'I don't think there's much chance of that, Joan,' she said.

'You never know,' said Joan. 'But, look, there's no use in fretting over something you can do nothing about, is there? Jenny's been there all these years, a bit longer won't hurt.'

'Hmmm. Well, I'm going to ask Miss Rowland again.'

But there was no chance to ask Miss Rowland for quite a while. The Hall was filling up again with more and more casualties, patients at earlier stages than they had been at before, so Dr Hardy had to have another local doctor to help him, and an army surgeon, Major Scott, was assigned to help Major Davies, attending three mornings a week. Of course, most patients who needed operations had already had them when they arrived at

Newcomb Hall, but some of them only a week before, and consequently, they needed expert care. Elizabeth found herself taking over more and more nursing duties; she was learning fast because she had to.

She had seen little of Jack in two days because she had been working on the ground floor, where what had been a drawing room opening out into a dining room had now been combined to make a large ward for the more acute patients who needed careful watching. She had given up her day off to help out too, though she agonised over missing a visit to Stand Alone Farm and Jenny. But she had scribbled a postcard to her sister and hoped Peart would read it out. In fact, she had written on it that he should. But would he?

'If you could help me to do the dressings on this floor?' Nurse Turner said one morning when Nurse Middleham was on her day off. Nurse Middleham insisted on taking all the hours off she was due, saying she needed them if she was to maintain her health and be any good to the patients. Elizabeth had noticed Nurse Turner smiling grimly at that.

'I am expected downstairs,' Elizabeth said hesitantly. She felt torn. How could she be in both places at once?

'Yes, well, we'll be quite quick and then you can go, it will be all right.'

Elizabeth's heart beat a little faster when they opened the door of what she thought of as Jack's room. But it didn't look the same. There were two beds in there and both were occupied by strangers.

'Where's Captain Benson?' she asked, her voice sounding odd in her own ears.

'Discharged,' Nurse Turner replied. 'Now, we'll begin with Captain Johnson. He has a shrapnel wound in his back and it's suppurating . . .'

Elizabeth moved forward, took the hydrogen peroxide from the bottom of the trolley and poured some into a kidney dish while Nurse Turner scrubbed up at the wash-stand in the corner.

'He's gone home. He didn't even tell me he was going,' she whispered.

'Did you say something, Nurse?' queried the officer, lying prone on the bed, his head turned to face her.

Elizabeth stared at him in utter misery. 'No, sir,' she said, then coughed. 'No, sir,' she said again, louder.

'Come on then, Nurse, get on with it.' Nurse Turner was standing by the trolley, her hands held up, pink and glistening from the scrubbing they had received. Elizabeth took a pair of forceps and handed her a clean dressing towel from the trolley on which to dry them.

Chapter Thirteen

'I don't think you should be going. If you make yourself ill it will be I who must bear the brunt of it,' said Mrs Benson. She stared in disapproval across the breakfast table at her son. He was wearing his captain's uniform, his Sam Browne belt and brass buttons gleaming from the polishing he had given them the day before.

'If I stay loafing about here, Mother, I shall go mad,' he replied. He got up and walked to the sideboard, a trifle stiffly but he did it without any outward signs of discomfort. He looked well, Olivia Benson had to admit to herself. He looked remarkably like his father when he was the same age. Before he had drunk and gambled himself into an early grave. But still . . .

'You can get the mine manager to bring the books up here, there's no need to go down there.'

'No, I want to see for myself what is happening.

Morton Main is the only mine left to us, I must see it does well.'

'I need the carriage myself this morning. It's the Ladies' Guild morning. We are working for the war effort.'

'Are you, Mother? Well, don't let it worry you, I can drive the trap myself.'

His mother compressed her lips into a thin, hard line. 'Well, if you must, you must. I see nothing I say has any influence on you at all.' She flounced out of the room and Jack grinned wryly. He had seen her enact the exact same scene so often with his father when he was alive. She was a strong-willed woman; no wonder his father had turned to drink. But if he himself were to stay here, at least for a while, he had to go his own way.

It wasn't far to the mining village. Later, when his legs were stronger, he should be able to walk down there, but for now it was enough to be out in the fresh air on his own. He had been dependent on other people for so long. It was a fine winter's day, the air sharp with frost, the sun coming through the bare branches of the trees to the side of the track. He whistled softly as he went, his thoughts turning to Elizabeth as they always did these days.

He loved her, he had to admit it to himself. But could she love a man crippled as he was? There was Christmas night, every detail etched on his memory. He had thought she loved him then but had he just caught her when she was vulnerable, seduced her? Her attitude since then, the way she went out of her way to avoid him when he was at the Hall, had given him cause for doubt. He looked down at the highly polished shoes over his false feet. For that's what they were. False. He was sure they fooled nobody.

Don't become maudlin, he told himself. Think of all the poor beggars who haven't made it back, all the ones with injuries so much worse than his. He lifted his head and began whistling again. The pony pricked up his ears and trotted on and the trap turned into the pit yard at Morton Main and came to a halt outside the offices. The yard was busy with men going to and fro. They all glanced at him in curiosity but then got on with their business. The winding wheel whirred round; loaded tubs were being taken out of the cage. There was the sound of sawing from the carpenter's shop, a hammering from the blacksmith's. The manager looked through the window of his office and came hurrying out to greet Jack.

'Captain Benson! I didn't expect to see you, not for a long while yet,' he exclaimed. He held out one hand. 'Can I assist you to a chair in the office?'

'Good morning, Dunne. I can manage.'

Jack got down from the trap, careful to stand straight, refusing to acknowledge any difficulty though he did pick up his stick from the seat and use it to steady himself.

'Lead the way, Dunne.'

'Yes, sir.'

Mr Dunne held the door of his office open and Jack negotiated the two steps to it successfully, but he was glad when he could sit down before the desk. So far, so good, he told himself.

'Nice morning, isn't it?' he said pleasantly. 'I'll have a look at the books, Dunne.'

'Mr Jones inspected them on Friday, sir,' said Mr Dunne, raising his eyebrows. 'I'm sure he found nothing wrong.'

Jones was the mining agent employed by the family when Jack's father had died. It was Jack's intention, and he had been thinking about it all weekend, to take over the agent's job himself. After all, Jones was agent for a number of mines, it wouldn't affect him much, and Jack reckoned he could do it. He had dreamed of an army career, but that was out of the question now.

He looked over the books for most of the morning, asking Mr Dunne questions about anything he was unsure of, making notes in the notebook he had brought with him. The hooter sounded at the end of the fore shift and the wheel whirred and the cage ran up and down, clanging open and shut as it disgorged the black-faced miners into the yard. Jack watched with interest. Some of them were mere boys, he realised, some older men, bent and with worn faces that no amount of coal dust could hide.

There was a knock at the door and the horsekeeper put his head round. 'Will I feed the pony, sir?' he asked. He had a nosebag in his hand, obviously expecting an affirmative answer.

'Thank you,' Jack replied. It was one o'clock before he closed his notebook and sat back in his chair. 'I'd better go back to lunch,' he remarked to the manager who was still sitting on the other side of the desk, working on papers, or at least ruffling them and putting ticks and crosses on them at intervals for all the world like a schoolmaster. Obviously he did not intend to leave the office while Jack was there.

'Will you be returning today, sir?'

He smiled. 'Not today, I think. But I'll be back soon.' He glanced at the telephone. Dunne would be ringing the agent as soon as the trap left the yard, he thought. In fact, he would bet on it. Well, let him. Jack himself would be calling too.

Just then the telephone rang. He waited as the manager picked up the receiver and suddenly the hooter sounded again, short, broken blasts, the signal that something was wrong in the pit. Dunne was on his feet, still talking. 'Right, I'll alert the Ambulance room,' he said. 'Just the one, did you say? Right.'

He put down the telephone and looked across at Jack. 'Sorry, I have to go. Accident. One of the putters trapped between tubs.' He wasted no more time talking. Jack followed him out into the yard where there was a sudden flurry of activity around the shaft. Jack waited. This side of mining he had never seen. He wondered if the man was badly hurt. But when the cage reached the bank after what seemed an age, he realised with a sick feeling inside his stomach that it was a boy, not a man, lying so still on the stretcher they brought out. He watched in horror as the stretcher was carried to the Ambulance room. The boy was wearing nothing but his helmet and boots and a pair of short blue cotton pants. There was a dense covering of coal dust on his skin and his eyes were open, staring. From behind the gates a woman wailed. Jack looked up and saw there was already a knot of them standing there; they must have come the minute they heard the hooter.

The motor ambulance came and the gates were opened for it but the men who had brought the boy out of the pit were shaking their heads at the driver.

'The lad's a goner,' one of the men who had carried the stretcher was saying. The boy had been taken into the Ambulance room, out of sight of prying eyes.

'What was his name?' Jack asked the manager.

'Tommy Gibson,' he replied quietly. 'An orphan, poor little sod.'

There was nothing more for Jack to do but climb on to the trap and go, past the few women still lingering, the unwanted ambulance. The women and the driver looked up at him impassively. A short way along the road a figure burst from the woodland path onto the road, a girl, running full pelt, her hair loosened from its grips and falling over her face and shoulders, her face a twisted mask of fear.

'Whoa!' Jack called to the pony and climbed down, not waiting until the trap came to a complete halt and consequently having to struggle to keep his balance. He managed, though, and as the girl came up he put out a hand and caught hold of her.

'Elizabeth, wait!' he cried. She looked at him and he knew she hadn't even seen him, she was so intent on getting to where she was going.

'Let me go, I have to get to the pit, didn't you hear the hooter? Someone's hurt, might be our Jimmy. I was told it was a lad.'

Men were streaming out of the pit by now, the back shift, leaving the pit idle in respect for the dead boy. They came along the road in a stream, parting around Jack and Elizabeth and the pony and trap.

'It's not Jimmy, Elizabeth, do you hear me? It's not him,' Jack cried. She looked up at him blankly and he caught her by the shoulders and brought her to him. Some of the men looked at them curiously but went on.

'Not Jimmy? How do you know?'

'I've just come from there. It's a boy, a young boy. But not Jimmy. His name is – was – Tommy something or other, the manager said.'

Elizabeth sagged against him. 'Oh, God forgive me, I can't help but be glad. It's not my brother, it's another lad and I'm glad.' She began to cry; deep, silent weeping. Around them, the men were beginning to mutter, take notice. They looked hard at Jack, not sure what to think.

'Come with me,' he said. 'Come on, into the trap. We'll take a ride.'

Obediently Elizabeth got up beside him. 'Gee up,' said Jack and the pony trotted on, away from the pit head and the pit rows, past the turnoff for the Manor and up the rise beyond, leaving the houses behind until they were out among fields, ploughed fields, ready for the spring planting, ringed with bare-branched trees and dark brown hedges. The pony had slowed to a walk up the rise and Jack let him keep his own pace. Beside him, Elizabeth shivered.

'Are you cold? There's a rug behind you.' He found the rug and wrapped it round her; he could feel how cold she was, he had to warm her. They were entering a tiny hamlet, only a couple of farms and a few labourers' cottages, but there was an inn, the Plough, he remembered it from before the war.

'We'll go in here, warm up, have something to eat if there is anything,' he said.

Elizabeth said nothing, simply sat while he got down from the trap and tied the pony to a hitching post, came around to her side to help her down.

'Come on, love,' he said. 'You'll catch your death if you don't get warmed up soon.'

Obediently she allowed him to take her arm and help her down. She was tired, suffering from the after-effects of the terrible fright she had had, running through the wood certain in her own mind that Jimmy had been injured in the pit, sure of it from the time she had heard the hooter give the signal for an accident. She had been walking in the wood, getting some fresh air after night duty on the wards, relaxing so she would be able to sleep, something she found hard in the daytime. And then the terrible sound had come and she'd remembered Jimmy was on back shift and so would be in the pit. And she had run and run.

Now she looked at Jack as he led her into the inn, calling to the landlord for drinks, asking if there was a fire in the snug. And whether it was because her emotions were already heightened, she felt such a surge of love for him that she couldn't bear it, it seared her very bones.

'Only sandwiches, sir,' the landlord was saying. Jack must have asked for food too. 'Soup and sandwiches.' She was drawn to the fire. There was an inglenook sofa to one side; the coal was crusted over, smouldering, and the landlord took a poker to it and broke it up so that it burst into flames. The warmth sprang out. Elizabeth closed her eyes for a moment, feeling it, luxuriating in it.

Jack sat down beside her, his thigh touching hers through the thickness of their clothes, but it made her tremble she was so intensely conscious of it. Her thoughts were hazy, dreamlike. The landlord brought bowls of broth, ham sandwiches, hot toddies.

'Ring if you need me, sir,' he said, giving Jack an understanding glance. 'I'm busy in the other bar, I won't disturb you.'

They ate and drank, the toddy burning Elizabeth's throat but she drank it down and the warmth of it spread through her. She was hungry, she hadn't realised, ravenously hungry. Jack didn't say much. He ate and drank and watched with satisfaction when she cleared her plate. And afterwards, when she sat back with a sigh, he took her hand and held it in his, bringing it to his lips and the place where they touched tingled. Dimly, she realised that she was lost, about to be drawn into that glorious experience yet again and she would regret it, oh, yes, she would regret it but she couldn't help it. If he asked her, if he asked the landlord for a room and took her upstairs, she would go no matter how knowingly the landlord looked at them, she would go and feel no shame at all. Deep in her belly, something moved, deliriously.

Jack didn't ask her, not yet he didn't. He was content to sit there with her, hold her, they had all the time in the world. They sat, their arms around each other, drowsy with the heat from the fire and the toddy and the food, in a magical world of their own, away from the cares of the war-life outside the little room.

'We must have a serious talk, my love,' said Jack. 'We shouldn't put it off. I don't want to take advantage of you.' He looked down at her face, rosy from the fire; her eyes, so dreamy, so deep a violet that they looked almost black. Liar, he thought. I do want to take advantage. I want to pick her up now and put her down on the rug and make love to her, grand and magical, perfect love. I want to pick her up and run upstairs and fling her on a bed—

This time he was brought up short all right, the bitter memory coming that he couldn't do that, no, never would be able to. Oh, he could pick her up all right, he could carry her, but run upstairs? He was a cripple, a man with no feet. She wouldn't want to be tied to him, of course she wouldn't, even if she was attracted to him. And she was, he knew that. Unless she did it from pity and he shied away from the thought. Not that, never. He dropped her hand, turned away from her, closing his eyes in agony.

Elizabeth felt as though she'd had cold water thrown over her. She sat up straight. What was she doing? She knew he would never marry her, where was her pride? He was an honourable man, he didn't want to marry her and didn't want to take advantage of her either. Most men would have taken her, she was offering herself on a platter, wasn't she? But not Jack Benson, no, that last time had been a mistake.

'I must get back,' she said, and he made an

involuntary gesture of appeal towards her but her face was averted, she wasn't looking at him.

'I must too,' Jack said stiffly. 'I must make sure there is a proper inquiry into that accident, I suppose there will be an inquest. He was an orphan, you know, Tommy . . . Tommy . . . Oh, for God's sake, I can't even remember his name!'

'Tommy Gibson? It wasn't Tommy Gibson? Oh, no, it can't be, surely?'

'That was it, yes,' said Jack. 'Did you know him?'

'Jimmy's best marra – he was Jimmy's best marra! Of course I knew him, he was in the Home with us. I must go back, I must see Jimmy,' she cried. 'Oh, God, how selfish I am. How must he be feeling? His best friend killed and I'm not there for him. Oh, poor Tommy, poor Tommy, he had no one but us, no one. He was a foundling. He and Jimmy started work at the pit together.'

Elizabeth had jumped up, she was making for the door. Then she realised where she was and turned to Jack. 'Don't you understand? I have to go. Now.'

'Put your coat on first, Elizabeth.' He was on his feet too, picking up both their coats. 'Look, don't worry, I'll take you, of course I will.'

They were soon rattling down the road to Morton Main in the gathering twilight. At the end of West Row he stopped and Elizabeth jumped down.

'You can't come in, not today,' she said. 'You

wouldn't be welcome today.' She wasted no time in explaining that statement but ran down the row, disappearing into Mrs Wearmouth's back yard.

Chapter Fourteen

Jimmy didn't weep. At least he didn't where anyone else could see him. His face looked suddenly small and pinched and white and Elizabeth ached with compassion for him.

'Where've you been?' he asked as she went into Mrs Wearmouth's kitchen. He was unusually clean and tidy for even when he was not covered in coal dust he was usually grubby from hunting in the rabbit warren or roaming over the pit heaps which had belonged to Old Pit. Of which there was little left but an ancient wooden structure over the shaft. The heaps were half-covered with grass now, and in the summer, brilliant with rosebay willowherb and startlingly beautiful. They provided endless opportunities for imaginative games and Jimmy and Tommy were still young enough for boys' games. Except that Tommy was gone now.

All this went through Elizabeth's mind as she sat

down in Mrs Wearmouth's kitchen and accepted a cup of tea. She watched as Mrs Wearmouth spooned sugar into the cup, though she didn't take sugar. The old lady said it was good for shock.

'Drink it up, lass,' she said and Elizabeth drank the syrupy liquid.

'I'm sorry, Jimmy, I'm so sorry,' she said, and the words sounded inadequate in her own ears. 'I didn't know it was Tommy, I came as soon as I found out.'

'Aye.'

Jimmy looked away. He couldn't stand the sympathy, it threatened to unman him. 'Well,' he said, struggling to sound matter-of-fact, 'it happens in the pit, doesn't it? He just wasn't quick enough when they shouted "Gone amain!" He should have jumped out of the road.'

In her mind's eye Elizabeth pictured the scene: the tub running backwards down a slope, out of control, the lads behind in its path. She shuddered; she had heard of it happening like that. Nobody's fault.

'Listen, lad, why don't you have a walk out in the fresh air? It'll mebbe make you sleep,' Mrs Wearmouth suggested.

Jimmy stood up. 'I'll just go to bed instead,' he said. Perhaps he wanted to be on his own. In his bed he could cry, Elizabeth thought.

'I'm glad you came,' he said to her, pausing by the door to the staircase. She longed to take him in her arms

172

and hug him but she knew that would only embarrass him.

'I have to go now. I should be at work,'she said. 'You'll be all right?'

'Why shouldn't I be?'

'Right then, try to have a sleep. I'll see you tomorrow.'

When he'd gone the two women looked at each other in complete understanding. 'I'll look after him, lass,' Mrs Wearmouth promised. 'He'll have to go to work the morn, though, Tommy not being a relative, like.'

'Yes. I'm very grateful, you know that, Mrs Wearmouth.'

After she had gone, the old woman busied herself about, clearing the tea things. Tommy was already laid out in the front room, Betty Hoddle had helped her with that. And the pit would pay for the funeral, that was one blessing. Though the owners were getting off lightly, there was no one left to pay any compensation to. Sighing, Mrs Wearmouth got on with her work.

'You weren't back for lunch,' said Olivia Benson. She gazed accusingly at her son. 'I waited and waited for you, I was worried.' She looked more annoyed than worried, Jack thought, but nevertheless he apologised.

'There was an accident at the mine, a young boy was killed,' he explained.

'Isn't the manager there to see to such things?'

'Yes, of course, but—'

'Well, never mind now. But please remember in future that you owe it to Nancy to let her know when you won't be here for a meal. After all, she has enough to do.'

No asking what had happened, no sympathy at all, Jack thought as he bathed and changed for dinner. It was as though whatever happened at the mine or the village was nothing to do with the family which owned it.

His thoughts returned to Elizabeth as they did most of the time now. She was such a warm, sympathetic woman, she was so upset by the news of the accident to the boy. The contrast between her and his mother was striking. Elizabeth. He determined he would ask her to marry him, let his mother think what she liked. She loved him, he was sure of it. This afternoon in the inn he had become convinced of it. He had made up his mind, couldn't live without her by his side. Surely she wouldn't refuse him?

In her room, Olivia looked at her reflection in the dressing-table mirror. She was annoyed, oh, yes, annoyed and perturbed and generally out of temper with everything, though she had been careful not to let Jack know the real cause. When he had not come home for lunch she had rung the manager, she knew well enough about the accident. But she also knew that Jack had already left the office and that he had been at the Plough Inn with a girl, and what's more a girl from the lowest level of society. And how she knew was because the landlord's wife from the Plough was in the same ladies' group as she herself; they had had a meeting that afternoon in Bishop Auckland, one where they had discussed ways of raising money for comforts for the soldiers.

Oh, how chagrined Olivia had been when that odious, jumped-up Polly Parker had told her and everyone else in the room about Jack and the girl.

'I do believe they're in love,' the woman had said, with that silly smile all over her face. 'I saw them come in and they were so close together, Mrs Benson, anyone could see. It was written on their faces.'

'Nonsense!' Olivia had said. 'I shall sue you for defamation of my son's character if you persist in this tittle-tattle. He was simply comforting the girl, she was connected to the boy who was killed today.'

Polly Parker had flushed and subsided into her chair, looking as though she was going to deflate altogether. 'I'm sure I meant no harm, Mrs Benson,' she mumbled. Even the tips of her ears were beetroot red.

'You shouldn't make up silly stories then,' Olivia had retorted tartly. 'Reading things that aren't there into perfectly ordinary situations.'

Ah, but this was something she would have to put a stop to at once. She would find out all about that slut of a girl.

The funeral was on the following Monday. It was arranged for the morning at ten o'clock, a time when the men and boys who had been on the fatal back shift that day were on night shift and so able to attend. There was a good crowd to follow the coffin into the Primitive Methodist Chapel at Morton Main. Jimmy sang the Twenty-third Psalm and Elizabeth sat beside Mrs Wearmouth, nerves tight as a fiddle string, fearing he would break down in the middle. He didn't. His voice rose, pure and clear to the high ceiling and he kept calm for the whole of the service but Elizabeth could see beneath the surface and her heart broke for him.

Captain Benson was there, he had even prevailed on his mother to attend and the villagers were stunned by this unprecedented event, the mine owners attending the funeral of a lad killed in the pit. Elizabeth saw he was there but all her attention was focused on her brother and how he was going to come through the day.

'Take the shift off, Jimmy,' she advised the lad. 'Don't go in today, everyone will understand.'

'No, I'd best go down,' he replied, and nothing she could say would change his mind. She had to go back to the Hall, she was due back on duty herself at one o'clock. Elizabeth was in a very sombre mood as she walked back through a wood with the trees dripping rain and the path muddy with tiny rivulets from the relentless downpour. She dressed in her uniform in the attic bedroom and went down to the big kitchen which was used as a staff dining room. With a sinking heart she saw Private Wilson was there. She would probably have to spend the afternoon and evening avoiding him.

'The lad got off then?' said Joan as she slipped into the seat beside her friend. 'I was sorry I couldn't go but Cook wouldn't spare me.'

'It was all right. The chapel was crowded, he had a good turn out,' said Elizabeth. No one else mentioned Tommy's funeral. After all, what was the death of one boy in the pit compared with the soldiers dying every day at the front, those dying in all the thousands of hospitals in the country, including their own? Only yesterday she had had to walk behind a coffin in her cloak and cap as it was carried out to the mortuary, the traditional nurse's duty.

She was glad there was a lot of work to do on the first floor that afternoon, preparing two of the rooms for the influx of new patients they were expecting to come in from France that evening. A special hospital train was leaving King's Cross and bringing convalescent soldiers to the various temporary hospitals in the area.

Elizabeth was spreading a bottom sheet on a bed in one room, carefully stretching it and folding hospital corners as she had been taught, tucking a draw sheet across the middle in case of accidents, when she heard a sound at the door. Without turning round she picked up a pillow and pulled on a clean pillowcase.

'I'm almost finished here, Nurse Turner.'

177

The door closed behind her and she looked around in surprise; they didn't normally work with the doors closed. It was not Nurse Turner, it was Private Wilson. Elizabeth dropped the pillow and rushed to get to the door but of course she had to pass him and somehow he caught hold of her from behind, in such a way that she could not defend herself. He threw her on the bed and himself on top of her, trapping her arms and scrabbling at her skirt. She couldn't move, couldn't breathe.

'No Captain Benson here now, is there, whore? Your fancy man's gone away home and forgotten all about you, hasn't he?' Wilson mumbled thickly, catching both her hands in one of his and putting the other over her mouth as she opened it to scream.

'These old walls are thick,' he said, voice full of menace, and fear and horror rose in her. 'But still, you'd best not make a noise, had you?'

He took his hand away and clamped his mouth to hers. His breath stank like a badger's and she gagged. He was unbuttoning his trousers; she moaned deep in her throat.

'Nurse Nelson! Private Wilson! Get off that bed this instant, do you hear me?'

Miss Rowland's voice it was. Private Wilson rolled off her and stood by the bed, hurriedly buttoning up his trousers.

'She wanted it, Matron, she was dying for it. What can a man do?' he gasped. Elizabeth sat up, dazed. She was pulling her clothes together. All she could think of was the relief of getting him off her.

'Go to your room, Nurse Nelson.'

Matron's voice was cold and forbidding. Startled, Elizabeth looked at her. 'But he attacked me, Miss—'

'I don't want to hear another word, Nurse. Do you hear me? Go to your room this instant or I will have you removed.'

It was unreal, Elizabeth thought, it couldn't be happening. Surely Miss Rowland wasn't taking Private Wilson's word, was she? She'd known Elizabeth for years, how could she believe this of her? She stumbled across to the door, pausing as she came to the other woman.

'Matron,' she appealed, but the contempt on the other's face seared her and she broke off.

'I know what I saw, Elizabeth, now go. I don't want you consorting with any of the rest of the nurses. Go and wait there until I find time to see to you. Private, you can try to explain your actions to your commanding officer.'

Elizabeth waited in the attic bedroom, going over and over in her mind what she was going to say to Miss Rowland. In the event, she had no chance to say anything for the Matron refused to listen.

'I want you with your box packed and out of here within the hour, Elizabeth Nelson,' she said grimly. 'I will not have the young girls working here corrupted by someone such as you.'

'But, Matron, you know me. You know I'm not like

that!' cried Elizabeth. Miss Rowland held out a brown paper envelope which held Elizabeth's pay up to date.

'I thought I knew you, I realise now I did not. Now, if you are not gone by two-thirty I will have you put outside the gates. In the meantime you are not to speak to anyone in the Hall. Do I make myself clear?'

After she had gone, Elizabeth gathered her pitifully few possessions together, took her straw box from under the bed and packed it, tying it round with a belt, working all the time in a daze. How could this be happening? She couldn't believe it. Maybe it was a nightmare, maybe she would wake up. She wasn't even to be allowed to say goodbye to Joan. But nightmare or not, she found herself outside the grounds with the gate shut behind her, her box in her hand and ten shillings in her purse and no idea what she was going to do, where she was going to sleep that night.

Miss Rowland watched her go from an upstairs window. She had never been so disappointed in a girl, she told herself. She had felt physically sick when she had opened the door of that room (and anyone else could have opened it and gone in, it wasn't locked, thank God no young nurse had done so), opened the door to see that soldier and the orphan girl she had taken a special interest in, had offered to sponsor for training at a large general hospital. Had seen them doing such unspeakable things on a patient's bed! The punishment of the soldier was up to his commanding officer, but as for the girl . . .

she couldn't bear the sight of her. Elizabeth had to go
and go at once. Yes, she'd done the right thing, never
had she been so mistaken in the character of anyone
before.

Elizabeth stood at the gate of the Manor, gazing at the
windows, close-curtained in heavy velvet and shrouded
with lace net. She remembered the last time she had been
here, Christmas night. Oh, please, God, let Jack be in.
He knew how Private Wilson had pursued her, could
speak for her to Miss Rowland, perhaps even get her to
change her mind. Surely, surely, she would change her
mind? Tomorrow everything would be back to normal;
tomorrow she would be able to go back to the Hall to
work. Her heart beat wildly, hammering against her ribs.
On the way here she had been physically sick and now
her head throbbed. Worst of all, she could still feel the
hateful marks where Wilson's fingers had dug into her,
the small cut on her lip which his teeth had made when
he'd kissed her so violently.

Steeling herself, Elizabeth put down her box behind the
garden wall and walked up to the front door and pulled
the bell. It was answered by the old woman, Nancy, the
one she had seen that morning after New Year.

'Yes?'

'Is Captain Benson in, please?'

Nancy's eyebrows rose. She looked Elizabeth up and
down.

181

'No, he isn't.'

'Who's that, Nancy? Someone collecting for the war effort again? Tell her I've given a cheque this month – oh!'

Behind Nancy, Elizabeth could see Mrs Benson, Jack's mother. She remembered seeing her in chapel that morning.

'What do you want?' Mrs Benson said baldly, quickly recovering from her surprise.

'She wants to see the Captain, ma'am,' said Nancy.

'Never mind, Nancy, I'll deal with this.' Mrs Benson's lips compressed into a thin, hard line. 'You get back to the kitchen, I'm sure there's plenty to do there.'

'Yes, ma'am.'

When the kitchen door closed behind the old woman, Olivia Benson beckoned to Elizabeth to follow her into a small room to one side of the hall, brown and bare except for a row of pegs with macintoshes and a shelf holding boots and galoshes.

'What is your name?' Mrs Benson asked, with no preamble whatsoever.

'Elizabeth Nelson.'

'Well, Elizabeth Nelson, I've heard of you. How you are pestering my son, importuning him! What do you want with him? Though, I assure you, whatever it is, you won't get it. He wants nothing to do with you. He's told me all about you, how you follow him about . . . . Good Lord, you don't really think he could be interested in *you*, do you? Where's your sense of decency, girl? He doesn't want you, that's all. You should be ashamed of yourself, pestering a poor, injured, *crippled* soldier who's fought for this country . . .' Her voice rising, she advanced on Elizabeth, face a mask of hatred, and the girl stepped backwards. Yet she had to have one last try.

'But Jack said—'

'Jack? Jack, is it? How dare you call my son by his given name? A guttersnipe like you! Get out of my sight before I call the constable, do you hear me?'

She was shouting now, shouting as loudly as a fishwife herself, as no lady should shout, face purple with rage. Elizabeth turned and fled through the open front door, down the garden path and out to where she could hide behind the wall. She felt as though she could never show her face again to anyone, the shame was unbearable.

Chapter Fifteen

Elizabeth walked to the outskirts of the town before she realised her box was still behind the wall at the Manor, so she walked all the way back again, praying she would meet no one she knew on the way. In this at least she was lucky; she found the box and carried it into Bishop Auckland. The trouble was, she had no idea what to do when she got there. She stood in the road by the workhouse hospital and looked along the road to the Children's Home where she had been brought up, but there was no help there.

It was already getting dark, a hard, deadly, cold darkness which deepened by the minute and seeped into her bones. She had left her gloves at the Hall and her fingers went white and numb as she transferred the heavy box from one hand to another. Slowly she began to walk towards the lights of Newgate Street, the warmth of the shops. On Station Bridge she looked over and saw that the train for Weardale was standing at the platform. On impulse she hurried down the steps to the ticket office.

'A single to Frosterley,' she said. Then, 'No, I mean Stanhope.' Stanhope was just as close to Stand Alone Farm as Frosterley and it was bigger, there would be more chance of work there.

'Make up your mind, lass, or the train will be gone,' said the man behind the glass. 'That'll be fivepence.'

Elizabeth took five pennies from her purse and handed them over, putting the purse down on the counter as she changed the box to her other hand yet again. The guard was closing doors, lifting his flag, the train starting to move.

'Make sharp, lass, or you'll miss it.'

Grabbing the ticket, Elizabeth ran and the guard obligingly stood by a door until she reached it.

'Hey, lass . . .' The man from the ticket office was chasing her on to the platform but she was on the train, she didn't hear what it was he was shouting. Whatever it was it couldn't have anything to do with her, she'd paid for her ticket.

'I'll just have to put it int'lost property,' the man mumbled.

Elizabeth sat in a corner seat in the carriage, her box on the rack above her head. Slowly she began to thaw out. The carriage was warm, heated by the steam of the engine. There were a couple of women sitting opposite her, deep in conversation and ignoring their fellow passengers, and a man in working clothes obviously on his way back from work, sitting slumped in the seat with exhaustion plain to see on his face. She glared out of the window at her pale reflection in the glass.

Maybe she should have gone to Morton Main, asked Mrs Wearmouth for shelter? But the shame of what had happened burned deep; she couldn't explain to Jimmy or his landlady, not yet. Maybe if she had a job she could say she'd moved because she didn't like nursing . . . But that was silly. Jimmy knew she loved it and was looking forward to training at Durham. Not any more, though, she thought, that chance was gone forever.

She had thought, when she had so impulsively caught the train, that she could at least be near Jenny, and was filled with an uncontrollable instinct to hide from everyone she knew at home. Stanhope was as good as any other place to work; maybe she could get a job in the workhouse hospital, though she didn't have any references. Elizabeth closed her eyes in despair. Oh, Jack, Jack, she agonised. How had she been so completely wrong about his feelings? Was he really only being kind, even when he was making love to her? His mother had been so sure, she had been so emphatic.

Maybe he had been attracted to her, but mine owners didn't marry miners' daughters, she knew that, hadn't she told herself so over and over? But she hadn't really believed it, that was the problem. She had dreamed . . .

What a flaming fool she was! Well, leaving Bishop was the best thing she could do for him, leave him alone. He had enough to put up with, what with his feet, poor man. Poor, lovely man.

Elizabeth fell into a troubled dozing and dreaming in which she was looking for somewhere to stay, something to eat. And cruel face after cruel face mocked her and closed doors on her and she was horribly afraid. What was to become of her? She awoke with a start as the train slowed and the guard shouted, 'Wolsingham! This is Wolsingham!' The workman was getting out of the carriage, someone else got in. Two more stops, Frosterley then Stanhope. Then what was she going to do when she got there? She felt empty, realised she had had nothing to eat since dinner at one o'clock and now it was almost ten.

In Stanhope, Elizabeth walked up the bank from the station to the deserted streets. Most of the houses were dark, the occupants early to bed. She would find a boarding house, she thought, just for tonight. She couldn't possibly stay out in the open. The cold which she had felt in Bishop lower down the dale was here, a raw, penetrating, painful misery. She found a boarding house at last, a few yards along the main street, and there was, thank heaven, a light in the window. But before she went in she thought she had better check her money, though she knew to a farthing how much she had left. There were two shillings and four pence ha'penny and the brown paper envelope with her wages inside, folded up in one section of her purse.

Only she couldn't find her purse. She put down her box and looked carefully through her pockets, not allowing herself to panic. Obviously she had put it somewhere safe. She opened up the box and looked through her things. It wasn't there. Of course it wasn't, she chided herself, she had bought a ticket at the railway station in the town, hadn't she?

Elizabeth's heart dropped to her boots. She'd lost her purse – somehow, she'd lost her purse. Oh, God, what was she going to do now? Her nose and ears were stinging with the cold, she felt she would never be warm again. What was she going to do? The questions ran through her head. She tucked her hands under her arm-pits and tried to think. She considered finding the workhouse; at least they would give her a bed for the night even if she had to scrub all day tomorrow to pay for it. Her whole mind and body rebelled against the idea, though. She remembered her mother, how terrified of the workhouse she had been and with good reason, according to all accounts of people who had been inside one.

'Now then, what are you doing out on the streets at this hour?'

Elizabeth nearly jumped out of her skin at the sound of the policeman's voice. She hadn't heard or seen him coming. Would he put her in jail for vagrancy?

'Nothing! I'm not doing anything, sir,' she said. 'I was just having a rest after I got off the train. I'm visiting my uncle. That's it, sir.' She picked up her box and was backing away. 'I'm all right, really, I know where I'm going,' she said then turned up a side street.

The constable watched her, wondering whether he should follow her, make sure she really did have somewhere to go. But it was a bitterly cold night, enough to freeze the balls off a brass monkey, it was. His supper beckoned, the warm kitchen and his plump young wife waiting for him. And in his experience young women with nowhere to go didn't come to Stanhope in Weardale, it would be the last place on earth they would choose. He pulled his cape up to his chin and went on his way to the police station to sign off.

Elizabeth came to the end of the houses and continued walking up the road because she couldn't think what else to do. She thought she might find a shed, a hut, anywhere she could spend the rest of the night. But she wandered on until she realised she was on to Bollihope Common, recognised the junction where the track from Frosterley joined the road. There was a shepherd's hut fairly close by, she remembered it suddenly and quickened her pace, looking about eagerly. A full moon was shining now, a moon surrounded by a thick white ring that meant frost. It seemed lighter than it had been down in the town; close by there was a rustling sound. Only sheep, she told herself, but she walked in the middle of the road just in

189

case. At last the dark outline of the hut appeared over to the right of the road. There was no light from the pane of glass which served as a window so at least there was no shepherd in there. Elizabeth left the road, tried to thread her way through the heather, sank her foot through the thin covering of ice over a boggy patch, almost fell but at last reached the door of the hut and, she breathed a sigh of relief, it was not locked.

The door was stiff and she had to lean her weight on it to open it but she managed at last and fell into the musty-smelling room. It was dark but for a beam of moonlight through the window pane and she could make out an upturned box serving as a table, and on it a storm lantern with a box of lucifers beside it. Elizabeth put down her box and fumbled with frozen fingers at the lantern, willing them to work. At last she managed to open the lantern, strike a lucifer match and put it to the wick. Oh, please, God, please, she prayed as the wick browned and the lucifer burned down, please let it light. And then it did, the flame shooting up so that she had to turn down the wick. She closed the lantern and lifted it experimentally; thankfully it was almost full of fuel judging by the weight.

Looking around, she saw there was a pile of sacks in one corner, a stool and, oh, she could hardly believe it, a camp bed by the opposite wall with a pillow and a fleece. She held her hands around the lantern until the pain of them thawing out became too much, but already she was feeling warmer. It was shelter from the biting cold, she could manage here for tonight. She stumbled to the bed, lay down with her head on the pillow and pulled the fleece over her. Her mind just closed down as she dropped into a deep, exhausted sleep.

Elizabeth awoke with a start. She was cold again, deathly cold. The lantern had gone out, the hut was lit by a cold white light from the tiny window. She stumbled to her feet, teeth chattering, and opened her box, pulling on her only spare jumper on top of the one she was wearing and her coat back on top. She pulled open the door and groaned aloud. The ground was covered in snow, crisp-lying snow about two inches deep already, and it was falling thick and fast.

'I have to get out of here,' she muttered. 'I'll die if I don't.' Distractedly she looked about the hut. There was a cupboard on one wall, she had missed it in the dim light from the lantern the night before. It could hold something to eat, she thought, something, anything. She opened it. There was a tin of sardines, a rusty tin of something else she thought could be beans. And, oh, praise the Lord, there was a tin opener.

Half an hour later, feeling a little better at least with something inside her, Elizabeth closed the door of the hut behind her, put the belt of her box over her arm and stepped out into snow which came to the top of her boots. Bending her head in the face of the blizzard, she made her way back to where the outline of the road could be seen by the snow poles lining it. She trudged along by the poles, her box getting heavier and heavier on her arm as she went, the snow sucking on her boots like a bog. A wind was springing up. A bitter, cold northeaster, it was beginning to blow the fallen snow into drifts leaving bare patches on the road which were coated with ice. The journey seemed endless. In this white, barren world she feared she would miss the path which led down to Stand Alone Farm. Maybe she should have gone the other way, back to Stanhope and the comparative comfort of the workhouse.

She dared not take her eyes from the side of the road, the whiteness obscuring the heather and bracken, dazzling her despite the dark, leaden grey of the sky. At first she didn't see the board with the faded lettering on it, the snow had swept up against it so that only the top half was visible. Elizabeth blinked rapidly, shaking the snowflakes from her lashes, and there it was. 'Oh, thank you, thank you, God,' she said aloud.

There was an immediate lessening of the wind as the path dropped away from the road, a blessing in itself. But she was sinking into the drifts up to her knees now, her skirt was sodden and when she lifted it up the snow on the hem was beginning to freeze in hard, icy lumps. She had to get there; she had to. All her mind was concentrated on reaching the farm. She didn't want to die in this frozen world, she wanted to live. She dropped the box as she stumbled into a clump of heather. She couldn't pick it up, she couldn't. Every breath brought a terrible pain in her side and in her chest as the cold air hit her lungs.

At last she reached the gate to the farm yard though she would hardly have known it but for the rowan tree which thrust its bare branches upwards, laden with snow. But here she stumbled and fell, whether it was from the sudden easing of tension that she was there, was not lost after all, she didn't know, but she fell and hadn't the strength to get to her feet to walk the last few yards to the back door. Her eyes closed. Strangely she began to feel warmer. A close warm lethargy crept over her. Dimly, in some sort of dream she heard a dog bark.

'Stop that yapping or I'll stop it for you!' Peart snarled at his dog. Snuff had risen from his place in the corner and was standing, facing the back door, his neck stretched out and teeth curled up over his lip. But he slunk back to the corner as he heard the menace in his master's tone.

'Fetch me another cup of tea, lass, and be quick about it an' all.'

Jenny scurried to do his bidding, lifting the old brown pot from before the fire where a smouldering peat fire burned and filling the pint pot with the dark brown liquid. As she added thick spoonfuls of condensed milk from the tin, her stomach rumbled. She looked longingly at the heel of bread on the table, the jar of dripping.

But she daren't take any breakfast yet, never until Peart was out of the way. If she did he made nasty remarks about her eating him out of house and home, how she wasn't worth it, he would get rid of her.

Today she would have to eat quickly. He would likely go no further than the sheep fold and the barn. There would be no shooting on the moor, no poaching. She shivered.

Snuff barked again, startling Jenny. If he went on Peart would throw him outside, no matter what the weather. She willed him to be silent. But he was at the door, nose down to the crack at the bottom where the wind came whistling through. He barked again, whined in excitement.

'Bloody dog! There must be something there.' Peart swallowed the last of his tea and took his coat from the row of hooks by the door. He buttoned it round him, pulled a cap down over his eyes and a muffler round his neck, and casually kicked Snuff out of the way, making the dog yelp. As Peart opened the door there was a great blast of wind which sent sparks up the chimney and a billow of soot-filled smoke out into the room. He lifted his twelve-bore from behind the door, broke it and put in a pair of cartridges. 'Just in case there's something in the yard we can eat,' he explained, more to himself than to Jenny, and went out, Snuff squeezing past him to run up the yard. Peart closed the door behind him.

Jenny looked at it for a minute, as the sounds of

barking and Peart shouting at the dog became fainter, then she went to the table and cut two slices from the loaf. One she spread with dripping, the other with the condensed milk. One in each hand, she took them to the chair by the fire and bit into the one with the beef dripping, concentrating all her attention on the food. This was the best time of the day for her.

Outside, the dog was up by the rowan tree, barking at something which lay there. Peart grinned. It was quite big, it might even be a sheep. Not one of his, a stray no doubt, maybe even a ewe lambing early. It must have strayed from the farmer's flock further along the common. It certainly wasn't one of his, they were well fastened up, he knew that. Too bad, folk should look after their flock, lazy beggars. Mutton tonight. He closed the gun and walked through the snow to the mound in the snow.

'Get out the road, will you, you mangy cur?' he shouted at Snuff, and the dog backed off, still excited, still whining and giving the occasional bark. Peart levelled his gun at where he judged the head of the mound to be. The snow was blinding now. He rubbed his eyes with the back of his sleeve to clear them. Bloody hell, it was no sheep! There was long black hair blowing about. It was a woman.

Chapter Sixteen

There was a sharp pain in her back. Elizabeth tried to ignore it; she didn't want to wake up, she wanted to sleep on in this place where she could feel the heat from a fire soothing away the cold, the bitter cold which seeped through to her very bones, the aching cold that was still lurking there to catch her, envelop her. But the pain in her back was persistent, it was like a knife stuck in her ribs. Vaguely she began to worry about it. Was it a knife in her ribs? Did it matter, though? If only she could sleep on and on and never wake up.

'Wake up! Howay, lass, wake up, will ye?'

She felt a slap on her face, and another. She moved her head in protest, tried to turn over but she couldn't, it was too much effort.

'Open your eyes, damn ye! Come on, you're not dead yet.'

The voice was familiar. Now where had she heard it?

Elizabeth opened her eyes reluctantly and right above her, only an inch or two from her nose, was that man, that awful man, Jenny's foster father, Peart. Groaning, she closed her eyes again and felt him catch hold of her by the shoulders and lift her head from the pillow and shake her.

'All right, all right, I'm awake,' she shouted, or thought she had shouted, but what she heard was barely above a whisper. Then, magically, the pain in her back eased as she was lifted. It was not a knife then, she thought hazily.

'An' about time an' all,' said Peart. 'Jen? Where the hell's that hot tea you were making for her? Do you want a clout, girl?'

'It's here, Peart.'

Elizabeth moved her head and saw her little sister standing at her feet, a chipped cup in her hands.

'Aye, well, come on, give it to her.' Peart moved back to a chair on the opposite side of the fire and watched as Jenny helped Elizabeth to sit up and then held the cup to her lips. She sipped the hot syrupy tea, the smell of the condensed milk making her gag a little, but as soon as it was down she began to feel better.

'Thanks, love,' she said and even managed a tiny smile for her sister. She looked around. She was lying on the old battered settle by the side of the fire in Peart's house. She couldn't remember for a few minutes just how she had got there, only the snow, the cold and the

branches of a tree above her as she slid into uncon-
sciousness. She looked at Peart.

'Did you find me?' she asked.

'I did. A good job an' all. A bit longer and you'd have
been a goner. Old Snuff I suppose it was really, he
sniffed you out. I thought you were a sheep. I was going
to shoot you. Pity, I could have eaten a nice shoulder of
mutton.'

A tart reply sprang to Elizabeth's lips but was not
uttered. She was so tired, so terribly tired, and she just
couldn't be bothered. She slid down on the settle, felt the
pain again and put a hand behind her. It was a broken
spring that had been sticking in her back. For some
reason she found that funny and laughed weakly.

'I don't know what's so funny?' snapped Peart. 'You
could have died out there anyroad. You wouldn't have
found *that* funny.'

'No, I'm sorry. And thank you for saving my life,'
Elizabeth said meekly.

'Aye, well. I couldn't leave a dog out in that, could
I?' He looked from her to Jenny who was hovering
nearby with that habitual anxious expression on her face.
'What are you doing here, like? It's not Sunday. And
nobody but a crack-brained fool would venture on the
moors on a day like today.'

'I . . . I was coming to see Jenny. I thought I would get
work in Stanhope, be able to see her more often. But I
couldn't find anywhere to stay . . .' She didn't feel up to

telling him the whole story, not yet.

'What bloody fools women are,' said Peart. He wagged his head from side to side. 'Well, I cannot stand gabbing here, I've the sheep to see to. I'm off. Mind you, lass.' He nodded his head at Jenny. 'You'd best get the dinner on. I'll be ready for it when I get back.'

After the door closed behind him, Elizabeth looked at her sister, still hovering at the foot of the settle.

'Come and sit down, pet,' she said. 'You can spare five minutes, can't you? We can talk.'

Jenny nodded, still not speaking. She sat down on the end of the settle where Elizabeth moved her legs to make room for her.

'Would you like me to live close by, Jenny?'

She nodded her head shyly. Elizabeth sighed. Every time she came she succeeded in drawing the girl out of herself but when she came back Jenny was as quiet and timid as ever. She watched her sister as she picked up a small roll of old cotton cloth and nursed it like a baby.

'Jenny, where's Petal? Where's your dolly?'

Jenny looked down at the roll of cloth. She laid it on the edge of the settle and began pleating the threadbare skirt of the dress.

'Jenny?'

'Peart threw Petal in the fire,' the child said at last.

Elizabeth drew in a sharp breath. 'In the fire? Why?' She felt a spurt of anger lifting her out of her fatigue and sat up on the settle.

'It was my own fault, I was lazy,' her sister whispered.

'Lazy? What do you mean?'

'The dinner wasn't ready when he came back. The . . .' Jenny hiccuped softly, her voice breaking. 'The taties weren't cooked, they were too hard. I'd been playing with Petal so he threw her into the fire.'

Elizabeth stared at the bent head, the black hair tousled and unevenly cut. The rotten, flaming sod, she thought.

'Come here, pet,' she said softly to Jenny who looked up, surprised, as Elizabeth held out her arms. After a moment she crept into them and laid her head on her sister's breast. Elizabeth held the thin little body. She could feel Jenny's ribs, her knobbly backbone. Oh, Lord, what was she going to do? What if she couldn't get work here? What if she had to go away? Wildly she thought of running off with Jenny, taking her as far away as she could gct. But common sense told her they would have to live on something; she hadn't even the money to buy them a meal, rent a room. It was hopeless. But she would find a way, she would. Oh, yes, indeed. She gave Jenny an extra hug.

'Come on now, pet,' she said, 'I'll give you a hand with the dinner and whatever else you have to do. Then Peart won't be mad at you, will he?' But when she got to her feet, she found her legs were wobbly and her arms trembled with weakness after the ordeal of the night before. Still, she forced herself to walk to the table where

Jenny brought a battered enamel dish with a few potatoes and carrots ready to peel.

'This isn't enough for three of us, is it?' Elizabeth asked in surprise.

'It's just for Peart,' said Jenny. 'I don't eat dinner.' She paused, brow knitting in perplexity. 'Eeh, I don't know whether I have to do some for you, though.'

Elizabeth ignored the suggestion that she wasn't going to be fed. Of course she had to be. It was still snowing outside, there was no way she could possibly leave the farm. Peart wouldn't starve her, would he?

'Do you not like meat and potatoes, Jenny?'

'I don't know.'

Elizabeth was dreadfully tired, she had had enough of this. Surely the bairn was fed? 'Fetch some more, Jenny. I think we should do enough for us all.' Jenny bit her lip but she was so used to doing exactly what she was told that she went back to the pantry and brought more. She carried an iron pan out, put in water from the pail and set it on the fire. Then she brought a rabbit, already skinned and cleaned, chopped it into small pieces expertly and threw them in the pan. Elizabeth watched, amazed. The small girl had all the practised movements of an experienced housewife like Mrs Wearmouth.

When the stew was cooking to her satisfaction, Jenny picked up the rag she had been nursing as a doll and began to dust the few bits of furniture. By this time Elizabeth was so exhausted she had crept back on to the settle and was half dozing in the heat from the fire. She was just too tired to think about it any more.

'Flaming hell, it's as cold as death out there!' It was the door banging which brought her back to full wakefulness with a start. She had been dreaming that Jack Benson was walking slowly up the track from Frosterley, calling her name, and she couldn't shout, couldn't speak to make him hear. She looked up to see Peart had her box with him.

'Oh, thanks for bringing that in,' she exclaimed. 'It's got everything I own in it.'

'What were you bringing it here for?' he demanded. 'You needn't think you're going to stay here for long, I can't afford to keep anybody else an' I'm not going to neither.'

'But . . . I can't go out in this, can I?'

'I'm not saying I won't shelter you till the road opens, but as soon as it does, you're gone.'

Elizabeth was filled with humiliation, but resentment also. Somehow she managed to bite her tongue, stop herself from giving the hot reply which sprang to her lips. She saw Jenny hovering in her nervous way, looking anxious, remembering how Peart had got rid of the doll. An act of cruelty it was against a small girl. The doll had been harmless. She would tell him so an' all. But not while Jenny was present.

'I intend to find work in Stanhope,' she said now, trying to keep her tone even, hide her feelings. 'Don't worry, I won't stay a moment longer than I have to. But I want to live in the dale, near my sister.'

'Aye, well. Think on,' said Peart, and turned to Jenny. 'Get my dinner on the table and be quick about it,' he snarled.

She hesitated a minute. 'Emm, will I put some out for Elizabeth?'

'I reckon so,' said Peart, though he shook his head begrudgingly.

'You get three plates, Jenny,' said Elizabeth. 'I'll bring the stew to the table.' Jenny looked scared. She looked from one to the other of them.

'Go on, lass, before I put a bomb under ye!' roared Peart, and she scuttled to the cupboard and brought the plates.

'An' mind you damn' well eat it,' he said. 'I'm not traipsing over the moor to get rabbits to fill your mouth just for you to leave it on the plate.' He slid a glance at Elizabeth as he spoke, watching as she put the heavy pan on a board at the end of the table and began to ladle out stew, bending over so that the front of her dress fell open, revealing the slender neck and the shadowed hollow below. He licked his lips.

Jenny obediently began to spoon the stew into her mouth as soon as her sister put the plate before her, chewing carefully, savouring it. She kept looking at

Elizabeth as though for reassurance and she tried to smile her encouragement. Peart gobbled his in his usual manner but his eyes were as much on the elder sister as they were on his food, something which she couldn't help noticing but tried to ignore.

By evening Elizabeth was still weary and stiff from her ordeal in the snow and found herself waiting, eyelids drooping, for when she could go to bed, something she was determined to do only when Jenny did. By now she was feeling uncomfortable at the way Peart watched her. Surely, surely, it wasn't going to happen again, as it had with Private Wilson and Uncle Ben? Revulsion rose in her like bile.

Peart had brought out a bottle of some evil-smelling spirit. She couldn't be sure what it was. He sat drinking in the armchair by the fire, watching her as she talked quietly to Jenny, only rousing himself to shout at the child for hot water, tea, or bread and cheese.

'Jen? Jen?' Sometime during the long, dark evening he awoke from a snoring sleep to shout.

Jenny, who had been sitting on the settle beside Elizabeth, jumped to her feet and ran across the room to him, yet, Elizabeth noticed, stayed just out of his reach. She seemed a bit more confident with Peart in this half-drunken state.

'Get away and check on the flock, lass, do I have to remind you every night?' He grabbed her arm and drew her close so that her face was inches from his. 'Do you want to sleep with the ewes for the night?' He released her arm and she jumped back, rubbing the place which was already reddening.

'Well, do you?' he roared.

'No, Peart,' she whispered.

'Well, go on then.' He grinned and picked up the bottle by the neck, took a swig, leered at Elizabeth who had sat up, trembling, ready to intervene should he really hurt her sister.

'Wait, I'll come with you,' she said to Jenny, though in fact she was so tired now that her legs felt leaden.

'No, you won't,' said Peart. 'She knows well enough what to do.'

'But it's dark—'

'Is it now? Do you think the ghoulies will get her?' he mocked. Jenny had already lit a storm lantern, was opening the door. She gave Elizabeth a small smile and slipped out, Snuff at her heels like a silent shadow.

'Do you fancy a drop of this?' asked Peart, proffering the bottle.

'No, thanks.'

'Suit yerself.' He shrugged and tipped the bottle almost vertically against his lips. He sank into a torpor, his eyes closing. Outside the wind howled, frozen snow lashed against the window, the door rattled. Elizabeth got to her feet and went to the door. She had to make sure Jenny was all right.

'Where the hell do you think you're going?'

The growled question took her by surprise. She stopped in her tracks. 'I wanted to see—'

'The lass's fine, did I not tell you? Don't go out of that door now or you'll not get in again. I'll be master in me own house or know the reason why.'

Peart had not even turned to face her; he was still slumped in his chair, still dangling the bottle from one hand.

'But she might be lost . . . she might have fallen in a drift, many a thing.'

'Not Jen. I cannot get rid of her that easy.'

Elizabeth stared at the door, willing it to open and Jenny to come in safely. What did he mean, get rid of Jenny? She'd just realised what he had said. Would he let the bairn go if she, Elizabeth, could take care of her? No, it was just talk, surely? By, but it was a hope she could cling to, wasn't it? If only she had a job, a home. If only Jack— Her thoughts cut off at that. She couldn't bear to think of Jack Benson, no, she couldn't. Anyway, hadn't she enough on her plate now?

There was a scrabbling on the door, a brief bark. The latch lifted and the door swung slowly inward, bringing a foot-deep bar of frozen snow with it. Oh, thank God, it was Jenny, Jenny and Snuff, icy white balls stuck to the hair of his belly so that he walked stiffly, painfully, to his corner and proceeded to lick them until they melted away.

'All there, Peart,' Jenny reported to the man slumped

before the fire, sweating with the heat and the whisky. The child was shivering, her face pinched and blue with cold.

The blizzard blew itself out during the night. By morning the sun shone brightly in a pale blue sky. Elizabeth woke in the double bed which was the only furniture in Jenny's room. Oh, how thankful she had been to see it the night before, to realise she didn't have to spend the night on the settle.

Whether Peart went to his bed at all she didn't know and cared less. He had, in the end, drunk himself into oblivion and she and Jenny had crept upstairs to the icy bedroom. Elizabeth had stood her box against the door, just in case Peart got any ideas. She would at least be warned. Jenny had watched without comment. Jumping into bed, the two girls had warmed themselves in each other's arms.

Now it was morning, light from the uncurtained window streaming in. Elizabeth looked at her sister, still fast asleep, dark smudges under her eyes. She tucked the blankets round her thin shoulders and dropped a kiss on the brown hair.

'I'll swing for that man, mind if I don't,' she said to herself. 'If I don't get you away from here, I swear I will.'

She climbed out of bed and went to the window to see a world of white, dazzling white edged with pink by some trick of the sun. It was a featureless white, she could see no humps of bushes or anything else, just a deep, white blanket of snow. This was the front of the house, away from the farm yard and the sheep fold and barn, there was not even a tree in all the expanse before her.

Shivering, Elizabeth dressed. She would have to wash later, there was no jug or basin in the room.

'Eeh, I'll get *wrong*!'

The cry from the bed made her turn to see Jenny tumbling out, pulling on her dress, tugging on her boots.

'Hey, it's all right, it's not late,' cried Elizabeth, but Jenny was already at the door, pushing aside the box and running downstairs. Elizabeth hurried to help her. There would be no getting away from Stand Alone Farm today, and maybe not for many a day after that.

Chapter Seventeen

'I am thinking of getting a motor car, Mother,' said Jack.

'Well, it will leave the carriage for me, I suppose,' Olivia answered. They were sitting at breakfast in the morning room at the Manor, sun streaming in through the high window, giving an illusion of a warm spring day outside.

Olivia looked at her son over the letter she was reading. He looked happy enough, she thought, he couldn't be missing that slut of a girl she had sent away the week before. Men soon got over these things. He would find someone else, someone more suitable, she was sure. After all, if he was going to bring a wife here she needed it to be someone she could associate with herself, someone of their own class. Oh, yes, she had done the right thing, sending that girl away with a flea in her ear.

Jack buttered a piece of toast, spooned marmalade. Today he had made a decision. He had thought and

209

thought and knew where he was going. It gave him new confidence in himself. His legs were hardening nicely, he could walk without the aid of a stick now, almost at normal pace too. He was learning the ways of the mine, could bring a fresh approach to some of the problems, he was certain. Mining was in his blood. His father was a mine owner, and his grandfather before that. And now Jack was going to carry on the tradition.

But not only that, he told himself, he was going to Newcomb Hall as soon as he'd finished what he had to do at the colliery offices. He would take Elizabeth out to lunch, insisting that Matron allow it. And then he would ask her to marry him and come to live with him at the Manor. He had thought it all out. He would take her little brother out of the pit, have him educated, train him as a mining surveyor or something. And he would have a separate flat made for his mother, part of the Manor but apart, self-contained. Oh, yes, he had it all planned. Elizabeth would not be able to resist such a bright future as they would have together. Not if she loved him, and he was convinced she did.

Jack finished his coffee and got to his feet. 'I'm going out now, Mother. I may not be back for lunch.'

'You'll have to take pot luck if you are, then,' she remarked. Olivia watched him as he left the room, only a little awkwardness betraying his disability. She had to admit that he had not become the burden she'd feared he would.

Jack drove down the track to the road in the governess cart, his head filled with ideas for the future. Everything was going to be fine. Today he would go to Bishop Auckland and buy the 1914 Austin tourer that was on display in the Motor Supplies. A pity it couldn't be a spanking new one but Austin was into production of aeroplanes and trucks for the duration. With a motor car, after an hour or two's instruction, he could get about much better, keep an eye on the Home Farm and the mine. There was no reason why he shouldn't get the estate back to the position it was in before his father gambled so much away. Oh, he would work hard, especially if he had a family, a son, to pass it all on to. Jack was filled with optimism.

Mr Dunne was behind his desk in the colliery office. He rose from his chair as Jack came in. 'Morning, sir,' he said. 'I have the books all ready for your inspection. There has been a deputation from the men too. The roof supports on number two level are inadequate, they say. I told them that it was the business of the management to say whether they need replacing or whatever. There is a war on, after all.'

Jack favoured him with a sharp glance. 'I don't see what the war has to do with it, we must have adequate safety precautions, Dunne,' he snapped. 'Have the overman in, get his opinion. If necessary, I will go down and inspect the level myself.'

Mr Dunne's manner changed. 'Of course we will see

to it. But timber is in short supply, the problems with shipping . . .'

'Nevertheless, Dunne, I'll have no skimping.' He sat down behind the desk and went through the books meticulously before taking his leave. Mr Dunne watched as Jack drove out of the yard and took the turn for Bishop Auckland. A new broom, he thought, well aware that safety precautions were being ignored all over the coal field with shortages caused by the war the excuse. The previous agent had been very cavalier in his attitude. Well, thank goodness for Jack Benson. Neglecting safety measures was a dangerous, false economy.

Jack's next stop was Newcomb Hall. It was lunch-time, surely Elizabeth would be free? He hummed under his breath as he negotiated the front steps to the portico. Lizzie had such an open expressive face, he could just imagine her delighted smile when she saw him unexpectedly. The entrance hall was deserted. He was right about the staff being at lunch, he could hear the buzz of conversation from the kitchen quarters where the green baize door stood propped open. He hesitated then turned to his right and knocked on the door of Matron's office.

'Come in.'

Miss Rowland was standing by the window. She looked round and when she saw who it was, smiled and went to meet him, holding out her hand.

'Captain Benson! How lovely to see you. And

walking so well too! It's so very good of you to come back to see us. Not many of our patients do, you know.'

'Well, I don't live very far away, Matron.'

'No, of course not. Would you like a cup of tea? Or coffee perhaps? I can easily ring for some.'

'No, thanks, Matron, not now.'

He sat down in the chair which she indicated with a wave of her hand. He sat back and crossed his legs, smiling. He had a feeling of pleasant anticipation. He would see his Lizzie in a few minutes.

'Actually, I really came to see Elizabeth Nelson. You know, the nurse's aide who worked on my floor?'

Matron's face changed completely. She sat down on the opposite side of the desk and frowned. 'Miss Nelson? What can you possibly want with her?'

Jack almost said that that was his business, but he didn't. Today he was at peace with the world. 'Oh, I just wanted to speak to her,' he said instead.

'I'm afraid that is impossible.'

'It is? Why?'

'Elizabeth Nelson was dismissed last week for lewd and immoral behaviour. I don't know where she is now.'

'What? What are you talking about?' Jack's euphoric mood disappeared in an instant.

Miss Rowland gazed grimly over her spectacles at him. No doubt he had been taken in by the girl's innocent looks, she thought, just as they all had been. Why, she had known Elizabeth all her life and had never guessed what she was really like. The picture of the two figures on the bed when she had opened that bedroom door came back to her. Disgusting!

'I'm not prepared to discuss it,' she said.

'But we must,' said Jack. 'Just what are you talking about? I have a right to know.'

'You have no right at all,' she replied. 'But since you insist, I will tell you. Elizabeth Nelson and Private Wilson were caught in . . . well, in circumstances which left no—'

'Private Wilson?' Jack interrupted. 'Did you say, Private Wilson?'

'I did. Not to beat about the bush, they were found on a bed together.'

As she said it, Matron blushed. This was not a subject she liked discussing with a man, especially a young, personable man. But she felt he was not going to be satisfied until he heard the whole story. Well, so be it, if it meant that he was stopped from making a dreadful mistake.

'I don't believe it! Or, if it's true, he must have caught her in the room and attacked her. She hated the man, she really did. And this wasn't the first time he'd assaulted her, you know. I've warned him before.'

'Private Wilson says she led him on,' Matron said. She had risen and was looking out of the window, anywhere but at Captain Benson. Oh, dear, this was *so* embarrassing. 'And evidently his commanding officer believes him, though he was transferred immediately. Oh, dear, I was so very mistaken in that girl . . .'

'I'm telling you, Matron, I don't believe she has done anything. If she was on the bed she must have been forced onto it by the orderly. Poor girl, she must be in a terrible state. Have you no idea where she went?'

'No, I haven't. What I do know is she won't get work in another hospital in this area. Not without a reference from me.'

Matron had a moment of self-doubt. Maybe the captain was right, maybe Elizabeth had been taken advantage of. Her friend, Joan Simpson, had come to ask what had happened to Elizabeth and been horrified to hear she had been dismissed, arguing for her friend. But still, girls from the Home did stick together. No, she'd done the right thing, she was sure. Best to get rid of a problem girl. She could not allow the Hall to get a reputation.

'I'm afraid I must ask you to go now, Captain,' she said. 'I have work to do.'

'But have you no idea where she can be?' he insisted.

'I'm afraid not. And I would strongly advise you not to seek her out.' Miss Rowland picked up some papers from her desk and adjusted her glasses to signify that the interview was at an end.

Jack went out to the governess cart, fuming with frustrated anger. If he could get hold of Wilson now, he would choke the truth out of him, by hell he would. He sat for a moment or two, glaring blackly down the drive, promising himself he would seek the man out and do just that. But first he had to find Elizabeth. He tried to concentrate on where she could be. Why, oh, why, hadn't she come straight to him?

Jimmy . . . Her brother was working in the mine at Morton Main. Galvanised into action, Jack picked up the reins and clucked at the pony, setting off down the drive at a spanking trot.

'Jimmy Nelson's address? Yes, of course we have it,' said Mr Dunne, and called through to the girl who had taken his clerk's job when the man was conscripted. 'Eliza Jane, fetch the folder with the men's addresses, will you?' If the manager was surprised to see Jack back so soon and with such an unusual request he didn't show it. He reckoned he had enough to do catching up on his work after a morning spent answering the owner's queries about the books. Besides, he hadn't had his dinner yet and it was already getting on for two o'clock.

Mrs Wearmouth, 5 West Row, that was where Jimmy lodged.

'Thanks, Dunne,' said Jack as he headed for the door.

'Mind, the lad won't be off shift for another hour and a half,' the manager called after him.

Damn and double damn, thought Jack irritably. Well, he would go to see the woman anyway. Who knows? Elizabeth might be there. Cheered at the thought, he hurried over to the colliery rows, leaving the pony by the edge of a patch of grass so that he could graze.

The house was a typical miner's cottage, no proper road to the front, a back yard to the rear. Unlike Saltaire or Bournville, thought Jack, both built by enlightened men who cared for their workers. Not to be thought of for mere pitmen. If he ever had the money he would try to do something about the colliery rows with their ash closets, he vowed. He walked up the yard of number five and knocked at the door. It was opened by a middle-aged woman wrapped around with a pinafore. There was a smell of meat and suet cooking. He felt suddenly hungry, he'd had no lunch. But he hadn't time to eat, not until he found Elizabeth.

The woman holding open the door raised her eyebrows to see Jack, still in his army uniform for he hadn't had time to see his tailor and the clothes he had from before the war were too small. She tipped her head to one side in mute inquiry.

'Excuse me – Mrs Wearmouth, isn't it?' She nodded her head. 'I'm looking for Elizabeth Nelson, I understand her brother lodges with you?'

'He's not in.'

'No, I know. But – look, may I come in?'

'Aye, if you like.'

Mrs Wearmouth opened the door wider and he followed her into the square kitchen. It was spotlessly clean, he noted, the range black-leaded and polished to a shining brilliance. The floor was flagged, the stones scrubbed clean and covered in places by hand-worked rag mats. Hookey mats, he believed they were called. The lid of the pan on the fire lifted and a bubble of water escaped, hissing down the side to the flames.

'Excuse me, sir, I'll just have to attend to the pot pie,' she said and bent over the pan, pulling it slightly back from the heat. 'Young Jimmy will be in soon, he's on back shift,' she explained. 'The lad's always starving with hunger. You know what young lads are.'

'Yes, of course,' Jack replied. As Mrs Wearmouth straightened up he went on. 'Actually, it's Elizabeth I'm looking for.'

'Aye, so you said.' She compressed her lips. 'I take it you've checked at the Hall, then?'

'I did. She's not there.' Jack didn't want to explain further. 'I thought she might be here?'

The woman shook her heard. 'Nay, she's not. An' I know for a fact she's not at her auntie's house neither. I was hoping she was back at the Hall. Young Joan Simpson came looking for her – last Friday it was. She was in a right taking an' all. Said something about Elizabeth being sent packing. I can't believe it, I can't. The lass is a good lass, I'd swear by it. Joan never said any more, I never did find out the ins and outs of it. Hey, it wasn't over you, was it? Did you get the lass into trouble? 'Cos if you did, it was badly done, I'm telling you! An' Jimmy's in a fair taking an' all, as if he hadn't enough to put up with, losing his best marra in the pit not all that long since neither, an' —'

'Tommy Gibson?' Of course, Tommy, how could he have forgotten? Jack bit his lip as Mrs Wearmouth looked at him with surprise.

'You knew? Now, wait a minute, you're Captain Benson, aren't you?'

'I'm sorry, I didn't introduce myself, did I? Yes, I'm Captain Benson.'

'The owner.' Mrs Wearmouth looked sourly at him. 'What do you want with Elizabeth? Sir?' The last an obvious afterthought.

'I mean her no harm, I just want to help her. I think it was a mistake, what happened. I'm sure she's done nothing wrong.'

'Aye. Well, we'll see. Anyroad, we've seen neither hide nor hair of her here.'

'I think I'll go back to the mine, meet Jimmy as he comes to bank,' said Jack. 'He may have some idea where she might have gone.'

'Aye. Well, if you do find her, tell her she's welcome to lodge here with her brother. I don't care for any gossip, folks can say what they like.'

Jack smiled warmly at the woman, her grey hair scraped back in a bun, face wrinkled, hands work-worn. Why, she must be younger than his mother, he realised suddenly. His soft-skinned, sweet-smelling mother whose hair was always piled on top of her head in elaborate waves and curls.

'I'll tell her,' he promised. 'I'll find her and tell her.' He would too, he told himself. Even if it took the rest of his life. A moment of doubt assailed him. Why, oh, why, had he not married her straight away? Rushed her off her feet? Why had he let anything get in the way?

As he drove into the pit yard, the hooter was going, signalling the end of the back shift. The night shift was already congregating at the entrance to the shaft, some already gone down. He wouldn't have long to wait for Jimmy, then. Jack decided not to go into the office, simply sat in the cart and waited. The men passing to and fro treated him to curious stares but he was oblivious of them, watching only for the young boy he had seen only a few times before.

Jimmy stepped out of the cage and walked through the crowd on his own, his shoulders hunched up around his ears, his face glum. He handed in his lamp and tokens to the cabin and came on towards where Jack's governess cart was standing, by the gate. The pony was taking advantage of slack reins and nibbling at the tips of the coal-blackened grass by the side. Jimmy noticed none of this, he was simply heading home through the gate, uninterested in anything around him.

'Jimmy!' Jack had to call again, 'Jimmy! Jimmy Nelson.' Jimmy hesitated, looked back at the cart. Slowly he came back to it.

'Aye, sir?' This was the big gaffer, he knew that, not just the manager gaffer but the owner. He hesitated again as the gaffer indicated to him to climb up onto the seat beside him. Jimmy looked around at the men, streaming from the yard, most of whom he could see now were watching with interest.

'Come on, I just want to speak to you,' said Jack.

Jimmy climbed up. 'I'll dirty the seat, sir.'

'Never mind.' He looked at the young boy, his whole person black from coal dust up to the line where his helmet had rested on his brow, showing startlingly white above it. 'Can we go up the road a little way? I'd like to talk to you about your sister.'

Jimmy's face was instantly creased with anxiety. 'Nothing's happened to her, has it, sir? I mean—'

'No, nothing's happened, or not that I know of.' Jack took up the reins and negotiated the pony and cart out of the gate and along the road, away from the pitmen and the rows and any other prying eyes. Outside the village he slowed the pony to a walk and then halted and turned back to Jimmy.

'I thought you might have some idea where Elizabeth is?'

Jimmy shook his head. 'Well, I haven't. I wish I had.' He looked suspiciously at Jack. 'What do you want to know for? Was it you that got her into trouble – was it?' His fists, still small but hard as iron, doubled up, his chin jutting forward aggressively.

'No, not me, I just want to find her, that's all. I think an injustice has been done.'

Jimmy laughed. 'Injustice, is it? That word has nowt to do with us, Mister. Words like that mean nowt at all here.' He had not relaxed his fighting stance, his knuckles gleaming white through the coal dust. 'Are you sweet on our Elizabeth, is that it? You want her for yourself, don't you? Well, you just leave her alone, she's a decent lass, she is. Chapel, we are!'

'I want to marry her,' Jack said. 'I want to find her and marry her, and that's what I'm going to do.'

Jimmy blinked. 'Marry her? Do you think pit lads are dim and daft then? Why would the likes of you want to marry our Elizabeth?'

'Because I love her.'

Jimmy gazed at him uncertainly then climbed down from the cart. 'Aye, well,' he said, 'mebbe you do. But I'm telling you: if I knew where our Elizabeth was, do you not think I'd have gone after her meself? Go away, man. The gaffer you may be but you're a fool for all that. An' now I'm off for me dinner.' He marched down the road towards Morton Main and Jack watched him until he disappeared into the colliery rows.

Chapter Eighteen

Elizabeth stood at the window, looking out at the snow. It had been two weeks since that awful day she had first come to Stand Alone Farm and still the snow stood as high as the window sill; in places, where it had drifted in the ever-present wind, it was higher. It felt as though she had been here forever, always waiting for Peart to come back from wherever he went, or else, if he was in the house, always on tenterhooks in case he told her to get out.

He was confusing, she thought as she gazed out at the whiteness. She never knew how he was going to be. Only yesterday he had come in with yet another rabbit in his bag.

'You're still here, then?' he had growled. 'Do you expect me to keep you all your bloody life?'

'I . . . How could I get away? The path's blocked, isn't it? It's still snowing.' She had gone out into yet another blizzard a couple of hours ago, taking Jenny by the hand, trying to find a way out to the road. Surely there had been other people up there, a horse-drawn snow plough perhaps. And there were snow poles on the road, showing the way back to Stanhope. She was even at the stage where she could actually contemplate asking the workhouse for help, or for shelter while she looked for work. But the path was completely obliterated, there was no sign even of Peart's footsteps. He must go somewhere else, she reckoned.

He had thrown the rabbit at her. 'Make yourself useful,' he'd ordered. 'A man could be nearly dying wi' hunger before you two would think to have a meal ready.'

'There wasn't any meat,' Jenny had stammered, visibly trembling. 'We couldn't, could we, Elizabeth?'

'Stop your bloody moaning or I'll give you something to moan about!' he snarled, and aimed a blow at the girl's head. Fortunately she was expecting it and managed to evade the worst of it: the hand only caught the edge of her shoulder. Nevertheless, she staggered.

'Leave the lass alone!' Elizabeth shouted at him, pulling Jenny behind her. 'Don't you hit her again, do you hear me?'

Peart grinned and his mood changed. Suddenly he was grinning. 'Sparky thing, aren't you? Aw, don't worry, I'll leave her alone. Just so long as you both mind me. Now get the dinner on like you're told!'

But now the dinner was eaten and Peart was dozing in the chair before the fire. Jenny was nursing a rag doll Elizabeth had made for her, though casting anxious glances behind her at Peart. She never usually played with the doll when he was in the house but today she had chanced it while he was asleep.

Elizabeth turned from the window, sighing. Already the day was beginning to darken. But at least the snow seemed to be coming down less heavily.

'Jen, get away upstairs to bed,' said Peart. Jenny jumped. She put the hand holding the doll behind her back.

'Go on, when I tell you!' he roared and the little girl fled. Elizabeth stared at him. He was gazing back at her, a peculiarly intent look on his face. 'Come here and sit by me,' he said to her and smiled as he rubbed his stubbly chin with one hand. Elizabeth was reminded forcibly of Private Wilson. Dear God, not again. There must be something about her which made men think she was like that, she thought miserably.

'I was thinking I would have an early night, go to bed with Jenny.'

'No, no. Howay, man, come and sit on the settle at least,' said Peart. 'Now, wouldn't you like a drink? I've got some whisky.'

'No, thank you,' she mumbled. Still, she went and sat on the settle opposite him. She daren't antagonise him – suppose he put her out? She put a hand up to her nose.

She couldn't help it. Close to, the dirty, musky smell of him, made stronger by the heat of the fire, was powerful.

'It's nice to have a woman about the place again,' he said. 'I've been lonely, you know.'

Elizabeth looked at him. 'I wouldn't have thought it,' she replied. 'I thought I was a burden to you, just another useless mouth to feed?' It was an expression he'd used once or twice.

'You mustn't mind me, I say things I don't really mean.' He leaned forward suddenly until his face was six inches from hers. He looked down at the swell of her breasts under her dress, his eyes glistening. 'Come on, pet, give us a kiss.'

He leaned further forward and pressed his lips to hers; they were wet and slobbery and the smell was rising from him in waves at this range. Elizabeth couldn't help herself she gagged.

'What the hell's the matter with you? Have you never kissed a man before? Who the hell do you think you are anyroad? I've a good mind—' He reached forward but she was too quick for him. She ducked and ran to the bottom of the stairs.

'What's the matter with *me*? What's the matter?' Elizabeth was past caring whether he threw her out or not, so long as he didn't touch her. 'The stink of you, that's what's the matter! When did you last have a bath or even a good wash?' She was on edge, trembling all over, poised to flee. But Peart didn't lose his temper and come after her. He just looked puzzled.

'A bath? In the middle of winter? Have some sense, lass, do you want me to catch me death?'

The tension left Elizabeth then. She turned and ran upstairs to the bedroom she was sharing with Jenny, undressing in the dark, or rather by the pale white light which came in at the window, the moon reflected from the snow. She need not be too frightened of Peart, she thought, he wasn't another Private Wilson. Nevertheless, she jammed her box against the door just in case. Jumping into bed, she lay close to her sister, feeling the warmth from the small body. The warmth slowly seeped through her and she was dropping off to sleep when she suddenly jerked awake. The moon! She hadn't seen a break in the clouds since she'd come but now there was moonlight. She got out of bed and crossed to the uncurtained window. It had stopped snowing, the wind had died down too. Across the field she could see movement: a hare, or maybe a rabbit, was jumping along in the snow. An owl hooted from close by. The scene was incredibly beautiful. Heartened, Elizabeth got back into bed and fell asleep.

If she expected any change in Peart's manner the next day there was none. He came down to breakfast in the same filthy shirt and trousers, growled at Jenny, making her spill a drop of the tea she was pouring, glared at Elizabeth and muttered about the house being a home for waifs and strays now. Then he pulled on his filthy old coat and tied his muffler round and round his neck, pulled his cap over his eyes and shouted for Snuff.

'I'm off,' he said to no one in particular. 'You, Jen, be careful with that wood. An' there's only a handful of coal in the coal house, mind, *an'* the peat's running low an' all.'

He banged the door behind him and could be heard through the gaps, cursing as he tramped up the yard through the snow.

'Where's he gone, Jenny?' asked Elizabeth.

'I don't know.' She was tipping the last of the water from the pail into the kettle, putting the kettle on the fire. 'I have to wash the pots and clean the floor before the fire goes out or there'll be no hot water.' She was wearing that same worried frown as she hurried about the chores.

'But why should the fire go out?'

'You heard Peart. He doesn't want us to waste the fuel there is.'

'Oh, Jenny, he didn't mean we shouldn't have a fire, surely?'

'He did.' Jenny was positive. Elizabeth gazed at her sister. Jenny had come out of her shell in the days since Elizabeth had been here. She spoke more often, ate at the table with them though carefully watched Peart when she took a piece of bread or a potato, just in case he should object. Elizabeth felt her old resentment of him stir at the thought of it.

'We can't let the fire go out, Jenny,' she insisted. The girl didn't reply. She was pouring water from the kettle into the enamel bowl, adding soda crystals and shaved soap, ready to wash the dishes. Elizabeth picked up the drying cloth to help her.

'I thought I would try to go into Stanhope today,' she said when the dishes were done and the room swept and tidied.

'You're coming back, though, aren't you?' Jenny asked, looking anxious.

'I don't think Peart wants me to stay here,' Elizabeth replied. 'But I'll come back to see you.'

'Take me with you.'

'I can't, I have nowhere to stay and no work either,' replied Elizabeth, biting her lip.

'Please,' said Jenny. She didn't cry, made no fuss, but she had her hands clasped together tightly in her lap and she was rocking slightly backwards and forwards.

'Jenny, I can't. I might have to go into the workhouse until I get a job. You wouldn't like that, would you?'

'If you were there . . .'

'But we wouldn't be together, you'd have to go in the children's end. And anyway, I think they would send you back here.'

Jenny said no more. She went over to the corner where

she had hidden the rag doll and picked it up, hugging it to her thin chest.

'I'd best go now, while the light holds,' said Elizabeth.

'Go on then.'

'I'll come back for my box.' She pulled on her coat, tied the scarf around her head. Then she went over to the little girl and hugged and kissed her.

'There's a sledge hanging on the wall in the barn,' said Jenny. 'Peart brings coal from Stanhope on it sometimes, when we haven't plenty of peat.'

'Is there? Why didn't you tell me before? I might have got through yesterday.'

'I didn't want you to go,' said Jenny.'

'Ah, petal,' said Elizabeth, and her heart ached for the little girl. 'I'll come back for you,' she vowed. 'I promise I will.'

Elizabeth sledged down the last bank to the frozen Tees at Stanhope. She crossed gingerly over the ice at the ford and halted on the other side to catch her breath. Her arms ached, her head throbbed and her fingers felt as though they would drop off at any minute. But she had reached the little town. All she had to do now was climb the bank to the main road which ran through it and find the workhouse. The workhouse . . . She could feel herself go cold inside at the thought of it. But there was nothing else for it. She certainly couldn't stay out in this weather; she had no food, no work, no money. But she would get work, oh, yes, she would, she vowed. She would find a job and lodging and get out of the workhouse. Why, she wouldn't be in it more than a day or two at most. She could work, she only had to have the chance. Besides there was Jenny to consider.

'You look fit enough to work for yourself to me,' said the Master. He surveyed Elizabeth from under huge bushy eyebrows which sprouted over his eyes and, she was sure, must obscure his vision. 'Where did you say you were from?'

'Bishop Auckland, sir.'

'You haven't come from Auckland today,' he said sharply and looked at her as though he'd caught her out in a lie.

'No, I was on Bollihope Common, got caught out in the blizzard.'

'Bollihope Common? A pretty daft place to be, wasn't it, with a blizzard coming?'

Elizabeth sighed. 'I was going to visit my sister, sir,' she began, and told him the story of losing her purse, getting caught in the storm and sheltering at Stand Alone Farm. 'I was a nurse's aide before that, sir,' she finished.

'Why didn't you say so? You can work in the old people's ward, earn a living, not battening on the guardians of this parish.'

'Oh! Yes, I will, sir!' Elizabeth was filled with hope. If she had a proper job in the hospital end, she could find lodgings outside, maybe even have Jenny to live with her. For she was confident that if only she had the room, she could get her sister away from Peart.

'Right, you can start now. We've lost most of the staff with any experience at all in this damned war,' said the workhouse Master. 'Just give me the name of your previous employer.'

Elizabeth's heart sank. Would Miss Rowland give her a reference? She had said she would not. But surely she wouldn't be so cruel? The Matron had known Elizabeth for most of her life, how could she believe Private Wilson before her? No, she would not.

An hour later, wearing an overall and cap which were far too big for her, Elizabeth was working on a ward which seemed to be almost exclusively for aged pauper women. She fetched bedpans, which were usually too late, and cleaned up beds and gave bedbaths, with the help of an inmate only a year or two younger than the patients. She had been tired by the effort of getting down from the moor into Stanhope. Now her arms ached from lifting and carrying.

It was very different from the hall where the patients had been wounded officers, mostly housed in separate rooms. Here the patients were truly infirm and kept all together, with little space between the beds. But they didn't complain, just lay quietly for the most part, only speaking when the need for a bedpan became urgent. Elizabeth's sensitive nature had been sorely bruised by what she saw at the hall; here it was bruised just as badly by the plight of the old women.

It was two o'clock and she was almost faint with hunger when Sister came out of her office and beckoned imperiously to her.

'Nelson!'

Elizabeth sped down the ward to her. 'Yes, Sister?' It must be dinner time, she thought with relief.

'You're to go to the office,' said Sister, looking grim.

An hour later Elizabeth was working in the laundry, scrubbing stained sheets. She had been unable to eat her dinner of potatoes and pease pudding, being too upset and humiliated. Miss Rowland had refused to give her a reference when the Master had telephoned her.

'Immoral character,' he had said as Elizabeth stood before him. 'You will find that no good comes of lying to me. I don't think you should be allowed on the wards, no indeed. You will pay for your bed and board by working in the laundry.'

She scrubbed away for the rest of the day then sat down to supper with the rest of the paupers. In the narrow, uncomfortable bed that night she fell asleep from sheer exhaustion. And so it went on for a fortnight, every day working herself into a stupor so that she didn't have to think; every night falling into bed bone-weary. And still she couldn't think of a way to get out, not with 'an immoral character'. She barely noticed the snow melting away, the signs of budding trees, the birds beginning to sing. She was permanently weary, in despair. She didn't write to Jimmy or Jenny, all she wanted to do was hide away.

It was a Sunday morning, before the paupers went to church in a long crocodile of grey-dressed women and shuffling, bent old men. Elizabeth sat on her bed thinking of nothing, glad of the respite Sunday brought from the hard, unremitting work, when a woman called to her.

'Elizabeth Nelson? You're wanted at the door. There's a chap wants to speak to you.'

'Eeh, go on, lass. Mebbe he wants to take you away from all this, eh? Ask him if he has a friend for me, will ye?'

There were chuckles, ribald laughter going round the room, but Elizabeth didn't hear. She was filled with a sudden wild hope. It was Jack, it had to be, he had been looking for her all along and now he'd found her! She sped down the stairs and into the front entrance, to the open door where sunlight streamed in, highlighting the drab paintwork.

It was not Jack and her heart dropped to her boots, the disappointment cut so deep. Peart stepped forward, cap in hand, face shining from soap and water and his hair brushed carefully to each side with a parting in the middle. She stared at him, he was so different, and for a moment or two she couldn't think what it was. Then she knew: the smell was gone. Not altogether: there was still a slight whiff about him, but that awful goatlike stink

234

was gone. Peart had had a bath. His clothes were clean too.

'Hello, lass,' he said. 'I thought I'd call and see how you were doing. Jen was crying for you.'

Elizabeth stared at him, disappointment blurring her vision. It was a minute before what he was saying penetrated.

'Jenny crying for me? Since when do you care if she cries?'

'Aw, howay, lass. Don't be like that. I've come down here to see ye, haven't I?'

Elizabeth felt like crying herself. She gazed at him, his face screwed into an ingratiating smile. Absently she rubbed the fingers of her right hand with her left. The constant use of washing soda was taking its toll, even on her work-accustomed skin.

'Nelson, who told you you could leave your work? Get back to the laundry at once, do you hear? And you, sir, you're an intruder. No visitors allowed during working hours. No visitors, I say.'

Elizabeth spun around. The workhouse Master was standing outside his office, legs astride, a thunderous expression on his face.

'I came to see her about her sister . . .' Peart began.

'I'll have no followers here, do you understand me? None of your lewd ways here!' the Master shouted at Elizabeth, ignoring Peart.

Indignation boiled up in Elizabeth and she turned on

him. 'What do you mean? What do you think we're going to do? Don't you call me lewd!' she replied, her voice rising to match his. Doors around the hall opened, faces peeped out. Nothing much out of the ordinary happened in the workhouse, a scene like this was great entertainment.

'Now, hold yer hosses!' said Peart, his speech broadening, 'I'm here to offer the lass a job as me housekeeper. I thought you'd be glad to be rid of her?'

The Master stepped back, calming down. 'Oh! Well, you know, the proper procedure is to ask me first. But step into my office, Mr . . . er . . .'

'Peart.'

'Yes, Mr Peart. There are a few formalities to be gone through.'

Half an hour later, Elizabeth was walking across the frozen Tees towards the steep bankside which led up to Bollihope Common, pulling the sledge behind her, laden with a couple of bags of coal.

'An' don't you take that again without asking first,' said Peart, turning to watch her struggle up to the path from the river behind him.

Chapter Nineteen

'I have a proposal for you, Jimmy.'

Jack Benson sat in Mrs Wearmouth's front room on the edge of a horsehair sofa. The horsehair penetrated the fine wool of his trousers, irritating the skin at the back of his knees. He shifted his position and crossed his legs, swinging one foot across in its polished leather shoe. Jimmy glanced at it and away, blushing slightly, and Jack put it back on the floor.

'Yes, sir?' Jimmy asked politely. He was wearing his good suit, his Sunday suit, and his hair was brushed back from his forehead, still wet from his bath. It was the middle of the afternoon, a warm day in May. Sun slanted through the narrow window of the room, the light patterned by Mrs Wearmouth's lace, dolly-dyed curtains. Jimmy was on fore shift, the afternoon lay before him and he had hoped to spend it out in the sunshine. Asking around the district for his sister, it was

237

true, he was still out in the sunshine. But here was Captain Benson, the mine owner, and Jimmy must be properly respectful.

He had heard Mr Dunne, the gaffer, lamenting the fact that Captain Benson had taken over from Mr Jones, the former agent. 'He pokes his nose into far too much, if you ask me,' Dunne had said to the under-manager. 'The government shouting for more and more production to help the war effort and him – an owner, mind you – going on about safety.'

But what did Captain Benson want with a putter lad like himself? Jimmy didn't believe the owner was on the side of him and his marras. It wasn't natural, was it? If he thought Jimmy was going to spy on his mates for the bosses, he was wrong. And if he wanted to ask about their Elizabeth again, well, Jimmy had told him all he knew last time. Still, best be polite.

Jack watched the expressions chase across Jimmy's face, wondering what he was really thinking. Surely the lad must hold a clue as to Elizabeth's whereabouts? A girl just didn't disappear into thin air, not in County Durham she didn't.

'I have a proposition for you, Jimmy,' he said.

'Aye?'

'How would you like to go back to school?'

Jimmy stared at him. The man had taken leave of his senses. 'I cannot go back to school, man, I'm over the age,' he pointed out reasonably.

'I mean, you could go to the grammar school at Bishop Auckland. King James's.'

Jimmy stared at him. The gaffer was definitely crackers. How could he go to the grammar school? He had no scholarship, hadn't even sat for one; and even if he had he couldn't pay for the uniform. And how could a putter lad pay fees?

It was as if Captain Benson could read his mind. 'I would be willing to pay the fees and give you a living allowance.'

'But why?'

Jack had thought this question might be asked and had worked out his answer. 'You're an intelligent boy, if you had an education you could go far. Be a credit to Morton Main and the colliery too. Haven't you ever dreamed of doing something better than mining?'

'There's nowt wrong with working in the pit,' Jimmy said flatly.

'No, I didn't say there was,' Jack said hastily. He well knew the miners' pride. Then he had a sudden inspiration. 'But you could train as a mining surveyor, couldn't you? If you had the education. So what do you say?'

'There's no catch?'

'No catch.'

Jimmy stared out of the window for a few minutes then turned back to face Jack. 'This has nothing to do with our Elizabeth, has it? I mean, you're not doing this because you feel guilty about her, are you, sir?'

Jack sighed. 'No, I don't feel guilty about her, except that I wish I'd kept an eye on her, stopped what happened to her. She was a good nurse, Jimmy, and I hope to heaven she has found another place somewhere, in some hospital where she can train properly. But, no, I want to do this for you. In fact, I was thinking of starting a fund. If you do well, I will sponsor another boy after you.' God, listen to me, he thought. What do I sound like? A Victorian do-gooder. I never thought of myself like that until this minute. He thought of what Elizabeth would think if she heard him. She'd look straight at him with those fabulous violet eyes, so like Jimmy's, and see straight through him.

When he had first thought of doing this, in the middle of a sleepless night when his body ached for her, when his arms felt empty and useless without her, he hadn't thought beyond how much he wanted to have her there so he could give her the world – but he couldn't and it was his own fault. He'd lost her because he hadn't seized her when he had the chance, made her marry him. But he could do something for her brother. Jack cast about in his mind and realised what it was. He could get Jimmy out of the pit; at the very least, lift him above the hard, poorly paid life of the miner.

In the morning he hadn't been so sure, but had watched the boy for a while, asked discreet questions of the manager. Jimmy was intelligent. He could do well, given the chance.

'Well, what do you say?' asked Jack. 'You'll have to sit some tests, show what you're made of first, of course.'

Jimmy nodded. 'I'll do it,' he said. 'But not today. There's one or two folk I want to see. Mebbe they know where our Elizabeth went.'

Hope flared in Jack, showed in his eyes. He stepped forward, opened his mouth to speak, but was forestalled by the boy.

'I'll let you know if there's anything,' he said. 'Now I'll just have to tell Mrs Wearmouth there'll be no more pit clothes to wash. Not for a long time anyroad.'

Jimmy strode along the field path which had once been a trail for the donkeys, taking coal in panniers from the bell pits of the area to the coast. The sun shone from a cloudless blue sky. There was May blossom out in the hedges, smelling sweet and fresh, and birds were singing sweeter than ever the canaries did in the pit.

Jimmy moodily kicked a stone in front of him as he walked. Everything would be grand if only he knew where Elizabeth was. He was coming to the path which led off to Coundon. He'd had this idea that she might, just might, have gone to see his sister, Alice, before she went wherever she was going. He turned on to the path, strode up the hill and there was the village. Alice didn't live in the pit rows, the family she had gone to were tradesmen. They had a substantial detached house in the main street, next to the haberdasher's they owned and ran. This spring afternoon the door was closed, the windows shrouded in lace. In the small front garden there was not a blade of grass out of place on the squares of lawn to either side of the path. A regimented row of rose bushes were in bud under the windows.

Jimmy stepped up to the door and rang the bell. He could hear it echo loudly in the house. There was no reply so he tried again.

'What do you want? Hey, you, boy, I'm talking to you.'

Jimmy turned to see a girl of about twelve standing outside the shop. She had long black hair tied back with a green ribbon, a pale green dress with a white pinafore worn over it: one of the frilled sort, for show not for work. He walked round to her.

'Hello, Alice,' he said. 'You haven't seen our sister Elizabeth, have you?'

Walking back along the path not ten minutes later, he seethed. Stuck-up little madam that she was, that Alice! She should have had her bum tanned. He picked up a stick and slashed at the hedge as he walked along.

'Elizabeth who?' she had asked, face set and straight. 'I haven't got a sister.'

'An' I suppose you'll say I'm not your brother!' Jimmy flared, then calmed himself. 'Look, Alice, our Elizabeth's gone missing and I have to find her.'

'Well, she's not here, I haven't seen her, even if I

knew what you were talking about,' said Alice, and waltzed off into the shop.

Jimmy fumed, but it was no use, he knew that. Alice was an unfeeling little . . . No, she wasn't, she had her new family now. Why, she hardly knew him or Elizabeth. Best leave her alone. At least he knew now that she had no idea where Elizabeth was. He tried to take his mind off his sisters. Finding a good, grassy bank he sat down, leaned back and crossed his legs. Small white clouds chased across the sky and in spite of his worry, his mood lightened. It was a grand day. Jimmy let his mind dwell on Captain Benson's proposal. It was a great chance, he knew that. And Elizabeth would be proud as punch of him if he went to the grammar school. The pit wasn't the same since Tommy went and he couldn't even pretend to be eighteen and enlist in the army for another year at least.

He'd give it a go, he decided, getting to his feet. Make something of himself, he would.

Next morning, Captain Benson was standing in the office doorway as Jimmy walked past from the cage. He beckoned to him and the boy left the crowd of miners and went over to him. Some of the men looked at each other and raised their eyebrows but that was all.

'Did you hear anything?' Captain Benson asked without preamble.

'No, sir.' Jimmy shook his head. Tiny bright specks of

coal dust dropped from his hair and eyebrows at the movement. He looked up in time to see the acute disappointment in the gaffer's face. Blimey, he really *did* care about Elizabeth, Jimmy realised, and couldn't help warming to him. He glanced round at the other men streaming past, most of them openly curious by now. Especially Mr Dunne, poking his head round the inner door of the office, all eyes and ears.

'I'll take you up on that offer. An' don't worry – our Elizabeth will get in touch, I know she will,' Jimmy said rapidly, and walked off quickly to the pit gates. She better had an' all, he said to himself as he hurried on down to the rows.

'I might let Jen go to school, what do you think about that?' asked Peart, smiling craftily. He was pleased with himself, Elizabeth could see, reckoned he was getting what he wanted now. She had been back at the farm for a few weeks and felt trapped, in spite of her relief at getting out of the workhouse. Lying in bed the night before, she had gone over and over in her mind what she could do. If she wrote to Jimmy surely he would help her, or at least give her the money to get away. But Jimmy was no doubt disgusted with the story of why she had been dismissed, it must be all round Morton Main by now. Elizabeth cringed at the thought. She couldn't bear to face the people she knew.

Especially not Jack Benson. He meant so much to her

and must despise her now. How could she face him? Her thoughts slid back to Jenny. Jenny, who was a different girl since she had been here. Her sister looked up to her, admired the way she stood up to Peart, was pathetically grateful for everything Elizabeth did for her. She would be heartbroken to be left without her.

'Well?' Peart demanded, bringing Elizabeth's thoughts back to the present.

'She should be at school anyway,' she replied. 'I cannot understand why the kiddy-catcher hasn't been after you before now.'

'Nay, they won't come all the way up here,' he said. 'Besides, she couldn't go in the winter, could she? Not wi' the snow an'that.'

'It's not winter now. It's May, the beginning of the summer. She could go to school now.'

'Aye, well, isn't that just what I've been saying?' Peart looked across at her as she stood by the fire, the frying pan in her hand. By, she was getting a fine figure on her, was the lass. He felt his loins stir as he looked at her. A lovely smell of bacon frying filled the room, he had brought it in from Stanhope only that morning.

Elizabeth lifted the bacon onto a plate and put it in front of him. Going back to the pan, she put in two slices of bread to fry in the bacon fat, one for her and one for Jenny. At least the little girl was eating better now, she thought. And she had known all along what Peart had in mind when he brought her back from Stanhope

Workhouse. It was a wonder she had been able to put him off until now. But the thought of him touching her after Jack . . . She shuddered.

'I'll think about it,' she said.

'Hmmm,' Peart snorted, and began to eat his bacon, cutting great pieces and stuffing them into his mouth, chewing noisily, wiping his plate with a heel of bread. Fat ran down his chin. He wiped it away with the back of his hand.

'Come on, Jenny, eat this,' said Elizabeth. She was hovering in the background as she usually did when Peart was in, but these days she came to the table when Elizabeth bade her. She sat down as far away from Peart as possible and began to eat the fried bread but still he turned on her, taking out his frustrations on her.

'You, you little beggar – feed the dog before you feed your face. Haven't I told you before?' he snarled.

Jenny reverted to her old self, scuttling into the corner for Snuff's dish and filling it with scraps. She stayed in the corner with him, not coming back to the table.

'Leave the bairn alone,' Elizabeth protested. He was so unpredictable, she thought despairingly, one minute trying to ingratiate himself with her and the next turning nasty like this. 'Come and eat your bread, Jenny,' she coaxed the child, but Jenny just gazed at her with large, troubled eyes. Elizabeth sighed and sat at the table opposite Peart. At least he had never tried to force her, she thought. He was not so bad as Private Wilson. But she knew he wouldn't wait much longer.

'Are you talking about getting married?' she asked.

Peart sat back and rubbed his lips with the back of his hand. 'Married? Why the hell should I get married? It costs over much, man. Just a Minister saying words over us, isn't it? Nay, we could just go on as we are, 'cept that you would move into my room.' He watched her reactions slyly.

Elizabeth shook her head. 'No,' she said, and rose from the table and went over to Jenny. 'Come on, pet,' she said. 'We'll go out for a breath of fresh air, will we?' Taking the girl by the hand, she drew her to the door and out, while Peart glowered at them and Jenny kept glancing back at him timidly. Elizabeth expected him to roar and shout after them to come back but he didn't and the girls escaped into the yard and then through the weedy pasture at the front of the house to the path leading to the high moor.

'He'll be fair stotting, he'll be that angry,' Jenny said as they gained the freedom of the moor. She clasped Elizabeth's hand tightly and looked up, her little face like an old woman's with the worry lines.

'Ah, so what?' said Elizabeth. 'He'll get over it.' Though in truth she was worried herself.

'You won't go away again, though, will you?'

'No, I won't, not without you, pet,' she answered and wondered if she could keep the promise.

The day was bright and sunny. The heather was tipped

with green shoots and in the small patches of grass there were tiny daisies. Further up, the sheep were calling to their lambs while nibbling away at the new growth. The lambs skipped and played. Peewits cried; a curlew rose suddenly in front of them, skimming away over the heather, calling plaintively, trying to distract their attention from its hidden nest.

In spite of everything, the sisters felt their spirits rise as the warm spring breeze lifted their hair. They began to scramble for the top of the moor from where they could see other farmsteads and know they were not completely alone in Stand Alone Farm. There were dark clefts over by Stanhope, where stone had been quarried for centuries, a blue mist on the horizon. And most of all there was the vast, blue sky.

And as they raised their faces to the sun, a lark rose to become a mere speck in all that vast blue and his trilling song was sweet and pure.

Jenny leaned against Elizabeth. 'It'll be all right, Elizabeth,' she said. 'I know it will.' And as Elizabeth smiled down at her she saw the worried lines smoothed away. Jenny was smiling, a rare, relaxed smile. The moor had worked its magic.

Chapter Twenty

Peart was a more complicated man than she had realised, Elizabeth thought as she sat by her sister on the settle that evening. They had got back from the moor by five o'clock and there was no sign of him or his dog. Elizabeth had breathed a sigh of relief. She had persuaded Jenny to go upstairs and play with her doll, out of his way should he come home in a foul mood. By the time he did come in, she had a pheasant he had brought in the day before (never mind that it was out of season) broiling on the fire, fragrant with herbs. There were new young nettles and potatoes left over from the winter stock. Maybe the dinner would put him in a better mood, she told herself.

But as it happened he was in a good mood anyway, or seemed to be. He had sniffed the air appreciatively.

'Grand,' he pronounced. 'I'm fair clemmed wi' hunger.'

She had called Jenny downstairs and dished out the food and Peart had even smiled at the girl so that Jenny was encouraged to sit at the table again and eat her share of the dinner. At this rate, Elizabeth thought, the bairn would be putting a bit of weight on her bones.

Jenny was tired after the fresh air and the good food; her eyes drooped and she leaned against Elizabeth as though for support.

'Get off to bed, young 'un,' said Peart, and Jenny's eyes flew open warily. But he smiled at her and felt in his pocket, bringing out a paper bag. 'Here, have one of these,' he said, holding out the bag. It was full of sweets like black bullets. She looked warily up at him.

'Go on,' he said again and she took one, gazing at it as though she wasn't sure what to do with it.

'Suck it, Jenny,' said Elizabeth, 'you'll like it. Then we'll go to bed.'

'Nay, it's far too early for you,' Peart objected. 'Stay and keep me company.'

Elizabeth wasn't sure. Staying with Jenny had been her protection up to now. Yet he *hadn't* forced her to do anything she didn't want to, had he? And it was early for her. But Jenny was so tired. She could handle him, Elizabeth thought, only a trifle uneasily.

'All right,' she said. 'Jenny, you go up, I won't be so long.'

They sat in silence for a while after she had gone. It was uncomfortable for Elizabeth. Every time she looked up, Peart's eyes were intent on her, like a cat watching a cornered mouse. If only they'd had a gramophone, some music, she thought. Something to take her mind off him. One of the patients at Newcomb Hall had had a gramophone. It had been lovely. She gazed at the embers of the peat fire, trying to see pictures in the red, grey and black.

'Do you want one?'

His voice made her jump. She looked quickly at him. He was holding out the bag of black bullets. She took one with a rapid, nervous movement and put it in her mouth then wished she hadn't. It was large and sweet and sticky. She stood up and made to move away.

'I'll just get the mending.'

'No. Stay here. I want you to stay here,' he insisted. He caught hold of her arm, moved from his chair to the settle and pulled her down to sit beside him.

He's not going to do anything, Elizabeth told herself silently. Keep calm, that's the thing. She felt slightly sick. She took out her handkerchief, one that Jimmy had bought her for Christmas, and put it to her mouth, spitting the black bullet into it. She took a long breath.

'I think I'd best be going to bed.'

'Not yet,' he insisted. 'Howay, give me a kiss first.'

His face was very close to hers. His breath didn't have its usual smell of cheap spirit, she noticed. His body smelled clean and only slightly musky. The main smell was of mint and sugar from the sweets. She leaned away from him. Embarrassment and confusion made her face red; in fact, she felt red all over.

He pressed against her. 'Just one kiss? You're not shy, are you?'

Elizabeth turned her face to his. Maybe she could escape to bed if she let him kiss her. He smiled slightly, grasped her around the waist and pressed his mouth to hers. She stayed compliant. His teeth pressed against her lips. His tongue darted out and forced her mouth open. She steeled herself to endure it. He pulled back and gave a triumphant smile.

'I'll go now,' she said but he did not release her.

'I'll let the bairn go to school,' he said. 'It'll be all right, you'll see. And I'll marry you. Later on, in the winter mebee, when I'm not so busy.' She could tell he was being as nice as he could.

Could she do it, for Jenny's sake? The girl had had no sort of a life up 'til now; she would be broken altogether if Elizabeth were to leave. Jenny trusted her, she was the bairn's only chance. Oh, she must go upstairs, give herself time to think. Fleetingly, images of Jack came into her mind: Jack smiling; Jack making love to her. Pure agony rose in her. She had to push it to the back of her mind, forget him. She couldn't bear to think of him, it was too painful. She had to think what she could do now. Jack didn't want her, his mother had made it clear.

'What do you say?' Peart's voice was low in her ear, persistent. 'Come on, pet, I want ye. I love ye.' He ran his hand down her arm, across her breasts, down to her hips.

'Upstairs,' said Elizabeth. 'Not here, not where Jenny might come down and see us.'

Peart sprang to his feet. He seized her hand, holding it clasped so tightly she could feel the hard calluses across his palm. Just in case she changed her mind, she thought in a detached, dull sort of way. But she wouldn't, there was an inevitability about what was happening. She allowed him to lead her upstairs, past Jenny's room (she kept her eyes averted), to his, a room which smelled strongly male from the years he had slept there, in his dirt, in this bed.

'I don't know why you want to waste your time and money on that pit boy?' said Olivia. She stared at her son, distaste plain to see on her face. 'What your father would have thought, I dread to imagine. That was something he wouldn't hear of. "The working classes won't thank you for interfering in their private lives," that's what he used to say.'

'Yes, Mother,' said Jack. 'He also said that they were shiftless, drunken and needed a firm hand, didn't he?' Jack gave her a meaningful smile. He hardly remembered his father sober, and as for gambling – well, he could teach any pitch and toss school of miners a thing or two about gambling. He'd very nearly driven the family to ruin and now his son was slowly rescuing it.

Olivia put her nose in the air and favoured him with her haughtiest look. 'I don't know what you mean, Jack.'

'Don't you, Mother?'

He picked up the book he had been studying and started to walk out of the room. At the door he paused.

'I will, no matter what you say, be helping Jimmy Nelson to get a decent education, Mother.'

'Jimmy Nelson? Of course, *that's* his name,' said Olivia as though she had just heard it, though Jack had introduced him to her only an hour ago. The boy had come up to the Manor to hear how Jack's plans were progressing and Jack had given him books to read and set him some elementary maths problems he judged would be about the level of a fourteen-year-old.

'Nelson? Isn't that the name of the girl who was dismissed from Newcomb Hall for immoral behaviour? She came here, the impudent young hussy, looking for you, would you believe? I—'

'She came *here*? When did she come here?'

Jack let go of the door he was holding open. It closed silently behind him as he strode back into the room and confronted his mother. Hope flared in him. Perhaps Elizabeth had been recently. Perhaps she had left a clue as to where she was living.

'Oh, ages ago, winter it was. I remember we had snow . . .'

'In the winter? You mean she came looking for me when she left the Hall?' Jack could feel a cold rage beginning to stir deep within him. He had to keep a firm hold on it to stop himself from shouting at his mother.

'Don't look at me like that, young man,' she said testily. 'Yes, I suppose it would be just after that incident. It was just as well you weren't here, you're such a softie. I told her you wanted nothing to do with her, of course you didn't.'

'Where did she go?' asked Jack, his voice low and menacing now so that his mother faltered and looked away.

'How would I know? I'm not interested in where such riffraff go,' she snapped. 'But forget about her. I was talking about this boy, her brother. He's probably no better than she is. Jack, I can't understand—'

But he was gone, out of the house and into the car which was parked outside, driving away rapidly before he became guilty of matricide.

He drove along the road which led to Morton Main colliery and the rows of miners' houses. He had an appointment with Mr Dunne at the mine. He had decided to go down with the night shift men, see for himself the state of the safety precautions. But he was too agitated for that now, he realised. It was something which could only be done in a calm, collected frame of mind.

Pausing at the entrance to the village, he decided to take the road beyond, through Old Morton and on, driving along any country lane which took his fancy. Not that he saw much of the scenery. His thoughts were bitter

and black and all about how he had wasted any
opportunity he'd had to secure his future with Elizabeth.
And it was his mother, his own mother, who had ended
the dream once and for all.

A cat streaked in front of him, narrowly missing the
wheels of the Austin tourer. He braked sharply. Jack had
been driving automatically on the almost empty lanes
but now he looked about him. He was entering the
hamlet where he had brought Elizabeth on that fateful
day, the one when Tommy Gibson had been killed. He
was almost at the Plough, the inn where he had taken her
for something to eat, the inn where they had been so
close. The remembrance was so sweet, so precious to
him, the thought that he might never see her again an
aching wound inside him. He stopped the car and stared
at the inn, the gaudy sign with its painted plough hanging
straight and unmoving on this warm, windless day.

Two small boys had appeared and were looking at the
car with round, wondering eyes.

'Eeh, can we have a ride, Mister?' one was brave
enough to ask but Jack was definitely not in the mood.

'No. Get away. You don't want to be run over, do
you?' he snapped and turned the car around, heading
back the way he had come.

If only he knew where she was, if she was all right. He
had this anxious feeling deep inside him, one which
intensified as time went on and he had no news of her.
There was something wrong, she was in danger and he

had to take some of the blame for it. He tried to tell himself that of course there was something wrong, she had no money, he didn't know if she had found work. He worried about whether she had enough to eat and a home. But no one starved to death in the twentieth century, he told himself. Still, the feelings persisted.

His gloomy thoughts were interrupted as he saw a boy sitting on a grassy bank, leaning against a wooden fence. It surrounded a rabbit warren, known locally as the bunny banks, a wild bit of land, plagued by small pitfalls from ancient workings. It was shaded in part by the copse which grew to one side, a good place to sit and read.

So this was where Jimmy came to get away from the other lads, a place of peace and quiet. Jack stopped the Austin and Jimmy closed his book and walked over to the car.

'Afternoon, sir,' he said. 'I was just trying to make sense of this Pythagoras bloke.'

'Yes. Well, I'll give you a hand with that, if you like?' said Jack. 'Get in.' He spent the next half hour patiently explaining the theory.

'What's the point of it, though?' said Jimmy. 'I mean, what use is it?'

'Surveying, architecture, lots of uses,' said Jack, and used the only straight tree in the copse to demonstrate it. But he couldn't keep his mind on it. Thoughts of Elizabeth intruded all the time.

'Look, Jimmy, can you not think of anywhere else your sister might be?' he asked finally.

Jimmy closed the book and stuck the stub of pencil he had been using behind his ear. He had been all eager attention when discussing the geometry; his eyes, so like Elizabeth's glowing with intelligence and the chance to use it. Now the smile was wiped from his face. He looked as worried as Jack felt.

'I don't know, sir,' he said. 'I've tried to think.'

'You're sure? I mean, did she ever say anything about anywhere she fancied seeing? London? Australia?' Dear God, not anywhere so far away, please, Jack prayed in sudden panic.

'Well . . . She might have gone up to see Jenny. But, no, she wouldn't stay there. The old fella wouldn't let her anyroad. Not when she had no money.'

'Jenny?' Jack saw a gleam of hope. The blood jumped in his veins. 'You didn't mention her before!'

'No, well, Jenny's me little sister. She was adopted up the dale. But Elizabeth couldn't stay there. Like I said—'

'Which dale?' Jack had no time for details, he got straight to the point.

'Why, Weardale, where else? Up above Frosterley. We went there once, me an' our Elizabeth. But the chap who took our Jenny, he was a rum 'un. According to our Elizabeth he—'

'What was the name of the farm?'

Jimmy pursed his lips. 'Nay, I can't remember. Up on the fells it was, though, a tumbledown sort of place, miles from anywhere.'

'Will you show me? We could motor up there today, it won't take long,' Jack insisted.

'I cannot,' Jimmy replied. 'How can I? I have to go on shift.'

'Take the shift off,' he said impatiently. 'You're leaving at the end of the week in any case.'

They had arranged for Jimmy to have special tuition from a retired schoolmaster in the town; he had to be able to pass the entrance standard for the grammar school.

'I can't, man, I can't let me marras down. With a putter short they'll not make the wages. Next week'll be different, they'll have another putter then.'

Jack had to give in. In any case, when he thought about it logically it would be almost dark by the time they got to Weardale and some of the roads on the moor were mere tracks, none of them properly made. The car would make heavy going of it, especially in the dark.

'When then? Saturday?' It was two days to Saturday, forty-eight hours to be got through somehow.

'Aye, all right. Saturday,' said Jimmy.

'I'll pick you up on the end of the rows, nine o'clock sharp,' said Jack. At least he was doing something now. The frustration of the last few weeks had been driving him slowly crazy.

*

Saturday morning was cold and rain drizzled down. In the gutters from the rows coaly water ran, dirty from where the miners' concessionary coal had been dumped in heaps for them to shovel into the coal houses when they came off shift. The back street of West Row was deserted. No washing lines were being put out, the wash would have to be dried inside today. A small child ran out of the end yard, crying, and stopped long enough to gape at the Austin tourer, his mouth open.

'Away wi' ye!' shouted his mother. 'I'm waiting for the messages!' The boy hunched his neck into the collar of his jacket and ran on, wiping his nose on the back of his hand. Jack considered shouting him back and offering him a lift but thought better of it as Jimmy came running out of Mrs Wearmouth's yard. He climbed into the passenger seat beside Jack, huddled up to escape the drops of water dripping from the canvas hood onto the celluloid weather protector above the door.

'Nasty day, sir,' he observed.

'Yes,' Jack replied. 'Give the starting handle a turn, will you? This weather's a bit hard on the starter motor.'

Jimmy did as he was asked, grinning in triumph as the engine spluttered into life. He was going to enjoy this ride up the dale anyroad, he thought. None of his marras had been in a motor car. And Jimmy was young enough to revel in the fact.

'By, it's grand, isn't it?' he commented as they rolled

along the lanes at a fairly steady speed of thirty miles an hour.

'You sure you can find the place?' asked Jack.

'Why aye, man,' said Jimmy, and Jack nodded, satisfied. Soon, very soon, he could be seeing Elizabeth. His pulse raced at the very thought.

Chapter Twenty-One

They drove into Frosterley at about half-past ten, the wheels throwing up droplets of water as they ran through puddles. But the sun was shining on the wet streets, lighting up the terraced rows which had been built in the first place for lead-miners and marble-quarriers.

'Now which way?' asked Jack, and Jimmy stared around him in dismay. He couldn't remember which way.

'We were walking,' he said lamely.

'Well, then, we'll stop the car and walk along the road. Do you not remember the name of the place at all?'

'Something Common, it was. And I think the man's name began with a P.'

They left the car and walked along the street. Women with shopping baskets over their arms and shawls on their heads gazed curiously at them. A butcher came to his shop doorway and watched their approach. Jack stopped before him.

'Morning,' he said, and the butcher nodded silently. 'Is there a common near here?' Jack asked.

The butcher stared at him stolidly and folded his arms across his striped apron. 'Bollihope Common, does tha' mean?'

'That'll be it. Was it, Jimmy?'

Jimmy nodded. The butcher pointed his thumb to the next opening between the houses. 'That road,' he said and went back into his shop.

'More of a track than a road,' said Jack as he drove the car up the bank side. He stopped and considered for a moment. 'I think I'll go into Stanhope and get on to the common from there,' he decided. 'It's bound to be a better road.'

Jimmy nodded. The track was full of holes and strewn with stones. In the car it seemed worse than when he had walked up it. Besides, he was enjoying the ride. Now the sun was out, Jack had put the hood back and the fresh moorland air, untainted by coal or coke gases, was like wine. By, life was good, the boy thought, allowing himself to feel happy and optimistic about his future after so many setbacks and disappointments in his life. He thought sadly of Tommy for a moment, how he would have loved this ride out. And there was Elizabeth, the daft lass. What a carry-on it was finding her. He'd give her what-for when he did, he would an' all.

In a farmyard beside the track, only a hundred or so yards from where Jack had turned the car around and gone back to the main road between Frosterley and Stanhope, Elizabeth was working as a labourer. She was cleaning out the hen house. It was back-breaking work. There was an accumulation of years of hen muck like a dry, hard carpet beneath her feet. She dug and shovelled and filled the barrow and took it outside to tip on the muck heap, forcing herself to go on and on until the floor was clear. She paused once, standing with her head cocked to one side. Was that the sound of a motor on the track? Of course she had seen motor cars before but never one here on the moor. She went to the gate, sparing herself a couple of minutes to look, but the car was disappearing around a bend in the track, going back to Frosterley. She went back to shovelling muck.

Jack drove the three or four miles into Stanhope, along the wide street to the market place with the old church in the corner watching over it. He parked by the church.

'May as well have some lunch,' he said to Jimmy. 'It's after twelve. Then we'll go on up. It's the Middleton road, I know it.'

They ate mutton pies from the baker's shop and drank dandelion and burdock pop, sitting in the comfortable leather seats of the car. Jimmy was young enough to stare with an air of superiority at the youngsters who came to touch and see. Afterwards, Jack drove them over the ford and up the other side to where the road was

264

joined by the track from Frosterley. Eventually, they found the path leading to Stand Alone Farm. Leaving the car on the road, they set off, walking through the heather. Just as well he'd brought a stick, Jack reflected. The terrain was very difficult for anyone, let alone a walker disabled as he was.

'It's deserted,' said Jack. They had knocked on the door, gone round the side and shouted, 'Anyone there?' to no avail.

'Aye,' agreed Jimmy. 'Though last time Jenny was locked in, poor bairn.'

'We may as well go back,' Jack decided. He leaned on his stick. His legs throbbed and ached with walking over the rough terrain. He had been so sure he would find Elizabeth. Now she wasn't here he felt that all the spirit had been knocked out of him and he was deathly tired.

'Leave a note,' Jimmy suggested. Jack tore a leaf from his diary and, resting it on his knee, wrote:

'Dearest Elizabeth, Jimmy and I came to see how you are. If you're here, please, please get in touch. I love you, Jack.'

He folded it in two and wrote her name on the outside then stuck it between the door and the jamb. They were halfway up the slope, going back to the car, when they were hailed.

'Hey, you! What do you think you're doing?'

'It's him. The fella from the farm,' said Jimmy.

'I'm looking for Elizabeth Nelson,' said Jack when the man reached them. In spite of his aching legs, he drew himself up to his full height and looked down his nose at Peart with a hauteur which would have been a credit to his mother. He felt an instant dislike for the man, standing there with his dog at his heels, gun broken over his arm, chin covered in greyish-brown stubble. There was an unpleasant smell coming from him. Jack recognised it from the trenches. His nostrils flared. This man hadn't washed in weeks, he reckoned.

'Are ye' now? An' what would ye' be wanting wi' me wife?' asked Peart, sticking out his chin aggressively.

'She's my sister,' said Jimmy, intervening quickly. 'An' so's Jenny. And I want to see them.'

'Well, you can't,' Peart replied sharply. 'Jen's at school and Elizabeth's out. I won't have you lot coming here pestering us, like.'

'Come on, Jimmy,' said Jack. 'We'd better go.' He was reeling with shock. He had to get away before he took this man by the neck and choked the life out of him.

'Aye, an' don't come back!' snarled Peart.

'You tell her to write to me,' said Jimmy. 'You tell her, do you hear?'

'Go to hell,' said Peart.

Elizabeth was working as a day labourer on the farm near Frosterley. Peart had come in one evening from his wanderings on the moor and as he was eating his supper had looked up, his mouth full of fried onions and meat. He had spluttered half-chewed food across the table.

'You're to start work the morn. Seven o'clock sharp, mind, the bloke said.'

Elizabeth had gazed at him in astonishment. 'What bloke?'

'The farmer, of course. Down by Frosterley, it is. So Jen can go wi' you for a couple of hours before she goes to that bloody school, then come back to you at four until you finish at six. Ten bob a week. Mind, I know how much you'll be getting so don't think you can keep any back. The lass'll get half a crown. Though, if I wasn't so bloody soft, she'd be working wi' you all day, never mind wasting time on book learning. The man has no wife and no labourer and now his lad's gone off and joined the army. So mind what I tell you, seven o'clock sharp.'

Elizabeth had stared at him dumbly. It was a good two miles away, she knew the farm he meant. 'But what about your supper?' she asked at last.

'I don't mind waiting till you get home,' he said magnanimously, and started to clean out his ear with a matchstick, inspecting it with interest before wiping it on his waistcoat.

Elizabeth walked across to where Jenny was sitting on the settle by the fire and sat down beside her. Her sister had been listening mutely to Peart. Now she slipped her hand in to Elizabeth's.

'Never mind,' she whispered. 'I'll help you when we get home, I will. I'll do the taties and that.'

Elizabeth squeezed her hand. 'I know you will, petal,' she whispered back. She sighed. Her body ached from Peart's attentions every night, her days were filled with work and she seemed no nearer to getting Jenny away from here. The one bright spot was that her sister was going to school now and, what was more, doing well. She never spoke of it when Peart was in the house but when the sisters were on their own she would chatter away to Elizabeth, telling her of the other girls she had met, how nice the teachers were, how they were all knitting socks for the soldiers at the front.

'I can turn a heel now,' she said. 'And I didn't drop a single stitch.'

'Well done! Oh, well done, Jenny,' Elizabeth exclaimed. She washed out Jenny's knickers and pinafore every night, staying up late to iron the pinafore because Jenny didn't have another one to change into. Clothes weren't really a problem, though, because most of the children came from hard up families in any case.

She didn't really mind going to work, thought Elizabeth after Jenny had gone up to bed. At least it meant time away from the dread of Peart coming home unexpectedly and demanding sex, no matter what she was doing. He didn't defer to her at all now; she supposed he thought he didn't have to. And he was back to his snide remarks about having to keep her and feed her and wasn't it time she was earning her own bloody keep? He would take her quickly and roughly, and if she tried to stop him he slapped her hands away and took her anyway.

At least Jenny is happier, she's going to school, Elizabeth told herself again. But she knew she should do something about the situation. She wasn't completely a doormat, was she? Yet she was so tired, so worn out. She would plan something tomorrow, when she felt better. Every day, every night, she thought about Jack. She dreamed they were together again and happy, Jack loving her, she loving him. But she knew it was just a dream. Any life she might have had with Jack Benson was over before it had had a chance to begin.

As Jack and Jimmy climbed into the Austin tourer, Peart was entering the back door of the farmhouse. He saw the note stuck in the door frame and took it out, taking it over to the window to read in the fading light. He smiled grimly. So the toff loved his Elizabeth, did he? He pictured the man, standing before him and looking at him as though he had just crawled out from under a stone. Well, he wasn't going to get what was Peart's, he damn' well wasn't. Peart grinned and crushed the note in his dirty hand, throwing it amongst the peat on the fire.

'She got married and didn't even tell us!' said Jimmy as he climbed back into the car after winding the starting handle. 'I can't believe it of our Elizabeth, I cannot.'

The captain said nothing. Jimmy glanced at him. Jack's knuckles gleamed white as they gripped the wheel, his face set and dark. The scar on his face, which somehow Jimmy had hardly noticed at all since he'd got to know Jack better, stood out in an angry red line surrounded by white.

'Mebbe he wasn't telling the truth,' the boy ventured.

Jack looked at him for a second, a cold, bitter look, but said nothing. They were both quiet all the way back to Bishop Auckland, Jack only speaking to ask Jimmy to get out and switch the headlights on as the electric switch in the car had failed.

'You haven't changed your mind about me going to school, have you?' Jimmy ventured at last. They were coasting down the main road from Wolsingham to Witton-le-Wear, not far from home now. He had been worrying about it all the way down the dale.

'What do you think?' asked Jack.

'I don't know, that's why I'm asking.'

'No, I haven't changed my mind. But you'll have to work like the blazes to catch up, you know.'

A wave of relief swept over Jimmy. He had been holding his breath for Jack's reply. 'I will, I promise I will,' he said. 'I'll do anything.' He looked over at Jack, grinning all over his face, but Jack hardly noticed.

He was staring into the dark, the meagre illumination from the gas streetlights casting ghostly shadows on rows of houses lining the road as they entered the town. His thoughts were a whirl of confusion: bitterness, fury at the fates which had led to this. And a sense of betrayal – why had Elizabeth married that dreadful man?

Jimmy felt guilty and didn't intrude on his companion's thoughts again. He knew he should be unhappy about his sister but if he was honest he had to say, all he could think of now was his future, whether he would fit in at the grammar school, if he could do the work. Elizabeth was married. So he hadn't liked her husband much, but there was nothing he could do about that, was there?

'Where have you been?'

As Jack opened the front door of the Manor, he was met in the hall by his mother who was obviously furious with him.

'Don't start, Mother,' he replied wearily.

'Don't start? Is that all you have to say? Here I've been, worried out of my mind wondering where you were. If anything had happened to you in that dreadful contraption you insist on going about in. Out of my mind, do you hear me?'

'I hear you, Mother.' Jack took off his hat and coat, looked at himself in the hall mirror, hardly recognising the hollow-eyed man staring back at him.

'Do you know, I've had Mr Dunne asking where you

were? He was expecting you at the mine, he said. Your father would never neglect to keep an appointment like that. Your father—'

'I'm sorry, Mother,' he said, his voice even, will-power keeping it so. 'If you don't mind, I think I'll go straight up now.'

'But aren't you at least going to have the courtesy to tell me where you've been? And what about supper? Have you eaten?'

'I don't want anything, Mother. I'm tired, I'll just go up, as I said.'

Olivia was left staring at his back as he disappeared up the staircase.

Once Jack had the bedroom door closed against the world, he flung off his clothes and got ready for bed mechanically. He sat on the side of the bed and unstrapped his feet, letting them drop to the floor any old how. He lay back on his pillows and closed his eyes.

Instantly, images of Elizabeth with that man rose to torture him. Why, oh, why, had she done it? Was it simply for a meal ticket for life? Or to be near the little sister Jimmy had mentioned? The questions ran round and round in his brain. He was filled with the hope-lessness of it.

It was all his fault too. If he'd done something about Wilson that first time, gone to the commanding officer, he could have had the man transferred, saved Elizabeth from being dismissed. He could have been there when she came looking for him. If only he had been! His fault, not his mother's. She had only done what was to be expected of any class-obsessed woman.

If only he'd spoken out, insisted Elizabeth marry him. Why had he hesitated? There were a thousand 'if onlys', but it was too late now. He turned over in bed restlessly. His legs hurt but at least it took his thoughts away from the greater agony in his mind. But not totally, nothing could do that. His life stretched before him: grey, dull, ugly, spoiled. And it was all his own fault.

Chapter Twenty-Two

'Jenny! Ah, Jenny—'

Jenny Nelson paused in her work to look around her. What was that? She pushed her thick hair back from her face, leaving a trail of mud on her forehead. Did someone speak or was it just a voice in the story she was telling herself in her mind? One of the stories she told herself all the time when she was out in the frozen fields, chopping away at the turnips – snagging them as the farmer called it – to provide extra feed for the sheep and cattle.

All was quiet, the field deserted. Nothing moved except the curl of smoke from the farmhouse in the distance, a dark stormy grey yet barely perceptible against the leaden colour of the sky. Where was Elizabeth? Jenny rose to her feet, as stiff as an old woman, after a couple of hours crouched on the hard, icy earth. Elizabeth could snag turnips standing up but Jenny had to get closer to them. After all, she was only ten, going on eleven, and her wrists were as thin as matchsticks, much like the rest of her.

'The lass doesn't look strong enough to snag turnips,' the farmer had said to Elizabeth that morning.

'But she is,' Elizabeth had replied. 'She's good at it an' all. Will she show you?'

Jenny had stood as tall as she could in her old black boots with the cardboard soles Elizabeth had cut for her only the night before. 'We'll get them soled in Frosterley on Friday, pet,' Elizabeth had said then. 'Both of us together. We'll make a deal of money in a week, me and you, see if we don't. And we'll buy tickets to Auckland, go to Morton Main . . . our Jimmy will help us.'

Jenny wasn't too sure about the money. In her experience they never did make as much as Elizabeth thought they would. But it would be grand to go on the train at last, as Elizabeth had always promised they would. See Jimmy. She could hardly remember him from the day he had come with her sister that very first time. But there had been a letter at Christmas and they had found it before Peart. He didn't like them to get letters.

Sighing, Jenny bent over her work. Elizabeth must have gone into the coppice at the side of the house, that was where she'd told Jenny to go when she had to answer a call of nature. Anyroad, she thought as she chopped the top from a mud-caked turnip, the farmer hadn't really cared whether she helped her sister or not. All he was interested in was that the work was done and done cheaply. As Elizabeth said, there was always farm work to be done and with the men away at the war, the farmers had to employ anyone they could get, no references needed here.

Peart didn't know they'd got this job. He thought Jenny was at school and Elizabeth out looking for work.

'I can't afford to keep you both,' he had snarled at them before he'd gone out that morning. Where he was going they didn't know, but lately when he'd gone he was out all day so Elizabeth said he would never know they were earning money and then they could actually keep it.

'Jenny? For God's sake, where are you, Jenny?'

She sprang to her feet this time. Oh, yes, that had been Elizabeth calling and by the sound of her there was something desperately wrong, she sounded funny. She began to run towards the coppice.

'Elizabeth? What's the matter?'

The cry burst from Jenny as she struggled under a straggling branch of hawthorn and saw her sister lying on the ground, hands clutching her belly, face whiter than the frosted leaves on the bushes around her. And even as she watched, Elizabeth's hands loosed their grasp and fell to the ground to either side, palms uppermost, open, fingers bent and broken nails pointing to the sky. Her eyes were closed and the only colour was in the pool of red soaking the earth around her, staining her patched working skirt. A stain which was growing wider even as Jenny watched for a frozen second before snatching up Elizabeth's old shawl which had caught on a bush and been pulled from her shoulders.

Jenny knelt by her, covering her with the shawl, taking the one from her own shoulders and pushing it under her sister's inert body. Frantically she tried to warm Elizabeth's hands, patted her cheeks.

'Elizabeth! Oh, Elizabeth!' she cried, a wailing desolate sound. And Elizabeth opened her eyes and looked at her and Jenny turned and ran for the farmhouse. The farmer's wife would be in even if the farmer wasn't.

The farmer's wife was not in; the back door was firmly closed. There was no sign of the farmer or his wife. Jenny was distraught, didn't know what to do. She hesitated, wringing her hands, then knocked again on the back door of the farmhouse. When there was no reply she went round to the front door which had that air of never having been opened. Jenny began to sob. She thought of running into Frosterley, but no, she knew in her heart there wasn't time for that.

'Sweet Jesus,' she prayed aloud, 'don't let Elizabeth die.' A cat mewed beside her, the rangy old farm cat. It rubbed itself against her legs and then, evidently deciding that Jenny was not going to feed it, stalked off to the open barn door where Jenny could hear kittens mewing excitedly. If she could only get Elizabeth into the barn, thought Jenny, she could cover her with hay, make her warm.

Elizabeth was not asleep, nor unconscious, nor yet awake. She had felt very cold a few minutes ago but now she was warmer. The pain in her belly was still there but somehow it was something apart from her altogether. She was floating somewhere, she wasn't sure . . . She was a bairn again, working in the field with her mother, they were snagging turnips. Only she had fallen down. She would have to get up and get on with the work because Mam wasn't very well and they needed the money now Da had run off. Mam was badly, she kept holding her back.

'What's the matter?' Elizabeth asked her. 'Mam, are you all right?'

'Just get on, Elizabeth,' her mother said, and Elizabeth got on her feet and found her snagger and bent over her work. But when she looked up, her mam was gone. Maybe she was in the little wood at the side. Elizabeth was working and working and Mam didn't come back. Maybe she was having a rest. Elizabeth worked on but then she thought she would go and find her mother and wandered over to the wood and something was moaning in there, an animal, it sounded like, caught in one of the farmer's traps. She went in under the trees but it wasn't an animal moaning at all, it was her mam. Elizabeth cried out, 'Mam! Mam!' in a desperate cry of panic and fear.

She came to with a start. Everything was whirling round her. She was in a wood, all right. After a minute she recognised it; it was the coppice by the side of the turnip field. For a moment she panicked. Oh, God, she was going to die, she was going to die just like her mam had died, out in the fields like an abandoned animal. And what would happen to Jenny then, who would look after her little sister?

'Somebody will.'

Elizabeth wasn't sure if the voice was real or in her head. But, strangely, she believed it. All she had to do was let go and she would float away. There was nothing to worry about now, nothing at all, because none of it mattered.

A blackbird was pecking about on the ground close to her head, its brightly coloured beak chipping at frozen leaves, turning them over. He must be finding something to eat, Elizabeth thought dreamily, though what, she couldn't imagine. Quietly she waited, not quite ready to go, but she would soon, in a minute. There was a patch of blue above her, a gap in the overhanging bushes. Another bird flew across, landing near. It was a hen blackbird. She too began pecking industriously at the floor. A drop of water fell on Elizabeth's face, splashing into her eyes so that she blinked. The ice was melting. Soon it would be spring, she thought, and closed her eyes and drifted off.

A sound filtered through, dragging her back to consciousness. It was a blackbird singing. Reluctantly, Elizabeth opened her eyes. She didn't want to wake up, no, she didn't. Still the blackbird sang so gloriously. There he was, sitting on an elder branch, a proud, perky little thing, puffing out his chest and singing to his mate, full of the promise of the spring which was coming.

'I'm not my mother,' Elizabeth said suddenly, barely above a breath but loud in her head. 'I'm me and I'm not going to die.'

'Elizabeth? Oh, Elizabeth, you're not dead, are you?'

It was Jenny. She was back, with a bogie, a low four-wheeled cart with a rope handle to pull it along which she'd found in the farmer's barn.

'I'm not dead. And I'm not going to be, pet,' said Elizabeth, her voice a little stronger. She was even able to help herself a little as Jenny pulled her onto the bogie and covered her with old sacks she'd brought from the meal house. Jenny was sobbing as she hitched the rope over her thin shoulder and pulled, leaning forward, almost bent double with the effort. Elizabeth wanted to tell her not to cry, not to worry, she had decided to live after all.

They reached the barn at last and Jenny made a nest in the hay, piling it round her sister then standing back to view her work, then bending to smooth hay and thick black hair away from Elizabeth's face.

'The farmer's out, you see, and the farmer's wife an'

all,' she said. 'I'll go down into Frosterley and get the doctor. Will you be all right, our Elizabeth?'

'I will, petal. I'm as warm as toast now, you've done grand.'

Jenny surveyed her doubtfully. Elizabeth had a half-smile playing around her mouth but she was so white, as white as the frost on the ground.

'I don't know if I can leave you.' The girl fretted and chewed her lip in indecision.

'Go on, I'll be all right now,' Elizabeth encouraged her, and Jenny ran out of the barn, boots clattering on the stones in the yard then fading into silence as she went down the road which led to the village. Elizabeth closed her eyes. She was tired, so tired.

She had lost the baby she didn't even know she was carrying. For a moment she mourned for it, but it was Peart's baby too, and she didn't want her baby to have Peart for a father, did she? Safe in the arms of Jesus, she thought. That was what someone had said when her mother died, and that was where her baby was too.

She knew she would get better now, she was no longer bleeding and, most important of all, she had the heart now, more than she had had for months, the heart to take charge of her own life and do something with it. Never again, she told herself, never again would Peart or any man use her without her consent. She was eighteen years old or very soon would be. A woman. She would shape her own life and look after Jenny while she was doing it.

'Hey, what's going on here?'

It was the farmer, Elizabeth didn't even know his name, she had been working in his fields for only a day.

'I . . . I took badly,' she said.

His round red face came closer as he squatted on his haunches and stared at her. 'Mind,' he said, his tone changing, 'you look it an' all. Hang on a minute, I'll get the wife.' He went to the door of the barn and hollered across the yard. 'Dot! Dorothy! Howay here a minute, will you?'

Within a very few minutes Elizabeth was installed on the sofa in the farmhouse kitchen. The room was warm from the fire which had been coaxed into a blaze in an instant and Dorothy, the farmer's wife, handed her a bowl of beef broth from the great iron pan on the bar and was encouraging her to eat it.

'Just a mouthful or two, lass, it'll put new life into you.' Dorothy, as fat and red-faced as her husband, hovered over her. 'A little more then, surely you can manage a little more? You'll never get better if you don't eat,' she said.

Elizabeth blushed as she thought of what the woman had done for her, changing her out of the blood-soaked clothes into one of her own nighties and giving her clean monthly clouts to keep her decent. By the time Jenny got back with the doctor, a broad, squat Scot from Glasgow, she already had a little colour in her cheeks as she lay, propped on pillows, looking a different woman from the one Jenny had left.

'Well,' he said, frowning heavily, 'I thought, judging by the lassie here, you were at death's door. I left my dinner to come up here, young woman.'

Jenny was unabashed. She was too busy grinning all over her face with relief as she gazed at her sister. The doctor examined Elizabeth, prodding her stomach hard and making her wince, asked about the blood loss, hummed and hawed with his fingers rubbing his chin.

'You've been a lucky lassie, I can tell you that,' he pronounced. 'I thought I'd have to take you into the cottage hospital, that's if I found you alive. But now . . .' He looked up inquiringly at the farmer's wife.

'She can bide here, the bairn an' all,' said Dorothy. 'That is . . . unless you would like to be taken home?' She gazed at Elizabeth then Jenny. Somehow, Dorothy didn't think either of them wanted to go home, wherever that was, though she had heard stories of that bugger Peart who was more pig than man having a fancy piece. By the look of dismay on the little 'un's face, though, if that was where they came from they certainly didn't want to go back. Dorothy smiled, satisfied, when Elizabeth assured her that they would love to stay here.

After all, it was lonely on the farm when her man was out working and it was going to be nice company for her.

A couple of days later, Peart appeared at the farm gate as the farmer was taking his two milking cows into the dairy.

'Have you seen owt of a young lass and a bairn – about ten, the bairn is?' asked Peart.

'No, I haven't,' snapped the farmer, looking him straight in the eye. 'An' I'll thank you to get out of my way, I have work to do.' Hell's bells, he thought, how had that nice young lass got herself tangled up with an excuse for a man like Peart? Neither use nor ornament he was, a disgrace to the dale.

Peart went on his way, shuffling and stoop-shouldered, his eyes bleary and his head thumping from the liquor he had consumed the night before.

It was ten days later when Elizabeth stood by the door of the farmhouse, Dorothy's second-best shawl on top of her clothes, the sovereign which the farmer had insisted on lending her safely secured in the inside pocket of her skirt.

'I'll never be able to thank you enough,' she said, leaning forward and kissing Dorothy's plump and weather-worn cheek. 'I promise you I'll write to you, just as soon as we're settled.'

'Aye, do that,' she answered. Then, unused to open expressions of sentiment, shouted over to the farmer, 'Hey, Alf! don't forget to fetch me sewing cotton from Stanhope, will you? One reel of black and one of white, think on, mind!'

'Aw, woman, I said I would, haven't you given me a list?'

'Aye, well, see that you do. And mind yourself an' all.' It was their usual way of saying farewell.

At Stanhope, Alf took Elizabeth and Jenny down the hill to the station, bought their tickets to Bishop Auckland and saw them onto the train. Elizabeth's heart was beating painfully. At any minute she expected Peart to walk into the station and grab Jenny, if only as a way of forcing them both back to Stand Alone Farm. She felt like hiding on the train rather than leaning out of the window to speak to the kindly farmer, but she forced herself.

'I'm grateful, Alf,' she said. 'You'll never know how grateful for all you've done for us. I'll write, I promise I'll write.'

The engine was getting up steam, the guard had his flag at the ready. Alf stood back, smiling broadly. 'Aye, be sure you do, mind, Jenny an' all. Or Dorothy's going to be awful disappointed.' The train began to move. He walked after it. 'Mind yourselfs, you two lasses!' he cried over the sound of the engine as it chugged away. Elizabeth could hardly see him for the steam which swirled around and enveloped him.

They sat back in their seats, Jenny's small face showing her excitement and delight. After all, this was the first time she had been on a train; she had never been further down the dale than Frosterley in all her young life.

'It goes fast, doesn't it?' she said, and the two soldiers in the carriage looked at each other and grinned. A woman with a large basket on her knees took an apple from under the cover and handed it to Jenny who went pink with gratification. She sat, holding it in her hand, until Elizabeth told her she could go on and eat it.

Elizabeth sank back in her seat and gazed out of the window. She had only a hazy idea of what she was going to do when she got back to Bishop Auckland, though she did want to see Jimmy. She refused to let herself think about Jack, though she was acutely aware that she was getting ever nearer to him. The familiar lump came into her throat as she thought of him. Jack, oh, Jack. Why had he acted the way he did?

Chapter Twenty-Three

The Saturday before Elizabeth and Jenny started their new life, Jack was standing on Darlington Station seeing Jimmy Nelson off on his great adventure. The train to London was late, the station crowded with men in uniform, tearful families gathered around them.

'I don't know why Elizabeth didn't write back,' said the boy. 'I wrote and told her I'd got the scholarship to Dartmouth. I thought she would have written back.'

'Maybe she didn't get the letter? The post can be erratic these days when most of the real postmen are in the army,' Jack replied.

'It's the only thing that worries me,' said Jimmy. 'It would have been nice to know how she was doing.'

'I'll do my best to find out,' promised Jack. 'I'll go up to Bollihope Common and insist on seeing her, I promise you.'

His emotions were mixed: excitement at having an

excuse to go to Stand Alone Farm, actually see Elizabeth, and dread at seeing her married to that man, maybe with a baby in her arms and another on the way. At the thought he was filled with pure jealousy. How could he bear it if that was the case? He gazed along the platform to where the track curved on its way from Durham and Newcastle. He pretended he was watching for the train to cover up his emotions.

'Another ten minutes, the stationmaster said,' Jimmy reminded him. 'A delay at Durham.'

Jack turned and smiled at him. 'Yes, I know.'

Jimmy had been so keen to get the scholarship to the Royal Naval College at Dartmouth, and Jack had to admit he had worked all hours to achieve it. Only a few months after gaining entrance to the grammar school at Auckland he had taken the examinations and won the place. The school was enormously proud of him. At least he had made it possible for Elizabeth's brother to get where he wanted, thought Jack. Something he had done in the first place for Elizabeth's sake, though now he felt it had been totally worthwhile for the boy's sake alone. Jimmy had proved himself not only to be above average intelligence but also to have an incredible capacity for hard work. It made Jack wonder if there were other boys in his mine who, given the chance, could go on to make their mark on the world. Perhaps he could award an annual scholarship, a modest one just to the grammar school. Say a hundred pounds a year.

Jack sighed. He thought of his mother only that morning at breakfast, how she had done her best to denigrate the boy's achievement.

'Mark my words, it's a waste of tax-payers' money,' she had said. 'How could a boy from a pit family ever come to anything in the navy? Even if he does manage to graduate, the other officers won't like it. Blood will out, I'm telling you. A pit lad does not make a leader of men and he'll fall on his face. Then you'll be sorry you helped him.'

Jack did not bother to answer her, remind her of Peter Lee, the great miners' leader. And there were others. There wasn't time anyway, he had Jimmy to pick up to take to Darlington. He had to report to Dartmouth by six o'clock that evening.

'Well, don't forget I've invited Dolly Hope and her parents round for dinner this evening,' said Olivia. 'I expect you to be nice and talk to the girl. She just needs bringing out of her shyness, Jack. And don't forget, she's an heiress in her own right. Her grandfather left her those farms in Northumberland and people say she has ten thousand a year besides.'

'I won't forget,' he said grimly. He had at last learned not to argue with his mother, just not to take too much notice of her either. It made for a quieter life. Now, travelling back from Darlington, he had to wait at the level crossing at Heighington; the local train from Bishop Auckland was coming through. He thought about going up to Bollihope Common. Perhaps he could go today, not go home, drive up to Stanhope now. Suddenly he was filled with a sense of urgency. Silly really, he told himself. How could it be urgent? Elizabeth had a husband to look after her, hadn't she? Not much of one but a husband nevertheless. He glanced up as the train went rushing by, the windows of the compartments flashing in the sun. It was quite full, he noticed, but then they always were since the beginning of the war. He sat up straighter and blinked. There was Elizabeth! He had seen her plainly, sitting by the window, her face close to the glass, watching the vehicles waiting at the crossing: a pony and trap, a Thornycroft lorry with an open cab, the driver hunched over the wheel, and the Austin tourer. It was only a second and then she was gone. The train chugged off round the bend, heading for Darlington.

He was really in a bad way, Jack told himself, if he was seeing her face everywhere he looked. Only a few days ago he had seen a girl with black hair walking down Newgate Street a few yards before him and had been sure it was Elizabeth. He'd run after her and touched her arm, and the girl had stopped, and of course it wasn't Elizabeth but someone entirely different.

The gate of the level crossing opened and he followed the lorry across. He drove on until he came to the turnoff which led up to Weardale. At Frosterley he bought himself a pie and a bottle of pop as he had done that day he and Jimmy had gone up to Stand Alone

Farm. He sat in the car and ate the pie and drank a mouthful of the pop then set off to drive to the lonely farm on the moor.

Earlier that morning, Elizabeth walked with Jenny from Bishop Auckland to Morton Main. It was just the same as it had always been, she thought – the rows of miners' houses, the chapel at the end of one row, the inscription above the door carved in the stone: Primitive Methodist Chapel, 1889. Beyond the houses the slag heap towered, with the engine house and winding wheel beside it inside the pit yard. It seemed like another life when she had last seen it.

Walking down West Row to Mrs Wearmouth's house, she could have sworn the same tea towels were on the washing lines, the same hopscotch bays marked out in the back street in yellow, for they were marked out with bits of sandstone as chalk was hard to come by. Even the children playing looked the same.

They walked up the yard and knocked on Mrs Wearmouth's door, Elizabeth wondering apprehensively if she would be welcome. After all, there was the old scandal of her abrupt departure from Newcomb Hall.

She needn't have worried. When Mrs Wearmouth opened the door her face broke into a welcoming smile.

'Eeh, lass, you're a sight for sore eyes!' she cried. 'Howay in and let's have a good look at you.' Opening the door wide she led the way into the kitchen. 'I'll have the tea made in a couple of shakes, the kettle's just on the boil,' she went on. With the teapot in one hand and the spoon in the other as she spooned tea leaves, she suddenly noticed Jenny, hiding behind Elizabeth's skirts.

'An' who's the little lass?' She looked closer. 'She reminds me of somebody, I'm not sure . . . Eeh, don't tell me it's little Jenny? It's not, is it? Are you Jenny Nelson, pet?'

Jenny nodded her head gravely, acknowledging that she was. She caught hold of Elizabeth's skirt, as a timid toddler might catch hold of her mother's. Oh, dear, thought Elizabeth. I'll have to try to bring her out of her shyness and before she gets much older too. She spared a bitter thought for Peart. He had a lot to answer for.

'I've got fairy cakes in the pantry, Jenny. I just made them yesterday but now Jimmy's gone away I don't know who's going to help me eat them. Do you think you could manage one?'

'Jimmy's away? Where? I thought he must be on fore shift,' she broke in.

'Did he not write to you? I'm sure he did, he asked me for an envelope,' Mrs Wearmouth said, her brow knitted. 'Just a minute, I'll see to the bairn and make the tea and then we'll talk.'

When they were settled round the table with Jenny nibbling at a sweet bun and Elizabeth barely able to contain her impatience, the older woman took a sip of tea and sat back.

'A lot's been happening since you went away, lass,' she said. 'Jimmy left the pit and went to the grammar school, did you not know?'

'Left the pit?' Elizabeth was stupefied.

'It's a shame you missed him an' all, he just went to Dartmouth this morning. Away wi' the larks they were.'

'Dartmouth?' Elizabeth repeated.

Mrs Wearmouth looked irritable. 'What's the matter? Can you not understand or something? Repeating everything I say.'

'I'm so surprised,' said Elizabeth. 'I came to see our Jimmy today and you say he's gone to Dartmouth? Why on earth has a young lad like him gone there? Do you mean the Dartmouth in Devon?'

'Where else? Eeh, I thought you'd be over the moon about it, I did an' all. The lad got a scholarship to that Naval College, that's why. I must say, I'm surprised he didn't let you know.'

'I . . . I moved. If he wrote I didn't get the letter.'

'Jimmy said you were married?'

'No, I'm not married,' said Elizabeth and blushed. She looked at Jenny, still nibbling at the edge of her cake. 'I stayed up the dale for Jenny's sake, she needed me.'

'Oh, I see.'

Mrs Wearmouth gazed thoughtfully at her. 'You don't look too clever yourself, pet,' she remarked. 'Have you been badly?'

'I was but I'm better now. I'm looking for work. I

thought I could stay here, if you'd have me. Find something nearby.'

'Eeh, lass, I'm sorry, I'm giving this place up, going to live with my sister over by the coast. With Tommy gone, you know, and now Jimmy . . . I'm getting on. It's lonely. Your aunt doesn't come over to see me very often neither. Too wrapped up in your Kit, she is. I know Jimmy was bothered about leaving me but he's done well, I wouldn't stand in his way for the world. He was that excited this morning when he went for the train. By, you must be proud of the lad, eh?'

'I am. Oh, I am.' said Elizabeth, though she was still bewildered as to how Jimmy had even got the chance to go to the grammar school never mind be able to afford to take up a scholarship. The Naval College, for goodness' sake? It was another world.

'I tell you what, though,' the older woman said suddenly. 'I had a letter this morning from my niece in Darlington. She was saying how hard it was to get staff.' She looked speculatively at Elizabeth. 'She has a boarding house along Albert Hill way. I'm sure she'd jump at the chance of having you, there'd be a room an' all . . .'

An hour later, Elizabeth and Jenny were back on the station platform at Bishop Auckland, having caught the bus only by racing after it, a letter from Mrs Wearmouth to her niece, written in record time, clutched in her hand. This was her chance and she wasn't going to let it go by, not if she could help it. Surely, with a recommendation from her aunt, the niece in Darlington would not go checking up on her previous employers? Jenny clutched her hand, looking white and bewildered.

'Don't worry, petal,' said Elizabeth, trying reassure her. 'Everything's going to be fine now, you'll see. You'll like it in Darlington, I promise you will.'

The train came and she quailed a little when she realised it had come down from Weardale but hurried the child into a compartment, telling herself that of course Peart wouldn't be on the train and even if he was she could handle him. Before long they were on their way.

It was only as she sat looking out of the window at the fields and villages flying past that she had time to think about Jimmy again. How had he managed to do what he had done? A scholarship was all very well and she knew he was bright enough to gain one, but he had to live in the meanwhile and Mrs Wearmouth only had her pension. They had left that morning, Mrs Wearmouth had said. Who were *they*?

As the train puffed past the level crossing at Heighington, Elizabeth watched the queue waiting by the closed gates. A pony and trap, a lorry and . . . yes, it looked like the car which had been on the road above the farm one day ages ago. But there wasn't time to check, the train had passed now, and soon they would be in Darlington and they could start their new life. Nothing was going to go wrong this time, she wouldn't let it, she told herself fiercely. By her side, Jenny had fallen into a doze, leaning against her sister. Elizabeth cuddled her, made her head comfortable in the crook of her arm. The poor little lass was tired out. But it was worth it. Optimism rose in Elizabeth. They weren't just going to be all right, they were going to be successful and happy, and Jenny too could go to the grammar school if she wanted to.

Chapter Twenty-Four

The room Elizabeth and Jenny shared was on the top floor of the boarding house in Albert Hill. There were views right across the town from the window and Jenny loved to sit on the deep window seat and gaze out towards the Cleveland Hills. She could sit and stare for hours, Elizabeth reckoned.

'Do your homework, Jenny,' she said one sunny evening when the hills in the distance were just dark shadows in a blue haze. 'Come on. How about your French? I'll sit with you, help you with your irregular verbs if you help me with the pronunciation.'

The trouble was all her young life Jenny had been used to the moors with their endless horizons, the wide, undulating vistas which had been all around Stand Alone Farm. She fretted if she couldn't see the far horizon.

'Will you take me to Guisborough on Saturday if it's fine?' asked Jenny. 'Oh, please. We can take a picnic, it won't cost much, just the bus fare.' She looked at Elizabeth with those big hazel eyes and Elizabeth felt her heart melting. 'You know I have to work on Saturdays,' she said. 'The shop is busy then.'

'All right, Sunday,' Jenny insisted and Elizabeth nodded.

'After Sunday School. But mind, we can't afford to spend any money. It'll be just a walk and a picnic'

'Oh, yes, I know,' said Jenny, her eyes alight now she had got her way.

Elizabeth smiled. Somehow the moors were part of Jenny; she knew that when they got to Guisborough all the girl would want to do would be to walk as far as they could up on to the North York Moors. They had been in Darlington for almost a year and Jenny was settled into the grammar school and doing well too, though she had had to work hard to get there. But Jenny was no stranger to hard work, thought Elizabeth now, as she watched her sister take her books from her leather schoolbag and set to work.

She herself was learning fast too. Everything which Jenny learned at school, Elizabeth learned in the evenings, often sitting up late at night after her sister had gone to bed. But French pronunciation was something she couldn't learn from books, not properly.

Elizabeth got on well with Laura Hicks, her landlady. When she had first arrived at the boarding house she was grateful to be taken in on the strength of the letter from

Mrs Wearmouth. She'd worked hard and long hours but it hadn't taken her long to realise that she wanted more than working as a maid, of all work, in a boarding house catering mostly for working men.

'I'll work for you on my day off,' she'd told Laura finally, 'if that's all right with you? But I really want to work in a fashion shop and now I have the chance of getting into Anderson's.'

'Eeh, don't worry, pet,' Laura had replied. 'Now I've got Mona coming in from next door, I'll manage.' Mona had just left school. She was a big girl with plump cheeks and a permanently cheerful smile. 'She hasn't a lot on top,' Laura went on, 'but she's willing.' She'd looked thoughtful. 'I tell you what, you work for me in your time off and you can have that room rent-free. I'd have a job renting it anyway, up at the top of the house like that. If I let it to one of the men from the factory, chances are he'd fall down the stairs one Friday night after they'd all been on the beer.'

'Oh, are you sure?'

'Why not? Anyroad, I like you being here, you and the little lass. Gives the house a bit of class, having a kid in grammar school uniform going in and out.' She laughed comfortably. Laura had been almost as pleased as Elizabeth when Jenny had passed the scholarship. She had no children of her own, and her husband was in the army: 'Not in the trenches, thank God,' she had said to Elizabeth when she'd first come. So the boarding-house keeper was more relaxed than most army wives, smiling and cheerful and always looking forward to the weekends when her husband had leave.

Elizabeth loved working at Anderson's. She found she had a natural flair for choosing clothes that would sell. The shop had a section for bespoke customers and dresses too and Elizabeth was fast learning to use the sewing machines and often lent a hand in the finishing of garments.

Mrs Anderson, a lady in her sixties, would take Elizabeth with her to the fashion houses in Newcastle and Harrogate, deferring more and more to her assistant's judgement. She had a feel for cloth too, instinctively picking out the best fabrics: sheer silks, fine tweeds and linens. Even in the fourth year of war there were still good fabrics to be bought, at a price, of course. And some of Anderson's customers could afford the prices. Darlington, in its small way, was a boom town since the war.

They were happy there, she and Jenny, Elizabeth mused. Jenny was at last coming out of her shell. She had begun to speak to the other girls at school, was even invited to a birthday party. It wasn't the invitation which pleased Elizabeth so much as the fact that Jenny went instead of being overtaken by a fit of shyness and refusing. But still her eyes had a faraway look in them sometimes and Elizabeth knew that in her imagination she was running through the heather of her beloved moors.

On Sunday they caught the bus to Guisborough, one of the new covered buses which carried as many as twenty-four passengers and had a roof on top. Elizabeth carried a basket with egg sandwiches and a bottle of liquorice-flavoured water and an umbrella, just in case. It was, after all, only April and though they were going through a warm period, there was a possibility of rain.

There was only one bus on Sundays. It returned at five-thirty, so as it was twelve by the time they got to the old market town, the ancient capital of Cleveland, they had plenty of time for a walk. They found a footpath behind the old priory, the impressive arch of which stood bare and gaunt against the sky, the outlines of the church and monastery the monks had built so long ago still there, marked out in stone.

'It's nice, isn't it, Elizabeth?' said Jenny as she half-skipped up the bank out of the town. Around them the fields were beginning to green with the promise of summer; there were daffodils poking their heads out from beneath hedges, just coming into bloom.

'Yes, it is,' Elizabeth answered.

They walked until they reached the edge of Guisborough Moor before finding a spot in the lee of a stone wall to eat their sandwiches and drink their liquorice water. Around them the moor was peaceful; even the lambs with their mothers were fairly quiet, almost as if they knew it was Sunday. Elizabeth leaned back against the wall and closed her eyes, breathing in deeply of the sharp upland air. It tasted fresh and clean, no hint of coal smoke or smelting iron and steel which was usual in Darlington, so usual that it almost went unnoticed. Jenny picked a blade of grass and blew through it, producing a whistling sound. She smiled secretly, delighted with herself. Elizabeth just caught the edge of the smile as she opened her eyes at the sound.

Inevitably, for even after all this time it still happened with her, Elizabeth thought of Jack. How he was, what he was doing, if he had grown more accustomed to his wooden feet, if he ever thought of her. Or was it as his mother had said that awful day, the one which stood out in her memory, the horror-filled day when she had gone to the Manor to see him and ask for his help and his mother had told her he didn't want to see her ever again? A stab of pain went through Elizabeth at the memory, a stab of pain so familiar to her now yet as agonising as the first time. She moved restlessly and opened her eycs. Jenny had wandered away to a small hillock across the field and was gazing out over the moor, the brown heather just beginning to bud.

'Come on, Jenny,' Elizabeth called. 'We're going on now.' She stood and packed the remains of the picnic in the basket. Obediently Jenny came running, her hazel eyes bright and a pink blush on her cheeks from the fresh air. Her legs, growing long and coltish now, flashed over the ground and the bright black plait of her hair flew out behind her.

'We might see pheasants an' all,' she said as peewits skimmed the ground, calling their plaintive cry.

Or maybe a nesting pair of blackbirds, thought Elizabeth, as a lark rose to the sky, singing its heart out. A blackbird's song was the sweetest. They walked on, across the moor, keeping to an ancient pack trail until, reluctantly, they had to turn for Guisborough and home.

'It was a lovely day,' said Jenny as she leaned against Elizabeth on the bus, her eyelids drooping sleepily. 'It's not Weardale but it *is* nice.'

Jack drove up the Great North Road, Dolly Hope by his side. He glanced at her. She sat with her handkerchief pressed against her lips; every few moments she dabbed her eyes with it, sighing audibly. Her eyes were red with crying, her nose red and blotchy. Her black silk dress, the newer, shorter length, had ridden up and was showing her bony knees. She looks a sight, he thought, and was immediately struck with compunction. The poor girl had just lost her father. Jack was taking her to her aunt and uncle's home in Hexham.

'Jack will you take you, my dear,' his mother had insisted, 'of course he will. He has nothing else to do, have you, Jack?'

'As a matter of fact—' he'd begun, but Olivia had shot him a warning glance full of daggers and interrupted smoothly.

'I'm sure he'll be pleased to, *won't you*, Jack?'

He had been going to say that he had arranged to go over the books of the farm tomorrow morning but he kept quiet. After all, a drive up to Northumberland wouldn't hurt him.

So here he was, driving past Durham City, automatically looking over to the peninsula and the imposing view of the cathedral as everyone did, and wishing with all his heart that the next hour or two were over and he was safely on his way back to Bishop Auckland.

'You can take the opportunity to get to know the girl better, Jack,' Olivia had said, almost as a command. 'I'm sure you could use the hours alone with her in a car to show her you care about her and will look after her. That's all a girl like that wants, Jack, a well-brought up, sheltered girl like Dolly. And in the emotional state she's in . . .'

The implication was, Jack thought grimly as he passed by Framwellgate Moor and Pity Me and headed for Chester-le-Street, that he should take advantage of the girl when she was vulnerable and bully her until he got her promise to marry him.

He didn't want to marry Dolly and reckoned it was a fair bet she didn't want to marry him. At least she hadn't shown the slightest inclination towards him, no matter what hopeful signs his mother saw in her attitude. When she had been invited to dine with them at the Manor she had come and sat through the meal saying barely a syllable, hardly even looking at him.

'She's shy,' Olivia had declared. 'She'll get over that. You can draw her out of it, Jack.'

In his heart, he thought she was about as interested in him as he was in her, which was hardly at all. It was all in his mother's mind, he thought, and smiled mirthlessly.

'Would you like to stop at all, call at an inn to refresh yourself?' Jack said delicately.

Dolly stared at him, her pale blue eyes large, even with their lids puffy from weeping. 'No, thank you,' she whispered. 'I would rather just get on. Unless you wish to stop, of course?'

Jack shook his head. He drove on in silence, taking the turn west which led to Hexham. The road was a little quieter than the Great North Road but not much. Dolly began to sit up and take notice of the countryside around her. Her tears dried and a half-smile played around her mouth. Jack was faintly surprised; until he remembered that of course she had spent a lot of her young life in Northumberland, not far from Hexham, when her grandparents were alive. They turned off the main road before they came to the town, onto a track pointed out by Dolly. Here Jack had perforce to drive more slowly for the track was not paved and though it was reasonably straight and the worst of the ruts had been filled in with stones, nevertheless the springs of the Austin squeaked and groaned in protest. They hadn't gone far along it when a lone horseman came into view, cantering towards them on a big grey. A cavalry officer, Jack was interested to notice, and slowed the car to a snail's pace just in case the grey should take fright, ready to stop if need be. He was so concerned about the reaction of the horse to the automobile that at first he didn't notice the change in his charge.

Dolly was sitting forward, lips parted, eyes shining. She rubbed hastily at her cheeks, wiping away any trace of tears, sniffed daintily and patted at the hair showing below her cartwheel hat.

'Hallooo there!'

The cavalry office cantered up to the car as Jack applied the brakes to bring it to a halt. The horse pranced about for a second or two and the officer cried, 'Steady now, steady,' expertly controlling the grey which finally stood still, snorting.

As an entrance meant to impress a young lady, thought Jack, it could not be beaten. He couldn't help smiling as he at last took notice of Dolly who was blushing a becoming pink; even the effects on her eyelids of all the weeping she had done seemed less obvious now. She was smiling tremulously, putting back her veil over her hat.

'Oh, Percy, Percy!' she breathed.

'Dearest Dolly!' cried the officer. He dismounted gracefully from the grey and stepped over to the car. Putting one brilliantly polished riding boot on the running board, he leaned forward and took her hand, kissing it with a flourish.

Jack started to chuckle and quickly covered it up with a cough. Percy, as Dolly had called the officer, looked up.

'Dolly, aren't you going to introduce me to your friend?' he asked politely.

'Oh, I'm sorry,' she said, all confusion. 'This is Captain Benson, one of my father's . . . our neighbours in Auckland.' Her lips trembled as she remembered her father's passing.

'You poor darling,' Percy murmured, before holding out his hand to Jack. 'Lieutenant Writeson at your service, sir. How do you do?'

'Well, thank you,' Jack replied, and smiled at the earnest young man. 'On leave, are you?'

'Yes, sir. From France. I was coming down to Durham to see Dolly when I heard . . . Your aunt told me you were coming this morning, Dolly.' He grinned and suddenly looked of an age for the sixth form, thought Jack, feeling old and jaded beside him.

'Oh, how clever of you to know when we would get here!' cried Dolly.

'Not really, I've been up and down the lane three times already this morning,' he admitted.

'Well, shall we get on?' Jack suggested gently. 'I would like to get home by two, I have an appointment this afternoon.'

Later, he drove back on the Edinburgh to Darlington road, the undulating hills through Riding Mill and

Castleside which tested his brakes to the limit. But the views were spectacular, the countryside glorious and Jack felt like a change anyway. He laughed aloud as he thought of his mother. She had worked so hard to bring Dolly and him together, woven plans of how they would marry and settle down near her. She could hold on to the Manor if Jack had Dolly's estates, and everything would work out satisfactorily for her. Oh, dear, what a nasty shock she was about to receive.

The young couple were so happy, it was obvious to anyone that they were in love and would probably marry as soon as the war was over, which surely couldn't be long now? How lucky they were, thought Jack, his expression sobering. He wondered how Elizabeth was faring. Was she all right in that place in the wilds of Bollihope Common?

Stand Alone Farm, he mused. There were a few farms with similar names dotted around the north, dating from the time of the Enclosures when common land was fenced off and small farmers who had always lived in villages were forced to live on the patch of land they farmed. There was Once Seen and Never Seen, even a No Place. Jack smiled wryly. They had a sense of humour at least, those old farmers. But how lonely they must have been.

Almost as lonely as he was himself, he thought, in a rare burst of self-pity. Oh, Elizabeth, Elizabeth. He hadn't seen her when he went up to the moor that second time a year ago. Just that oaf of a husband of hers.

'Get off my land,' the man had said. His gun was broken over his arm but he had snapped it shut threateningly.

'Stop pestering us. Anyroad, it's none of your business what letters my lass gets.'

'Ah, but does she receive her letters?' Jack persevered. 'Her brother wrote—'

'I've warned you!' Peart had shouted, abruptly angry. 'If she got a letter from her brother, that's her business. If she doesn't want to answer, that's her business an' all! An' she doesn't want to see anybody, do you hear? Now get lost, will you?'

Jack had retreated. He had had to face the fact that Elizabeth didn't want to see him. They were standing in the yard, she must have heard the commotion. If she'd wanted to see him she would have come out.

Peart watched him disappear up the track, using his stick as a lever, walking with a stiff gait. Then he swore at Snuff and aimed a kick at him which the dog was able to evade. They went into the house, where the fire was out, no dinner cooking. Peart was filled with rage. Aye, but he'd find the pair of them, those bitches, and he would drag them back by the hair on their heads, he would an' all.

Now, as he drove through Witton-le-Wear on the last lap for home, Jack went over the confrontation with Peart in his mind. The man had been more unkempt, dirtier than ever. There was no smoke rising from the chimneys of the house . . . A thought struck him. Was Elizabeth even there? Or was Peart bluffing him? He would find out, he vowed to himself he would.

He had written to Jimmy to find out if he had had any word at all from his sister. But Jimmy had not replied as yet, which was strange for he wrote dutifully every week normally.

It was possible that the boy was at sea and Jack worried about that. There were U-boats lurking round the British coast, he knew, it was reported in the papers often enough. The boy sailors from Dartmouth did go to sea as part of their training. But surely Jimmy was too young?

Jack drove the car into Morton Main and the colliery yard. It was two o'clock and time for his appointment with Mr Dunne. He refused to worry about Jimmy, of course he was too young to go to sea. But at the back of his mind a thought lurked. If Jimmy had, and anything happened to him, then he, Jack Benson, would be to blame for he had encouraged the boy.

Chapter Twenty-Five

The war was over. 'Is it true?' Laura asked as rumours swept through the town. Elizabeth could only nod her head.

'In three months of epic fighting the British armies in France have brought to a sudden and dramatic end the great wearing-out fight of the last four years . . .' So the Commander in Chief of the British Forces, Field Marshal Haig, was reported as stating in his Despatch. The Armistice was signed on November 11th, 1918 and people poured into the streets to celebrate in joy and relief.

'What does Armistice mean? What will happen?' asked Jenny. She could scarcely remember when there hadn't been the war with Germany.

'There'll be no more fighting, the soldiers will come home,' Elizabeth replied. And Jimmy will be safe, she thought in her heart.

They had a street party. Laura made cakes and pies and Elizabeth sliced bread and made sandwiches. The women put trestle tables up in the road along the streets of Albert Hill. Union Jacks hung from most of the windows; red, white and blue bunting was strung across the streets like so much colourful washing.

But the men were slow to come home, most of them not arriving until 1919. In the end, the people of Darlington went back to work and the women worried about their jobs, for now the men were coming back there would be no place for them.

Elizabeth was busy. Everyone wanted the new shorter skirts and those who could afford it came to Anderson's to be measured for costumes with a figure-hugging skirt and tailored jacket. She was taking over the running of the shop more and more these days for Mrs Anderson, who had lost her only son in the early days of the war, was becoming sadder and more wan-looking every day.

'What was it all about?' she asked Elizabeth one day. There was a lull in the shop and she was standing in the doorway which led to the workshop at the back. Elizabeth was turning up a hem by hand, putting tiny feather stitches along it which would not be seen on the outside of the garment but would be strong enough not to break or come out with wear.

Elizabeth looked up from her work, knowing exactly what the older woman meant. Here she was herself, thankful that the war had come to an end before Jimmy was old enough to get involved, when there were so many women like Mrs Anderson who had lost husbands and sons. German women too, she mused.

'Come and sit down, Mrs Anderson, you look all in.' Elizabeth put her work aside and moved towards the older woman, putting an arm around her and leading her to a chair. 'I'll make a cup of tea, shall I? It's five to twelve anyway, I'll close the shop early for dinner.'

Mrs Anderson allowed herself to be led without protest; indeed, as Elizabeth touched her she could feel the heat rising from her through the layers of clothing. She looked closer, concerned. This was more than a moment of grieving. Mrs Anderson's eyes were febrile and even as she watched, a fine sheen of moisture appeared on her brow.

'You're running a fever!' Elizabeth exclaimed. 'Can't you feel it?'

'I don't feel too good,' the older woman admitted.

'I must get you home and into bed,' said Elizabeth. 'Who is your doctor?' A fever was not something to be trifled with, it could be anything and the thought of what it might be filled Elizabeth with dread.

'No, no doctor,' said Mrs Anderson. 'Just let me rest awhile. I'll be right as rain after, you'll see. I'm never ill, never had a day off work in my life. I'm just tired.'

She was still protesting in a weak, fretful sort of way when the shop bell tinkled.

'Oh, blow!' said Elizabeth. 'A minute more and I'd have had the closed sign up.'

'Go and see whoever it is, I'll be perfectly all right,' insisted Mrs Anderson.

'Sure?' Elizabeth didn't like leaving her.

'Go on.'

It was a woman who'd come to pick material for one of the new skirts. She hovered over them, choosing first one design and then another. 'What do you think?' she twittered, and Elizabeth forced herself to apply her mind to the choice though she felt like screaming at her to get on with it or go away. Her ears were attuned to the back room, listening for any sound from her employer.

She unrolled a fine tweed, picked off the shelf at random. 'What do you think of this?' she asked, her fingers smoothing the cloth. 'I can have it made up by next Monday, madam,' she said, when suddenly there was a crash from the back room, a smothered scream and then silence. Leaving the customer in the shop Elizabeth ran through the doorway, brushing past her chair with the half-hemmed skirt, knocking it heedlessly to the floor.

'Mrs Anderson! Mrs Anderson!'

The figure on the floor was still and steam was rising from her skirt and one leg, which was sticking out where the skirt had ridden up as she fell. Elizabeth knelt by her side and lifted her head. Her eyes were closed, she was white as a sheet. Elizabeth bent her ear to her mouth. Mrs

Anderson was breathing; barely, but breathing. Thank God she wasn't dead.

'Can I help?'

The customer was in the doorway, craning her head forward, avid with curiosity.

'Get a doctor, now!' shouted Elizabeth and the woman scuttled away, the shop door opening and closing behind her. Elizabeth turned back to her employer. She glanced at her leg. Mrs Anderson had been wearing cotton stockings under her long skirt but still she had scalded her shins. The kettle was lying on its side on the floor in a pool of still steaming water. When it boiled Mrs Anderson must have felt well enough to make the tea. The pot was still clasped in her hand, the spout broken where it had hit the floor. Gently, Elizabeth removed it. She found a cushion and put it under the unconscious woman's head. She was never so pleased to see anyone in her life as the bustling figure of the doctor with his black bag as he came through the door.

'Come away, come away, give me room to look at the patient,' he snapped, barely looking at Elizabeth. He took only a few minutes over his examination then folded his stethoscope into his bag.

'I thought as much. You'll have to keep her warm. Plenty of fluids to drink, no solids. Keep her in bed. Get her regular doctor to call on her.' He was almost to the door, Elizabeth watching open-mouthed when he turned. 'The burn is only first-degree. A cold boracic lotion dressing should do the trick. Should I send the bill to the shop?'

'But, Doctor, what is it?'

'Influenza of course! People are going down like ninepins. You should engage a nurse, she'll need proper barrier nursing. But her own doctor will see to that, I have enough to do with my own patients.'

Elizabeth was left staring after him as he rushed through the shop and banged the door behind him. She stood for a moment, trying to organise her whirling thoughts, then she went outside and called a cab, getting the driver to wait outside for a moment as she wrapped Mrs Anderson in a roll of warm cloth from the shop. She got the driver to help her out with the sick woman who was now recovered enough to totter to the cab, her weight supported by Elizabeth and the driver.

'What's wrong with her, lass?' he asked. 'She looks drunk to me.'

'I don't know,' lied Elizabeth. 'Been working too hard, I expect.'

The next few days were hectic for her. She found it was impossible to hire a nurse, they were all engaged as the strange fever which was so much stronger than any flu Elizabeth had ever known raged through the town and, according to the papers, through the country and most of the world as well. 'A plague to equal the Black Death!' the headlines screeched from every news board.

'I don't know what the Black Death was, Jenny hasn't done it yet in history,' she said to Laura at the door of Mrs Anderson's house in West Auckland Road. Elizabeth had got a letter to Laura by a passing urchin. Now her landlady stood outside the house, handkerchief over her mouth and nose at Elizabeth's insistence.

'For the love of God, don't let Jenny come here,' begged Elizabeth. 'You'll look after her, won't you? But I can't abandon Mrs Anderson now, poor soul.'

''Course I will. You mind yourself, though. What would the lass do if you caught it . . . if anything happened to you, like?'

'Make Jenny eat up her vegetables, get her an orange every day. I'll pay you, I will, Laura. I don't want you to be out of pocket.'

'Don't be so soft!' she said. 'Look, I'll call round most days if I can, see how you're getting on.'

What would she do without her friend? Elizabeth asked herself every day. Her thoughts were clouded with worry all the time as she tended to Mrs Anderson, trying to get her to take barley water with a lemon squeezed in it and some sugar, sponging her down when her temperature threatened to burst through the top of the thermometer. She dressed her scalded leg; poulticed her chest with hot linseed when the infection caused congestion of the lungs; listened through the long hours of the night as she talked brightly to her dead son in her delirium; wept for her.

Most mornings there was a knock at the door and when she opened it there was Laura, stepping two paces back from the basket she'd left on the top step, anxious eyes showing her relief when Elizabeth answered the door.

'You'll make yourself ill next,' she said. 'Is the old woman no better then?'

'Not yet,' Elizabeth would reply. 'How's Jenny?'

'Ah, she's fine, don't worry about the lass,' Laura said. 'She's helping me now. Mona's caught it, you know. She's badly, poor bairn. They've closed the school for the time being, did you know?'

'No. A good thing, though. Give Jenny my love and tell her I said she should be good and help all she can. I'll see her soon.'

'Aye, I'd best be off. Ta-ra.'

The doctor came in some days. A dapper little man, this one, though with a permanent expression of anxiety. 'You're doing a fine job, Miss Nelson,' he said. 'Have you ever thought of becoming a nurse? You'd make a good one, I'm sure.'

Elizabeth gave a noncommittal answer but when he had gone, depression settled on her. 'Oh, yes, I have thought of having a career in nursing,' she said aloud as she minced beef to make beef tea for Mrs Anderson and a cottage pie for herself. 'I have indeed. Once it was a bright future for me.'

Mrs Anderson was showing signs of recovering.

When Elizabeth took the tray up to her room, with the beef tea and a couple of pieces of toast and a rose from the garden in a bud vase, Mrs Anderson was awake, pale and wan-looking but with her eyes open and properly focused. Her temperature had broken.

'Oh! You're better,' Elizabeth cried. 'Isn't that grand?'

Mrs Anderson smiled. 'I feel like a wrung out dish-cloth,' she confided. 'But, yes, I can think now without bringing on a migraine.'

Elizabeth put an arm under her shoulders and helped her to sit up, propping her up with pillows. 'Come on then, you'll have to eat some of this, that's the only way to get your strength back.'

Mrs Anderson started well enough but after a few mouthfuls fell back on her pillows. 'I'm as weak as a kitten,' she confided. Elizabeth persuaded her to take a little more but then gave up. Her employer was going to be all right now, time would heal her, she reckoned.

'What about the shop?'

Elizabeth smiled at the question. It was a sure sign that recovery had set in.

'Closed. I had the shutters put up and a notice on the door. There was nothing else I could do. It's not the only business in Darlington that's closed because of this flu. Quite a lot are. All over the country too, apparently.'

But Mrs Anderson seemed to have lost interest. She had slumped down on her pillows and her eyelids were drooping. After a moment, Elizabeth quietly left the room.

'I might be coming home shortly,' she said the next time Laura called. 'Mrs Anderson is a lot better, she's going to get over it.'

'Just as well,' her friend answered. 'Jenny is beginning to fret for you. Moping around the place, she is, since the school closed.'

'I think she could probably come here with me for now. I'll ask if that's all right.'

But it wasn't to be, though the doctor agreed the danger of infection was past and Mrs Anderson said she would be delighted to have the girl. The news that Elizabeth had been dreading came by messenger, a neighbour's lad. Both Laura and Jenny were down with the dreaded plague.

She had to go, of course. Now that the epidemic was almost over the doctor managed to procure a nurse for Mrs Anderson and Elizabeth was free to go back to Albert Hill. She ran all the way. The next bus wasn't due for an hour and her nerves couldn't bear the wait. Her heart beat painfully against her ribs, she had a stitch in her side by the time she got to North Road and had to lean against a wall, gasping for breath.

'Nothing's going to happen to Jenny, nothing. She never gets a cold, never mind anything worse. It's a mistake. By the time I get there she'll be fine.' Elizabeth repeated it over and over to herself like a litany. Then she began to pray. 'Dear Lord, Jenny hasn't lived yet, you wouldn't be so cruel – no, don't let anything happen to Jenny.' The bells of St Cuthbert's sounded in the distance, faint and muted but nevertheless Elizabeth recognised the tolling for the departed and despair descended on her like a cloud. It was like an omen, she thought. It *was* an omen.

Her hand trembled as she turned the brass handle on the front door of the boarding house. There was a red mist of fear before her eyes, she was so terrified of what she might find inside. She rushed up to the bedroom under the eaves which she shared with Jenny, opened the door to see the still figure on the bed. A very still figure. Elizabeth's heart dropped, she felt all her fears were realised.

'Laura? Laura, is that you?'

The voice from the figure was weak and fretful but very much alive. Elizabeth rushed to the bed and gathered her sister in her arms, rocking her, crying over her.

Oh, thank God, thank God!' she sobbed and Jenny struggled to be free. But the tensions of the last days, combined with the shock of the news that morning, had strung Elizabeth's nerves to breaking point.

'Let go, let go, Elizabeth! What's the matter with you?' Jenny at last succeeded in freeing herself and Elizabeth sat back and laughed and laughed.

'I thought . . . I thought you were . . . I thought you had this awful influenza,' she managed to say in between hiccuping with laughter. 'That's what he said. You know, the boy from next door.'

'Billy? He's daft that lad. No, I had a bilious attack, me and Laura. It was the pies we had for supper last night – they were bought from the shop because Laura hadn't had time to bake. I was sick. I hate being sick, Elizabeth, it leaves a funny taste in your mouth.' Jenny pulled a face to show her disgust.

'You don't feel sick now?' she asked anxiously, unable to believe that her fears, her headlong dash across the town, had all been unnecessary. She was staring into Jenny's face for signs of illness.

'No. I've had a sleep and I want to get up now but Laura said I should stay in bed. I don't have to, do I, Elizabeth?'

'We'll see. Maybe this evening it will be all right. I'd better go and see how Laura is now.'

'That Billy, he always gets things wrong,' Laura said. She too was in her bedroom but in the process of dressing, buttoning up her frock. 'I'll tell that woman in the pie shop next time I see her,' she vowed. 'Me and the bairn were as sick as dogs, we were. But now I think I could just do with a nice cup of tea.'

'I'll make it,' said Elizabeth. 'I can stay here now, Mrs Anderson is over the worst and has a nurse in to see to her. I'll call back in the morning, see if I'm needed.'

Next morning, Elizabeth woke after sleeping deeply for twelve hours with a feeling of happy well-being. She lay on her back and stretched her arms above her head, yawning widely. Everything would get back to normal now.

She was in the kitchen cooking scrambled eggs for breakfast when the postman came. There was a letter for her from Morton Main in Mrs Wearmouth's spidery handwriting. Elizabeth gazed at it a moment, wondering if it was a mistake. Mrs Wearmouth did keep in touch but usually through her niece.

'You'll never know what it says unless you open it,' Laura advised. She was back to her old self today, happy because her husband was expected back at the weekend.

Elizabeth opened the letter, her eyes skimming over the words. Then she put it down on the kitchen table.

'Well?' asked Laura.

'Our Jimmy's dead,' Elizabeth said. 'He died of the influenza.'

Chapter Twenty-Six

There was no funeral in the chapel at Morton Main for Jimmy Nelson. How could there be? Elizabeth asked herself. Midshipman James Nelson had died at sea, Mrs Wearmouth had said.

'But he was too young to go to sea,' Elizabeth protested to Laura. 'How could he die at sea? He was only sixteen.'

There were many questions she wanted answers to, her mind was awhirl with them. She wrote to the Officers' Training College at Dartmouth; that was the only address she had for there had been no letters from Jimmy in her time at Darlington. She supposed if he had written it would have been to Stand Alone Farm. No, Jimmy was ashamed of her over that scandal at the Hall, she was aware of that, he had a puritan streak in him. Jimmy was dead. She had to remind herself of the fact over and over again.

In the meantime, Elizabeth was kept pretty busy with Mrs Anderson and the shop. She had opened up again and was struggling to get through the full order book of bespoke costumes which were evidently all the rage in the more prosperous circles of Darlington society after the austerity of the war.

But Mrs Anderson was slow to get her strength back. She seemed to have lost interest in the shop and almost never called in. When Elizabeth took the books to show her she skimmed through them, her lack of interest obvious.

'You do the banking, Elizabeth,' she would say. Or, 'You can go to the wholesalers yourself, can't you, Elizabeth? You have better taste than I do in any case. I have every confidence in you.'

Sometimes Elizabeth felt like screaming at her that she had a life of her own, she had her own grieving to do, her own affairs to sort out. But she didn't. Mrs Anderson had been good enough to give her an opportunity to make something of herself and Elizabeth was grateful. She was not prepared however for what her employer had to say to her one day when she went to West Auckland Road to report on the business and there was another visitor, Mrs Anderson's solicitor, Mr Kennedy. For once there was a tinge of colour in the older woman's face, a sparkle of interest in her eyes.

'Come in, Elizabeth,' she said. 'You know Mr Kennedy, don't you?'

Elizabeth nodded and took the solicitor's outstretched hand. 'Yes, of course, how are you?' she murmured.

'I have invited him here today, Elizabeth, because I asked him to draw up the papers and now he needs both our signatures.'

'Papers?' Elizabeth was mystified.

'Yes. For a partnership. I have decided to make you a full partner in recognition of your good work and all you did for me in my recent illness. I will always be grateful to you for that. I don't know what I would have done without you.'

Elizabeth sat down suddenly. She couldn't believe it. 'Thank you,' she said as though she were accepting a cup of tea or a biscuit. But she didn't know what else to say. She listened in a daze as Mr Kennedy explained the legal phrases in the partnership document, taking very little in. When at last he came to the end she signed her name where he indicated and watched as Mrs Anderson did the same.

'There now, my dear,' Mrs Anderson said as she put down the pen. 'I hope you'll be very happy as a partner in Anderson's. I'm sure you will be – you deserve to be at any rate. Now, the first thing I would like you to do,' she smiled, 'if you agree, of course, is to look out for an assistant. I will not be coming in to the shop on a full-time basis again, I think, and you will need more help.'

'Oh, but surely, when you feel better—'

'No. I have decided to go into a sort of semi-retirement. I know the shop is in good hands now, I can afford to relax a little.'

Elizabeth nodded in understanding. Mrs Anderson had worked hard for years to build up the business, she knew.

'Congratulations, Miss Nelson,' Mr Kennedy broke into the conversation. He shook her hand again. 'Now don't worry, everything is arranged at the bank. All business cheques will require both your signatures, it's perfectly normal.' Now that the main business was over he was brusque, putting papers away in his attaché case and rising to his feet.

Elizabeth was still in a state of mild shock, she simply smiled and nodded.

When eventually she found herself back on the street she walked back to the shop feeling unsure what her reaction to it all was. But once there, after taking off her hat and coat and hanging them up in the back room, she paused and gazed around her. She was a property owner now, a businesswoman, she realised. Her hard work would now be for her own benefit as much as Mrs Anderson's. Oh, Jimmy, Jimmy, she thought suddenly. If you could see me now! And she sat down suddenly on the chair where she did all her hand-sewing and wept, hard bitter sobs which racked her body, deep, gulping breaths which hurt her lungs.

The shop bell rang, warning of a customer, and swiftly she dried her eyes and splashed cold water on her face. She called, 'I won't be a moment,' then patted her face dry with a towel. Casting a swift glance in the mirror which hung by the door, she smoothed her hair behind her ears and went out into the shop.

'Can I help you, madam?' she asked.

'Eeh, I'm right pleased for you,' said Laura when Elizabeth told her and Jenny the news as they sat round the table for supper. 'You've worked hard for it, though.' She nodded her head for emphasis.

'A lot of people work hard and long in shops and never get to be the boss,' Elizabeth pointed out. 'I've been lucky, that's all. It means one thing, though, I won't be able to help you in the house now but I can pay you a proper rent.'

'Aye, well, we'll see,' said Laura.

On the first Sunday morning they could, the two sisters took the train for Bishop Auckland. As the engine puffed its way out of Shildon Tunnel, emerging into the bright sunshine of a spring morning, Elizabeth looked around her at the familiar vista of undulating hills and long rows of pit villages, with their attendant winding wheels, idling mostly as it was a Sunday, with the black waste heaps beside them. It was all so familiar: the ploughed fields with young barley, oats or wheat pushing up green shoots, the lambs frisking beside their mothers in the meadows, side by side with the signs of the coal industry; the town itself coming into view, the train slowing as it came into the station. Elizabeth's thoughts were sombre as she alighted with Jenny. She was dreading going to Morton Main with its memories of Jimmy.

'By, lass, I'm right glad to see you,' said Mrs Wearmouth as she opened the door to the sisters. 'Come away in, I've got the dinner just about ready, I thought you'd be here about now.'

Elizabeth had written to tell her that she was coming. She'd thought they could go to the six o'clock service in the chapel as a small remembrance of Jimmy.

'Oh, you shouldn't have made dinner, Mrs Wearmouth,' she exclaimed. 'I wasn't expecting it, it wouldn't be fair.' The smell of roast beef and Yorkshire pudding filled the kitchen and the girls' mouths watered. It was a long time since breakfast in Darlington.

'It's nice to have someone to cook for,' Mrs Wearmouth said mournfully. 'I was going to live with my sister but I thought I'd miss Morton Main.' She put her arms around each of them in turn and hugged them. 'Your Jimmy was a good lad, a clever one an' all. Sang like an angel in the choir, he did. He'd be missed when he went to the navy, I'm sure. I tell you, it's a fact that only the good die young.'

Elizabeth said nothing, she was too full of emotion. The lump at the back of her throat threatened to choke her. Her hunger had disappeared. When she sat down at the table she had to force herself to do justice to the older woman's cooking. Afterwards, as she helped with the washing up and Jenny sat quietly on the sofa, she asked after Jimmy.

'Did he write to you, Mrs Wearmouth? From Dartmouth, I mean?'

'Oh, yes, he always wrote. He was a good lad, your Jimmy, as I said. Wrote every week, he did. He was that excited he was going to sea. Signed his letter Midshipman J. Nelson, he did. He was as pleased as Punch he was.' Mrs Wearmouth wrung out the dishcloth and put it away in the pantry along with the enamel washing up basin and the drying tray. Then she spread a green chenille cloth over the scrubbed table and put an aspidistra plant in the centre. 'There now, all tidy for Sunday afternoon,' she said.

'He didn't write to me,' said Elizabeth, a catch in her voice. 'He was ashamed of me, I suppose?'

Mrs Wearmouth looked at her, her eyebrows raised.

'Well,' she said, 'I think you're wrong there. I expect he thought it was a waste of effort after all the times he wrote to you when you were up the dale. He even got the gaffer at the pit to take him up in his motor car once.

'I told him, I did, "You wouldn't catch me riding about in one of those contraptions, especially not on some of those steep banks up Weardale. If the Good Lord wanted us to ride about in such noisy, dirty things—"'

'Jimmy went to Bollihope Common? To Stand Alone Farm?'

'Well, aye, of course he did. He wanted to tell you he didn't believe a word that Miss Rowland said, not one word. At first he just went up there on the off-chance, thought you might be there with little Jenny, but that man told him no—'

'Peart said I wasn't there?'

'I think so.' Mrs Wearmouth's brow furrowed as she tried to remember. 'Something like that.'

Elizabeth felt like crying. Mr Dunne had actually taken Jimmy up to Weardale, he had been near them, and Peart hadn't told her? He'd lied to Jimmy, too? Oh, it was too much! A slow, deep anger was beginning to burn in Elizabeth. She could have come back to Morton Main when life became so awful with Peart, she could have just run. She knew now that he would not have followed her; she had been naive to think he would just because she'd taken Jenny. He had used her, and had lied to her brother when he came in search of her.

'Damn him, damn him!' she whispered, half to herself. 'The dirty rotten swine!'

'Elizabeth! Such language!' Mrs Wearmouth cried, shocked to the core. 'On a Sunday an' all.'

'I'm sorry, but it's enough to make a saint swear,' she replied. 'I'll go up there next week, I will, and find out what else Peart's done. I'll wring it out of his neck, I will! Oh, I wish you'd told me about this last time I was here.'

'Well, I never got chance, did I? You were in and out of here that fast, with having to catch the Darlington train. We were thinking of the job, weren't we, anyroad?'

Jenny, who had been sitting quietly watching, came over to her and slipped her hand into Elizabeth's. 'We're not going to Stand Alone Farm, are we, Elizabeth? Not when Peart's there?' Her voice was soft and fearful.

'I am. I'll—' She suddenly felt the hand in hers tremble and looked down at Jenny. 'No, petal, you don't have to come. I'll go myself, I will.'

'Don't go, Elizabeth, don't!' said Jenny. 'What will I do if you don't come back?'

'I'll come back.' Elizabeth saw the depth of fear in her sister's eyes and changed the subject abruptly. 'Never mind now, Jenny. We'll go for a walk, shall we? And maybe we'll call on Auntie Betty and see our Kit. I bet he's a big boy now, I won't hardly know him.'

Mrs Wearmouth looked tired, ready for her afternoon rest. Elizabeth promised to be back in good time for tea before they went to chapel, and the girls went out, leaving Mrs Wearmouth composing herself on the settee before the fire.

Jenny was always glad to be out in the fresh air. Elizabeth walked along briskly, making for the pit yard and then Old Morton village, passing the Black Boy and the Pit Laddie public houses and walking to the end of the village before turning back and making for the row of houses where Auntie Betty lived.

'I like it better on the moors, Elizabeth,' said Jenny, wrinkling her nose as they walked past the slag heap and pit buildings, the winding wheel and engine house. There was the smell of coal dust over everything, though the yard was tidily swept and fresh pine pit props stacked in squares to one side.

Elizabeth almost said, 'What, even with Peart there?' But she didn't. Jenny had been brought up on the wide, windswept moors, it was natural she should feel like that. She remembered the day they had spent on Guisborough moor. How good it had been to breathe sweet, clean air.

Auntie Betty was in the house with Kit, who was sitting at the kitchen table, colouring in a picture book. He looked up briefly but continued what he was doing.

'Eeh, look who it is, Lizzie and . . . is it Jenny? Mrs Wearmouth said you were coming. I don't know why you didn't come here for your dinner, we are family after all.' Betty bridled slightly.

Elizabeth felt her tongue forming the words, 'Elizabeth, not Lizzie,' but she didn't speak. After all, she thought wearily as she gazed at Kit, what did it matter?

'Mrs Wearmouth wrote to me about our Jimmy,' she said instead. 'I thought we'd go to the service at six o'clock, as a mark of respect. He sang in the choir, didn't he?'

'Like an angel,' Auntie Betty agreed. She glanced at the ceiling. 'I don't know about Ben, but we'll go, me and Christopher. He's in bed, he was on the beer this dinnertime.'

Elizabeth said nothing, hiding her relief that Ben Hoddle wasn't going. He would only have disturbed her concentration, she thought. Jenny was standing beside Christopher, watching as he coloured in an outline drawing of Christ standing before a closed door, a lantern in his hand, knocking. The crayoned pink with which he had coloured in the face glistened crudely.

'Can I do the flowers?' asked Jenny.

Christopher gazed levelly at her. 'All right,' he conceded. 'Mind, it's for my Sunday School class so don't make a mess of it. Don't go over the edges.'

'I won't,' Jenny said solemnly. Elizabeth watched as their two heads bent over the book, the tip of Jenny's tongue protruding from the corner of her mouth as she concentrated. She has a light touch, Elizabeth mused, and a tidy nature. More so than I have. The edges of her leaves didn't show any errant green.

There was a thud from upstairs and both women looked up, Betty's forehead knitting. After a moment Ben came clattering down, coming into the kitchen with his braces hanging, grey stubble on his chin. The lines of his face had slackened since Elizabeth saw him last; his eyes showed the effect of too much beer. He came and sat down in what was obviously *his* chair by the fire, first taking a half-smoked cigarette from the high mantelshelf and lighting it from the fire with a piece of paper torn from a newspaper.

'Now then, Lizzie,' he said when he had pulled on the cigarette until it glowed and burned down a half-inch. 'What's brought you here, then? It's not like you to grace us with a visit.'

She stared at him, the scene from a few years ago when he had molested her in this very pantry vivid in her mind.

'Lost your tongue, have you?' he went on, and grinned, fixing her with his bold eyes. 'By, Lizzie, you're just like your mam, you are an' all.'

'Leave her alone, Ben,' Auntie Betty said sharply. 'She's come because our poor Jimmy died, we're going to the chapel tonight.'

'God preserve us from the Holy Joes!' said Ben and spat in the fire before looking back at Elizabeth. It made her feel uncomfortable, the way he stared. Her skin itched.

'I'll be going back to Mrs Wearmouth's now,' she said. 'Are you coming, Jenny?'

Chapel that evening was full, for most of the miners and their families were Methodists. Quite often the service was conducted by a lay preacher but this time it was the Minister who, after the first hymn and prayers, looked around the congregation and saw the friends and

7

relations of Midshipman James Nelson. He paused, added some thoughts to the notes in front of him and changed what he had been about to say.

Elizabeth and Jenny sat with hands clasped as he spoke of the brief life of Jimmy, the great gift of his singing, how proud the choir had been when he'd gained a place at Naval College and how sad to hear of his death. Afterwards, they sang the Twenty-third Psalm to the tune of 'Crimond' and linked hands to say grace together. And Elizabeth walked out of the church with head high, her grief for her younger brother assuaged at least a little.

'Come back for a bite to eat before you go,' said Mrs Wearmouth.

'I think we'd best be on our way,' said Elizabeth. 'Thank you all the same. And thank you for all you did for Jimmy.' She said goodbye to Auntie Betty and Kit and, as the buses had stopped at six o'clock that afternoon, she and Jenny walked along the track which led along the top of the woods to Bishop Auckland. Now that the war was over, there was talk of a bus starting up from the villages to Darlington, but for now the train was the only way and the last one went at seven-thirty.

They were about halfway through the wood when they heard the sound of rapid footsteps behind them. Jenny kept glancing back but Elizabeth hurried her on.

'We don't want to miss the train, do we?' she asked. 'Come on, it's only someone else walking into the town, no one to hurt us.'

'It's Uncle Ben,' said Jenny. 'Look! There he is, cutting across by that oak tree.'

Elizabeth's heart quickened though she told herself not to be silly. He couldn't hurt her, not now she was fully grown. She wouldn't let him. He was a coward at bottom, of course he was.

'You go on, Jenny, I'll catch you up. Likely we left something behind, that's all.'

'Righto. I'll wait at the stile,' said Jenny and ran off. Elizabeth turned to face Ben Hoddle.

'What do you want?' she demanded.

'Hey, now, don't be like that, Lizzie,' he said, panting a little after his rush after her.

'Don't call me Lizzie!'

'Ooh, touchy, aren't you?' he said. 'Howay, lass, give me a bit of what you gave that soldier boy – Wilson, wasn't it? He told us all about it, you know, in the Pit Laddie, the night before he got transferred out of here.'

'Then he was telling lies,' Elizabeth said, fighting to keep her voice even for Jenny would still be in earshot and she didn't want to frighten her.

'Aye, of course he was. They all say that don't they? Aw, come on, lass, just behind this tree. No one will know. Just a feely, eh?' He held out his hand to her, leaning forward to gaze at the white skin showing at the neck of her dress.

Elizabeth stepped back and tripped, falling onto the grassy bank by the side of the track. She scrabbled at the earth to get leverage as he bent over her and her hand closed round a stone. As his head came close to hers, she lifted the stone and hit him on the temple. For a moment, surprise replaced the grin on Ben's face and then he slumped, rolling on top of her and off through a patch of mud on to the stony track.

Elizabeth scrambled to her feet and backed away from him, still holding the stone in her hand. Her breath came in heavy rasping bursts; her heart beat so hard she felt as though it would burst through her skin. Then she turned and ran, throwing the stone away from her as she went, round the bend to where Jenny stood waiting at the stile. At the bend she stopped suddenly as a horrible thought came to her. She hadn't killed him, had she?

She looked back and saw him getting to his feet. He swayed for a long moment and she thought he would fall again. But then he lurched off in the direction of Morton Main.

Chapter Twenty-Seven

That night Elizabeth dreamed the old dream again for
the first time in years. She was in the turnip field with her
mother, only sometimes she changed abruptly and was in
another turnip field with Jenny. She felt the pain, the
dragging ache which became more and more agonising
until she crawled into a copse – and there was her baby
on the ground, a tiny, perfect baby, no bigger than her
thumb. And it opened its mouth and cried.

'I'm coming,' she said to it, 'I'm coming.'

Abruptly she was a little girl again and sitting in the
kitchen, on the settee in the corner, and Mrs Wearmouth
was saying to Auntie Betty, 'What I'd like to know is,
who put the babby in her anyroad?'

And Auntie Betty flushed and mumbled and said that
it wasn't her Ben, no, it wasn't. Then she caught sight
of Elizabeth and shouted at her to get out, she wasn't
wanted there, she was as bad as her mother and could

get to the workhouse with the other brats. And Elizabeth woke, drenched with perspiration, and her heart thumping painfully against her chest.

Turning on her back, she pushed off the bedclothes and allowed the cool air to wash over her heated face and neck. She remembered now. She'd been about nine years old, she reckoned, when Mrs Wearmouth had asked that; nine years old and her mother had died in just the same way as she had nearly died herself. Her poor mam. But how had she had a miscarriage when Da had gone away so many months before? For the first time, Elizabeth wondered about that. Mrs Wearmouth's question made sense now. And why had Da gone away? Her memories of him had been good ones. He had often played with them, given them piggy backs, played ball games. And then there was the awful night, the night when she had woken, terrified, and Jimmy and Alice had crept into her bed, huddling against her. And Da had bellowed and shouted and they'd pulled the bedclothes over their heads. She could hear him now, in her head.

'Jane! Jane, I'll swing for you, I will, you and your fancy man. I believed you once, I forgave you—'

'I didn't *do* anything!'

'No? Then why is that bugger telling all the shift that Betty is barren. It's not him that can't have any, he's got a kid: our Kit!' His voice was rising. Suddenly the bedroom door burst open and Mam ran in. She ran to where they lay, all of a heap in Elizabeth's narrow bed, and tried to climb in beside them.

Her mind shied away from the memories which were surfacing after being so long suppressed. Oh, surely, they hadn't happened? But she couldn't stop her thoughts from running on. How Da had run into the room after her mother and he hadn't looked a bit like their da then, no, he hadn't. His face was contorted like the face of the Devil in a book she'd got from Sunday School as a prize. He had pulled Mam from the bed and turned her over and smacked her hard. And mam had cried out and Elizabeth jumped up and shouted at him.

'Leave her alone! You're a bully, our Da! A big bully.' Da had looked at her then, seemed surprised to see her there. Slowly the mad light left his eyes and he let go of her mam, and Elizabeth put her arms around her and sobbed. Da had walked out of the bedroom, his head sunk on his chest.

'Don't worry, pet, it's all right, I'm all right,' Mam had whispered. 'Howay now, don't cry, you'll upset the bairns. Go on, cuddle them in and I'll go and see to Da. He's not been well, you know, he didn't mean to hit me.'

But Elizabeth knew he had. She watched as her mother went out of the bedroom and into the one shared by her and Da. There was a murmur of voices, low now, the anger burned out. Jenny was sobbing quietly, curled into a ball between Elizabeth and Alice. Elizabeth cuddled her in.

'It's all right now, petal,' she said. 'Come on, go to sleep. I think Da just had a nightmare.'

The images faded from Elizabeth's thoughts. She couldn't remember what had happened after that, if anything had. A while later, it could have been weeks or months, she had no idea, Da had gone.

'He'll come back,' Mam had said, 'he will, I know he will.'

Well, thought Elizabeth, it's been a long wait so far. She got out of bed and went to the window, drawing the curtain and looking out over the rooftops of Darlington. A pale, ghostly light lay on the town, silvering the slates, casting the chimneys into black shadow. It was something to do with Ben Hoddle, she decided. Yes, indeed. Had Ben pestered her mother the way he'd pestered her? Did Aunt Betty know? Was Christopher . . . but no, she wouldn't allow herself to think any further than that.

Indeed, there was little time for her to think about anything other than the shop in the next few weeks. The order book was full and besides that there were new fashions coming into the shops. Elizabeth was kept busy travelling to Leeds and Newcastle, once even to London, to fashion shows and wholesale houses.

Anna, the girl she had taken on the week after she was made a partner, was becoming a great asset. In a very short while Elizabeth could safely leave the shop in her hands when she herself was out.

'I'm thinking of getting extra help, Mrs Anderson,' she said one day during her customary visit to West Auckland Road. She had to go there as often as she could because Mrs Anderson had given up saying she was coming back to the shop. She was lethargic, not getting out of bed until eleven o'clock sometimes, her face pale and her expressions lacklustre.

'Melancholia,' the doctor said, 'it's common in patients recovering from influenza. Try to take her out of herself, interest her in something.'

Elizabeth tried her best, taking her out to tea on the High Row, talking to her about what was happening in the shop, anything which might kindle her interest again. Jenny (bless her, thought Elizabeth) took to popping in to visit the old lady occasionally, making a detour to West Auckland Road on her way home from school. She had the most success. Mrs Anderson would sometimes play Ludo with her, though at other times she would simply shake her head.

'Not today, Jenny,' she would say. 'I'm too tired today. But thank you for coming to see me.'

'You do what you think, dear,' she said now to Elizabeth. 'I'm sure you know best.' Elizabeth despaired of her ever regaining her former bright spirits.

'I want to go to Weardale as soon as I can,' she said to Laura one evening when Jenny was in bed and the two women were sitting round the fire supping cocoa. 'I would like to see Peart, face him, ask him what he did with my letters.' The letters from Jimmy, she thought sadly, I must make time to go up there and get the letters from him. 'I can't go on a Sunday, though, I don't think I can take Jenny. It might just send her back into her shell when she's doing so well at school, making friends and everything.'

'She's certainly a different girl,' Laura agreed. 'How on earth anyone responsible for children could have let that man foster her, I just don't know. Criminal it was, they should be put up against a wall and shot.'

'Well, I daresay I could have got her away a lot sooner if I hadn't been so ignorant about what to do,' said Elizabeth. She sipped her cocoa reflectively.

'You were just a bairn yourself,' Laura replied. Over the months she had learned all about Stand Alone Farm and Peart, and the Children's Home at Bishop Auckland and Miss Rowland.

'I suppose,' said Elizabeth absently. She was busy in her mind, trying to arrange her schedule for the following week to include a visit to Bollihope Common. She wondered about taking on a seamstress to help her with the bespoke work. Goodness knows, she could do with the help and the shop was doing very well. The profits could surely stretch to one. But it was just a thought for now. It seemed no matter what she was thinking about lately, plans for the shop ran through her mind. And in any case, she couldn't possibly get a seamstress and be able to leave her to work on her own within the next week or two. And after that came the school holiday; she couldn't go to the farm without Jenny wondering where she was and worrying.

'I tell you what,' said Laura, 'I was thinking of going to see my sister in York next Sunday. I could take Jenny, I'm sure she'd like to come. We could take the ten o'clock train from Banktop Station and come back on the five. What do you think?'

'Oh, Laura, that would be grand, I'd be so grateful.'

'Aye. Well, I can say we want Jenny to see York Minster. It'll be good for her education.' Laura smiled triumphantly. 'That's a good idea, isn't it? I do have some, you know.'

And so it was arranged.

Alighting once more at Stanhope Station, Elizabeth shivered though it had nothing to do with the cold. Memories came crowding back of the other times she had been here, especially that first time in the snowstorm when she despaired of finding anywhere to stay. Best forget such things, she told herself firmly. Memories didn't help.

There was a bus standing with Middleton-in-Teesdale showing on its destination board. The service must have started up since the war ended, she thought. On impulse she approached the driver who was leaning against the side of the bus, smoking a pipe.

'Do you go by way of Bollihope Common?' Elizabeth asked him.

He took the pipe out of his mouth and spat into the gutter. 'Aye.'

'Will you stop by Stand Alone Farm path?'

'If you tell us where it is.'

Elizabeth climbed on to the twenty-four-seater bus, hardly believing her luck, and took a seat by the window. At the stroke of eleven the driver got in and they set off.

'Threepence.'

Elizabeth jumped. She had been staring out of the window, thinking of what she was going to say to Peart when she saw him. Oh, she was a very different girl now from the one he had used and bullied, she told herself.

'What?'

'I said threepence. You didn't think the ride was for free, did you?'

It was a man who had been sitting on the front seat. She noticed now he had a dun-coloured shop coat on and a money bag over his shoulder. In his hand was a roll of tickets.

'I'm only going to Stand Alone Farm,' she objected. 'Isn't threepence a bit too much? Or is that a return?'

'No. It's threepence anywhere along that road. Now if you don't want to pay we can stop the bus and you can get off. A return is fivepence.'

Tuppence was an amount to look at twice before spending, and she might not be able to catch the bus back. Elizabeth sighed. 'All right, I'll pay.' She handed over her threepence and resumed looking out of the window. There were roadmen working on the track, a cart loaded with small stones and men raking them over the surface. A steamroller and vat of tar stood off to the side. The council was making up the road, she thought, a sure sign that the war was over.

It was only a few minutes to the place where the path led off to the right; the same sign, looking only slightly more weathered, was still hanging on the rotten wooden post. Elizabeth jumped to her feet; she couldn't believe they were there already.

'Here – let me off here,' she called to the driver. He overshot but not by much. 'What time do you come back?' she asked.

'Two o'clock from Middleton,' the conductor replied and the bus trundled off. Elizabeth set off down the path which widened in places to a track. Perhaps, once, all of it had been wider, but heather and bracken had grown in on it. She glanced anxiously upwards. Clouds were lowering, threatening rain. She hurried on until she came to the broken-down fence and the gate which led into the farmyard. As she gazed at the back of the house, still looking as derelict as it ever had, she couldn't help a feeling of apprehension which made her heart beat faster.

'Come on, he can do nothing to you now,' she said aloud. Jenny was safe from Peart's clutches and she herself had enough resources to fight him if need be, something which had always stopped her before. Money counted for everything if you hadn't any, she thought grimly as she went through the gate and up to the back door of the farm. Lifting a resolute fist, she knocked hard on the door.

Under the eaves birds twittered. At her second knock a couple rose into the air and flew off to the rowan tree. She could hear nothing else. Although, yes, she could. There was a soft whining and a snuffling from behind the broken boards of the dilapidated door.

'Snuff?' she called. 'Snuff, is that you?' The whining became louder. There was even a weak bark. Elizabeth pushed at the door; it wasn't locked, but something was stopping it from opening easily. She pushed harder and found she was pushing the dog who lay just inside, emaciated to the point of being almost unrecognisable and only just alive. As she stepped inside Snuff managed to raise his head and give a little whimper.

There was a smell in the room such as Elizabeth had never smelled before in her whole life. It made her retch and gag so that she turned abruptly and went back outside into the blessed fresh air. She stood and took deep, gulping breaths of it, until her stomach settled down and her head cleared.

There was something dead in the room, there had to be. And she was filled with the dread of what it was, what it could only be. How else could the dog have got into such an appalling condition? She felt like fleeing up the path, running to the nearest human being, begging for help. Even if it meant going as far as the farm where she and Jenny had worked the turnip field, or to Stanhope if need be. But she knew she couldn't leave Snuff now she had given him hope, she had to see to him. And she had to find out what horror was in the room.

Steeling herself, holding her handkerchief over her mouth, she forced herself to go back in. In front of the chair by the fire there was what looked like a huddle of old clothes and there was no doubt that this was where the smell came from. Walking closer with slow, hesitant footsteps until she was near enough to peer at him she saw the face of the man, unrecognisable almost in its advanced state of decay. But it was Peart. By his hand was an empty whisky bottle; the shirt he had on was one she had patched herself. She stared, paralysed with shock, her mind unable to think. Then the dog whimpered again, breaking into the silence and her sense returned.

In her mind she was screaming; in reality there was no sound except her ragged breathing and that of the dog. Walking over to the door, she bent and half carried, half pulled Snuff out into the open then closed the door on the horror in the house. She looked at him thoughtfully then went to the water butt on the end of the barn, found the old ladle which she had used so often in the past and brought the dog a drink. It lapped, slowly at first, then frantically, licking every last drop from the battered tin. She went back to the butt and refilled the ladle.

'Slowly, this time,' she said. 'Steady, Snuff. You'll be fine now, lad.' When the dog was finished she put down the ladle and rose to her feet.

'I'm going for help, Snuff,' she said. 'Don't worry, I won't abandon you.'

Walking up the path, Elizabeth tried to remember the name of the farmer and his wife, the ones who had been so kind to her when . . . no, she couldn't think of that, not at this minute. Doris, she thought, no, that wasn't right. Albert was the farmer, she thought doubtfully. She was ashamed that she couldn't remember when they had been so kind. But her mind had frozen, she reckoned. Head down, thinking hard, she came to the road. Oh, if only the bus was coming. She looked to the left and to the right but there was no sign of anything or anyone. She began to walk to the bend in the road, head down, scouring her brain for the names. And suddenly there was a car, almost running into her as it came round the bend. And in the driving seat was Jack Benson.

Chapter Twenty-Eight

Jack came out of the colliery office on Friday evening and stood on the step, breathing in the particular smell surrounding a coal mine: coal and engine oil, a faint taint of sulphur from the coke ovens. He had been going over the books, over and over to make sure he made no mistakes. The fact was output from the mine was up. The men, including those returned from soldiering in France and Belgium, were cheerful and optimistic. Their rates of pay, though modest in Jack's opinion, were the best they had ever had in peacetime.

There was trouble brewing, though, he mused. The Association of Mine Owners wanted to reduce the rates now the war was over. They couldn't be sustained, demand was falling and stocks were rising, was the argument. He had wanted to spend the weekend preparing a paper to read at the owners' meeting next week, but he was blowed if he knew how to start. Oh, yes, the owners had made good profits during the war and they couldn't have done so without the workers, but they didn't see it like that, not at all. They had the upper hand now. In their opinion the miners needed to be sat on, they were getting too big for their boots.

Jack sighed, thinking of Jimmy, his talented protégé, the son of a miner. Given-education boys like him did well. The two he had sponsored since Jimmy were doing well in the grammar school, though the parents of one were threatening to take him out and put him to work.

'He can work in the pit, bring in some money. A great lad like him, idling his time away at school,' his mother had said when Jack visited her. But she had half a dozen other children around her and was obviously close to having another. She would need the lad's money all right if the wages were reduced to pre-war levels.

Jack was sick of thinking about it. He walked to his car, cranked the handle, and when the engine burst into life climbed in. Thinking of Jimmy made him think of Elizabeth and the usual ache in the pit of his stomach started up, spreading melancholy like a malignant growth. Elizabeth . . . what was she doing now? And how could he face her after Jimmy's death, even if he found her? He had been responsible for it, it had been he who had enabled the lad to go to Dartmouth.

'You see,' Olivia had said to him, 'no good comes of interfering in other people's lives.' She had sounded smug, as though she was somehow vindicated in her opinions by Jimmy's death.

On impulse, Jack drove to the miners' rows, to West Row in fact. His longing for Elizabeth was so great, his sorrow at Jimmy's death combining with it into a heavy load. He had to try to shake himself out of it, he had to. But he would have a word with Jimmy's landlady first, try to lay a few ghosts.

Parking his car on the end of the row, he walked up the street to Mrs Wearmouth's cottage. It was the first time he had been here since the boy's death. He knew he should have called weeks ago but he had put it off, so shocked by Jimmy's dying like that of such a random thing as influenza.

He didn't allow himself to hesitate now though, as he opened Mrs Wearmouth's back gate and walked up the yard to knock on her door. It was answered immediately. She must have seen him coming and been on her way to the door even before he knocked.

'Captain Benson!' she cried. 'How good of you to call. Come away in, do, I'll make a nice cup of tea.'

'Thank you, Mrs Wearmouth, but—' Jack had been about to refuse the tea but seeing her expression, changed his mind quickly. 'Of course, Mrs Wearmouth, I'd love a cup of tea.' He followed her in and sat down, watching as she bustled about, bringing out a treasured china cup and saucer, brewing tea. He remembered how good she had been to Jimmy, how the boy talked so much about her and with such affection, and warmed to her himself.

'I was devastated to hear the news about Jimmy,' he said, and she paused, teapot in hand.

'Aye, it was awful.' She took a hanky out of her apron pocket and wiped away a sudden tear. 'I was just saying to his sister – you know, Elizabeth – how good you'd been to him . . .'

'Elizabeth? She was here?'

In his surprise, Jack jumped to his feet and stepped towards her urgently.

'Well, aye, yes, she was. We went to the service in the chapel and the Minister spoke that nicely about Jimmy. It was such a comfort, for Elizabeth and Jenny especially. Oh, yes, very nice.' She paused and looked at him strangely. 'Is there something wrong?'

'No, no. Just that Jimmy and I were trying to get in touch with Elizabeth before he died. Didn't you know?' Remembering his manners, Jack sat back in his chair.

Mrs Wearmouth shook her head. 'No one said anything to me,' she replied. 'I could have told you where she was – where she's been for this last year anyroad.'

'Where? I thought she was married and living in Weardale. But her husband is an awkward sort of chap. Oh, I'm sorry, Mrs Wearmouth, you see I need to get in touch with her.' Jack took the cup she was offering him, waiting while she spooned sugar into it.

'Huh! Well, she left him, a cruel beggar by all accounts, treated little Jenny something shameful, he did. Elizabeth's well out of *that*!'

'But where is she now?'

'Living in Darlington with my niece. Doing well for herself an' all. Working in a dress shop, she is. Would you like one of my Shrewsbury biscuits? New made yesterday, they are, an' though I says it meself—'

'No, thank you, Mrs Wearmouth.' Jack's mind was in a whirl. Elizabeth in Darlington? And she hadn't got in touch with him? Not even when Jimmy died. Oh, she must not want to see him, that was it. He must have done something to upset her so badly, she didn't want to know him. But he would go to see her, he would go now, waste not a moment more. It was just a pity it was too late to go tonight. Oh, what a fool he'd been. Of course Mrs Wearmouth was the obvious person to ask and it had taken him all this time to do it. He stood up, anxious to be off.

'I'll go to Darlington to find her,' he said. 'Thank you very much, Mrs Wearmouth, for your help.'

'Do you not think it would help more if I was to give you the address?'

'Oh. Yes, of course. If you would be so good?' He took a diary and fountain pen from his inside pocket and waited expectantly.

She shook her head, smiling a little at his obvious desire to be off immediately. 'What's your hurry, lad?'

she asked. 'It's a bit late to go tonight, why don't you wait for the morn?'

Jack smiled wryly. She was right, of course. 'I'll go tomorrow,' he agreed. He wrote down the address to her dictation and, putting the book and pen away, held out his hand. 'Thank you very much, Mrs Wearmouth,' he repeated.

She watched him speculatively as he went down the yard. He looked for all the world like a lover in pursuit of his lass, she thought. Pity he hadn't been as keen before Elizabeth went up to that blooming place up the dale. Still, better late than never. Mrs Wearmouth was an avid reader of *Woman's Weekly*, she loved the little romantic stories in it, couldn't wait to get her hands on it every week.

As it happened, Jack couldn't set out for Darlington until Sunday after lunch. There were problems at the mine and at the farm which it seemed only he could resolve. But at last he was free to go. Eventually he found the boarding house in Albert Hill. He knocked on the door, his heart beating fast, so that he had to smile at himself. Acting like a young lad in calf love, he told himself. Get a hold of yourself.

'Yes? What do you want? The missus is out, gone to York she has, her and the little lass.' It was a girl wrapped in an all-enveloping overall two sizes too big for her who opened the door. Mona was harassed. She had been left with all the washing up after the big Sunday lunch and already she had been interrupted by three calls at the door. Two people wanting rooms and now this chap. She eyed him. Well-dressed he was but probably only wanting to sell summat. And she had the teas to see to soon.

'I'm looking for Elizabeth Nelson,' said Jack. 'I understand she lives here?'

'Aye. Well, she does,' said Mona, and Jack's heart leaped. He took a step forward but the girl held on to the door, barring his way.

'May I see her?'

'No, you can't,' said Mona.

'Why not?'

This was maddening. He felt like taking hold of the girl and shaking her but kept his voice quiet and polite.

'She's not here, that's why.' Jack waited and after a moment Mona went on, 'Gone out she has an' all. Leaving me with everything to do. I don't know how I'll manage by meself. An' people at the door all the time . . .'

Jack felt in his pocket and found a sixpence. 'I understand,' he said and dropped the coin into the front pocket of the apron. She looked down at it and started to grin.

'Eeh, thanks, Mister.'

'Can you tell me where Elizabeth went to?'

'No, not exactly.' Seeing his disappointment she

asked, 'You don't want your money back, do you, Mister?'

'No, no, you keep it.' He stepped back from the door.

'It's somewhere up the Dales she's gone,' Mona said, 'Weardale, I think,' and closed the door firmly before he could change his mind.

Weardale? That could only mean Bollihope Common, Jack thought, and hurried out to his car. If he set off now he had plenty of time to reach Stand Alone Farm before dark. He only hoped Elizabeth hadn't decided to go back to her husband.

Two hours later, Jack was climbing up the fell from Stanhope and looking out for the track which led off to Stand Alone Farm. His mind was full of Elizabeth, memories flooding back of how she had felt in his arms, how beautiful she was with her black hair and dark violet eyes, her white skin, the way her lips curved slightly into a half-smile. He imagined kissing her again after all this time. Oh, he would save her from that man, whatever it was that had driven her to go back to him. The picture of her he carried in his thoughts was so vivid that when he actually saw her, scrambling on the stony, rutted, unmade road, he thought he was hallucinating. But suddenly she stood stock still and looked straight at him, her mouth opening in a perfect oval of surprise.

*

Afterwards, looking back on it, it would seem like a miracle that Jack should appear like that, just when she needed him so much. But at the time, late on Sunday afternoon, after the horror she had left at Stand Alone Farm, it was more than that: it was like a burst of unbelievable happiness so bright she couldn't help being lit up by it. Elizabeth stood for a moment, stunned, and gazed at him and he climbed out of his car, gazing back at her, and then, slowly at first, then faster, they ran to each other and Jack took her in his arms and held her as though he would never let go again.

Neither of them was thinking of anything, no questions were being asked, no explanations sought. It was enough that they were in each other's arms. For Elizabeth the feelings of safety and love and coming home were overwhelming. She let them wash over her, lap around her, aware of nothing else. Gradually other things did impinge; the remembered smell of him, his own individual scent, combined with a faint clean tang of soap and something else that was indefinable.

His face was buried in her neck and hers in his. When she at last lifted her head to gaze into his face, his hazel eyes and her own were wet and luminous with tears.

'Elizabeth,' he said huskily. 'Oh, Elizabeth.'

She clung to him. Her arms slid round his neck and she lifted her lips to his. Their kiss was wild and sweet and satisfying after what felt a lifetime of being denied it. How long they stood there neither of them was aware, it would have been longer but for the sudden blaring of a hooter.

'Howay, man, the pair of you! What do you think you're up to, standing in the middle of the road, holding up the traffic? Get out of the way, will you?'

Jack lifted his head, they both did. Elizabeth's eyes were dreamily dazed. She was unable to stop smiling all over her face. It was the bus from Middleton-in-Teesdale they had halted, the driver leaning forward to gesticulate and blow his horn, the conductor clinging to a rail as he leaned out of the door, shouting.

'Should be locked up, you two, no shame you haven't. Don't you know it's broad daylight? Get out of the road, will you? Save your carryings on for somewhere private!'

Jack's arms tightened around Elizabeth. Deliberately he bent his head and kissed her again and from inside the bus, where four or five young lads lounged, there came the sound of wolf whistles. He grinned, then, taking his time, drew Elizabeth to the side of the road and gestured with his free hand for the bus to pass. The conductor went back inside, the bus went on and so did the whistling until the bus was round the bend and out of sight, going down the bank towards Stanhope.

'Oh, Jack,' said Elizabeth, rather inadequately, 'I'm so glad to see you. So glad.'

He smiled tenderly. 'I rather gathered that,' he murmured. 'Oh, Elizabeth – Lizzie – why did you go away like that? Why didn't you come to me? You know I wouldn't have believed that oaf Wilson rather than you, you must do!'

Elizabeth stared at him, remembering the scene with his mother, how she had said Jack wanted nothing more to do with Elizabeth. 'But your mother—' No, she couldn't tell him what his mother had said that day, couldn't blacken his own mother to him. Instead she simply gazed at him. She seemed unable to take her eyes off him.

'I thought you were happy here with that man,' he said. 'And then, when Mrs Wearmouth said you'd left him . . . and later, when I thought you were going back to him, I nearly went mad.'

'Oh!'

Meeting Jack had driven all that she had seen at Stand Alone Farm out of her mind. She couldn't believe she had forgotten such a dreadful thing, felt stricken.

'Oh, Jack!' She faltered. 'But . . . Oh, I should have told the people on the bus. Oh, God, Jack, I forgot—'

'What? What is it? Told them what? Come and sit down in the car, sweetheart, you've gone as white as a sheet and you're trembling. What is it?'

'How could I just forget? Oh, Jack, the most awful thing has happened . . . I'll have to go to Stanhope, or maybe just to the farm along the road. I have to get help.' She was beginning to babble now, she knew she was. She turned this way and that. Meeting Jack had done more than make her forget, she couldn't even decide the best thing to do.

'Calm down, pet, calm down. It's all right, come on now, I'll see to whatever it is. If you want me to face him, I will. Just you wait in the car, I'll see to it.'

'No. No, Jack, it isn't that.'

Elizabeth leaned her head against his chest. Oh, indeed, indeed the temptation to leave everything to him was overwhelming. Then she told him what she had found when she came to the farm earlier that day.

'The smell, Jack . . . It smelled like a dead rat.' Elizabeth began to cry, tears running down her face. The emotions of the day had finally broken through her self-control. 'But I'll have to go back. There's the dog, you see.'

'No, you're not,' he said calmly. He thought of the smell of death. Oh, a man got well used to that if he was in the trenches during the war. But she should not have had to face it. No, indeed. He started the car. 'I'm taking you down to the police station in Stanhope. We'll tell them what happened and you can stay in the hotel there. I'll come back with the police, bring the dog with me if you insist. He'll be all right until then, now he has water.'

'But—'

'No, Elizabeth, you've had enough for one day. So just do as you're told for once, will you?'

He drove down the pot-holed and stone-strewn road to where the roadmen had laid the tarmac, appreciating the smoothness under his tyres there. He made conversation, ordinary conversation, commenting on the way the moors were becoming criss-crossed with proper roads now the war was over. All the time he kept a watchful eye on her, seeing how white she was, how tired she looked in spite of the luminosity in her eyes when she gazed at him. A great tenderness filled him. He would look after her now, oh, yes, he would indeed.

At Stanhope he drove her to the hotel and ordered tea and hot buttered toast, sitting with her while she ate a piece of toast and drank a cup of tea. Elizabeth began to look a little less white, she'd stopped trembling.

'Stay here now and I'll go to the police station,' he said.

Elizabeth nodded. She felt deathly tired. All this was surely a dream? She closed her eyes and opened them again. Jack was still there. 'Don't be long,' she said.

Chapter Twenty-Nine

Jack went back to Stand Alone Farm with the police. There they found Snuff, able to hold up his head now after the reviving water which Elizabeth had given him. He even managed a small wag of his tail when he saw them coming down the track, a belated bark which sounded more like a cough.

'Poor sod,' said the police sergeant, gagging at the stink. 'They say dogs have a stronger sense of smell than us an' all.'

'Been dead a couple of weeks or more, I'd reckon,' the police surgeon told Jack, nodding at the body. 'How did you say he was found?' He repeated what Elizabeth had told him.

'Lived apart, did she?' the surgeon asked. They watched as men brought in an aluminium death wagon and gingerly moved the remains of Peart into it, closing the lid. The police sergeant tried to open the window but the sash was obviously long gone, the window stuck fast.

'Just leave the door open,' advised the surgeon. 'Now the body's gone so will the smell.'

'His wife found him, did you say? She'll have to make a statement,' said the sergeant.

'Not today. She's had too much of a shock, Sergeant,' Jack insisted, and the policeman nodded reluctantly.

'OK.'

Somehow, the police van and the hearse had forced their way down the overgrown track to the farm. When Jack went outside there were flattened bushes and clumps of bracken.

'I thought it was just a footpath,' he remarked to the police doctor. The man glanced at him shrewdly. It was the sort of inconsequential remark made by someone after a shock.

'Come on, we'll get you back to Stanhope and your . . . er . . . lady friend.'

'I'll take the dog,' Jack offered. A policeman had had the foresight to bring dog food and was feeding it slowly to Snuff. Jack had an idea that Elizabeth and her sister wouldn't like the idea of the dog being put down or worse, left to roam.

He had left his car by the hotel entrance and put Snuff in the back seat before going in to Elizabeth.

'You'll bring her round in the morning, Mrs Peart?' the police sergeant stated rather than asked, and Jack promised he would. There was a meeting of the Mine

Owners' Association but that would have to go by the board.

Inside, he found Elizabeth slumped in the residents' lounge. She looked anxiously up at him as he went in, his stick tapping on the polished wood floor. Jack sat beside her and took her hand.

'It's all right, sweetheart. They reckon the drink did it. The police took the body away.'

'Snuff? The dog? Is he all right?'

'He's fine. Been fed and watered. He's in the back of the car now, perking up grand, he is.'

Elizabeth sank back in her chair. 'Poor man, poor Peart.' Jack had his own opinion on the man but didn't air it.

'Look, the police want you to give a statement about your husband, how you found him. Tomorrow will do, they said. So I thought—'

'He *wasn't* my husband.' Elizabeth blushed scarlet. 'Not really. I mean, we weren't actually married.'

'But . . . he said, when I went up to the farm with Jimmy, he *said* you were his wife. He wouldn't let us see you, said you didn't want to.' Jack remembered the times he had been up there, leaving letters for Elizabeth. Jimmy too. They had been so desperate to know she was all right, she and Jenny.

'No, we weren't married. I stayed because of Jenny. Oh, Jack, she had a life no child should have to suffer through and I didn't have the money to take her away.

Anyway, Peart and his legal wife had taken her from the guardians. Miss Rowland said I could do nothing about that.'

Jack stared at her. 'But you could have come to me! You could at least have written to Jimmy.'

'I was a fool not to, wasn't I? But I thought you didn't want me. Your mother—'

'My mother? What about her? What did she say to you?'

'Nothing. It wasn't her fault.' And Elizabeth realised that it hadn't really been Mrs Benson's fault, it had been her own feelings of worthlessness and shame which had made her so ready to accept that neither Jack nor Jimmy wanted anything more to do with her. And when neither of them had got in touch . . . What a fool she had been!

'Oh, Jack, I've been an idiot, haven't I?'

He squeezed her hand and in his own mind dismissed the months, even years, of longing and unhappiness he had gone through. It was worth it now, he reflected. 'Forget it now, darling. But look, I've been thinking. Shall I book rooms here for the night? Then you won't have to travel up again tomorrow. I think that's the best idea.'

'I have to go back to Darlington! There's Jenny, she'll be worried. And there's my work, I work in a dress shop, I have to open up tomorrow.' Elizabeth's brow furrowed. She had to work something out for tomorrow, she realised. But Jack, bless his heart, was a resourceful man.

'These are modern times. There's the telephone, isn't there?' Telephones were still fairly rare in Darlington but Mrs Anderson had recently had one installed in the house; her recent illness had made her frightened of being unable to contact others.

Within an hour they were sitting at a table in the dining room, eating dinner. Mrs Anderson had been alerted by telephone and declared herself well enough to open up the shop. 'Take as long as you like, Elizabeth,' she had said. 'Oh, what a terrible experience!' It seemed the emergency breathed new life into her, Elizabeth thought as she handed the telephone back to Jack after the call.

It was more difficult with Jenny as Laura Hicks was not connected to the telephone. But Jack was not deterred. He simply rang 'Telegrams' and that was that.

'They'll think someone has died,' said Elizabeth doubtfully, and for a moment failed to see the irony of her words. But somehow the death of Peart seemed remote now. No one would mourn him. No one she knew at least.

'I'll allow for a pre-paid reply,' said Jack. He was not to be gainsaid now, not when he had his love with him at last. And the reply had come: 'Don't worry. Stay. Everything here fine.' It was signed by both Laura and Jenny.

'But I wonder, though, if Jenny will be sad about

Peart,' Elizabeth said doubtfully. 'After all, he was the only father she knew.'

'That's enough, Elizabeth,' said Jack. 'We will be back by tomorrow afternoon in any case.'

The dinner was plain but good: thin slices of succulent local lamb with rosemary and afterwards a game pie. Cotherstone cheese from over in Teesdale, white and crumbly and delicious. And wine, a rich ruby red wine which made Elizabeth ever so slightly light-headed. She had thought she would not be able to eat a bite but somehow or other her plate became empty and was replaced by another which became empty too. She was enjoying herself, floating on a cloud, though at the back of her mind she was aware that she would have to rejoin the real world soon. But not yet.

Jack watched her expressive face, changing as she smiled and laughed and was surprised by the taste of something, the effect of the wine making her eyes and cheeks glow more than ever. He would never let her go again, he swore to himself. Never, never, never. The dining room, no more than half full the whole evening, emptied until at last the waiters were hovering at the side, watching the lovers, glancing at the grandfather clock by the wall. But Elizabeth's eyelids were beginning to droop in spite of her desire that the evening go on forever.

They went upstairs hand in hand to a chorus of: 'Goodnight, sir, madam.' They didn't notice that the lights in the dining room went out before they were halfway up. Jack had booked two adjoining rooms. He stood at her side before her door and kissed her tenderly.

'Goodnight, my darling.'

Elizabeth's eyes flew open. 'Oh! I thought you would be coming in with me?'

'You're not too tired?' Even as he said it he had the door open and they were in the room, the door closing softly behind them. It was a fairly small room, the double bed taking up most of the space, covers turned down invitingly. Elizabeth felt a thrill begin in the base of her stomach, and grow and swell.

'I have no nightie,' she whispered.

'No need,' Jack answered. His hands went to her blouse, opening the buttons one by one, slipping it over her arms and folding it carefully before laying it on a chair. He loosed her skirt and it dropped to the floor and she stepped out of it. He picked it up and laid it over the back of the chair. Then he kissed her gently: on the lips, the nape of her neck, the tops of her breasts where they swelled above her bust bodice. Pushing down the straps, he found the rosy buds and kissed them one by one, until they were hard and erect. He moaned with longing.

Gently she pushed him down onto the bed and began undressing him. As if it was the most natural thing in the world, she unstrapped the hated wooden feet, kissed the skin reddened from the day's activities, gently massaged it. Then she slipped off her drawers and climbed into the bed with him and they lay, breast to breast, belly to belly, arms entwined around one another. She could feel his excitement mounting, her own body more demanding, an exquisite pain.

When he laid her gently on her back and entered her she almost fainted, she felt the sensations were almost too much to bear. And afterwards, when he collapsed on top of her, she was filled with a great sense of elation and triumph, a happiness transcending even that she had felt that night in the Manor, the time he had first made love to her. And then, abruptly, she was deeply asleep as though nature knew she had reached the limits of emotion, at least for one day.

Jack, his face close to hers as she lay in the crook of his arm, watched her in the moonlight which filtered in through the open curtains. It dappled her face, pale light and dappled dark, enhancing its beautiful planes and lines. She looked like an angel lying there, his angel. He would go through hell for her. Then he too fell asleep, deeply and dreamlessly.

Sunlight streamed in the window on to the bed where they lay, moving across Elizabeth's face so that she woke and blinked, wondering for a moment, but only a moment. She had such a deep feeling of well-being and peace. She felt Jack's arm across her breast and turned to face him on the pillow.

Jack slept on, his face boyish, untroubled. She took a

finger and traced the scar which ran down his cheek, fainter than when she had first met him but still discernible. Funny how she hadn't even noticed it yesterday – only his kind hazel eyes, his frank expression. She decided she liked the scar, it was all part of his character-filled face.

Jack opened his eyes and gazed straight into hers. 'Morning, my love,' he said, his voice a caress. He kissed her gently, then with increasing passion, and once again Elizabeth felt herself carried away on an irresistible tide. They were interrupted by a discreet knock at the door.

'Yes?'

She answered as they remembered just in time that this was her room.

'I have a message for Mr Benson, madam,' a man's voice said. 'He's not in his room.'

'Oh? He must have gone for a walk.'

'Yes, madam.' There was just the faintest touch of disbelief in the voice. 'Will I leave it with you, madam?'

'Just a minute.'

Elizabeth struggled with a fit of the giggles as she hurriedly pulled her blouse and skirt over her naked body. She sat on the edge of the bed to button up the blouse and Jack put a hand inside, tickling her, making her give a strangled yelp and stand up in a hurry.

'Is everything all right, madam?'

'Yes, yes, I'm coming.' Elizabeth pushed her hair

behind her ears and opened the door, just a crack, foiling the man's attempt to see beyond her into the room. He handed her a note. 'Thank you,' she said, 'I'll see Mr Benson gets it.' Closing the door, she collapsed in a heap of laughter.

Downstairs the waiter said to the cook, who was breaking eggs into a large black pan on the range, 'Didn't even blush, the besom!' The cook smiled reminiscently. She was a big-bosomed woman in her forties but she was still able to remember how it was when she was twenty and her sweetheart came home from the Boer War. And that poor man upstairs, from what she had glimpsed of him the night before, was lame, she dare bet from the last war, and in her opinion, deserved all the happiness he could get.

Jack read the note then looked at Elizabeth.

'They want us there by ten o'clock, petal,' he said. 'The police, I mean. Are you sure you're all right about it?'

'Best get it over,' she replied. The giggling had stopped but the joy of the evening and night were still there at the back of her mind, a buttress against the world. She had nothing to worry about with Jack beside her.

In the event, the interview at the police station was brief. They simply wanted a statement from her saying how she had found Peart.

'You were his wife?' asked the sergeant.

'No,' said Elizabeth, and Jack looked quickly at her. She lifted her chin. 'My little sister was his foster daughter. I lived with him for a time as his wife.' She heard Jack draw in his breath sharply but the sergeant took it in his stride, simply carried on writing it all down. Elizabeth realised he must already know she and Peart weren't married, one way or another. After all, the area around Stanhope was fairly sparsely populated, he would know most things about everyone here. Her thoughts were interrupted as the sergeant handed her a pen and asked her to sign the statement.

'There will be a post mortem, of course. And an inquest. We will let you know the date, Miss Nelson.' He shook her hand and Jack's and then at last they were ushered out on to the street.

Jack was very quiet as he started the car and set off for Darlington. After about half an hour of driving he pulled into the side of the road.

'Why, Elizabeth?'

She just looked at him. Sometimes, when she looked back on it now, she couldn't understand herself. 'Because of Jenny,' she said at last. He was still gazing at her, his brow furrowed, so she went on, 'I was so worried about her. Oh, Jack, if you had seen the way she was when she lived on that farm with only him and Snuff.' She glanced at the back seat where the dog was sitting, quite alert now after a few feeds and plenty of water. His head went up and he looked at her intelligently as she spoke his name. Oh, Snuff, she thought, if only you could talk. You know what it was like.

Jack's heart suddenly melted. She looked so worried, like a little girl caught out in something naughty. His Lizzie. He had no right to worry her, she had had a hard enough life as it was. What did he care about the past now? Best to let it go. He leaned forward and kissed her gently.

'Don't worry, sweetheart,' he said. 'I only wanted to understand better but it doesn't matter. Now is what matters, now and the future. Today is the first day of our new life.'

He put the car into gear and drove down the main road to Darlington, a well-surfaced road so he could pick up some speed. He began to whistle a local nursery rhyme, 'Bobby Shafto', about a long-ago Member of Parliament for Durham who went to London and left his sweetheart behind. Something Jack himself was never going to do.

Chapter Thirty

'I will not have that . . . that slut in my house!' shouted Olivia. Her face was bright red, she was practically dribbling with rage. Jack, looking at her, wondered if she was going to have a apoplectic fit.

'Sit down, Mother, do,' he urged her. His mind had registered the insult to Elizabeth and he would deal with it later but for now, well, this was his mother and he was responsible for her well-being.

'I won't sit down! Don't patronise me, Jack! I have told you I will not have it and I mean it.' In spite of herself she sank into a chair, trembling.

'A common foundling from the orphanage, a pitman's daughter,' she said shakily.

'Hardly a foundling when she knows her parentage,' Jack pointed out. He waited patiently for his mother to calm down. He was certainly not going to give in on this no matter how many tantrums she threw. For that was all it was, he could tell as much now. Her colour was already improving.

'A pit brat, I said,' snapped Olivia, not exactly truthfully.

'Nevertheless, I'm going to marry her and you will just have to accustom yourself to the idea,' he said.

'Well, I won't attend the wedding and you won't bring her back to my house,' Olivia insisted.

'But this is *my* house, Mother,' he observed quietly.

'Oh, the cruelty of it!' she gasped. 'And will you put your own mother out on the streets?'

Jack smiled. 'As it happens, I have no intention of bringing her back here to live. We intend to live in Darlington where Elizabeth is a partner in a fashion shop.'

Olivia clutched at the region of her chest where she imagined her heart to be. 'That I should see the day . . .' she whispered, a catch in her voice as she changed tactics. 'That I should see the day when my own daughter-in-law should be engaged in trade. Oh, dear, dear.' She found a wisp of lace handkerchief and held it to her eyes, her shoulders shaking.

Jack eyed her, his lips compressed. 'You're wasting your time, Mother. You're not going to change my mind. Elizabeth and I are going to be married at the end of the month.

'You're abandoning me!'

'Mother, when I came out of Newcomb Hall you

didn't want me here, interfering with your way of life. You did everything to stop me. Well, now you can have your own way. Don't worry, I'll see to the upkeep of the old place. And as to Elizabeth, I doubt very much if she would want to live with you!'

This last sally knocked Olivia speechless. She glared at her son, forgetting her bid for sympathy, her role of poor old woman.

'Go then, get out! And I hope I never—'

He walked to the door. 'Don't worry, I'm going, Mother,' he said. Holding the door open he turned back to her and she gasped again at the cold, hard expression on his face.

'I have one last thing to say. If you ever bad-mouth Elizabeth again, to anyone, I will get to hear of it and will take appropriate action. And the first thing I shall do is to throw you out of here. Do you understand me, Mother?'

He stumbled slightly as he went out, having to lean heavily on his stick for a moment, but he recovered himself and continued on his way without looking back.

'You shouldn't, you know, Jack. You shouldn't have spoken to her like that. After all, she is your mother.'

'I had to be hard,' he replied. 'But I promise, I'll go back and apologise to her. After we are married, of course. And only on the understanding—'

'Oh, Jack!' Elizabeth interrupted him, and he smiled

and took her in his arms. 'Come on, we have more important things to talk about. Such as where we're going to live!'

'There's a nice house empty in West Auckland Road,' she said. 'If we were there, Jenny could carry on at the same school. She's going so well, Jack.'

'I'll see about it next week,' he said, lifting a hand to stroke her hair, loving the silky feel of it. He frowned. 'First of all there's the inquest to be got through, though.'

'And the funeral. We have to go to that. Not you if you don't want to but Jenny and I.'

He looked as though he were going to protest but changed his mind. 'You're not going without me, I can tell you that,' he declared.

Elizabeth leaned against his shoulder. She had been surprised when she'd mentioned it to Jenny, had thought the child wouldn't want to go to the funeral of the man she had feared so much. But her sister had insisted she wanted to.

The inquest was simply a formality, the verdict death from alcoholic poisoning as expected. The funeral was arranged for a few days later, at two o'clock in the afternoon. On the morning they travelled up to Weardale together, Elizabeth sitting beside Jack in the front of the car, Jenny with Snuff in the back. She had wanted the dog to go, begged that he should be allowed to, in fact. Not actually in the church but back to Weardale and to Stand Alone Farm.

'He'll want to say goodbye,' she said. Elizabeth and Jack had looked at each other with raised eyebrows.

'He's only a dog, pet,' said Elizabeth.

'I don't care, I want him to go.' Jenny could be stubborn when she liked.

They arrived at the ancient stone church in Stanhope and went inside. There were no other mourners except for the police sergeant. Jenny held on hard to Elizabeth's hand. They rose to their feet when the coffin was carried in and the vicar began the liturgy. Afterwards they followed it to the churchyard where Roger Peart, for that it turned out was his name, something which rather surprised Elizabeth, though she didn't know why, was laid to rest.

'The little lass gets the old place,' said the sergeant as he shook hands with Elizabeth. 'I made inquiries. Well, if there was no one else then it was up to us to put it in hand.'

'Thank you for everything,' said Elizabeth. And sadly, flatly, they shook hands with the vicar and Jack drove them up to Bollihope Common. As they drove away the sergeant stood by the side of the road and watched them out of sight. Then, whistling, relieved to be rid of the whole business, he turned for the police station. There was the more important job to see to of sheep rustling on the high moor. He reckoned it was probably an unemployed gang from further down the dale.

Jenny sat quietly on the back of the car, looking out at

the moor. Eventually, Jack turned the car down the lonnen to Stand Alone Farm, following the tracks made by the police vehicles that fateful Sunday. The gate was open, hanging drunkenly on its hinges, and Jack drove into the yard by the old muck heap. All three of them sat and stared around. The place looked even more derelict and abandoned, he thought. Dead grass the colour of hay filled the cracks between the cobblestones. In the corner a patch of rosebay willowherb showed purple against the lichen-covered stone.

'What about the sheep? I forgot about them,' Jenny said, suddenly worried. Her voice broke the silence; no animals called, no birds twittered here.

'It's all right. The farmer down the road is looking to them,' said Jack. 'Look, flower, do you want to stay in the car while we go in?'

'No, I'm coming,' she said, and scrambled out of the car. 'Come on, Snuff,' she commanded. But he didn't want to. He crouched down on the seat and whimpered then gave a little wag of his tail just in case she was angry with him.

'Leave him, Jenny.'

Elizabeth remembered vividly how the dog had been when she'd found him here, and no doubt he did too. Thank goodness he was looking more his old self. At least his backbone didn't stick through his coat now. She took hold of Jenny's hand and steeled herself to follow Jack into the big living room-cum-kitchen.

There was no sign of the horror that had been here the last time she'd called. The police had cleaned everything up. But the room was cold and cheerless. Bits of hay and old leaves had drifted in through the holes in the bottom of the door.

Jenny went straight to the staircase. After a startled glance at Jack, Elizabeth followed her and Jack came after them.

Jenny stopped in front of what had been Peart's bedroom door.

'Oh, come on, pet,' said Elizabeth. 'You don't want to go in there, not today.'

'I do,' said Jenny. 'There's something I want you to see. I can go in myself if you don't want to. I know you hated it in there.'

Elizabeth blushed. She looked helplessly from her sister to Jack and back again. Scenes flashed through her mind, the nights she had lain there, enduring what Peart did to her, the sexual act without love, not caring what she felt but only about his own satisfaction. She had endured it for Jenny's sake. How had her sister known she hated it so much? Elizabeth hadn't realised she had betrayed her feelings so clearly. She looked at Jack. Oh, loving him was a world away from *that*. She knew she could never, ever endure that again.

'Now then, love,' said Jack, and his voice was calm and ordinary and reassuring. 'We'll go in with you, there's nothing to hurt anybody. Come on, let's get it over, whatever it is Jenny wants.'

The room was cold and bare, the bed unmade, a fusty smell coming from the bedding so that they wrinkled their noses. Jack went over to the window and opened it wide.

'Just been empty and closed for a long time,' he said, smiling. He and Elizabeth watched as Jenny took hold of the bottom of the iron bedstead and pulled it out of position.

'Hang on, I'll help you with that,' Jack said, but he was too late. Jenny had already moved it out of her way. Under the bed was a dilapidated old trunk and this too she wanted moved, allowing Jack to help her this time.

'Shall I open it for you?' he asked but Jenny shook her head absently. She was gazing at the oblong patch of clean floorboards which stood out from the rest because they had been underneath the trunk. She evidently saw what she was looking for because she knelt down and inserted a finger in a knot hole. She pulled but was unable to lift the board.

'I'll do it,' said Jack, kneeling albeit awkwardly with his disability. He could get sufficient leverage, however, and easily pulled up the board.

Elizabeth gasped. She had been in this room so often, cleaned it regularly when she lived here, and she had never realised what was under the bed. Under the floor there was a cavity and in that cavity a biscuit tin with a picture of a plump girl with roses. Jenny gave a grunt of satisfaction and seized upon it, holding it tight in her arms.

'I knew it was there!' she cried. 'I've seen him go in it many a time.'

She jumped up and sat on the edge of the bed and took the lid off the tin. Inside were letters, half a dozen at least, all addressed to Elizabeth. 'Oh!' Jenny gasped with surprise and disappointment. 'I thought he kept money in it.'

Elizabeth didn't hear her. She had stepped forward and picked up the bundle of letters. She recognised Jimmy's hand immediately and a great wave of anger and grief washed over her; anger at Peart who had kept the letters from her and grief for Jimmy. If only she had got the letters she might have seen her brother before he went to Devon. Now she would never see him again. She began to weep, great gulping sobs which she found herself powerless to control.

Jack took her in his arms. 'Oh, sweetheart, sweetheart, don't,' he whispered. 'Please don't.' He held her until the storm of tears was past and she was still in his arms. Then he handed her a large white handkerchief. 'Come on, blow your nose. Think of Jenny.'

She watched them solemnly, still holding the biscuit tin. As Jack mentioned her name she looked away, down at the box. 'Look, I knew it was there! I knew it was money, I did,' she shouted. Inside the box was a bundle of notes: five pound notes, then pound notes, even twenty pound notes. A fortune. She looked excitedly from Elizabeth to Jack. 'I knew it!' she repeated and then her smile wavered. 'It is mine, isn't it?' she asked. 'I can do what I like with it?'

'Within reason.' It was Jack who answered, Elizabeth was staring at the money in disbelief.

'I'm going to have the house done up so it doesn't rain in, put new paint and paper on the walls . . .' She noticed the strange way Elizabeth was looking at her.

'What?' she asked.

'You knew it was there, all the time? Even when we were desperate for money to get away?'

Jenny hung her head. 'I was frightened you'd go and leave me,' she confessed after a pause. 'You might have gone away and not come back.'

'But I would never have done that, Jenny. Never, never.'

Jenny said nothing. Carefully she put the lid back on the box. All the excitement drained from her and suddenly Elizabeth forgot her own feelings. Swiftly she went to her little sister and took her in her arms. 'I would never, ever leave you. You are my sister and I love you,' she said. 'Howay now, we're going home. It's been a long day.'

She picked up her bundle of letters, two of which she saw now, were in Jack's writing. She would save them to read later, in bed, on her own when there was time to savour each and every word.

The key to the door was on the mantelshelf so this time Jack locked the door as they went out, Elizabeth clutching her letters, Jenny her biscuit tin. Snuff had been watching the door anxiously. When they came out he began to bark joyously and in the car he licked all three faces, one by one.

Chapter Thirty-One

Elizabeth travelled over to Morton Main on the following Tuesday. It was a good day to leave the shop, Monday being market day in Darlington and the day women came in from all the outlying districts to meet up, get in the weekly shopping and, if there was time, browse through the clothes shops. Consequently Tuesdays were fairly quiet.

'I'll call for you, go with you to the village,' Jack had suggested, but Elizabeth wanted to go on her own.

'We can see the Minister later,' she said. They had decided to be wed in the Wesleyan Chapel in Morton Main. 'But if you don't mind, Jack, I'd like to go myself first, see my aunt and uncle and Kit, tell them. I'm meet up with you later, if you like.'

She travelled through on the bus which had recently started up, serving the rural villages and mining communities. Elizabeth smiled to herself as she gazed out of the window, seeing little, for her thoughts were totally on Jack and the amazing knowledge that he loved her after all, that they were going to be together for the rest of their lives. Even now she could hardly believe it, felt a slight anxiety that it might all be an illusion and she would wake up soon. The wedding was four weeks away and she couldn't wait, yet she had so much to do first, so much to settle.

She thought of the letters from Jack which had been in the box under Peart's bed. If only – no, it was no good thinking of that. The past was done, it couldn't be changed. But Jimmy's letters . . . oh, it was such a bitter regret not to have received them. To know he had not blamed her for what had happened, to have been able to tell him how proud she'd been of him. Wherever you are, Jimmy, she thought, I hope you know that.

'Morton Main!' called the conductor and she picked up her bag and moved to the exit. The familiar smell of coal dust hung in the air. On the opposite side of the road from the rows two children of about four years old sat on the farmer's fence, balancing themselves on the top rail with their booted feet on the second, watching as she descended to the pavement. They watched her curiously. It wasn't often anyone who didn't live here got off the bus. One of them, a boy, jumped down and ran across to her as soon as the bus had gone.

'Who're you wanting, missus? I can show you for a penny.'

Elizabeth smiled. 'I know where it is, thanks,' she said, and his eager grin faded.

'I just thought,' he mumbled.

'But I'll give you a ha'penny if you carry my bag for me,' she suggested. 'You'll have to share it with your marra, though.' After all, enterprise should be encouraged, she told herself, and the bag was pretty light.

They set off for Auntie Betty's house in one of the middle rows, the children holding the bag between them carefully so that the bottom didn't scrape on the dusty ground. At the gate Elizabeth solemnly handed them a halfpenny.

'Eeh, thanks, missus,' they chorused and ran off to Meggie's, the shop at the end of the rows. Elizabeth was still smiling as she knocked on the Hoddles' door.'

'Oh, it's you,' said Ben, as he opened it. He stood, still holding onto the handle. He was unshaven, braces hanging down the sides of his trousers, shirt collarless, feet bare. He blinked bleary eyes at her then turned his head and shouted behind him, 'Betty! It's Madam, come to have a word with her subjects.'

Elizabeth pushed past him, ignoring the sarcasm. Her aunt was coming out of the pantry, wiping her hands on a tea towel.

'Mind,' she said, 'I didn't expect to see you here. According to Mrs Wearmouth, you're a shop manageress now, ready to take over Darlington, like.'

'Well,' said Elizabeth, sighing inwardly. 'I came to tell you I'm getting married, to Jack Benson, and I'd like you to come to my wedding. Christopher too. I want my sisters and my brother at my own wedding.'

'Do you, now?' said Ben, who had followed her in and stood before the fire in his bare feet, rocking backwards and forwards on his toes. 'And what if we don't want to come? Nor let the kid come either?'

'Ben,' Betty said weakly, and attempted to divert the conversation from where it was heading. 'Jack Benson, eh? You mean, the gaffer?'

'Kit's my brother and he's coming to my wedding,' Elizabeth said, ignoring Betty for the minute. She was staring at Ben, unable to keep the contempt from her expression. She shuddered as she remembered the feel of his hands on her.

'Don't you look at me like that, you little slut!' said Ben, his own expression becoming ugly. 'That's all you are for all your fancy ways – a slut. Just like your mother.'

'Ben!' said Betty, more strongly now. 'Watch your mouth, will you?'

'My mother wasn't a slut,' said Elizabeth, fury rising in her so that she was unable to keep quiet, even though common sense told her she should.

Ben smirked and cast a glance full of meaning at Betty, who blushed furiously. 'How do you know? You were just a bairn when she died,' he said. 'Or mebbe I should tell—'

'Shut your mouth! Shut your dirty, filthy mouth!' Elizabeth shouted suddenly. She couldn't bear to hear another word from him. She clenched her hands to her sides. It was all she could do not to attack him with her fists, scratch his smirking face with her nails.

He laughed, a sniggering, hateful laugh, and her arms flew up almost of their own volition. She clawed at his face and the laughter was cut off abruptly. He grabbed at her arms and thrust her back against the square wooden table, so violently that she bent over backwards, catching her shoulder a glancing blow on the aspidistra pot in the centre of the chenille table cloth. She hardly felt it, she was so furious.

'You swine,' she said, gulping for breath as she straightened up. 'You couldn't keep your hands off me when I was young. You unspeakable, perverted maniac! You should be crawling on your belly like the worm you are, you . . . you . . .'

But before she could think of the word she wanted, her aunt was between them, slapping her across the face and screaming at her. It was a while before Elizabeth could work out what it was that her aunt was screaming, her face was so contorted, words running into each other from her slavering mouth.

'Don't you touch my Ben!' Betty cried. 'Don't you

dare. I'll swing for you, I swear I will. I'll cut your pretty little face so that man of yours, that stuck-up gaffer, won't look at you. I'll . . .'

Elizabeth was silenced, bewildered by the onslaught. For Betty was saying more, she was saying unbelievable things. They weren't true – oh no, they weren't true. Not about her mother.

'It's a lie,' she faltered.

'Indeed it's bloody well not!' Betty yelled, beside herself with rage. 'Why do you think that father of yours left, eh? Why, tell me that? Because of your mother, your own bloody mother, and her carryings on, that's why. Not content with her own man, she had to go for mine. And that's another thing. Why do you think I wanted Christopher? Because he's *mine,* that's why. He was Ben's, and Ben belonged to me. Christopher should have been mine, I tell you.'

'It's not true, it's a lie!' Elizabeth repeated. Out of the corner of her eye she could see Ben Hoddle standing to one side, grinning, enjoying himself hugely. He lit a cigarette, smirking. He folded his arms across his protruding stomach and leaned back against the wall, grinning.

'It's no bloody lie,' cried Betty. 'Jane wouldn't leave my Ben alone. He told me how it was – chasing after him all the time. And then she had the brazen face to lie about it, say he forced her. My Ben? He wouldn't force anybody, I know he wouldn't!'

'He had a go at me,' Elizabeth shouted back. 'If I hadn't got away—'

'You're a bare-faced liar an' all! You're just like your mother, just like her. She always had the men buzzing round her like bees round a honeypot when we were young. She always took any lad I wanted, by heck she did! I told her, and I told that man of hers an' all, I said he should keep her under lock and key . . .'

Elizabeth was speechless. She stared at her aunt, stunned. It was all coming out now. It had been Betty who had driven Da away, leaving Mam and her bairns to God and Providence.

'Who put the baby in there anyroad?'

Clear as a bell the question rang in her head, the one posed by Mrs Wearmouth that day so long ago when Elizabeth was nine and they'd had to go to the workhouse. 'Who put the babby in there anyroad?'

'What? What did you say?' Betty was screaming with rage. She wiped the spittle from her mouth and chin with the back of her hand. Elizabeth realised she must have spoken aloud.

'Who do you think? She chased after Ben again, he told me all about it. She said he caught her out on the lane up by the bunny banks and raped her just like that first time when she fell wrong with Christopher, but you couldn't believe a word she said. She was always panting for it, the mucky filthy trollop that she was . . .'

'Shut your mouth, Betty Hoddle, or I'll shut it for you

as sure as eggs is eggs,' said Elizabeth, not shouting now, her voice low and dangerous so that Ben stopped smirking and stood up straight, scowling at her.

'You'll do nowt of t'sort, I promise you that,' he growled.

'Don't even speak to me,' snapped Elizabeth. Contemptuously, she turned her back on him and spoke to her aunt.

'You're blind as a bat when it comes to him. You let him take down your own sister. *You let him.* I don't believe you took his word, a man like him. It's because of you two that my father went, my mother died and we were sent to the workhouse. Betty Hoddle, I hope you rot in hell for that!'

'I didn't, I didn't! It was all our Jane's fault – I told you what she was like.' Betty looked suddenly uncertain in the face of Elizabeth's fury, all the more terrible because everything she'd said was in a quiet, almost unemotional tone but telling in its intensity.

'And if you think I'll leave my little brother to be brought up any longer by a rotten pair like you, you're sadly mistaken. I'll go to the law about you and expose *him–*' here Elizabeth jerked a thumb in the direction of Ben '–for what he is. A dirty rapist of little girls and defenceless women. I will, I promise you.'

'You'll not get the bairn! No, you won't. I told you, he's mine – mine. He was always mine!'

'Will I not, then? When I tell Jack what happened

here, when I tell how that man of yours tried to rape me in *that* pantry,' Elizabeth pointed to the door, 'do you think they'll let you keep the lad?'

'I'll tell them you're lying, I'll tell them—'

'Save your breath, Betty. The slut has the high and mighty gaffer behind her now, she can do what she wants with the likes of us. She'll be in the money when she marries him, like, won't she?' Ben leaned forward until his face was barely six inches away from Elizabeth's and involuntarily she shrank back from his fetid breath, his air of menace.

'Mind, you money-grabbing little strumpet, we all know why you're marrying him, don't we? A cripple like Jack Benson? Nobody would marry him if he was a poor sod from the rows like me, would they? Not half a man with no feet.'

Hardly knowing what she was doing, Elizabeth swung her hand and slapped him so hard his head went back.

'Don't you dare say—' she began, but the next thing she knew she was lying on the floor of the kitchen, her head on the clippy fireside mat, the kitchen swimming round her. And, magically, there was Jack's face before her, his arms lifting her up as she descended into a velvet blackness.

Mrs Wearmouth had been to the Co-op store on the edge of Old Morton and was on her way home with a laden basket. She was happy, for Elizabeth had said she would call in to see her later on in the day. She had some news, apparently, and Mrs Wearmouth had a good idea what it was. These days, Mrs Wearmouth's life was a bit short of news. It seemed to her, since Jimmy had left, that the days were all the same, grey and uniform. She got up in the mornings and made herself a bit of breakfast and tried to keep herself busy during the long day, every day the same except for Sundays when she went to chapel and Thursdays when she went to the Women's Fellowship. A visit was an event and she had gone to the shop for treacle and ginger spice. She would make some ginger snaps for tea. Everyone complimented her on her ginger snaps.

Passing the middle rows, she glanced down and noticed practically every gateway had a woman standing there, looking at each other. Every one but Betty Hoddle's, that is. From there came the noise of raised voices, Betty's and Ben's and, yes, Elizabeth's, who of course was visiting her Aunt Betty today before she came to Mrs Wearmouth's.

'A right carry on in there, it's as good as a play,' remarked the woman in the end house. 'I bet they can hear it in the next street.'

Ben was shouting now, menacing rather, thought Mrs Wearmouth. I hope he's not going to hit our Elizabeth. 'Here, hold my basket for me, will you, Alice?' she asked the woman. 'I just have to go somewhere.'

Thrusting the basket into a surprised Alice's hand, she turned and set off for the colliery offices at a pace she hadn't reached in years. She had noticed Jack Benson's motor there when she came past.

Chapter Thirty-Two

Elizabeth opened her eyes, she couldn't think for a moment where she was. There was a strange face looking down on her, a man's face, keen-eyed though smelling ever so slightly of whisky.

'There now, young woman,' he said. She recognised him now as the local doctor. 'You've been very lucky. A bump on the head, but nothing that a couple of days' rest won't heal.' He stood back and Jack took his place. He knelt and picked up Elizabeth's hand, kissing it fervently.

'Oh, Lizzie, Lizzie,' he whispered. 'What did you get yourself into?' She opened her mouth to answer and he went on quickly, 'No, never mind. Just lie quiet, sweetheart. You're going to be fine, the doctor says so. Everything will be all right now, I'll see to it all.'

He kissed her lightly on the lips before rising to his

feet with a smile of such relief that her heart flooded with love for him. Vaguely she realised that she was still in Auntie Betty's kitchen, lying on the settee. Mrs Wearmouth was by the window, hovering anxiously. Elizabeth wondered idly where the Hoddles were then closed her eyes and in spite of the throbbing down one side of her face, drifted off into sleep.

'Well, Doctor?' asked Jack.

'Just as I told the lassie, Mr Benson,' Dr Short replied. 'She'll have a headache for a day or two and should take it easy, but there's no lasting damage. There could have been, though. She could have fractured her skull if she'd hit the table leg. A nasty business altogether.' He stared at the door which led into the other room, his expression hard. 'Indefensible, I'd say, a man like that hitting a woman not even his wife. Or indeed his wife,' he amended, seeing Jack's expression.

Dr Short was the doctor for the mine and the panel doctor. The miners paid a few pence a week so that he would attend to their families besides themselves. He would never make a fortune, Jack thought, but he had a reputation as a good doctor and a dedicated man.

'I'll deal with them,' Jack said grimly. 'Meanwhile I'll take my fiancée back to the Manor.'

The doctor nodded. 'I'll look in tomorrow after surgery,' he promised. 'But I'm sure there's nothing to worry about.'

After he had gone, Jack checked on Elizabeth, who

was sleeping peacefully. 'Watch her, Mrs Wearmouth, will you?' he asked.

'Aye, I will.'

Jack went into the other room where he found the Hoddles sitting opposite each other before an empty grate. The room had an unused air. He guessed it was only used for visitors or at Christmas time. Both of them stood up when he came in, though the man wore a defiant expression.

'She started it,' said Betty. 'It wasn't my Ben's fault.'

Jack cast a steely glance at her then turned to her husband. 'I want you out of Morton Main within the week.'

'What? You mean . . . you can't do that!' cried Ben.

'On the contrary, I can.'

Betty sat down suddenly, her face showing her shock and dismay. 'Eeh, what are we going to do?' she wailed.

'We could have you prosecuted for assault,' he went on as though she hadn't spoken. 'I will wait to hear what my fiancée has to say about that. Meanwhile,' he looked directly at Ben, 'you can collect any wages due to you from the office.'

'You have to give proper notice. I'll go to the Union . . .'

Jack smiled thinly. 'Do so. I think you'll find they will do nothing. Now, I'm taking Elizabeth out of here. Please remain in this room until we have gone. I do not wish her to have to see you again.'

'But I'm her aunt,' said Betty. 'We have her brother. This has nothing to do with you, really, it's a family matter.'

'Anything to do with Elizabeth is my business now,' said Jack, and turned on his heel and walked back into the kitchen. Bending over the settee, he whispered in Elizabeth's ear soothingly and she stirred and smiled. He almost lifted her there and then but cursed to himself when he remembered his feet. He couldn't chance falling with her and couldn't use his stick and carry her at the same time.

Mrs Wearmouth was ahead of him in thinking of it. 'I'll get a couple of lads who are off shift to help, will I?' she asked and Jack reluctantly agreed. He had never felt his disability so keenly. But there was no shortage of volunteers; the fore shift men were home and bathed for the most part and not yet in bed themselves. Elizabeth was soon installed in the capacious back seat of the car.

'Where are we going?' she asked, the fresh air bringing her wider awake.

'The Manor, sweetheart.'

'Oh, no!' Her eyes opened wide. She couldn't cope with Mrs Benson, not just now. 'Mrs Wearmouth—'

'Take her to my place,' that lady, who had followed them out to the car, said. 'It's not as though I haven't got the room for her. And I'll be glad to have her.'

Half an hour later, Elizabeth was installed in the front bedroom in West Row with Mrs Wearmouth's best

Durham quilt, the patchwork depicting an elaborate pattern of roses and trailing ivy, tucked around her.

'What about Jenny?' she asked as she settled her aching head on the pillow.

'Don't worry, love, I'll fetch her from school,' said Jack.

By, it was lovely just lying back and leaving everything to your own man, she thought. For the first time in her life too. Tomorrow she would think about things but just at the minute she could be a helpless little woman and it was grand.

Three weeks later, on a crisp autumnal Saturday morning, Elizabeth gazed at herself in the portable mirror which stood on top of the chest of drawers in the same front bedroom in West Row. Her thick black hair was piled high on top of her head; her eyes, gazing back at her, were almost indigo in contrast to her white skin. Behind her, Jenny and Alice hovered in identical dresses of pale lavender, the new length too, just below the knee and trimmed with self-coloured lace. Elizabeth would have liked to have made the dresses herself but there had been no time.

'I want to marry you now,' Jack had said. 'I know it's daft but I feel if we wait, you might disappear or something.'

'I won't! Oh, indeed I won't,' Elizabeth had assured him.

Now she waited as Jenny lifted the coronet of lilies-of-the-valley which held her cream lace veil in place and settled it on her head. Cream, not white, Elizabeth had been determined on that. She was not starting her new life with a lie.

'It's lovely, it is! You look lovely, our Elizabeth,' Jenny breathed. 'Doesn't she, Alice?'

The other girl nodded quietly. She was still a bit standoffish with her sisters though when Elizabeth and Jack had gone to see her, and her adopted family realised Jack was gentry and a mine owner, they had thawed noticeably towards Alice's natural family. Elizabeth didn't care what the reason was, she was happy to have both her sisters here for her wedding after all the years of separation. But for Jenny she would always have a special affection, dear Jenny.

'I'm going to live on the farm, I'm not going to sell it,' she had told Jack when he'd offered to see to it for her. 'I have enough money to look after it, haven't I?'

Jenny had looked at him with those clear hazel eyes under dark, straight brows which she'd inherited from her father. She was growing up now, Elizabeth told herself, she knew what she wanted. And so the land and the stint on the moor had been let to a tenant for five years, by which time Jenny reckoned she would be able to run it herself. Only she had big ideas for it; she wasn't going to let it go to rack and ruin as Peart had done. There were already builders repairing the walls and roof of Stand Alone Farm, the track had been cleared properly and a tarmac surface laid.

The important thing was that Jenny was happy in her school in Darlington, happy to live in the Victorian villa which Jack had found them, conveniently placed on West Auckland Road so that he could easily get to Morton Main. But happiest of all in the knowledge that one day she would be going back to her beloved Weardale in the northern Pennines, able to roam the high moor at will.

There was, naturally, one cloud which dimmed the happy prospect of the future. Jimmy was not there to give his sister away. And there was no one else, no one she felt would be right.

Elizabeth's musings were interrupted by the sound of a car arriving and Mrs Wearmouth calling up the stairs.

'Jenny! Alice! Howay now, it's time.'

The two girls went off down the stairs, and Elizabeth heard the car start up and go. Mrs Wearmouth was sharing it with the bridesmaids so Elizabeth was left in a suddenly hushed house. She stood up and went to the window. From here she could see the yard next door where she had played in the days when the family were all together. She felt the familiar ache of regret. But only for a minute. She was too happy today. The past was over, dead and gone.

'Can't you help Ben get a job somewhere else?' she had asked Jack when she'd heard how he had sent the

Hoddles away from Morton Main. 'Kit will hate us forever if he thinks it's my fault they had to leave.' And, bless him, Jack had got them a place at Chilton, seven miles away, a hewing job for Ben in Chilton pit.

'You're not sending them an invitation to the wedding, though, are you?' he had asked.

'Well,' she looked doubtfully at him, 'to the church? There's Kit, you see.'

The car was coming back for her now. She could hear it turning the corner into the back street. Elizabeth smiled and her face lit up with radiant happiness. She went to the bed and picked up her bouquet of wine-red roses and went downstairs to the car.

'On your own, pet?' the driver asked, surprised.

'On my own,' she said.

'Good luck,' someone shouted from the knot of women gathered at the gate to see her off. 'You be happy, hunny.'

'Thank you, thank you!' she answered. 'I will.'

At the red-brick chapel, only a couple of streets away, Jenny and Alice were waiting for her in the porch. Jenny rushed to straighten her veil and place the train of her dress in just the right position, and then the organ began to play and Elizabeth started off down the aisle with her sisters behind her. The congregation rose to its feet and she saw Auntie Betty and her brother Kit near the door. Betty looked uncertain but Elizabeth smiled brilliantly at them both and they smiled back, even Kit, affected by the aura of joy which surrounded her.

'They're all here, Jimmy,' she whispered. 'All the family.' Even he was here, in spirit at least, walking beside her, ready to give her away to Jack, her lovely man.

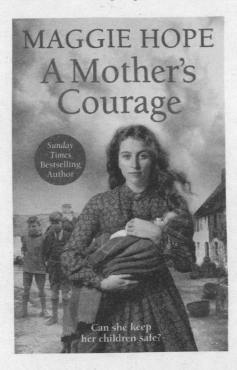

Will her courage be enough to protect her family?

Eleanor Saint spends as much time as she can helping in the community of her small mining town, even though her snobbish grandmother disapproves of her visiting the poor. When she comes of age, Eleanor is married to Frances Tait, a missionary, and she is delighted to have a husband who shares her passion for helping others.

It is not long before Eleanor starts a family of her own. But when Mr Tait's work takes their family far from home, her children face dangers that Eleanor could never have imagined. She will need to put her family first, before everything else, if she wants to protect them...

MAGGIE HOPE
The Coal Miner's
Daughter

Will they escape their
life of poverty?

A wealthy landlord's son, and a coal miner's daughter...

Growing up in poverty, one of six siblings, Hannah Armstrong never thought she'd know anything other than her little mining town. But then she falls for Timothy Durkin, a wealthy Oxford student...

Following her heart, Hannah sacrifices everything she holds dear and follows her new husband to Oxford. But will her new life of luxury be everything she expected – or will she find that once a coal miner's daughter, always a coal miner's daughter..?

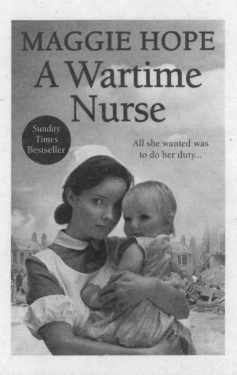

MAGGIE HOPE
A Wartime Nurse

Sunday Times Bestseller

All she wanted was
to do her duty...

As bombs begin to fall, her strength will be tested...

A newly qualified nurse, Theda Wearmouth is delighted to gain a
place at Newcastle Hospital. But the onset of war brings tragedy
when her young soldier boyfriend is killed in action before he can
make good on his promise to marry her.

Broken-hearted, Theda finds herself re-assigned to a special unit
of the hospital dealing with German prisoners of war. Her duty is
clear. But will she be able to cope with nursing the very men her
fiancé died fighting...?

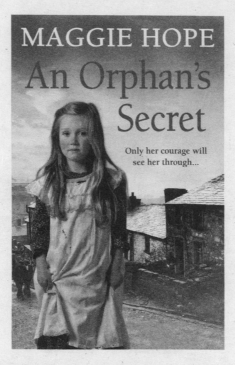

MAGGIE HOPE

An Orphan's Secret

Only her courage will
see her through...

Life is a long, tough struggle for Meg Maddison...

Growing up caring for her brothers after the death of their mother,
it is only her indomitable spirit that gets her through the hard times.
And when she marries and starts a family of her own, it seems as if
the hardships are over.

But the return of a darkly menacing figure from her past threatens
to destroy all she has fought for...